BLOOD MAGIC

A Novel

JENNIFER LYON

BALLANTINE BOOKS • NEW YORK

A Ballantine Books Mass Market Original

Copyright © 2009 by Jennifer Apodaca

Excerpt of *Soul Magic* copyright © 2009 by Jennifer Apodaca

Published in the United States by Ballantine Books, an imprint of The Random House Publishing Group, a division of Random House, Inc., New York.

BALLANTINE and colophon are registered trademarks of Random House, Inc.

This book contains an excerpt from the forthcoming book *Soul Magic* by Jennifer Lyon. This excerpt has been set for this edition only and may not reflect the final content of the forthcoming edition.

ISBN 978-0-345-50634-4

Cover design and illustration by Jae Song, based on a photograph © Werner Bokelberg

Printed in the United States of America

www.ballantinebooks.com

OPM 9 8 7 6 5 4 3 2 1

The whispers were nothing new.

Darcy MacAlister followed behind her mother's graceful white casket with the elegant raised scrolls as they left the MacAlister Funeral Home for the cemetery next door. She would not let the whispers affect her.

"They used to call her Dark Mac in high school."

"Some say her father was afraid of her."

". . . Drove him to drink."

"There's something strange about that one . . ."

Darcy stiffened her back, her black sheath dress sliding around her legs. She focused on the coffin and inhaled the briny, damp ocean air.

The warmth she felt vanished, replaced by a deep chill.

It was nine o'clock by the time Darcy arrived home to her little apartment. She went into her bedroom and took a shower to wash away the day's aches, then poured a glass of wine, which she carried with her to check her email.

Her computer dinged indicating she had a new email message. The subject line said, *Warning*. Without even thinking, she clicked it open. It read: *The hunters have found you! They will kill you!*

What hunters? Why would they look for her? Darcy looked up to see who had sent the message.

This didn't make any sense.

The email was from *her*.

To all the readers
who desire a little magic in their lives—
this book is for you

ACKNOWLEDGMENTS

Thank you to my agent, Karen Solem. I wouldn't be here without your support, guidance, honesty, and hard work. Much appreciated, Karen!

And to my editor, Liz Scheier, thank you for working tirelessly to develop this book to its fullest potential. You rock, Liz!

This book went through many transformations, but one thing held true: I could not have done it without my friends. They believed in my idea, they spent hours working with me on world building, developing characters, pondering the paradoxes of magic, and reading pages. Their generosity, support, laughter, and occasional butt-kicking helped bring this book to life. So Marianne Donley, Michele Cwiertny, Maureen Child, and Laura Wright—thank you! See you all at the next lunch—you know, where they make us sit outside because we laugh too often and too loud. How dare we have that much fun!

1

The whispers were nothing new.

Darcy MacAlister followed behind her mother's graceful white casket with the elegant raised scrolls as they left the MacAlister Funeral Home for the cemetery next door. Being the funeral director eased the knot of grief and sorrow in her throat. She was honored to oversee every detail of the service that celebrated Eileen MacAlister's life, and show the community how well-loved her mother had been. She would not let the whispers affect her.

"They used to call her Dark Mac in high school."

"Some say her father was afraid of her."

". . . Drove him to drink."

"Hush! Darcy took care of your grandfather when he passed. She's been nothing but kind to us."

"She found my cat for me when he got lost. Just knew where he was."

"There's something strange about that one . . ."

Darcy stiffened her back, her black sheath dress sliding around her legs. She focused on the coffin and inhaled the briny, damp ocean air.

Joe's arm slid around her shoulder, pulling her close to his side.

She looked up at her cousin. Joe hovered around six feet and weighed in at one eighty, and he knew how to kill, thanks to his years in the Special Forces. And right now, his jaw was so tight, she knew he wanted to hit someone. "Ignore them," she said softly.

He barely nodded.

Not a promise, but the best she'd get from him. It had been almost nine years since Joe had left the seaside town of Glassbreakers, California, full of excitement about changing the world. When he returned a few months ago, he was a different man, grim and disconnected, like he didn't care if he lived or died. Yet once he found out that her mom, his aunt, was terminally ill with a complication from lupus, he would show up at the house to do chores, barbeque, or take care of anything else that needed to be done. Any thanks just irritated him.

They stopped at the grave. The base of the casket was surrounded by flower arrangements; fresh greenery and baby's breath was woven around the poles of the canopy under which the guests sat or stood.

Darcy cleared her throat, feeling the weight of her mother's last gift; a silver Celtic knot pendant of loops and swirls that spread out like wings at her throat. "Thank you all for coming today. My mother asked me to tell you that she cherished each of you. That you all brought joy and happiness to her life. And now, she's asked that you don't grieve for her, but instead celebrate each of your days, and embrace your families and loved ones." She looked out over all the mourners, warmed to see so many that truly cared about Eileen MacAlister. "Once we do the final prayers, we will have a reception back inside. We would be pleased if you would join us."

She took her seat, grateful that she didn't have to worry about the reception. Her best friend, Carla Fisk, and her newest employee, Morgan Reed, were inside the mortuary right now setting up the sandwiches, salads, and cookies. Instead, she concentrated on the prayers and closing words that would send her mom to her final rest. For the last time, people streamed by the casket, cried, and hugged her. The day was nearly over.

"You've done your mom proud, darling," Reverend Jack Masters said, leaning down and kissing her cheek.

Darcy rose and walked with the minister to stand by her mom's casket. "Thank you, Jack. We planned this ceremony together. I just followed her wishes." Those last months had been a blessing and a nightmare. Eileen had struggled with lupus since her early twenties, but in the last year her lungs had given out.

Words from two stragglers floated to them. "Strange that she doesn't even cry for her mother."

Jack's face tightened, then he shook his head in disgust. "Eileen knew you loved her, Darcy. And I have worked with you on dozens of funerals. You're a professional through and through. This is your final gift to your mother."

She almost cried then, but hugged him instead. "Thanks, Jack. That really helps."

"Can I walk you in?"

She shook her head. "I want to stay here for a few more minutes."

He nodded and headed inside.

Darcy was finally alone. She inhaled the sea breeze mixed with the scent of recently cut grass and freshly turned dirt. Jack was right, she had done her mom proud. That felt good; it felt right. Her mom had adopted Darcy when she was only a few weeks old, and no matter how odd a child Darcy had turned out to be, Eileen's love had remained rock steady. Always.

Turning slightly, she swept her hand across the glossy surface of the casket. "I'm going to give the house to Joe, Mom. I've thought about this a lot. He needs something, an anchor. I can't live there, I just . . . can't. But Joe . . ."

The warmth she felt vanished, replaced by a deep chill. She snapped her head up and caught sight of a young couple walking along one of the sidewalk pathways directly in front of her. Sweeping her eyes left, she saw three people: two men and a woman standing by a headstone.

They all looked like normal visitors to the cemetery.

Dropping her gaze, she said, "Guess I'm tired. Anyway, about Joe and—"

She felt it again. This time chills raced down her back and the hair stood up on her arms. Her heart rate increased quickly. Dropping her hand, she whirled to look toward the canopy.

A man was suddenly there, standing by the chair she'd sat in earlier.

Her heart swelled and banged against her rib cage. The man was extremely tall and wore a long, black suede coat. But something was off, his face was too soft, almost feminine, yet his build was huge. *Pull yourself together, he's probably just a late mourner.* Taking a deep breath, she noticed a coppery smell then said, "You startled me. Are you here for my mom?" Perhaps he was an acquaintance of her mom's that she hadn't met.

Staring at her, he said, "I'm here for you, Darcy."

His eyes were a vacant and cruel green. She broke into a cold sweat. A voice in her head screamed, *Run!* Darcy shivered once, then turned and ran. The heels of her black pumps caught in the thick grass. She stopped, turned, and saw that the man was still standing there watching her, a nasty smirk on his full lips.

Fear washed up the back of her throat. She yanked off her shoes and looked back. The man was gone.

Vanished.

Run!

Unnamed terror pulsed deep inside of her and she ran,

heading toward the mortuary. It was too far! At least thirty or forty yards . . .

"Darcy!"

It was Joe, striding toward her from the left, Morgan at his side. Darcy turned and raced to him, her thighs burning. She couldn't get the metallic taste of fear out of her mouth.

Joe caught her in his arms, lifting her off the ground and turning with the momentum. "What's wrong?" He set her down and whipped back around, keeping her at his back.

Tears burned behind her eyes at the gesture. He had always protected her.

"Darcy, are you okay?" Morgan looked at her, her huge blue eyes full of worry.

Warm embarrassment began in the center of Darcy's chest and spread like a bad rash. What exactly had she panicked over? "I think I might have just made a fool of myself."

Joe did one more scan then turned to look down at her; both of his dark eyebrows raised over vivid blue eyes. "You looked terrified. What happened?"

She shrugged, then leaned down to slide one pump onto her damp foot. "This guy just freaked me out."

"That's a switch. Usually it's you freaking people out."

She rolled her eyes as she balanced on one high heel, brushed a couple blades of grass from her foot, and slid on the other shoe. Then she stood and said, "He startled me. I didn't hear him walk up, he was just . . . there. I asked him if he was here for mom, and he said 'I'm here for you, Darcy.' " Now that she said it out loud, she realized the man might have meant that he was there to support her at her mother's funeral.

Morgan jerked her head around to stare at Darcy. "What did he look like?"

The fear coming off Morgan prickled her skin and nearly made her step back. In high school, Morgan had been popular and sure of herself while Darcy had been awkward; always trying to figure out how to fit in. Something had changed Morgan. She tried to answer, "Black hair, really weird green eyes, and his face was . . . well, it seemed almost delicate."

"A small guy?" asked Joe.

"No. Big. Taller than you. He wore a black suede coat that went to his knees and black slacks under that."

Morgan's gaze darted around the cemetery, then she reached out and put her icy cold hand on Darcy's arm. She opened her mouth, then grimaced before saying, "I need to tell you something. But I can't seem to remember exactly . . ." She snatched her hand from Darcy's arm and started rubbing her temples.

"Morgan, you need to eat. You've been working since this morning," Joe said.

That was true, Darcy silently agreed. But she had felt the cold fear in Morgan's hand. After being gone from town for a few years, the woman had returned scared and troubled by something. But then again, Darcy herself had just raced across the cemetery grounds like something out of a horror movie was after her, so who was she to judge? "Let's all go inside. I'm acting like a nuthouse escapee and Morgan is forgetting things. We could all use some food, and we have guests waiting."

Joe took her arm. "I'll take a look around inside. If he's there, I'll get his story."

She looked up at him. "Thanks." It made her feel better that he took her seriously even when she felt like an utter fool. What had possessed her to run away?

It was nine o'clock by the time Darcy arrived home to her little apartment. The only thing that had gotten her through the last few hours was the promise of a hot shower and a big glass of wine. She lived in a ground-floor unit overlooking a sunny courtyard with propane barbeques and benches shaded by a couple of large oak trees with sprawling limbs that bent and twisted like broken fingers. Tonight, it seemed dark and shadowy with too many hiding places.

Her imagination was in overdrive.

She hurried to her front door, slid in her key, and unlocked it. Once inside, she closed the door, shoved home the dead bolt, and took a deep breath. Feeling calmer, she put her hand on the back of her blue couch and bent over to take off her pumps. As she stood up, she looked at the tapestry over the aged brick fireplace. It had hung there since she moved into the apartment, but tonight it looked . . . brighter.

It pictured a golden brown cat sitting on a silver box and looking down into a glassy-still lake. Behind the cat, lavender-shadowed mountains rose up. The cat and the mountains cast odd reflections into the mirror-like lake. It was mesmerizing to stare at the picture and try to make out the images on the lake surface. Sometimes it looked almost like the threads of the canvas were moving with the water in the lake. Tonight everything seemed clearer and more vibrant.

The tapestry was the only possession Darcy had of her biological mother's. Eileen had never spoken much about the adoption, but she had hung the tapestry in Darcy's bedroom while growing up. Her dad had hated it, but her mom wouldn't let him touch it.

Why had Fallon left it with Darcy?

She'd never really given it much thought; the tapestry had just always been there. But then her mom had dropped her last bombshell on Darcy before she died: She had signed Darcy up on an Internet birth parents search agency. She had told Darcy it was time to learn who she was and where she came from.

Should she follow up with searching for her birth parents?

Her grief for her mom was still too fresh to make any decisions.

She went into her bedroom, took a shower to wash away the day's aches, and put on a pair of gray sweat pants and a pink tank top. Leaving her hair wet, she went to the kitchen where she poured a glass of wine and fixed a plate of cheese and crackers. She carried them with her to check her email.

She had a few more condolence emails. When she was finished replying to them, she realized that her shoulders had relaxed, her headache had eased, and the murmuring voices in her head had quieted.

Her computer dinged indicating she had a new email message. The subject line said, *Warning*. Without even thinking, she clicked it open. It read: *The hunters have found you! They will kill you!*

Startled, she set down her wineglass. What the hell was this? The noise in her head grew into a thick buzz. Fear pounded in her chest. She told herself she was overreacting, just like she had when that man had shown up at the gravesite. She'd probably read the email wrong. She leaned in closer and read the message again.

The hunters have found you! They will kill you!

What hunters? Why would they look for her? Darcy looked up to see who had sent the message. Her mouth went dry and uneasiness skittered up her spine. The wine turned her stomach queasy.

This didn't make any sense.

The email was from *her*.

2

Axel Locke prowled through his nightclub and washed down his rising compulsion with another beer.

And another.

Alcohol didn't help. Only sex took the edge off of the building pressure to hunt and kill.

"Packed tonight." Sutton West walked up beside him.

Axel glanced over at his friend and shrugged. Axel of Evil had been an instant success since he'd opened the doors a year ago. The club filled up nightly with men looking for relief from the evil they carried inside of them. The brick and fire décor reflected that theme. The two long bars curved like a wicked knife and had a shiny black lacquer finish with the borders lit in red to make it appear as though fire were dancing along the edges. The dance floors were done with the same fire-edged lacquer. Two brick fire pits in black cages were surrounded by black and red leather seating. Archways that separated the rooms were intricately carved with gargoyles, fire-breathing dragons, and angry demons. Red, black, and purple lighting added to the dark, hellish effect.

But Axel knew Sutton hadn't come over to shoot the breeze. "What's up?"

The man's gaze kept searching the room. "Hell if I know. Something though."

Yeah, he felt uneasy too. Damn. "A witch?"

The big bald man's blue eyes darted to meet Axel's.

"Not a chance. I'd know and so would you." He looked over to the bloodred leather couch ringing one of the fire pits. "And so would they."

Axel narrowed his gaze on the men. Four of them, wearing casual clothes and jackets that concealed the long-bladed knives they always carried. They were witch hunters, but they didn't appear to be the usual kind who came in looking to hook up or relax. "Did you check their palms?"

Sutton said, "Smooth as a baby's butt."

"Rogue witch hunters." He drained the beer in his glass. Rogues had no lifeline, or for that matter any lines, on the palms of their hands. *That's what happens when you lose your soul,* he thought dryly. "More and more of us are losing the battle with the curse and going rogue. But the question is, why are the rogues here?"

"The hawk."

Yeah, he thought, they wanted to spy on the man wearing the hawk tat. See what he was going to do. The large tattoo on Axel's back seemed to grow warm. Ignoring it, he turned to stare at Sutton. "You know Key is just fucking with us. I told him I wanted a raven. He totally ignored me and tattooed a hawk instead. His idea of a joke."

"Bullshit, I was standing there, watching him ink your back with black feathers that turned gold and brown before the ink dried. The shape of the bird shifted, too. It was some freaky shit. The Wing Slayer chose you as a leader."

Axel finished off his beer. All they wanted to do was keep their souls. They had been born witch hunters, a breed of men with a centuries-long and honorable history of protection and justice. They'd been immortal and unstoppable guardians of the earth witches, highly evolved women with powers drawn from the earth's elements to protect, heal, and assist mortals while hunting down and killing demon witches. Now, thanks to a thirty-year-old blood-and-sex curse, Axel and Sutton fought a dark, soul-destroying compulsion for witch blood. "But more to the point, what do the rogues care if I have a hawk tat?"

"If the Wing Slayer is alive, then they are royally fucked. Your hawk tat indicates the Wing Slayer is alive. They come to the club to keep an eye on you and figure out what you're going to do. Something changed that tat and it wasn't Key."

"Sucks to be soulless rogues." Without their souls, when they died, they would become shades banished to walk the between-worlds in endless agony.

"Quinn Young has convinced the rogues that if they kill all the witches, the curse will break and their souls will return."

Axel snorted. "Young is the one who should be afraid of the Wing Slayer." He turned and fixed his eyes on Sutton. "That bastard renounced Him." And that renouncement combined with the curse of the demon witches caused the break between the Wing Slayer and his witch hunters.

"So you do believe the Wing Slayer is alive?"

Axel nodded. "I believe it, but what the hell I'm supposed to do about it is another thing. Why would he tag me to lead the Wing Slayer Witch Hunters? We can't protect earth witches, we can't even get within smelling distance or we risk losing control and killing the witches ourselves."

Sutton studied him, his teal-blue eyes thoughtful. "Bad tonight?"

When wasn't it? Sometimes he dreamed of sliding his knife into a witch and feeling the bliss of her power-laced blood coating his skin and sinking into him, then he woke in sheer, sweat-popping terror that he might really have done it. Or would do it. "Bad enough."

"Go. Get relief. I'll keep an eye on the rogues."

He nodded once and said, "Give Phoenix, Key, and Ram the heads-up that we have company." The other Wing Slayer Hunters were all somewhere in the club.

"On it," Sutton said and strode off.

Relief for witch hunters came from fulfilling the sex part of the curse. Sex eased back the craving for witch blood. He headed toward one of the bars where several women gathered, and zeroed in on one wearing a short tan skirt that revealed miles of leg. She had short black hair and was wearing a tiny green top, and flashed a dome smile when she saw him looking at her.

"Hi, I'm Tina."

Axel turned. Up close, he could smell the sweet tang of rum and coke, and see the pain in her eyes. *Join the club, babe. We all got problems.* "You got an itch, Tina?"

She moved up to him, settling her body over his thigh so that he could feel her heat. It went straight to his groin. "You got a place?"

He looked down into her face. "Yeah, upstairs."

She looked up at him and he saw a second of hesitation. He could guess what she was thinking. There were rumors about the men in the club. They were big men and they could hurt a woman if they weren't careful. He was always careful. Reaching out, he slid his hands around her hips, pulling her higher up his thigh. "I won't hurt you. I just need you."

She ran her hand up his arm. "Same goes for me."

Women who came to the club knew they were dealing with dangerous men. Some liked the danger, some had their own demons to fight, and a few were related to witch hunters and had the same sense of not belonging. He stood up. It didn't matter why she was there. It only mattered that she could give him what he needed.

Relief from the craving.

He took her hand, realizing she was only about five-foot-six. He'd been looking at her endless legs and hadn't thought about her size, or how much of him she'd be able to take. How much he'd have to hold on to his control. For a few seconds, he wondered if it was worth it. If he gave in to his animal side, he'd be able to let go and bury himself hard and deep in a woman, right up to the balls, without a thought for her comfort. Lust flamed lightning-hot through his gut and groin with the desire to give a woman everything he had.

Someone bumped into him, jerking him from his fantasy. He clenched his jaw. Self-control was what separated the man from the animal, and the witch hunter from the rogue. He let go of the woman's hand so that she could move in front of him as they made their way through the crowd.

He focused on her long legs and sexy ass. She'd bring him moderate relief from his cravings, and he'd make damn sure she had a good time.

Putting his hand on the small of her back, he guided her toward the staircase. He stopped short when he saw the man standing at the bottom of the stairs.

Before he could fully react, he felt Sutton move up behind him. He didn't need to look to know that Phoenix, Key, and Ram were on alert, spreading out to be ready for trouble.

He needed to get the girl out of the way. She had taken a step farther before she realized his hand wasn't on her back. She turned to look at him.

Axel gently took her arm, pulling her toward him then turning to hand her off to Sutton. "Take Tina up to my condo the back way and get her whatever she wants." Then he looked at her. "I'll be up as soon as I take care of something here."

She looked a little confused, but she nodded and followed Sutton.

Then he turned back to the man. Without looking, he knew the four rogue hunters that had been hanging out by the fire pit had closed in. But Axel focused on the man in front of him. "What are you doing here?"

The man held out a sheet of paper, revealing his smooth palm as he did. "You have one chance to prove your loyalty. Take care of this witch or you will be terminated."

He snorted. "Christ, Dad, that sounds like a bad movie line." At fifty-two, Myles Locke looked thirty. The blood of murdered witches kept him looking young. His eyes were the same green color as Axel's, but his father's eyes looked flat and dead. Merciless.

His dad took a step toward him. "You dumb shit coward. The Wing Slayer is dead. The witches killed him with their curse. Everyone is laughing at you hiding behind a dead, useless god, because you're too cowardly to man up and kill the bitches who cursed us."

He got a whiff of copper from his dad, the result of absorbing witch blood through the skin. Mortals usually couldn't smell it, but witches and witch hunters could. "Man up? You calling killing earth witches who can't defend themselves being a man?" It made him sick, but not as sick as the dark desire running through his veins. The craving to sink his blade into a witch and feel the kick of her power-laced blood covering his skin. Furious, he growled, "Get out of my club."

The two rogue hunters behind his father pulled out their knives.

Axel reacted, pulling his knife from the holster at the small of his back. Lifting his gaze to the two rogue hunters, he glared a challenge at them. He wanted the fight.

They sheathed their knives.

Disappointed, Axel struggled to get himself under control. Cowards. They never liked a fair fight, one where they ran the risk of dying without their souls and spending eternity as formless, empty shades. He knew that Key, Phoenix, and Ram were watching and, like him, they would protect everyone in the club. They might not choose to start a fight, but they'd sure as hell finish it. He hated days like this. All he'd wanted to do was sink himself between a willing woman's legs and give them both pleasure, and now he was dealing with rogue hunters led by his dad. And he didn't have anyone to kill to take the edge off.

The music stopped and restless murmurs arose. The tension thickened.

His dad dropped his gaze to the knife Axel held. The hilt was silver. "I don't see any wings magically impressed on there. The Wing Slayer can't return your immortality to you if he's dead. Stop being a sniveling coward and kill the witches."

Smiling coldly, Axel said, "I like my lifeline."

Myles flinched, then his face hardened. "We will be immortal once we kill all the witches and break the curse, then we'll have the immortal lifeline."

"Interesting logic," Axel said dryly. "Earth witches had nothing to do with the curse. It was demon witches."

"They were there, they didn't stop the curse. You're out of excuses and out of time. You have twenty-four hours to do your duty by killing this witch. If you don't, you're dead." He dropped the sheet of paper in his hand. It was still floating to the floor when the doors closed behind the hunters.

Axel snatched the paper before it touched the ground and looked down. He stared at the picture for a long moment. Her brown eyes were slightly tilted like those of most witches. Hunters couldn't always tell a witch by the way she looked, but they could always smell the power in her blood. This witch was an attractive woman. Vibrant. On the back side of the sheet was the target info he'd need to hunt and kill her. He searched for her name and found it.

Darcy MacAlister.

It wasn't his fight. All he wanted to do was keep his soul. He wouldn't kill her, he'd vowed he would never give in to the curse and kill an earth witch.

He crumpled the paper and stuffed it into his pocket.

SUNDAY: DAY TWO OF THE DEATH MARK

She was still asleep Sunday morning when the phone rang. Rolling over, she grabbed the handset off her nightstand. "Hello?"

"Hey, woke you?"

"Carla, yeah," Darcy sat up. "I was dreaming of a hawk. Weird, I haven't dreamed of him in a long time." She'd dreamed of him when she'd been scared as a little girl.

"Your safety hawk?"

Darcy laughed, clearing away the remnants of sleep. "Your psych PhD is showing again." Carla always referred to the hawk in Darcy's childhood dreams as her safety hawk. Just like her dreams then, this one had seemed so vivid and real. Back then, the hawk had come to comfort her when she'd been alone and in the dark. This time, he'd come to ease her grief.

"It's not surprising you'd dream of something comforting, you just buried your mom yesterday. And now I feel like a rotten friend because I have to cancel on you today, Darcy. I'm so sorry. An emergency came up," Carla said.

They'd planned to have breakfast and start going through her mom's stuff at the house. She pushed herself up in her bed. "Is it a problem with one of your clients?"

"Not exactly."

When she was this vague, Darcy left it alone. Her hypnosis clients had a range of problems, but she also worked with people who had been indoctrinated into cults and other forms of brainwashing. It was sometimes dangerous and Carla was cautious with both her clients' privacy and their safety.

"Let's do it tomorrow after work. I have to fly out for a consult on Tuesday, but I'm free all Monday night."

"You're working too hard," Darcy said. "As a doctor, you should know better."

"That's what your mom always told me," Carla said fondly.

Darcy smiled, running her hand over her jewel green comforter. Carla had been wonderful with her mom, going over and cooking dinner for her when Darcy was tied up with work, dropping in with herbal teas to ease her breathing, just being there. "She really liked you."

"Nah, she was just pumping me for information on you."

She laughed. "Probably. Off you go, we'll talk tomorrow. I'll tell you the story about how I freaked out on one of the mourners."

"When was this? I didn't see anything happen."

She felt stupid all over again just thinking about it. "I was by myself at the gravesite when it happened. You and Morgan were setting up for the reception."

"What freaked you out?"

That's what bothered her; she still didn't know. "Looking back, I'm sure it was the stress of the day, but at the time, it seemed like this man just suddenly appeared out of nowhere. And he looked odd. Anyway, I'll tell you about it tomorrow."

"Darcy, be careful. If this guy gave you the creeps, trust that feeling. Come to my house tomorrow. I have something important to talk to you about. We can start

on your mom's house later in the week or this week-
end."

"Is something wrong?"

"Not wrong, but I want to talk to you. And please, be
careful. I have to run."

"Nice way to build the suspense. See you tomorrow
night."

Axel leaned in and sank the eight ball. Three Days
Grace bemoaned "The Animal I Have Become" over the
speaker system.

"I can't work with Phoenix's chomping," Kieran
DeMicca snarled over the whir of the tattoo needle. Key
had been working on the multicolored dragon that
spread across his own chest for months.

"Christ, that's just sick." Phoenix Torq shoved another handful of Fritos in his mouth and chewed loudly,
managing to compete with the pounding music. He had
a single wing of the mythical phoenix tattooed on each
massive bicep. Since he wore a leather vest and no shirt,
the wings were plainly visible. He had his leather-clad
legs stretched out in front of him, ending in specially
made leather motorcycle boots.

Phoenix and Key had been bickering for a half hour.
They always argued. Phoenix was a mean bounty hunter
who enjoyed bringing back human scum alive. Just
barely alive. And Key was an artist whose dark draw-
ings writhed with evil.

Key said, "Chicks liked my tat last night. Both of
them."

Phoenix sat up. "Fuck me, you had two chicks? At the
same time?"

Axel rolled his eyes and racked the balls for another
game.

Key laughed. "*Fuck me,* that's what they both said.

How'd you know, Phoenix? You watching? Looking for sloppy seconds?"

Phoenix dropped the bag of chips then reached down to pull his knife from his boot. He caressed the blade with one long finger. At six-foot-four, he was two hundred and forty pounds of I-don't-give-a-shit-if-I-die menace. But right now, he was mellow. "Wonder how many chicks you'll get without a tongue."

Key held up the vibrating tattoo needle. "Probably more chicks than you can find to pull this out of your ass."

"Ouch," Ram muttered.

Axel made the break, then stood up and faced Ram. "My money's on the tattoo needle." They all had gone under Key's needle. Personally, Axel would rather face a couple of knife-wielding rogue hunters than a vibrating needle again.

Ramsey Virtos studied the position of the balls with his usual military precision, then made his shot. "That dragon is spooky as hell." Ram had chosen the wings of a mythical thunderbird for his tattoo.

Axel looked over at Key. He was the smallest of the five of them, but he had the biggest tattoo. The dragon had started out as a set of wings over Key's muscular chest. But he'd been adding a body, face, tail, and who knew what else would come. Yeah, Key might be the smallest, but he was both talented and deadly. "Wonder when he'll add flames to the dragon's mouth."

Ram laughed, the sound as measured and controlled as everything else about the man.

Key answered, "She'll tell me when she wants flames."

Axel left that one alone, noticing that Phoenix had lost interest in Key. He watched as Phoenix sheathed his knife, got up, and headed toward the monitor at which Sutton was staring. Sutton usually manned the security sytem's monitors that showed various angles of the warehouse and Axel's club next door. Since it was midafternoon, and the club wouldn't be open for hours, it was strange that he had seen something. Axel put his stick down. "What?"

Ram and Key also turned their attention to the monitors.

Sutton looked over at Axel. "Your mom and sister are on their way in."

"Are they alone?" He strode over to see for himself. Sure enough, his mom had his four-year-old sister in her arms, and she was heading up to the back door of the warehouse. It was unusual for them to do that. "Unlock the door."

"Done," Sutton said.

The music cut off and they all turned toward the door. Axel walked by the pool table in the middle of the cavernous room, past Key's tattoo station next to his drafting table, and headed to the door to open it for his mom and sister.

Eve Locke looked a little bit like a fifty-something, dark blond Catherine Zeta Jones. But today, there were lines of strain around her mouth and eyes, and her skin was pale.

Little Hannah saw him and immediately held out her arms.

Axel took her from his mom. His little sister, smelling like baby shampoo, put her soft arms around his neck and squeezed. "Hi Axel. Mommy said I could color with Key. Can I? Please?" She leaned back and looked at him. Her dark brown eyes sparkled with happiness. She had no idea what he and the other men were. She loved them all. And the men—witch hunters with a killer dark side they barely controlled—melted like ice cream around Hannah.

He looked at his mom.

She nodded.

Axel set Hannah on the ground. "Go ask Key if he wants to color." God, it sounded so ridiculous. Kieran had grown up on the streets and killed to stay alive. On top of that, Key had a dark comic series that made him wealthy. But he and Hannah would spend hours coloring. Key always had time for her. He saw exactly what Hannah's little stick figures and squiggles were supposed to be.

He watched Hannah run over to Key. Then he turned back. "Mom, what's wrong?"

She hadn't moved. She stood stiff and tense inside the door of the garage and workout area of the warehouse. She had to be the toughest, smartest woman he knew, but right now, she looked . . . fragile.

Phoenix, Sutton, and Ram gathered behind him. He could feel the tension building in the silence.

Eve looked at the men grouped behind Axel, then shifted her gaze to him. She took a shaky breath and said, "She has the mark. Hannah. She has the death mark."

He jerked like she'd hit him. The dreaded words pounded in his brain. His blood surged into a throbbing rage. *Not Hannah*. Sweet God, not her. He heard himself ask, "Are you sure?"

She nodded. "I'm sure. It's a death curse." She shivered, wrapping her arms around her waist.

Axel wanted to tell her she was wrong, but while Eve Locke was mortal, she wasn't ignorant about the other beings that lived alongside of them. She'd traveled the world as a flight attendant, then met and fell in love with his dad—and had accepted that he was an immortal witch hunter. That meant Eve would age and die while Myles lived, but Eve thought she could handle that. She wanted to believe the man she loved was doing something big and important. They'd married and had Axel. Then the curse happened and Eve had believed that her love would keep his dad from going rogue, and since Myles was no longer immortal, they'd grow old together.

She'd been wrong, and any innocence she'd held on to had been shattered as she fought to keep her son from the same fate.

Axel forced himself to stand still and to stay in control.

Tears welled up in her brown eyes. "It's on her forehead. She woke up with a pink dot this morning and I thought it was a bug bite. Then this afternoon, it was a perfect round circle. Oh God, Axel, I don't know what to do. I can't let my baby die." She shuddered, her entire body trembling.

His mom's pain added to the compulsion burning like fire ants deep in his veins. No matter how much he wanted to hold on to his soul, he had no choice. He had to hunt down the demon witch and kill her. It would destroy him, but it would free Hannah from the curse. The death curse started as a pink dot, and within hours it became a dime-size pink circle. The victim would sicken and die at the full moon. It was a new moon, which meant he had about fourteen days until the curse would kill Hannah. Keeping his hands loose at his sides, he looked into his mom's eyes. "I won't let her die. I'll find the witch who cursed Hannah and kill her."

"Axel . . ." Her voice was thick and tight.

He understood it. She loved him. So much so that she had stayed with his dad, even after he'd turned, because she knew Myles would kill her before he'd let her take Axel. Then when things had gotten too dangerous for Axel, the two of them went on the run until Axel had been old enough to handle his dad. Their complicated history—including the period of time when his dad had found his mom again and used his witch-hunter magnetism to seduce Eve and get her pregnant—changed nothing. She was being forced to sacrifice one of her children to save the other.

"You can't kill a witch. Just one witch kill will turn you." She looked over to make sure Hannah was busy with Key, then she added, "I'll do it. I want you all to find the witch, then I'll kill her."

Sutton shifted uneasily next to him. Phoenix growled low in his throat. "Eve, be careful," Ram warned.

Axel held himself still. The very idea of his mother encountering a demon witch made his head ring with rage. Hunters were born to both protect and kill. In spite of the blood curse, both drives still ran deep until they went rogue.

But Eve had her own powerful instincts—those of a mother trying to save both her children. He closed the space between them and put his arm around her shoulders. He loved her enough to take the decision from her. "Mom, only a witch who has given up her soul for demonic powers can cast a death curse. You would be too easy for her to kill. You have to take care of Hannah. I'll find the witch who cursed her."

He let go of his mom and walked across the warehouse, following the baby giggles and low male tones. Hannah and Key were sprawled on the floor with a six-foot-long piece of butcher paper and about a million crayons. Hannah had dark blond hair held back in two clips, with bangs that fell over her forehead. She was on her stomach, her legs bent at the knees, kicking her pink-tennis-shoed feet back and forth. She stuck her tongue out the side of her mouth while coloring with a pink crayon and wearing an intense look of concentration.

His chest hurt just looking at her. She and Key were working on one of their "projects," which was some kind of ongoing cartoon.

He hunkered down by Hannah. "What are you drawing?"

She looked up at him with a baby-teeth grin. "A story about flying puppies. Wanna help?"

He casually reached out to brush her bangs back and saw it—the perfectly round, dime-size pink mark. The compulsion to find the witch who'd cursed Hannah and spill her blood hissed in his bloodstream. His heart pounded, and his muscles twitched. He carefully pulled his hand away from his sister.

Key's gray eyes hardened with sheer hatred, but his voice was gentle. "You're stuck with me, Hannah. Your brother has business to take care of." Then he shifted his gaze to Axel. "Go take care of it."

Axel nodded. He knew exactly how Hannah had been cursed: His dad had tangled with a demon witch and she had cast a death curse on him. But witch hunters were immune to death curses, so the curse went down the bloodline, passing Axel and settling on Hannah.

3

A half hour later, he pulled up to the compound where his dad lived in the town of Glassbreakers; one of the odd little seaside towns in Los Angeles County. The compound used to be a veterinarian's house with an office and a kennel behind the house. He knew his dad had renovated the house, but he didn't know what he'd done with the veterinarian's office and kennel. The place was actually owned by the Rogue Cadre, but they gave Myles whatever he wanted for being a loyal witch killer. The idea of becoming a slave to anyone twisted Axel's balls, but he shook it off. He wasn't one of them yet, and the Wing Slayer Hunters would kill him if that day ever came.

With the death curse on Hannah, that day looked like a sure thing.

He left his truck on the street, leapt easily over the fence, and stalked up the driveway toward the sprawling house. He knew cameras were following him, but he didn't care. He wanted Myles to know he was there.

He reached the entry and pounded on the thick oak double doors.

The door opened and Axel blinked in surprise as recognition dawned on him. "Holden? That you?" It was Holden Mackenzie, the kid he'd played with until he was fourteen. He caught the copper scent and saw that his bulging arms were hairless. *Rogue.* That realization felt like a kick in the gut—his childhood buddy was rogue. "Christ, Holden, you're one of them?"

"Cut the shit, Axel. We're not kids and this isn't a game. The witches destroyed us. It's time we fought back and reclaimed our rightful heritage."

Axel thought of the rogues he'd killed when he worked private security on the club circuit. He hadn't singled them out, but when they came into the club and caused trouble of the deadly kind, he'd ended it. He'd always felt a tug of remorse, of pity for the witch hunter who had lost the battle with the curse. But this— seeing the man he'd known as a boy, the boy he'd played games of hunting demon witches with—it sickened and infuriated him. "You dumb fuck, you sold out our heritage."

Holden's nose flared with rage. His jaw was tight as he said, "Myles is upstairs."

He'd had years to deal with the fact that his dad was rogue, but Holden . . . that put the reality that he was only one witch kill from going that way, too, right in his face.

And that witch kill would happen to save Hannah's life.

Was he really any better than Holden? Or Myles?

He shook it off and strode into the tiled entryway. Another rogue stood at the bottom of the stairs holding a Glock. Now his dad had guards. What exactly was he doing that required guards? Not his problem, he reminded himself. He was here about Hannah. He took the stairs three at a time.

He found him in the master bedroom, lying on blue satin sheets, drinking Scotch, and watching a porn flick on the big-screen TV.

Myles looked over at him. "Is the witch dead?"

He knew he wasn't asking about the witch that had

cursed Hannah, but the one he had ordered Axel to kill. "Hell if I know." Myles was wearing a pair of boxers and there was an angry burn along his left side. It was from a fire-spell. They healed very fast, but a burn that bad would take a couple days. It looked like his dad had tangled with the wrong witch last night.

"Do you want to die? Young knows you've killed rogues, and that you've marked yourself in allegiance to a dead god. If you don't join us, you'll be killed."

Axel pulled out his gun and pointed it at his dad's heart. "I'm not interested in your threats, or Young's delusions of power. Did the witch that did this to you survive?"

Myles set the glass of Scotch on his bedside table. Ignoring the gun pointed at him, he answered darkly, "What do you care?"

"Hannah has been death-cursed."

He shrugged, then winced in pain. "So?"

Hate raced through Axel, from his heart to his trigger finger. It took everything he had not to kill him then and there. The only reason he didn't kill his father that very second was that he needed to know who the witch was. And killing him would bring down the guards in the house, and the wrath of the entire Rogue Cadre on him. Axel didn't need the headache while he tracked the witch who had cursed Hannah. "Who's the witch? What did you do to make her so angry?"

Myles picked up his glass and tossed back the remaining Scotch, then glared at Axel. "I did my duty. Exterminating all the witches is the only way to end this curse and get our souls back. How was I supposed to know her mother would show up?"

Axel's blood ran cold. He knew his dad was a monster, but . . . "You killed a kid?"

He snorted. "Not a kid; probably in her twenties.

Fought like a hellcat until I cut her enough . . ." He shuddered with pleasure at the memory.

Looking at his dad, he once again saw his own future. A cold-blooded, murderous animal. But Hannah . . . Myles didn't care that his daughter would die from a life-sucking curse, but Axel did. He shoved the gun into the raw burn on his father's side. "Who is the demon witch that cursed Hannah?"

"Don't know." Sweat rolled down the old man's face.

"Goddamn it, I won't let Hannah die."

Myles, half laughing, half grunting in pain, shook his head. "You think I give a rat's ass about that girl? You want the death curse lifted, go find a witch and force her to undo the curse."

"You make me sick." He wanted so desperately to kill the bastard, to watch his eyes drain of life, his body grow cold. He could do it with just one twitch of his finger . . . but he didn't. Not yet. He couldn't risk the rogue hunters getting in his way of saving Hannah. Or worse, going after his mom and Hannah in retaliation for his dad's death. "One day, I'll end your miserable life." He left the room before he gave in to the urge.

But he wasn't leaving empty-handed. Without meaning to, Myles had given Axel a possible solution. A way that might allow him to save Hannah and keep his soul at the same time. He would find another witch and force her to cast a spell to undo the curse. Earth witches were in hiding from rogues, and even if he found one, she would most likely refuse to help him since they had no protection from a pissed off demon witch. Casting a spell to undo a demon witch's curse would most definitely piss her off. But he would force the witch to do it. All he needed was the witch—and his dad had given him all the information he needed on one last night in his club.

Darcy MacAlister.

MONDAY: DAY THREE OF THE DEATH MARK

"We'll take good care of your mother," Darcy said to end the consultation and stood up in the conference room.

The four others in the room stood up. The deceased's two children and their respective spouses.

"Thank you," the daughter said.

Smiling gently, she took the woman's hand. "Don't worry about a thing. But if you have any questions or concerns, call me. I'm here to help you any way I can."

The daughter's husband nodded his thanks, then put his arm around his wife as they left.

Darcy steeled herself and turned to the son, Bryce Walker. She held out her hand and said, "Bryce, I'm very sorry about your mother. She was a lovely woman and we'll make sure she has a service that will honor her memory."

After a second of hesitation, he took her hand and muttered, "Thanks," while refusing to look her in the eyes. He dropped her hand quickly, took his wife's arm, and headed out of the conference room.

"What the hell was that?" Joe asked, coming in from the casket-display room.

Darcy fought back the tide of memories. "We dated," she said tightly, then picked up a folder from the conference table.

Joe moved up beside her, his blue gaze catching hers. "Did he do something to you? Hurt you?"

She sighed. "No. Nothing like that."

"Explain."

"No." She wasn't going to get into her sex life with Joe. Or lack of sex life now. She rarely dated anymore.

He touched her shoulder. "Darcy, you either tell me or I'm going to find out from Bryce himself."

She could feel Joe's concern in the warmth of his

hand. "We weren't sexually compatible, among other things." When they'd had sex, Darcy had felt his spooky thoughts wash over her.

Then he'd broken up with her by text message.

Bryce wasn't the only one, but he had been the last. So she hadn't dated in a while, hadn't opened herself to that kind of pain and rejection.

Joe brought her back to the moment by gently squeezing her shoulder and saying, "He wasn't good enough for you."

"Yeah, I know. He found a woman that was right for him. Cindy. She seems nice." So many people were getting married, finding mates; life partners. It made her feel lonely, frustrated, and out of place. But as much as she wanted to find a place she belonged, she didn't want to open herself to more rejection.

"You're tired and you just lost your mother. You shouldn't even be working this week."

"I want to work." What was she going to do? Sit home and feel sorry for herself? Her mom was better off now, no longer struggling for each breath. She was at peace. Darcy would not begrudge her that. To reassure Joe, she added, "I'm going to Carla's tonight. That'll be fun."

"Going dancing? Out to meet men?"

She shook her head. "Staying in." She wondered what Carla wanted to talk to her about.

He narrowed his gaze. "I've been home for months and I don't think I've seen you date once. What's up? Did you switch sides while I was gone?"

"Switch . . . Oh!" His meaning startled her into a huge laugh. She set down the folder and laughed harder. "God, Joe, I've missed you."

"That's because you had to run this place by yourself. Now you have me to boss around."

Her laughter died away. "I'm not your boss, Joe. This place is yours."

"Don't start with that shit. You pulled this mortuary back from the brink of bankruptcy. You saved your dad's ass, and he thanked you by leaving the mortuary to me. I wasn't even here, and he had the gall to order you to keep it running until I got out of the service."

Darcy had thought that her father would finally be proud of her. Finally see that she was worth his respect, if not his love. It seemed stupid now. But she didn't regret saving the mortuary. She felt like she was doing something important here, helping people in their times of grief. She waved off Joe's anger by saying, "Water under the bridge."

"I'm not taking this place from you. We're partners. Our fathers started the mortuary and you and I own it equally. And for now, you've earned the right to be the boss."

She picked up her files and walked out of the conference room into the lobby.

Joe fell into step beside her.

Grinning at him, she said, "Since I'm the boss, you're on call tonight." Glassbreakers was a small town, so they didn't get that many calls for a body pickup that couldn't wait until morning. But it was fun to give Joe the grunt work.

Joe ignored her, his gaze fixed on Morgan moving across the taupe carpet toward them. She wore tan slacks with a yellow sweater and a heavy silence that seemed to weigh down her every step. There was none of the cheerleader bounce that she'd had in high school.

Darcy watched the woman, remembering the confidence she'd had in school, the way she had known exactly where she belonged and where she was going. No one had been surprised when Morgan moved to San Diego and became an on-air journalist. It had always seemed like Morgan knew her course, understood her purpose in life. Darcy had envied that.

Morgan stopped a few feet away and said, "I've finished for the day. I was wondering if I could talk to you, Darcy."

"Sure," she said, and walked past Morgan into her office. Setting down the plans for the Walker viewing and funeral she took a seat and gestured to the chair facing her desk. "Sit down."

While Morgan settled into the chair, Joe stood in the doorway, hovering. When it came to Morgan, Joe always hovered. The two of them had flirted in high school, but they'd never gone out as far as Darcy knew.

Since Joe was half owner, Darcy decided he had every right to listen in. She looked at Morgan's pinched face. "Is something wrong?"

She took a breath and brushed her shoulder-length blond hair back. "No. Well, yes. It's complicated."

Darcy waited, but Morgan seemed to be uncertain, so she asked, "Is it a problem here? Morgan, you're an excellent employee. I don't know why you wanted a job here, but I was desperate when my last assistant quit while I was taking care of my mother. You stepped in and have proved yourself. If something happened, I, well Joe and I, will back you up." She meant that. Morgan was Joe's age, two years older than Darcy, and back in high school, she'd run with the cool cheerleader/jock crowd. But when those kids tormented Darcy—taunting her with names like Dark Mac—Morgan told them to stop, or managed to turn their attention to something else. She and Darcy hadn't been friends, but Morgan hadn't been cruel. And the one time Darcy had been in real trouble, it had been Morgan that led Joe to her.

Morgan looked down at her hands.

"If it's some other kind of trouble, I'll try to help."

She didn't have to look to see Joe straighten up and tense.

She clenched her hands. "I need to tell you something." She absently rubbed at her right temple. "It's about my husband, Eric . . ."

"Your husband?" Darcy prompted. She had heard that Morgan had married, but nothing else about her husband or where he was now. "Are you divorced?"

She shook her head, then raised her other hand so that she was rubbing both temples. She squinted as if the light was hurting her eyes. "No, I . . ."

"Morgan, are you sick?"

"A headache."

Darcy was curious as hell about what Morgan had been planning to tell her, but she could see the woman didn't feel well. "Go home, Morgan. Get some rest, we can talk tomorrow."

Morgan dropped her hands and stood up.

"Do you want me to drive you to your apartment?"

"I'll drive her," Joe said, moving into the room.

Morgan turned and seemed surprised. "Joe."

He kept her gaze. "Let me drive you home. We can pick up something to eat . . ."

She shook her head. "No, I'll be fine. It's just a headache. I can drive myself." She turned, clutched her purse to her stomach, and hurried out of the office.

"Don't," Darcy said, reading in her cousin that he was about to go after Morgan.

Joe shot his gaze to her. "She's sick."

"She's afraid. If you crowd her, it'll scare her more."

Joe's shoulders went back. "What has she told you?

"Nothing, but you know, when she brushes by me, I just . . . feel it. It's jumbled and complicated, but she's scared of something."

He didn't even blink. "Or someone."

"Joe, don't confuse nostalgia for a high school crush

for something real. She's not the same girl." She didn't want Morgan to hurt Joe or drag him into a dangerous situation that could hurt them both.

His stare crashed into hers. "Darcy, this is the shit that unsettles the men you date. You see too much sometimes. Or you feel it, or whatever it is you do."

"Thanks, Dr. Phil," she said. "Go away, I have work to do. You can figure out this attraction to Morgan by yourself."

He laughed and headed for the door. "I'm out of here. See you in the morning."

"Night, Joe."

He looked back. "Be careful. I'll lock the door on my way out." Then he left.

She heard the lock turn in the front door.

In the silence, the voice-sounds in her head started up. Sighing, Darcy grabbed her iPod to drown out the voices. While the Red House Painters sang, she kicked off her heels and stripped off her jacket. Comfortable, she got to work tackling the invoicing, filing death certificates, and seeing to the endless details of death.

Thirty minutes later, the knife scar on her upper left arm finally got her attention. It occasionally burned or itched. She realized she'd been scratching it while she worked. She looked down: It was red from all the scratching. She opened her desk to grab a bottle of lotion. Squeezing out a pea-size dab, she rubbed it into her scar. As she put the lotion away, she glanced at the computer screen and noticed a new email had arrived.

While her iPod continued to play, she clicked on the icon to open the email. Her heart skipped a beat, then sped up. Another email from herself, just like the one two nights ago. The subject line read: *Warning*.

She read the message: *They've found you! Run! Get out!*

An involuntary shiver raced down her back and quivered in her stomach. This was freaking creepy. Feeling like someone was behind her, she ripped out her earbuds and swung around in the swivel chair, but no one was there.

The only people left in the mortuary were her and two dead bodies. She needed to get a grip. Someone was screwing with her. But why? Who? She'd endured a lot of pranks growing up, but none in the last few years.

The phone rang and she grabbed it, glad to handle a normal activity. "MacAlister Funeral Home, how may I help you?"

"Run!"

Shivers danced over the skin on her arms. The voice sounded flat, computer-like. "Who is this?" She stood up and leaned over her desk to look out into the lobby. Nothing threatening lurked in her line of vision.

"Run!"

She slammed the phone down. She didn't know what was going on, but she was getting the hell out of there. Darcy grabbed her purse off the small shelf unit and dropped her iPod in it, then she snatched her jacket off the back of her chair and shoved her feet into her pumps.

Tension pulled tight across her back, neck, and shoulders. Quickly, she fished her keys out of her purse and walked out into the lobby. Her heels sank into the soft, thick taupe carpet as she crossed the lobby. Everything looked normal, she thought, as she caught the scent of the flower arrangement in a large crystal vase on the highly polished accent table. At the door, she unlocked the dead bolt, opened it, and went outside. She closed the door, then jammed her key in and locked it.

The night air smelled like the salty ocean mixed with a coppery odor that made her want to cover her nose and breathe through her mouth. She'd never liked copper, going so far as to avoid pennies when she was a kid.

Right now she felt like she had pennies in her mouth; that metallic taste and thick scent.

Like the man from the gravesite.

She shivered, struggling to keep the fear from overwhelming her. Everything else seemed normal. Crickets and frogs chirped and croaked. She took a deep breath to pull herself together.

Copper.

Why did she smell copper? The unease gave way to a real panic clawing at her. She believed the danger was real and close by, though she didn't know why. With her keys in her hand, she turned.

Two large men holding huge knives blocked the walkway to the parking lot.

Darcy froze, her muscles tightening with fear. Her heart rate kicked up. They hadn't been there when she had walked outside. Where'd they come from? She stuck her hand in her purse to grab her cell phone and said, "What . . . uh . . . can I help you?" She had the phone in her fingers, fumbling to dial 911.

The one on her right lunged toward her, caught her by the throat, and slammed her back against the wall. Her phone, purse, and coat slid to the ground. Her head rang. The taste of copper filled her mouth. The vivid smell induced an elemental fear so deep it made the scar on her arm throb.

Fight! Her mind screamed.

The second guy moved in.

Their knives flashed silver in the moonlight. The first one said, "Get the keys. We'll take her inside."

Like hell! She clutched the keys tighter and wedged her fist between her back and the stucco. But the second man yanked her arm out, wrapped his hand around her wrist, and squeezed. The keys fell from her numb fingers. He grabbed them and hurried to the door.

Terror clamped down on her lungs as mind-numbing

fear flooded her bloodstream. *Fight back!* Voices in her head screamed. Darcy linked her hands and brought them up between the arms of the brute holding her throat. The action broke his hold. She tried to run.

He caught her wrist, yanked her back, and threw her face-first into the stucco wall. It scraped her face and she tasted blood from a split lip. He shoved his huge body against hers, trapping her flush against the wall. "Hurry up with the door!"

"She's holding the door closed with witchcraft!" The second man screamed. "Cut her!"

Fear rolled and churned in her stomach. *Witchcraft?* What the hell were they talking about? The chatter of voices in her head hurt. The man holding her pushed her harder into the wall. "Your powers won't save you, witch." She felt the cold edge of his knife pressing into the curve of her neck, just above her shoulder.

The scar on her arm burned. Wavy images and words bounced in her head—*knives and blood.* She shuddered and struggled to get away. "No! Bastards! Get off me!"

The knife sliced a hot trail of fire across her skin. Then the man leaned in and hissed, "Smell that? Your blood's mine."

Red fear and pain rolled over her mind. Even the voices inside her head fled. They were going to kill her and she didn't know why. She barely knew what they looked like—just big with vacant, mean eyes. Warm blood welled up and ran down her back. The man holding her panted in excitement, and Darcy felt his eagerness for the kill. For her blood.

"Got it," the key guy said.

She heard the door open. Pain and fear threatened to overwhelm her. She had to block it out and think. Had to find a way to save herself. If she let them get her inside, she would die. The man behind her grabbed her arm just as the sound of an engine roared through the night. The noise grew, then she heard a screech of tires. With her body and face pressed into the stucco, she might as well have been blind. There were more sounds—flesh slamming against flesh, something wet and horrifying, metallic clinks as knives hit the ground, and grunts—then the man who had trapped her against the wall was gone. Yanked off of her.

She sucked in a breath, then turned around to see a large silhouette in the headlights of a big truck stick a knife deep into the chest of the man who'd been holding her. He dropped the body on top of the other man lying motionless in the truck's beam of light.

Horrified, she turned to the door. It stood open with her keys hanging in the lock. *Get inside and lock the door.*

A powerful arm wrapped around her waist and pulled her right off her feet. She lost her grip on the keys and the door, not to mention her sanity. She struggled in his hold, trying to kick him as he stalked over to the opened door of the truck. She took a deep breath to scream, but he slapped a hand over her mouth.

"Damn it, do you want to die?" He stepped up into the truck and tossed her onto the passenger seat.

Darcy bounced, feeling every ache in her body. One shoe slid off and hit the floorboard. She fought a wave of dizziness and struggled to get her breathing under control. The truck smelled like leather and night air. She wiggled to slide her foot back into her shoe and demanded, "Who are you?"

He slammed his door. "I just saved your ass. More rogue hunters will be coming. They don't leave messes and they don't leave witches alive." He put the truck in reverse and hit the gas.

She had to grab the seat to keep from flying through the windshield. As he shifted from reverse to drive, she saw her chance and lunged for the door handle.

He caught her left arm in a brutal grip.

She looked back and gasped at his cold green eyes and the knife in his left hand.

"Don't make me cut you. I don't want to hurt you, but I will if you fight me."

Oh, God. "Why are you doing this?"

His gaze traveled down to her bleeding mouth, and his hand tightened on her arm. "I need a witch."

Holy shit! *A witch?* What had he meant that more rogue hunters would come? None of this made any sense. "You'll have to kill me now. I'm not going to let you take me anywhere!"

His green eyes flared with a heat that nearly knocked her back in her seat. Pulling her forward, he brought her close enough to his face for her to get a nose full of his cedar scent mixed with sweat. "Do you want me to cut you?"

No! The back of her neck burned where the first one had cut her. The one she'd seen this man kill. Fear choked her. She couldn't answer him.

He nodded and let her go. "First-aid kit in the glove compartment." Then he set his huge knife on his thigh and drove.

Darcy shivered and reached for the kit while she tried to figure out how to escape.

4

Axel drove the truck up the quiet road to the safe house. It was nestled against cliffs that rose up over a lake. The property was located at the edge of Los Angeles, deep in a rugged forest that didn't attract much attention. The house was surrounded by rocky cliffs on three sides and faced the lake, providing good protection. No one except the Wing Slayer Hunters knew he owned this house and the surrounding property. He'd kept it furnished and stocked, ready for him to hide his mom and sister if they were ever threatened. He always knew the Rogue Cadre might decide to use them as leverage if they wanted something from Axel. He hadn't foreseen a situation where he'd be hiding a witch, but here he was with a witch that he knew the rogues were looking for. If anyone did find them, he had cameras and sensors that continually monitored the property.

He parked the truck in front of the house and sucked in a breath.

Smelled her blood.

Squeezing his fingers around the steering wheel, he ignored the burn, the need. Her wound had stopped bleeding but the smell of fresh witch blood still lingered. Still tormented him with the promise of cool relief to his burning need. *Get this over with.*

He heard the soft click as she tried to squeeze the door handle. Getting ready to shove it open and run. He picked up his knife, then moved so fast that he got around the truck in time to catch the passenger door as she shoved it open. He blocked her in. "Don't run from me. Don't." He barely had himself under control now; if she ran, the predator in him would surface.

She swung her head to look at him, her face pale in the glow of the cab light. "How did you . . . you were right next to me, then suddenly . . ."

Fear brightened her eyes and made their tilted shape even more prominent. The line of her jaw bulged with tension. "Witch hunters are fast. Now stop stalling and get out of the truck."

"Witch hunters?"

His gaze stopped on her smooth, full thigh beneath her black skirt. A flash of lust surprised him. Ignoring it, he backed up and said, "Get out."

She swung her legs around and slid down to the ground, her eyes darting from side to side.

Christ, the back of her silver shirt was black and gummy with dried blood. Strands of her hair stuck to it. He could see the white edge of the big bandage she'd stuck over the knife cut. She had to be in pain but she hadn't said a word. Fury rocketed through him at the memory of driving up and seeing the two hunters on her.

One sliding his knife across her delicate skin . . .

He wrenched his mind away from those thoughts. She was there for one reason: to spell the curse off Hannah—then she was gone.

She'll be dead within hours of him releasing her. He told himself that if she cooperated, he'd find a place for her that was safe from the rogues or the demon witch whose curse she was going to undo. He grabbed her arm.

She jerked back, trying to get free.

Axel took a breath and smelled her fear. Keeping a hold on her arm he said, "I'm not going to hurt you if you cooperate."

Defiance lined her face in contrast to the fear marking her scent. "Like I'd believe you."

"Keep it up and I'll drug you." He wouldn't risk drugging her, but as a threat, it worked.

"I'm allergic to drugs!"

He smiled. Now she was catching on. "I know." Witches were highly evolved creatures with an ability to heal using a combination of their craft and natural remedies provided by the earth. Synthetic drugs screwed that up and made them sick.

She recoiled. "Bastard."

"So we understand each other." He tugged on her arm and guided her up a flight of stone steps and over a flagstone path to the front door. The house was an optical illusion. It looked like a one-story house built on the flat stretch of land in front of the jagged cliffs. But that was just the top level of the house. There was an entire lower level hidden by a façade of dirt and rocks.

He unlocked and opened the door, then heard the faint hiss of the infrared sensors crossing the pathway. Pulling out his BlackBerry with one hand while keeping a hold on the witch, he coded the alarm to pause for fifteen seconds. When the faint hiss stopped, he walked her through the doorway. She stood still at his side, looking around. The living room held a heavy rust-colored couch, a leather recliner, a stone fireplace next to a dark wood bookcase built around a plasma TV, and a large rug on the cold tile floor. No sign that the house was wired with enough electronics to give Bill Gates a hard-on, nor was there any indication that there was another entire floor below.

"Come on." He walked past a hallway that led to three bedrooms and into a large modern kitchen right down to the stainless-steel appliances.

He stopped when he saw his mom sitting at the big trestle table with Hannah in her arms. "Is she all right?"

His mom had her hair up on top of her head and wore a pair of sweatpants and a T-shirt. Her face was heavy with worry. "She has a fever."

Hannah lifted her head up; her hair in a soft braid and Minnie Mouse tucked under her arm. Her tired eyes sparked with curiosity. "Who's that?"

Axel dropped his hold on Darcy and went to his sister. "She won't hurt you."

Hannah held her arms up to him.

Axel lifted her up and looked into her too-bright eyes. "Not feeling good?"

"Mommy gave me grape stuff to make me feel better."

He forced himself to stay focused. He had the witch and they were going to save Hannah. He turned to Darcy.

Damn, she looked bad, he hadn't realized how bad until now. Her face was scraped, her lip split and swollen, dried blood everywhere. There were some finger marks on her neck. He didn't want Hannah to see any of this, but there was nothing he could do but get it over with quickly. He'd just show Darcy the death mark on Hannah and get her to work.

Hannah held out her doll to Darcy. "Want to hold my Minnie? She makes me feel better."

Darcy looked at the doll then shifted her gaze to his mom. "Who are you people? You can't keep me here. I want to leave."

Axel reached out his hand and pulled the doll back to Hannah. "She doesn't need Minnie. You hold on to her." Then he looked at Darcy and said meaningfully, "Maybe she needs some medicine."

Darcy sucked in her lips and glared at him.

He didn't have time to regret not getting to her before the two rogues who hurt her. Instead, he focused on

Hannah. "We're going to show her the mark on your forehead. She's going to help you feel better."

She wrinkled up her little face. "It hurts. Make it go away."

Anger arced up like a waking beast inside of him. His hand itched to hold his knife and spill blood . . .

His mom's firm voice cut through the haze of the curse. "Axel, show her the mark. Darcy, I know you want to leave, and you can once you help Hannah."

Hannah didn't wait. In his arms, she leaned toward Darcy and pushed up her bangs.

Axel watched as Darcy's gaze fixed on Hannah's forehead. Her eyes went wide, her pupils dilated in shock. Fear stamped down hard on her face and she stepped back. She slapped both her hands over her mouth. "Oh, God!" She took another step. "This isn't happening!" And she turned and ran.

Darcy was going to be sick. She pulled open the front door, ignoring the warning beep of the security system, and stumbled outside onto the flagstone. She sucked in a breath of cool air. Her mouth watered and her stomach rolled.

She couldn't outrun the truth. She had seen that mark once before when she had been six years old. She and Joe had snuck in to see the dead man everyone was talking about.

They made it to the viewing room unnoticed.

It smelled like flowers and the wet scent of sad people. She wrinkled her nose. The family of the dead guy sat at the end of the coffin, and several people stood with their backs to Darcy while talking to the family. Joe tugged her to the shiny, brass-handled coffin.

They stood together at the side of the casket. She squeezed Joe's hand and looked in. It was a young man

*with short hair and a waxy sunken face, but her gaze
stuck on his forehead, on the coal-black round mark.*

*Her head started to spin. The voices in her head made
shocked hisses and moans and said, "Oh no. He has the
death mark! Get back, Darcy! The demon witch might
find you if you touch him!"*

"No!" She didn't want a black mark on her head!

Her dad's loud voice boomed, "Darcy MacAlister!"

*She turned to look at him. "It's a death mark, Daddy!
He has the death mark!"*

Her dad's face turned red.

A woman cried out and dissolved into weeping.

People gathered around.

*Darcy stared up at all the adults, trying to make them
understand. "The death mark killed him!"*

*Her father grabbed her arm, yanking so hard she
yelped in pain . . .*

The memory was so vivid even now. Seeing the pink
mark on Hannah brought it all back. That beautiful little girl inside the house was marked for death. She bent
over and put her hands on her knees, trying to find her
center and think. She wanted to run, but she couldn't
leave that child. Some force within her wouldn't let her.
She had to . . . what? What was she that she recognized
that death mark?

She knew what her dad had thought . . .

*Someone yanked her arm. She cried out, waking up
suddenly and feeling scared.*

*Her dad pulled her out of bed, holding her up with
both hands. The moonlight streamed in and she could
see that his eyes were red. His breath smelled bad, too.*

"I'm not raising a devil-spawn!" he yelled at her.

*"Gerry!" Her mom rushed into the room. "She's just
a little girl!"*

Darcy started to cry.

Her dad shook her. "There's something wrong with her! She's a freak! You saw her tonight!"

"You're drunk! Put her down, Gerry, or I swear to God, I'll call the police! Do you want the town to find out you're afraid of a little girl?"

His hands dug into her arms. His jaw was tight. "She embarrassed us . . ."

Her mom took her from him, hugging Darcy tight. "Go sleep it off, Gerry."

He stormed out.

Someone tugged on her arm, yanking her from the memory, and said, "You can't escape. You set off two silent alarms that alert me just running out the front door. My house is very secure."

Darcy snapped upright and jerked a step back from him. A wave of dizziness hit her. The cut burned on her back. Ever since that night, Darcy had stopped hearing the voices clearly. She'd stopped being different, weird, freaky unless by accident. She'd tried to be normal so her dad would love her.

Her kidnapper kept talking. "Not that I need electronics. Witch hunters can track you anywhere."

Pulling herself together, she straightened and ignored the pain from the cut. He'd called himself a witch hunter earlier, and he'd called those two men who attacked her the same thing. She thought of the emails warning her of hunters. But what did it all mean? "Who are you? What do you want from me?"

"Axel Locke. I need you to do a spell to remove the death curse from my sister."

He stood a couple feet from her, and *loomed*. He was well over six feet, and had sleek black hair that just touched his collar. His face was cut hard. His T-shirt couldn't contain the muscles, sinew and veins ripping through his massive arms. Everything about him was strong and threatening.

"Is this your way of asking? Scaring the crap out of me?" Darcy didn't like the deep fear writhing inside of her. It reminded her of her dad, of the terror that she'd be thrown out of the only family she'd ever had. The fear that her dad was right, that something evil lived inside of her.

"I was too busy saving your life to ask. But if I had, we both know what the answer would be. You witches don't care that a child will die . . ." He shut his mouth on the word, his jaw bulging with emotion.

She couldn't track this conversation. The whole thing was surreal. "What makes you think I can do it anyway? Your sister needs a doctor, not me." A witch? Her? Was such a thing possible?

"It's early in the curse yet, you should be able to do it."

More panic dumped into her bloodstream. "Are you drunk? Stupid? Crazy? I am not a witch!" She would know, wouldn't she?

He glared down at her. "Playing dumb won't help you. You're going to do the spell."

He was blocking the only way off the porch. She could try and run through the house . . . but to where? Somehow she'd lost her bearings on the way here. The house was practically set into a mountain with only one road out that she could see. Then there was that little girl. . . . Lifting her head and ignoring the pain searing down the back of her neck, she said, "Playing dumb? You're the one who kidnapped me! Now you're talking witches and hunters and death curses! I can't help you!"

He took a step closer. "You're telling me you don't know you're a witch?"

His voice was thick with disbelief. She had no way of knowing what he'd do next. Or knowing what she should do to save herself. Running the back of her hand over her mouth, she tried to sound calm and firm. "That's exactly what I'm telling you."

"Unlikely." Another step brought him even closer. "You made your lip bleed again."

She backed up into the wall of the house. His voice was a low growl that penetrated her skin. The need to know, to understand what was happening, burned inside of her. He was a single step from her. His green eyes looked feverish, his cedar smell was stronger, and it actually pulled at her. "Stop it! Whatever you're doing, just stop it! I have to think."

"I can't stop." In that growl, he added, "I wish to God I could. Your skin smells like lemons. But your blood smells spicy."

Her stomach fluttered as if a dozen butterflies were inside. She could hear a coyote howl in the distance, then the answering call from its mate. Crickets chirped. A body of water lapped softly against a shore not far off. She tried to process his words, but nothing was making sense. Except the closer he got to her, the bigger the feeling inside of her, the need . . . "What are you doing?"

His gaze narrowed on her mouth. "You're bleeding."

Her stomach jiggled. "You already said that." She was frozen in his intensity, caught in some web winding around the two of them.

"Your blood calls to me." He lifted his right hand and used the pad of his thumb to wipe the blood trickling down from the cut on her bottom lip.

The shock of him touching her blood vibrated through her right down to her bones. She felt the weirdest tugging deep inside, like parts of her that were closed off wanted to open up to him. She grabbed his wrist to pull his thumb away from her face, but a rush of dizziness caused her to hold on to his strength, keeping his hand against her face like an anchor. Nothing made sense. "How can I be a witch?" It was torn from her soul. If she was a witch, then was she the evil spawn her dad believed? Was that why her biological mother got rid of her?

He tore his gaze from her mouth, looked into her eyes, and said in a rough, claim-staking voice, "My witch now. I've touched your blood, you're mine."

Her heart thudded. His eyes burned into her, and then they changed, the green becoming mirror-like. She could see her own brown eyes in their depths, but it felt like a magnet, pulling her closer. Though she held his wrist, he easily slid his thumb over her cut and into her mouth. The voices in her head calmed to white noise. Erotic images mixed in her mind as the taste of his skin seared her tongue. She felt tears of recognition well up. She wanted—needed—to be closer to him.

He slid his thumb out and leaned down to kiss her.

"Axel," a female voice called from the house.

He made a threatening noise in his chest and slid his hand around the back of Darcy's head to hold her. Then he drew his tongue intimately across her lips. Her muscles softened and she leaned into him, needing him.

"Axel!" The voice was closer this time.

He went still, like a wolf about to attack. He lifted his head and looked down at her with a potent, *commanding* hunger. In the green reflection of his eyes, Darcy thought she glimpsed the shadow of a hawk, her hawk. Then he jerked his hand from her hair, and looked down at his thumb.

The smear of her blood was vanishing, disappearing into his skin.

His mother stood a couple feet away. "Axel, you touched her blood! Leave! Get in the truck and go. Get away from her. She'll destroy you."

He kept his intense stare on her. "Can't."

Eve moved to Darcy's side. "Let me take her inside. She's hurt and needs—"

"Don't," Axel barked. "Don't get between us."

She'd destroy him? He was destroying her! Forcing her to acknowledge something she didn't want to. Couldn't. His mom obviously recognized the danger inside of her, and thought it would destroy Axel. "I am not a witch!"

They both ignored her. Eve said, "We need her to spell the curse off Hannah."

Axel didn't move, just kept watching Darcy like some kind of feral beast. "She'll do it."

Darcy wasn't getting through to them. Taking control of herself, she remembered that she had skills of her own. Lowering her voice, she said, "I can't help you. I'm no use to you. Just let me go."

He narrowed his eyes on her. "Don't try to charm me with your voice. It won't work. The only chance you have of staying alive is to do exactly what I tell you."

"Axel . . ." Eve's voice broke in.

He cut her off. "Go inside, Mom. Now."

His mom turned and went in the house.

He grabbed Darcy's arm.

"No!" She tried to plant her feet and resist him. Why hadn't she run when she had the chance? "Don't touch me." She couldn't think when he touched her.

He dropped her arm and scooped her up. Without saying a word, he walked into the house, turned right into the hallway, and then left into a huge master bedroom. There was a heavy teak bed in the middle of the room and bunch of computer equipment set up against one wall. That was all she saw before he turned again and went through a big bathroom with a monster tub and took her into a walk-in closet.

"What are you doing?"

"Keeping you alive." His voice was rough and cold as he slapped his hand against a mirror hung deep in the corner of the closet.

A doorway-size piece of the closet wall opened up. They walked through and started down some stairs. The wall slid closed behind them.

Real panic shot through her. Visions of torture and rape and . . . Darcy struggled, trying to get out of his arms.

He tightened his grip, trapping her hands between her side and his chest. "Easy, I'm not going to hurt you. I need you too much."

Like she believed him! Furious and scared, energy welled up inside of her. She thought of the two men who attacked and cut her. Of Axel threatening her with his knife.

The knife! She'd seen him stick it in the holster at his back. Her heart rate shot up to high-speed terror. The knife. She concentrated on the knife, felt the energy form into a ball in her chest, then escape.

Axel stopped walking in the hallway with a look of surprise on his face.

His knife had slipped out of the holster and was flying around him in a circle. Shocked, she watched, feeling a weird connection to the knife. The hallway was so small that Axel would have to drop her to dodge the knife. She could get away. That's all she wanted, just to escape.

But instead of dropping her, he stayed still until the last second then he suddenly turned right and jerked his head to avoid the blade. Only the hilt of the knife glanced off his left cheekbone. He barely let out a grunt.

But a mere second later, pain slammed into Darcy's left cheekbone, making her head snap back with the force of it. Like *she'd* been hit by the knife. Her entire body bowed with shock. Pain radiated outward in hot waves. Her ears rang and a tear slid down her face. She squeezed her eyes shut.

"Jesus Christ, what did you expect?" Axel roared, his voice a thundering echo in the hallway. He lifted her closer to his face and said more gently, "Breathe. The pain will stop in a minute. Just breathe through it."

She struggled to do what he told her. Breathe in and out. Finally the pain began to dull enough to think. Had *she* made the knife do that? But it hit Axel not her, so what happened to her face? Finally she looked at him. There was a mild red mark on the left side of his face that was disappearing even as she watched. He must heal fast. Confused, she asked, "What happened?"

His nostrils flared. "You got emotional and stupid, forgot about witch karma, and used your powers to try to stab me with my knife. I barely felt it. But magnified three times, you gave yourself a black eye."

"Hey, I'm the one that got bitch-slapped by witch karma, what are you yelling at me for?" The pain settled down to a steady throb. Something sure as hell had slammed into the side of her face. She had most definitely felt the energy inside of her gather, then act.

He dropped his gaze to her and a grin twitched on his lips. "Point taken." Then his expression hardened and he resumed walking as if nothing had happened. He turned into a room the size of an average bedroom. It had a tile floor, bare walls, and overhead lighting. He set her down.

Without a word, he stalked out into the hallway, retrieved his knife from the ground, then returned to fill up the small room with his massive size. Sliding the knife into the holster, he said, "Get started. This counter used to be a wet bar that we converted into work space for you. My mom stocked everything she could think of in here. If you need anything, we'll get it."

She glanced at the dark granite counter, the sink, and the cupboards, but she still didn't understand; what exactly did they expect her to do? "Start what? I don't know . . ."

He sucked in a breath. "Stop. You just demonstrated

your witchcraft by trying to stab me with my own knife. Get started on the spell. That death curse will kill Hannah at the full moon. We don't have much time." He left, closing the door behind him.

She looked around, ignoring the ache in her left eye and cheekbone, to take it all in. The wall behind the counter was lined with neatly labeled drawers that contained dried herbs and assorted other items like salt, incense, candles, gemstones, and pieces of silver. She turned, catching sight of a twin bed in one corner.

This room was her prison. She was in deep trouble.

Once he was back in his room, Axel paced like an animal. He had a vicious hard-on for the witch. And nothing was making sense. As far as he knew, the curse made them crave the witch's blood, not sex. The sex part of the curse was just an increased sex drive, not this . . . painful yearning. He went to his computer, and keyed in.

Sutton appeared on the screen. "Yeah?"

Axel looked at the man's ice blue eyes and sharp bone structure. "What do you have on Darcy MacAlister?" They had the kill sheet that told Axel where she lived, worked, banked . . . all the places to track her.

Sutton frowned. "Did you get her?"

"She's in the room now. But she's claiming she doesn't know what she is." *Are you drunk? Stupid? Crazy? I am not a witch!* He'd heard the desperation in her voice, felt it, and he'd seen the shock on her face when she saw the mark on Hannah. Then she'd used her powers to try to stab him. Either she was incredibly stupid, or she hadn't known about witch karma. What witch didn't know that?

"You couldn't feel her power?" Sutton asked.

Oh, yeah, he felt it. He had smelled it in her blood, and felt the sizzle and kick of it when he touched her blood. Saw it with her attempt to stab him. But it was his reaction that was unusual. He hadn't wanted to kill her, he'd wanted to fuck her. He'd wanted to possess her.

Even her pain from the witch karma bothered him. "Felt it. She's a witch. But does she know she's a witch?"

He turned to look at the second monitor and all the blood drained from his brain. Darcy. She'd taken off her shirt, bra and bandage, and she stood at the counter with her back to the camera mounted in the corner. She had a white cloth and was trying to clean the blood off herself. Her skin was pale gold, stretching over her shoulder blades. She'd pulled her long auburn hair over her uninjured shoulder, and tried to dab at the weeping cut.

He saw her back contract with pain.

Damn it, there were herbs in the room she could use to ease the pain if she . . . shit, he was beginning to believe her.

"Axel."

Tearing his gaze away, he looked at Sutton on the screen. "What've you got?"

"One emergency-room admit for a deep cut to her left arm. She had a severe reaction to the meds and almost died. Nothing since. Her birth records indicate . . . oh shit."

"Give it to me."

"Darcy's adopted. Her adoptive mother had had a hysterectomy and couldn't have children. Darcy's mom has no allergy to meds."

He lifted his gaze to the witch. "Her adoptive mom's not a witch." While he stared, Darcy turned around with the bloody cloth in her hand. Her face was creased with pain and desperation. His eyes slid to an intricate silver necklace dangling between her breasts, and his lust ramped up to ball-squeezing need. "She doesn't know she's a witch." He believed her. "She won't know how to remove the curse. I'm so screwed."

"She can still undo the curse. There's time. We can help her," Sutton said.

Desperation and lust made his words hoarse. "I have to get her out of here."

"If you do, she's dead. I hacked into the Rogue Cadre's database, she's been moved to the number one kill. They want this witch all kinds of dead."

Axel thought about the rogues targeting Darcy. "If she doesn't even know she's a witch, why are they after her? How did she attract their attention?"

Sutton shook his head while studying the computer screens he was working on. "The only thing I can find is that she registered for a birth-parent search. But I don't know why that would get the rogues' attention. Something did, though; they are determined to kill her."

An odd, protective feeling rose in his chest. For a witch. He had no idea what to make of that, so he ignored it. "That doesn't solve my problem. I have a witch who doesn't know how to spell a curse and just seven days until the waxing gibbous moon." An earth witch could only spell the curse up until the waxing gibbous moon. After that, only killing the demon witch before the full moon would break the death curse. And once they hit the true full moon, nothing would save Hannah.

Sutton leaned back, looking directly into the camera. "Can you control your compulsion around her long enough for her to learn the spell? It can't be that hard to find a spell for her to do. It'd be easier and safer than trying to get another witch with the Rogue Cadre breathing down your neck."

Axel didn't look away. "No. I've touched her blood."

His blue eyes widened in surprise. Sutton leaned forward. "Is she still alive, A?"

He brought his hand up to cover the hollow place in his chest. It took everything he had to keep his gaze on Sutton and not look up to the monitor showing Darcy. "Yes. But she's in me now." He lost his battle and looked up. She was using the washcloth to get the blood out of her shirt. Her body was turned slightly so he could see her narrow waist, the swell of her breast beneath her arm as she moved. In a deep voice, he told the truth, "I need her."

"Can you have sex with her and not kill her?"

He shifted his gaze back to Sutton. Sweat ran down his back. "I don't know." He wanted her blood, too; he wanted all of her. What if he completely lost control during sex and cut her to get to her blood? Once he cut her, he wouldn't stop until she was dead.

"I'm going to gather what we know about spelling a curse. The way I see it, you can do one of two things. Send your mom to deal with the witch and you stay away from her."

He knew that wasn't going to happen. "Or?"

"We know that sex with mortal women helps us control the compulsion. Find out if the same goes with a witch."

"Find everything you can on spells and death curses. I'll worry about keeping the witch alive." Axel hit the key to break the connection and stood up. Darcy was like a magnetic pull that he couldn't resist. He went through his closet, down the stairs, and to the room. He had an office on this level, bedrooms, and a small kitchen. He built the safe house so they could hide on the bottom floor if attacked and escape through a hidden garage. There was also a supply of weapons. He had Darcy in the room across from his office. The lock on her room was specially made to engage a second lock if the first one was tripped, and a third if the second was tripped. It wasn't totally witch-proof, but it would slow her down.

But Darcy hadn't even tried to unlock it.

He used his palm print to fully disengage the lock and opened the door.

She swung around, holding the wet shirt in front of

her breasts. The action was so female, so vulnerable, that he felt a weird protective feeling again, mixed with lust. Then he caught sight of the scar on her upper left arm. It had to be the one she'd been admitted to the emergency room for. He closed the distance between them and reached for her arm.

She tried to jerk away, still clutching the wet shirt to her breasts.

Axel loosened his hold on her. As determined as he was to save Hannah, terrifying and hurting women disgusted him. He sure as hell didn't want to see her suffer a repeat of the pain she'd experienced from the witch karma. "Easy, I just want to see the scar." As soon as he touched the jagged cut, he felt the heat. "Another witch hunter attacked you. When?"

She looked at him with angry brown eyes. "Let go of me."

He realized that he had tightened his fingers possessively. Damn it, he forced his hand to let go of her arm. "Tell me what happened." His blood was already running hot. Her scent alone made him want more; need more.

She clutched the shirt tighter but she lifted her chin with determination. "I was fourteen. I was walking home from a party and was attacked by a psycho with a knife. Somehow in the struggle, my arm was cut."

He saw her backing away from the truth. A truth she didn't seem to want to know. "Your arm was cut with witch karma. Just like today, you probably used your powers to stab the hunter with his own knife. Witch karma causes any intentional harm done with magic to come back on the witch times three." He looked into her eyes. "You know exactly what happened that day."

She moved back from him. "No one believed me. He was going to kill me! I had to fight back, I couldn't stop the energy that grabbed his knife and cut his bicep. Seconds later, my arm just exploded open . . . there was so much blood and pain. I thought I was going to die."

She had been fourteen! What the hell was wrong with the witches allowing her to be adopted into a mortal family? She'd survived the hunter only to be damn near killed by the hospital staff when they gave her synthetic pain blockers. "What chased off the hunter?"

Clutching the shirt even tighter, she said, "My cousin. A friend of his, Morgan, had found out there really wasn't a party that night, that some kids were playing a trick on me. My mom had dropped me off, but when the parents answered the door, they had no idea what I was talking about. I was so humiliated. I didn't want to call home and tell my parents, so I decided to walk home. Anyway, the two of them got there and saw what was happening. They scared the guy off and called nine one one."

"Was he young, old?"

"Kind of old, I guess. He actually seemed horrified and shocked once my cousin and Morgan showed up. Like he'd snapped out of . . . I don't know." Her face was tight with pain, memories, and fighting a truth that seemed to scare her.

"Bloodlust. He lost control, but he wasn't rogue or you'd be dead."

"Bloodlust? What?"

She looked vulnerable and way too sexy holding her damp shirt to her breasts. The need to touch her strengthened with every breath. He reached over his shoulder to grab a handful of his shirt and pulled it off. He held it out to her. "Put this on and I'll explain."

She took it. "Turn around."

Not a chance. "Turn my back on you after you tried to stab me with my own knife?" He raised his eyebrows in a challenge to see what she'd do.

What she did was take his breath away. She set her

wet shirt on the counter next to her bra, and then pulled his shirt over her head. For a brief second, he saw her wearing only that silver necklace resting against the subtle golden witch-shimmer that no camera or mortal eye could see. Her breasts were full and rounded with dark pink nipples that made his mouth water and his dick stand at attention. She was even more beautiful in the flesh. He clenched his hands into fists to keep from touching her.

The spell. She was there to do the spell. He had to remember Hannah, and why they needed the witch.

Once she had the shirt down, she said, "Don't you see? I can't help you. I don't know how to do magic. I just want to go back to my life. My family and friends will be worried."

He cut her off. "You'll be dead inside of a day if I let you go."

"I don't . . . why?"

"Those men that attacked you tonight. They were witch hunters."

"Like you? You hunt witches?"

She needed to understand. "Not like me, not yet anyway. Thanks to witches, witch hunters are cursed to crave witch blood. If we give in to the craving, we lose our souls and go rogue. It's like a drug, the rogues can't stop killing the witches for the power in their blood. And now that they've found you, they aren't going to stop."

"But I didn't even know I was a witch!"

He had to make her believe it and grasp the seriousness of the situation. "They know. They found you and they have moved you to the top of their kill list. Those men tonight were just the first. More will come and they will keep coming. They will kill anyone who gets in their way: friends, family, strangers; anyone to get to your blood." He paused then said, "I'm your only hope of staying alive. You work to cure my sister and I'll protect you." Unless he gave in and killed her himself. He fought a new wave of heart-racing desire, lust, pain . . . all for sex, her blood, her very essence.

Her eyes flared with torment, fear, and determination. "But you're one of them. How will you keep from killing me?"

He hit the very edge of his control. The hot lust seized his balls, while the compulsion screamed for her blood. Sweat beaded and ran down his back. "Sex," he said. "I want to screw you more than I want to kill you." He had to leave, before he lost all control. He knew she was in pain and needed to heal. He couldn't risk sex with her while there was any blood on her, blood that would inflame him until he pulled his knife and killed her to get all of her blood. He knew it, and yet every nerve in him screamed to take her now. Rip that skirt off of her, shove her panties aside, and bury himself in her. Hold her against him while he filled her up and made her his. Only his.

Fury rushed into her face. "That's your solution? Let me screw you and I won't kill you? I'm not having sex with you! I won't let you force me."

His balls ached, his skin burned, and he was running out of patience. "I don't force women and I sure as hell wouldn't have to force you." He moved closer to her, close enough to feel the heat coming off her witch-shimmer, but he didn't touch her. He didn't dare touch her. He looked down into her angry eyes. "Would I, Darcy?"

She sucked in a breath. "What is that? Every time you get near me, I feel strange."

"Pheromones, hunters attract women using phero-mones. But this . . . this is something else." He stepped back, feeling the hot sweat of lust and need run down his back. "Maybe because I touched your blood."

She crossed her arms protectively over her chest. "Or

maybe you're an arrogant ass used to having women fall at your feet."

He blinked in surprise. He'd never met a woman who stood up to him like the witch. Hell, now he just wanted her more. It was time to get out of there. He turned and started for the door.

Her gasp stopped him. "It's a hawk."

His tat. That's all, she saw his tat since he'd given her his shirt. "Yes." He stayed where he was, looking at the door, telling himself to open the door. Leave.

She moved up closer behind him. "He looks so real."

Axel stiffened as her rich voice poured over his skin.

"It's almost like if I touched him, I could feel the feathers."

Axel opened his mouth, but it was too late. Her fingers landed on his right shoulder blade where the tip of the tattooed hawk wings began. The bird had his wings straight up like he was coming in for a landing, covering almost all of his back. Her fingers rode the wings down to the waist of his pants. Fire seared from her touch straight to his dick.

Then her touch was gone. He missed it instantly.

"Skin, not feathers," she said softly.

Axel turned. The sight of her wearing his shirt against her sparkling witch-skin made his hands itch to touch her; to lay claim to her in a primitive way. Before he thought about it, he took a step and scooped her up in one arm to bring her face-to-face. "Teasing me, little witch?" It came out in a deep growl.

"Put me down, or I'll . . ."

He kissed her, laying claim to her mouth, closing his lips over hers, while tracing them with his tongue.

Static crackled in the room; little pops of her undisciplined power. The brush of it against his skin made his dick twitch in painful arousal. He curled his hand behind her head to angle her mouth open.

Her small hands dug into his shoulders as she parted her lips.

He slid his tongue against hers and she tasted so damn good. So hot. He could feel her nipples pebble through the shirt pressing on his bare chest.

Her body spoke to his. He could smell her desire, a full spicy scent that was blooming around them both.

He slid his hand down her thigh and under her knee. Her skin was warm and smooth and he knew she'd taste like lemon and spice. He pulled her leg up high over his hip, forcing his shirt and her skirt to ride up, until she was exposed and vulnerable to him, with only her panties covering her. Then he pulled her into his erection straining to burst free of his pants.

He felt her damp hot need right through his pants. She was as hot for him as he was for her. Whatever it was between them, it was powerful. He kissed her harder.

Her small, startled cry pierced his raging lust.

Yanking his head back, he saw the blood well up on her lip. "Christ." He'd torn the newly forming scab. The smell was intoxicating, but her wince made him sick. He'd never hurt a woman he'd had sex with. Ever. He was always careful.

Abruptly, he set her on her feet. Dragging in a breath, he got another lungful of her warm scent spiced with fresh blood. "I have to get out of here." He turned to the door.

"Wait!"

He couldn't, he yanked open the door.

"I won't be locked up!"

The panic in her voice yanked him back around to look at her. Big mistake. She looked too vulnerable and vibrant at the same time. In as calm a voice as he could muster, he said, "You're perfectly safe in here. I'm going to get you help to figure out how to spell the curse off Hannah."

She took a step toward him. "Don't lock me up. I am not an animal."

Fear. He could scent it as clearly as he could her anger. Fear had a too-sweet smell and he didn't like it one bit coming off of her. But he needed to get away from her for her safety. And he had to keep her to save Hannah. Determinedly ignoring her fear, he said, "You'll be fine." He closed the door and engaged the lock.

Something hit the door and shattered. "Bastard!"

Bastard. She'd thrown the first thing she found—a small pottery bowl—when Axel closed and locked that door. She turned back to the dark granite countertop, her gaze drawn to the built-in drawers. She searched them and found every color and size of candles and holders.

Bending down to the bottom cupboards, she discovered all kinds of bowls, utensils, and towels. A small fridge was built in next to the cupboards and was filled with bottled water and various bottles of oils. Nothing that would help her escape.

She grabbed onto the leather seat of the big metal stool and pulled herself upright. Ignoring the bed on her left, she walked to the door on the right side of the room and looked into the small bathroom with the essentials: sink, toilet, and shower. Under the sink were towels, soap, shampoo, toothbrush, and other prison necessities.

Back in the room, the wall between the bathroom door and outside door had a little desk with drawers built in that held papers and pencils.

No magic key, no crowbar, not even a lighter to set the bedding on fire and force them to let her out.

With nothing else to look at, she turned her attention to the locked door.

She had to get out.

Carla would be frantic wondering what had happened to her. Joe would be furious. Worried, but furious. Darcy wanted to help that little girl, but she'd never been able to control whatever it was inside of her. She'd spent most of her life trying to keep it contained.

Fat lot of good that had done her. No matter what she did, her dad never loved and accepted her. And now she was in a mess.

But could she leave that little girl? Hannah's face was burned into her brain—with the horrible mark dead center on her forehead.

Running her hand over her face, she winced when she touched the sore area around her eye. From witch karma.

A witch. She couldn't hide from it anymore. Too many years and experiences added up. Then she had touched Axel's hawk and she'd felt the truth of what he was, and of what the curse had done to him.

But she wasn't going to let him lock her up, damn it!

She focused on the door. There was a brass door handle, then some kind of coaster-size brass plate with a black pad in the center. Thumbprint lock, maybe? Censor? Could she get the door to unlock?

Anything was better than staying locked up in the room. She was starting to feel as if the walls were closing in. She had to stay angry; keep trying to get out.

But how did she get the lock to open? She stared at it and kept thinking.

Earlier tonight, the two men insisted that she had kept the funeral home door shut with her powers.

And then there were the emails from her email account, and the weird phone call telling her to run.

Her powers? Something else? She truly had no idea.

She shifted her gaze back to the door, and felt a familiar choking sensation squeezing her chest. The sensation of being closed off from the world, like she was locked in a casket. She shivered, wrapped her arms around herself, and thought, *Let me out!* A wave of energy slid through her.

Was that a click she heard? She ran to the door and tried opening it.

Still locked. She was locked in a room, in a dungeon below ground level.

The panic started. Her breathing rate increased. Memories of being locked in dark places overwhelmed her.

Unable to endure the fear, she marched over, picked up the metal stool, and raised it up then crashed it down on the lock.

The loud clash echoed in the room. She tried the door—the lock held.

She was locked in. Trapped.

No fucking way.

She raised the chair and bashed the lock over and over until pain radiated up her arms.

She dropped the stool, staring at the scratched but still engaged lock. She looked around, panting and fighting the choking claustrophobia. Every time she'd gotten this frightened as a child, the hawk had come to her. His wings would wrap around her and make her feel safe.

There was no hawk here, no one to help her. The feeling of being closed in wrapped around her chest and throat and squeezed. She picked up the stool and raised it once more. Screw the lock, she'd bash the door until it splintered and she could escape. She raised it over her head . . .

A woman's voice yelled through the door. "Darcy! Stop! I'm opening the door."

Darcy backed up but held the stool. Her only weapon. Could she hit whoever it was and run? Her heart pounded in her ears as the door swung open.

Eve stood there. Behind her stood the little girl.

Darcy set the stool down. No way in hell could she hit

a woman while her daughter watched. Nor could she risk hurting the child.

"Come out," Eve said. "There's a little kitchen down the hall. Come on, we'll make some tea."

Was it a trick? "Where is he?"

"Axel's not here." Eve walked into the room, and took Darcy's hand. Her mouth went flat and when she looked up, her brown eyes were sincere with regret. "I saw you on the cameras, but I didn't get down here soon enough. Your hand is swelling. Come on, I'll get you some ice."

6

The ice on her hand eased the pain. Eve heated water on a hot plate and poured three cups; two cups of tea and one of warm milk with just a little tea for Hannah.

Darcy sat in a chair pulled up to a table barely bigger than a dinner plate, and considered her options. Eve said Axel wasn't here, could she get away from Eve and make a run for it?

But she didn't know where she was. She'd tried to watch where Axel drove her, but it was like her mind had been fogged. All she remembered was the wilderness surrounding the house. Then there were the two men who'd tried to kill her. Were more really out there looking for her?

"Do you like tea parties?" Hannah sat on her knees in the chair next to her at the small table. The little girl clearly felt better than when Darcy had arrived at the house.

The child watched her with huge brown eyes so she answered, "When I was a little girl." She had played tea party with her dolls and the voices in her head.

Eve put a mug of tea in front of her then sat down. The three of them barely fit around the table. "Darcy, I promise, we're not going to hurt you. We're desperate and we need you." She glanced left to her daughter. "For Hannah."

She could clearly see the worry in the lines around

Eve's eyes and mouth. Oddly, she could relate. "My mom got sick a lot when I was growing up."

Eve's eyes filled with sympathy. "That must have been hard."

She shrugged. "It just was. She had lupus all my life." What she didn't tell them was that her dad blamed her when her mom got really sick. Either Darcy had tired her out, or she brought on flare-ups with her freakishness. When Eileen was confined to bed or in the hospital, Darcy would be so scared and lonely. She'd sneak out into the moonlight, lie down on the grass, and talk to the voices. If her dad found her, he'd go ballistic. He'd tell her to stop that crazy shit and lock her in the hallway closet. Terrified, she'd cry herself sick. That's when her hawk would come, his big warm wings settling around her, making her feel safe again so she could sleep.

Darcy realized Hannah was talking.

"Axel's mad when I get sick. The spot on my head makes him really mad." She lifted her cup with both hands and sipped, then said, "Axel plays tea party with me and Minnie."

Darcy stared at the little girl and tried to picture it. The huge, overbearing man who'd killed two men at the mortuary, then snatched her, played tea party with his little sister and her doll.

Hannah rose up on her knees to lean her elbows on the table. "Do you want to see my room?"

"Maybe tomorrow, Hannah." Eve moved Hannah's mug back.

Hannah ignored her and kept chattering to Darcy. "It's not really my room, 'cause my room is at home. Axel says we have to stay here 'cause it's safer. But Axel moved some of my toys for me. But not my swing set. Do you like to swing? When Axel pushes me, I can touch the clouds."

Darcy tried to follow the twists and turns of Hannah's conversation. She was obviously a bright kid, very articulate, and she adored her brother.

"Do you?"

She looked down at the child's questioning face. "What?"

Hannah frowned, like Darcy might be a little slow. "Like to swing?"

For the first time tonight, she almost smiled. She couldn't help it, this kid was a charmer. "I love to. It's like flying." She remembered her mom or Joe pushing her as high as she could go and feeling like she was free.

Hannah sat back on her heels and bounced on the chair. "Sometimes my mom pushes me, I jump out and Axel catches me."

"He also gives you cookies when you two think I'm not looking," Eve said. Then she said to Darcy, "I should have stopped Axel from locking you in." She reached across the table and took Darcy's uninjured hand. "I'll do anything you want, but please help us. Help Hannah."

Darcy felt Eve's powerful love and fear for Hannah sink into her skin and touch her heart. If she did have the means to help this little girl, how could she walk away?

TUESDAY: DAY FOUR OF THE DEATH MARK

The sound of footsteps jerked Darcy awake. She bit her lip to keep from crying out. God she was sore.

Axel walked in wearing a dark tee and jeans, holding a steaming cup in one hand and a large paper bag with handles in the other. He dropped the bag on the desk and headed toward her. "Drink this. My mom made it to help with the soreness from your cuts and to keep your hands busy so you leave my furniture alone."

She sat up in the bed, frowning at him. "Your concern is so touching." She glared at the mug he held out to her.

"It's just tea with herbs."

"Like I'd trust you." She was too sore and tired to fight. She just wanted to go home. Her right hand hurt like she'd put it in a shredder. She opened and closed her fingers to try and work out the tenderness.

He wrapped his fingers around her wrist, while dropping down on his haunches to look at her hand. He set the tea on the floor.

She tried to snatch the hand back but he kept his grip firm, not painful.

Frowning harder, he said, "Not broken, but you bruised the hell out of it."

"Yeah, well, I thought I'd give the witchcraft thing a try to unlock the door. Those two that attacked me last night swore I was holding the mortuary door closed with witchcraft, so I tried to summon the same, I don't know, intensity I guess and unlock the door. It didn't work." It was a little insulting to be forced to acknowledge being something other than mortal, then to fail at that when she really needed the help.

Lifting his gaze, he said, "The locks are specially designed. Even if you had tripped one lock with your powers, a second lock would automatically engage. It's designed to do the same thing with physical force like smashing it with a bar stool."

She measured him with a stare. "I'm not going to be locked up." She would never stop trying to escape.

He stroked her wrist with his thumb. "I got that."

His touch eased the pain in her wrist. It made her nervous that she responded to him unlike she had to any other man. Was it the pheromones? "I want to go home."

He kept his hold on her, gently stroking her tender skin. "Can't. Make no mistake, the rogues are after you.

I ran into two of them last night at your apartment. You're safer here where I can protect you."

She struggled to take it all in. "You went to my apartment?" She was still catching up.

He kept gently stroking her wrist. "I got you some clothes and stuff you might need. You were perfectly safe. My mom is a crack shot if it came down to it."

"She didn't have a gun with her last night when she let me out of the room." Eve had had on sweatpants and a T-shirt; she hadn't had anywhere to hide a gun.

"The gun is to protect you, not hurt you. We just want to save Hannah's life. Mom was worried about you and wanted to reassure you." With his free hand, he picked up the cup of tea, holding it out to her so she could grasp the handle. "Drink it."

She took the tea. He didn't want her dead, at least not until she uncursed his sister, so she figured the tea was safe. "What about the rogues at my apartment?" It was creepy to think of them there, looking through her stuff.

His mouth flattened. "They're dead."

She almost choked on the tea. "What . . ."

He let go of her hand. "They attacked me, I killed them."

She blinked in the fog of her thoughts. He was kind to his baby sister, played with her, loved his mom, but killed that easily. Who was he?

"Drink your tea, take a hot shower, then come into my office across the hall. We'll figure out what to do next."

She sorted through that, glanced up at the two cameras mounted in opposite corners. "Are there cameras in the bathroom?"

His green eyes flared for a second as he rose to his feet. "No. Not in any bathroom in the house. The rest of the house is wired with cameras and different security devices."

"How do I know you're telling the truth?" She wasn't going to strip naked for his viewing pleasure.

He looked down at her. "I don't need cameras if I want to spy on you, Darcy."

She almost dropped her tea when he literally faded from view. Then materialized again. "What was that?"

"Witch hunters can shield their presence and they can be deadly silent. We're predators."

Her skin prickled while her heart hammered with the memory. "That's why I didn't see those two last night. But I knew something was there." She shivered and wrapped both hands around her steaming cup.

Anger pulsed in his voice. "You saw them when they wanted you to see them. Your terror drops adrenaline into your blood, giving them more power as they bleed you."

Axel, and those men who had attacked her, really were something other than human. "Can you teleport?" He'd driven his truck to find her though . . .

"No. But we can hide behind a shield so we're invisible. And we're fast."

She opened her mouth, wanting to know more.

He cut her off. "You'll have complete privacy in the bathroom. Your clothes are in the bag there." He gestured to the desk. "Get moving, we have less than a week for you to heal Hannah. Come across the hall when you're finished." He turned and left.

She felt the struggle in the air around her ease. She knew what it was because he'd told her. Axel was fighting not to become what those two rogues were.

She finished the tea and took a hot shower.

Fifteen minutes later, she walked across the hallway wearing her own jeans, T-shirt, and sandals. The fact that Axel got into her apartment and looked through her underwear drawer was unsettling, but not creepy like knowing the rogues had been there. That made her blood run cold. But having her own clothes to wear made her feel a little bit better, more in control.

The door to her room was open and she looked across the hall to see Axel behind a huge desk, holding a cup of something steamy.

He turned his head, his green eyes taking her in, sweeping over her from her damp hair to her shoes. She paused in the middle of the hallway. He looked massive sitting there, his shoulders spanning more than half the desk. His T-shirt stretched enough to show the ridges of ripped muscles. The size of his bicep nearly matched her thigh. Even his hand wrapped around the cup was huge, as if it were a child's teacup, not a full-size mug.

If he wanted her blood, what could she do to stop him? He had her isolated, out in the middle of nowhere. After seeing his disappearing act, she suspected he'd somehow shielded her from being able to track where he was taking her.

She didn't trust him.

But she was drawn to him, especially to the hawk. When she touched the hawk on his skin, she'd felt safe. And more, as if there was more inside of her and the hawk could show her.

Maybe she really was crazy.

"There's more tea in that thermos. My mom will bring down some breakfast for you in a little bit." Axel gestured to the carafe on the desk. "And coffee down the hall in the kitchen." His voice hardened. "Don't run, Darcy. Do not run from me."

She had started to look to her left toward the kitchen, but his last words caught her attention. "Yeah, yeah, big bad hunter, I get it."

He lowered his chin and glared at her. "You look like hell. Black eye, split lip, and too little sleep."

Annoyed, she stalked into the room. "Thanks. I'm trying a new look called Kidnapped and Pissed." The desk took up half of the office, the rest held a couch, side table, light, and bookshelves. One wall had a massive flat-screen TV. Turning back to the desk, she picked up the thermos and filled her cup with the fragrant tea. Until Axel opened his big mouth, she had felt much better. The herbs in the tea had reduced the pain and swelling.

She heard a snort. It didn't come from Axel. Darcy looked around. "Where'd that come from? Who else is here?" She remembered the way Axel had disappeared. Was someone else in the room?

Axel set his coffee down, hit a button on his computer keyboard and said, "Look behind you."

She turned to glance over her shoulder and almost dropped her tea. "Holy cow!" The TV came to life and a face materialized on the screen. Close-shaved head, piercing blue eyes, hard jaw . . . like some super-hot athlete, but his bulk looked real not steroid-grown. He was huge. The image was so clear, she could see the gold eagle pierced through one ear. "Where is he?"

Axel got up and walked around the desk to sit on the edge a few feet from her. "He's at our warehouse. Video-conferencing. Sutton's been looking for ways to link you to other witches. They won't have anything to do with us, but they should respond to you."

Darcy tore her gaze from the screen to look at Axel. He was three feet away from her, leaning his butt on the desk, his boots crossed at the ankles. "Sutton. He's one of . . . you?"

"Witch hunter."

"Rogue?"

"Show her your palm, Sutton."

The man lifted his palm up. Obviously, he could see and hear them, too.

Axel said, "See the lines?"

Sutton's palm was massive, but yeah, she did. "And?"

"Rogues have no lines on their palms. Once they lose their soul, their lifelines vanish."

"What does that mean?" Darcy believed in souls. She'd been around the dead all of her life and believed that the soul went on once the body died. So if the soul was gone . . .

Axel said, "When the rogue dies without his soul, he becomes a shade with no form and no world. He'll roam forever in a vast emptiness between the worlds."

A shiver went down her spine.

Sutton broke in, "See the screen? These are rogues."

Darcy looked at the TV. It went to a split screen with Sutton on the left. On the right, two men appeared. They were huge, bulging with muscles, but there was something off. Their faces didn't fit their physique; they almost looked feminine. They had delicate eyebrows and were missing the ruggedness of a beard shadow—as if they didn't have to shave. Dropping her gaze down their arms, she noticed they didn't have the darker smattering of hair most men had. Their skin appeared waxy. "Why do they look almost female in some places and very male in others?"

Sutton answered, "Witch blood is absorbed through the skin. All witches are female, so we assume that's what's causing the change."

Darcy listened but something bothered her as she stared at the rogues on the screen. They looked like the two that attacked her outside the mortuary but there was something else that kept bothering her. Finally, it hit her. "There was a man at the cemetery on Saturday. He looked like those rogues you showed me. His eyes were green and . . ."

Axel made a deep noise in his chest. "My father. He assigned me to kill you."

But he hadn't killed her, he'd rescued her from two other killers. "Your father? He's rogue?"

"Yes. Apparently, he was there to verify that you were a witch. Believe me, if he'd been there to kill you, you'd be dead."

What was it like to know your father was some kind of murderer? She had the insane urge to touch him, to try and ease the hardness that lived inside the man. But she ignored the impulse—Axel had kidnapped her and had already told her he could barely control his craving for her blood. He was trying not to become what his father was.

She focused her thoughts. "How did this curse happen?"

"It was about thirty years ago. Three demon witches captured three witch hunters. They planned to curse the hunters with a spell that would bind their souls as familiars, but the curse caught up all the earth witches and witch hunters working together to stop it. It basically turned into one clusterfuck of a curse."

"So back then, you talked to each other? Got along?"

Axel nodded. "We protected earth witches, and in turn, they cast protection spells over our families so that demon witches couldn't use them as leverage against us. If something like a death curse got through, the witches would heal the victim, then the witch hunters would hunt and kill the demon witch, and they would provide protection for the witch who undid the curse."

That caught her attention. "The demon witch will go after the one who undoes the curse?" So she was going to have a demon witch coming after her? How would she protect herself? Once Axel got what he wanted from her, she was on her own.

"Darcy," Sutton said, "you have to do this. Find the spell to break the curse on Hannah. We'll figure out a way to protect you. The only other choice is for Axel to find the demon witch and kill her."

"Then he'll go rogue," she said. What choice did she

have? She couldn't let that little girl die. She didn't want the responsibility of Axel's soul on her, but she wouldn't walk away. Besides, if she did, the rogues would find her. And they might kill others to get to her, she couldn't endanger people at work, her friends, or Joe.

Oh, God, Joe.

Snapping her head up, she said, "I'd like to call Joe. Just tell him that I'm okay . . ."

Axel shot up off the desk to his full height. "Joe? Who is Joe?"

"Shit, Axel!" Sutton's voice roared through the room. "Back off!"

She wasn't sure what changed him. He'd been tense, but not like this. She jumped off the edge of the desk and looked around for a weapon. Nothing lethal caught her eye.

Axel crowded her. "Answer me, Darcy. Who is he, a boyfriend?"

She looked up and saw that his pupils had enlarged and his jaw was tight. Anger took the place of fear. She was tired of this crap. She'd been attacked, kidnapped, locked up, and she was done being pushed around. "Who I sleep with is none of your business!"

Axel sucked in a breath, almost making the air around them tremble with his fury. "You're not going to go out and scratch your itch while I'm trying to save Hannah's life!" He turned around and stormed out of the room.

"Joe's my *cousin*! Get your mind out of the gutter!" God she was pissed. Who the hell did he think he was?

A slamming door answered her.

"Go ahead, run away, you bastard! Afraid of the witch?" What did she just say? It wasn't just Axel, she was acting insane. Insane enough to believe she was a witch.

Except she did believe it. Maybe some part of her had always known it. She'd always been different.

"You realize he's actually trying not to kill you. It's the bloodlust making him jealous and unreasonable."

She stomped around the desk and dropped into Axel's oversize chair. She had to calm down. "Does everyone bow down to that bully? I'm not going to let him push me around." Except for the part where he ripped her out of her life.

Sutton sighed heavily. "He'll kill you."

She stared at his face on the screen, noting the comfortingly masculine shadow of a beard around his cheeks and chin. "I refuse to buy the 'me cave man, can't help being a butthole' excuse. Besides, I'm not the type that cowers."

"Noted," Sutton said dryly.

She looked around the office and noticed there wasn't a phone. She'd find a way to contact Joe, but it was sinking in that even if she lived through this and cured Hannah, she couldn't go back home, back to her family. She'd endanger them by being a witch. The rogues would kill anyone to have her blood.

And then she was going to piss off a demon witch just to add to the fun and games.

Her dad had been right after all. She was a dangerous embarrassment. She'd worked so hard to prove him wrong, even after his death, to prove that she was worthy of acceptance and love. What a crock of shit that was. She was a witch, a creature of magic, chased by an evil that would force her into hiding forever. How could she ever fall in love and subject a man to that? Or a child?

Screw it. One step at a time. Find out how to be a witch.

*   *   *

She'd been at it for a couple of hours. The witch loops were rejecting her. They all told her the same thing— that these were very dangerous times and she needed two sponsors who knew her and could swear she wasn't a demon witch. It looked like rogues had used witch loops as hunting grounds by posing as witches, then luring out witches and killing them. Restless and frustrated, she shoved back from Axel's desk and paced around the office.

From the screen, Sutton said, "Axel said you used witchcraft to try and stab him with his knife. How did you do that?"

"Fear. He was dragging me down the stairs and I really thought he might kill me. I felt a ball of hot energy roll up from somewhere and into my chest, then rush out." She frowned, trying to understand it.

"Can you summon up that feeling?"

"I don't know . . ." She rubbed her temples. Whenever she got that scared, she wasn't thinking, she was . . . reacting. How could she re-create that?

"That's not good enough. Lives are at risk here, Hannah's and yours, along with Axel's soul. Concentrate, Darcy. Try."

She whirled around to face the image. *Try?* She had tried, damn it! She'd tried with everything she had last night when Axel locked in her that room. She didn't know how!

And he had the nerve, the audacity, to tell her to try?

Turning her back on the condescending idiot, she stormed over to the laptop, opened a blank email, and typed in Joe's address.

"What are you doing?"

"Sending an email to my cousin."

"No."

Jerking her head up, she glared at the bald man. "I've been kidnapped, locked in a dungeon, and pushed around enough. Joe will be worried. I'm going tell him I'm okay and you're going to let me."

His blue eyes narrowed. "It's not safe to contact anyone."

"Except witches," she shot back.

"We need them."

Fury climbed up her spine and made her jaw rigid. "Send this email, Sutton."

"Calm down. You're being unreasonable. You can't do magic if you lose control."

Calm down? Someone took the lid off the boiling pot deep in her belly and steam burst up. With a shaking hand, she punched the send button over and over on the laptop.

The email just sat there, taunting her.

"Go, damn it!"

The email faded away. Darcy stared at the Internet program.

"You're wasting time. All emails go through me. If you send that, I'll delete it."

She'd just sent it. Hadn't she? Did it bypass Sutton? Trying to figure it out, she said, "So I should just delete it?"

He nodded.

But the email was gone. She had to think. What exactly happened? Had she magically bypassed Sutton and sent the email to Joe? She couldn't keep staring at the computer, so she paced around the front of the desk.

She couldn't stand it and paced back, but she refrained from looking at the laptop so Sutton wouldn't get suspicious.

Could she do magic? Send emails with magic? What about those emails from herself warning her of hunters? Had she . . .

A female voice cut off her thought with, "Only you can hear me."

Startled, she swung around. Her foot caught on the roller of the chair, knocking her off balance and onto her ass. With her legs sprawled, she looked up at the laptop.

An avatar stared back at her from the computer screen. A wrinkled woman with white hair pulled back in an old-fashioned bun and intense pale blue eyes, nearly white.

The avatar spoke, "Darcy, don't let anyone know I'm talking to you."

Was she real? Who was she? Oh, God, what if she wasn't just hearing voices in her head now, but seeing cartoon characters to go with the voices?

"Darcy, what happened?" Sutton called out from the wall screen.

"I fell over the stupid chair." She climbed up to her feet, keeping her gaze on the avatar. The voice sounded distinctly female but with a digitized quality. "Uh . . ."

The avatar's eyes followed her. "Tell him you need a break. Take the computer someplace where he won't be able to see you."

She tried to think quickly. It wasn't like she could pick up the computer and run. "I need to take a break." But there were cameras in her room, so she couldn't talk to the laptop in there. Would Sutton even let her take the laptop? She stood there, shifting back and forth on her sandals trying to figure out what to do.

"We don't have time for breaks, Darcy."

She jerked her gaze from the laptop to the man on the big screen. "Tough. I think I cut my leg when I fell. I'm going to go in the bathroom and clean it up. Then maybe I can even have a glass of water. Or is water against the rules?"

Sutton's stare turned wary. "Okay. Go on."

She dropped her eyes to the laptop. Damn it, how could she get him to let her take it? Lowering her shoulders in a show of resignation or cooperation, she said,

"Look, I'll take the laptop in my room and work there for a little bit. I need to think."

"Fine. Remember, any emails you send will route through my computer and I'll see them."

She snatched up the computer. "Big Brother's watching, I get it." She faked a limp and got the hell out of there. Her heart slammed against her rib cage so hard, she heard the pounding in her ears.

Who was in the laptop? A witch? Some other creature? Or had her mind snapped? As she walked across the hall, she thought about the weird emails from herself. And that phone call. Going into the room, she glanced up to see the two cameras mounted in opposite corners of the ceiling.

Her only hope was the bathroom. She passed the desk on her right, turned into the small bathroom, and shut the door. Then she turned on the water for good measure. Finally she sat on the edge of the tub and put the computer on her thighs. "Who are you?"

The avatar looked back at her warningly. "Can anyone hear you talking to me? No one must hear you."

She shook her head. "As far as I know, they can't. Tell me who you are." She had a death grip on the edges of the laptop and forced her fingers to relax.

"I'll show you, but first, make absolutely certain no one can see the computer screen."

Darcy had believed Axel when he said there were no cameras in the bathroom. But just to be sure, she twisted so her back was to the wall at the edge of the bathtub, then angled the laptop down so that any ceiling camera wouldn't be able to see the screen. "I'm sure." Anticipation shot up her spine.

The pixels in the avatar faded then reemerged showing a new face. One she recognized. "Carla? How . . ."

"Shhh, don't say my name. Call me Crone when you talk to me." The picture did the same blurring of pixels then sharpened back into the avatar. "I called Joe about an hour after you didn't show up last night. You weren't answering your cell phone and I had a bad feeling, especially after you told me about the man who spooked you at your mom's funeral. Joe's been looking for you. When he told me what he found at the mortuary, I knew you'd been taken by witch hunters. I can't believe you're still alive. Rogues don't wait to kill."

Darcy heard the emotion in her voice. "Axel's not a rogue," she said without thought, her mind consumed by Carla—she was a witch? Her head buzzed with distant voices and spinning thoughts. Nothing and no one was what it seemed. She didn't even know her best friend as well as she had thought she did. "You're a witch? I mean . . . how are you contacting me? Sutton has the computer bugged or whatever."

The avatar nodded, the sage face kind and patient. "I'm a witch. I knew you were a witch when I first met you. You didn't know and you didn't seem to want to know."

"But . . ." Betrayal swirled in her relief and confusion. "Why didn't you say something?"

"Darcy, all of us witches are hiding these days. Our powers are weakened from the curse and we're being slaughtered by the rogues. I figured you were safer not knowing. Living as a mortal, I didn't think you'd get a rogue witch hunter's attention." She paused, then added, "We don't have time for recriminations. Let's get you out of there and someplace safe, then you can be mad at me all you want."

Darcy swallowed, and in spite of her shock, she felt less alone. Less scared. "How are you talking to me? Why didn't Sutton hear you in the other room?"

"I found you by searching the witch loops in the desperate hope of at least hearing something about you, and saw your emails requesting to join."

Darcy broke in, "My emails went through? I tried to send Joe an email, but I wasn't sure it worked."

"It must have. I'm projecting my avatar to you magically. The hunter didn't hear me because I was funneling my voice directly to your chakras, so only you could hear."

"My chakras? What's that?" She felt stupid and slow.

"Seven levels of magical energy inside of you. Every witch has them."

Her head felt thick. "I have so much to learn."

The crone avatar nodded. "I need to teach you enough to get you out of there, then you can learn all you want. Do you know where you are?"

"Not exactly, but I'm not leaving anyway." Stunned, she pressed her lips together. All she'd wanted last night was to get out, go back home. But now, she knew the truth—she couldn't leave Hannah to die. Not if she could save her.

"You have to! It's too dangerous . . ."

She tried to make Carla understand. "There's a little girl here, Hannah, she's four years old and she has the death mark." Darcy couldn't leave her, not yet. "I have to help her, Car . . . Crone."

"You can't," Carla said in a voice that cracked with regret. "It's spell magic, Darcy. We witches were there when the curse happened. It broke our bond with our familiars and magically weakened us. We can't do that kind of spell work without a familiar and we can't get familiars anymore."

She closed her eyes and saw that beautiful little girl with the death mark on her forehead. Then she opened her eyes and looked around the small bathroom, seeing her lotion and hairbrush that Axel had brought her. Such little things, but they made her feel better. He hadn't had to do that. He had her at his mercy, and yet, he'd gotten her the things he'd thought she would want.

She shifted her gaze to the avatar. "I have to try. Axel tells me that the rogues have put me at the top of their kill list. Two rogues caught me outside the mortuary last night. They'd already cut me once when Axel showed up, killed them, and took me. Maybe I'm safer here. He won't kill me, at least not before I save his sister."

The crone avatar closed her eyes and her face crumpled in grief and frustration. "We can both leave, go into hiding . . ."

Darcy was not going to get her best friend killed. "No. I can't get away right now anyway. I have to learn magic and you can help me. Please." She glanced at the water running in the sink. How long had she been hiding in the bathroom? Her neck tensed up. "I can't stay in the bathroom much longer."

"I'll help you."

7

Axel and Eve both tried to read to Hannah.

"No! I want Key to read to me!" She kicked her legs in protest where she sat on the couch between them.

Eve put her arm around Hannah. "Key isn't here. He can't come here, and it's not safe for you to leave."

Big tears welled up in her dark eyes. "It's because I'm sick. Key doesn't like me anymore because I'm sick." Her lower lip trembled.

Helpless rage wound through Axel as tears spilled down his sister's face. He pulled out his BlackBerry and hit Key's number.

Voice mail answered. "Shit."

"Shit," Hannah repeated with a sob.

Axel was torn between laughing and smashing something. Instead he reached over and lifted Hannah into his arms. "Hannah, you know that's a bad word." He wiped her tears.

"You said it."

"I'm a grown-up."

"Can I say it when I'm a grown-up?"

Hell yes. Let her make it to be a grown-up and she could say it every damned day. "Yes, you can. Now how about I call Key and you leave him a message on his voice mail?"

She laid her warm head on his chest. "Don't want to. Too tired."

He looked at his mom.

Eve returned his gaze, her dark eyes brimming with fear.

"All right, close your eyes and rest." She was already getting sick. His cheerful, bubbly, talk-nonstop sister was tuning into a cranky, fearful, sick child.

Eve stood, "Put her in her bed."

Axel rose and followed his mom. He kept a bed in the safe house for Hannah and his mom. But since they'd had time, he and Key and Sutton had moved a lot of Hannah's things to make her feel more secure, while Ram and Phoenix fixed up the room downstairs for Darcy. But none of that mattered if they didn't figure out how to stop this death curse on Hannah.

She was sound asleep by the time he laid her in the bed. His mom tucked her Minnie Mouse into her arms. Axel took a last look at his sister, then stalked down the hallway, through his bedroom, and downstairs.

The witch had better be making progress. She'd fed Sutton a story about a witch suddenly appearing on the laptop and agreeing to help her. Sutton said the witch was using magic to hide behind an avatar and he couldn't track her. They didn't know where the avatar calling herself Crone was located or why she popped up to contact Darcy when all the loops rejected her. She was using magic, so she had to be a witch, but what if she was a demon witch?

Stepping off the last riser, he heard Darcy say, "I feel it! It's opening!"

What was she talking about? He strode along the hall and turned into her room. Darcy sat on the cold tile floor, cross-legged and staring at a lit orange candle. There was an empty bowl next to the candle. He asked, "Feel what opening?"

Darcy jerked, lifting her folded hands off her lap. "Axel!"

A thin river of water shot from her hands and hit him in the middle of his chest. "What the hell?"

Darcy's brown eyes lit up with gold lights. "Water! I did water! The second chakra!" Then her face sobered. "Uh, you're wet. I was trying to get the water in the bowl."

Had she done it on purpose? He'd find out soon enough, so he waited, watching her.

"What?"

"Waiting to see if you get drenched by witch karma."

Leaping to her feet, she waved a hand at him. "Oh, please, it was just a little water. It didn't *harm* you."

"Too bad." He eyed her little shirt covering her breasts. He wouldn't mind seeing it wet and clinging to her. Sudden thick need filled his veins and made him hot. He inhaled, and caught her lemony scent, intensifying the need. It had to be from touching her blood.

She narrowed her eyes. "I'm going to try fire next. The third chakra."

Axel brought his thoughts under control. He was there to check on her progress. He pulled off his damp shirt and used it to wipe his chest.

"What are you doing?"

"Drying off." Or cooling off; running the cool damp material over his hot skin. But he didn't need to tell the little witch that. He tossed the shirt onto her bed. "So this Crone is teaching you something?"

Her excitement had dimmed. "Yes. But healing Hannah will be more complicated than I thought. The curse affected witches, too, so we can't do spell magic."

Axel forgot the water and his lust. His suspicion surfaced. What was this Crone telling her? "You will do this, Darcy."

"I'm trying! I have to learn low magic first; the magic in my first four chakras. And then I'll try to figure out how to do the high magic using the last three chakras, but . . ."

"Explain these chakras." Axel knew many things about witches, like how to cut them to disconnect their powers. His dad had taught him that. But he didn't know exactly where their magic came from, other than from the earth.

She leaned down and picked up the candle and bowl off the floor. "Witches have seven chakras. The first one is at the base of our spine, it's red and called the earth charka, the one that connects us to the earth. That's why I was sitting on the floor to try to access my second chakra—to be more connected to the earth." She blew out the candle and set it on the dark granite counter next to the clay bowl.

Axel noted the computer sitting opened on the countertop. Right now, it had a starburst screen saver on it. Was Crone behind that? Listening? Watching? Looking back at Darcy, he said, "The second chakra is water."

"Yes, it's here." She put her hand over her pelvis.

He looked down at her palm resting over the zipper of her jeans and was gripped by the desire to move her hand, unzip her jeans, and lay his own hand over her second chakra. Forcing his gaze up to her face, he said, "Go on."

"I was just feeling that chakra open when you came in."

Oh, hell. The thought of her pelvis opening . . . tried to push it out of his mind.

"Opening the chakras gives me access to the power. The fire chakra is yellow and located here." She put her hand roughly where her solar plexus was. "Then chakra four is air and it's green." Her hand slid up to rest over her breasts. "If I can open those four chakras, then I can pull the power of the earth elements through those chakras. With practice, I'll learn to direct and control the magic. See?"

He was trying not to see, trying not to visualize where those chakras were on her. Trying not to think of tracing them with his fingers or tongue. *Focus.* "But those chakras won't heal Hannah?"

She shook her head, her auburn hair swinging around her shoulders. "No. That takes high magic. Spell magic comes down through the higher chakras. Chakra five, the blue chakra, is here." She put her hand on her throat. "It's communication, where we bring elemental magic and spell magic together. I guess we need a familiar and that's another problem."

"Because?"

She fiddled with the bowl on the counter. "We can't get familiars. The curse broke our bonds with our familiars."

Bad news after bad news. "You can't do the spell without a familiar?" The hunters knew witches had weakened, but not the specifics. Since witches hid from them, they didn't exactly exchange information.

She stopped playing with the bowl and met his gaze. "I'm going to try. I have to get control of at least six of my chakras to do it. Chakra six, here,"—she touched her forehead—"is the third eye. It's indigo in color and that's where I will connect with the Ancestors and ask them to help. I guess since the curse, no one has connected with the Ancestors. The last chakra, seven, is violet and at the very top of our head. That one is knowledge and spiritual connection."

He was impressed . . . assuming this was true. But she had summoned water, so there was something to what she was telling him. "So the problem is that you have to learn the chakras and how to control the power, and find a way to get a familiar so you can do a spell, is that correct?"

"From what I know so far. Crone tells me there's much more to learn. But I have to start with the first four chakras and learn how to control them."

Which brought him to a point. "Who is Crone, Darcy?"

Her stare fell to his chest. "I don't know. She just popped up."

"Then why do you trust her?"

Darcy tried to pivot on the stool where she sat.

Axel stepped in, forcing her legs apart and trapping her. "Look at me. Not my chest, my eyes."

Her witch-shimmer darkened with a rosy blush.

Seeing that, Axel knew she was reacting to him physically. But was she lying too? Hiding Crone's identity? "Darcy."

She looked up. "Back off, Axel. I'm doing everything I can."

Was she? Or was she gaining her powers to escape him? The idea seeded in his belly. *His witch. His.* He knew it was the blood curse taking over and bringing out the animal in him. He fought it down, kept his hands at his sides. Breathed in and out to stay in control.

The moment stretched out. Darcy grew tense and agitated.

The spicy scent of power slammed into him. It ignited the burn under his skin, cramped his gut, and fogged his brain. He could take what he wanted from her, his knife in the holster in the small of his back . . .

The sound of rushing water exploded in the room. It shocked his bloodlust back to simmer.

Darcy jerked, almost falling backward off the stool.

Axel grabbed her and pulled her into his chest with the instinct to protect and shield her. He looked over Darcy's head and saw the water in the bathroom sink running.

Then turned his head to the left and saw the spigot there had turned on, too.

No threat to Darcy. Had she sensed his bloodlust rising? He eased her back onto the stool and looked down into her flushed face. "Your powers turned on the water?"

"I felt that chakra open, so I guess I turned on the water. It wasn't a conscious decision." Frowning, she added, "You made me nervous."

He'd scared her. He told himself he would have gotten control, he wouldn't have hurt her. Now that he was touching her, the bloodlust faded beneath the rush of sexual lust, and an almost choking need to protect her. He held her with one hand behind her head and the other on her shoulder. The water still ran. "Can you turn them off with witchcraft?"

She turned her head, looked at the stream of running water from the sink next to them.

It shut off.

He felt a single jolt. The curse reacting to her powers?

Whipping her head back, she looked up at him. "I did it!"

Something fleeting traveled through his guts, but he focused on her face, on her excitement. Her joy in learning what she could do. Her success. Her vibrant beauty that he wanted to taste. It was so opposite of what he was, what he had the potential to become, that he longed to have more of it, more of Darcy.

He lowered his head and touched his mouth to hers.

She exhaled into his mouth and it fired him up. That was what he wanted, needed; her very breath. Holding her tight, he pressed into her until she opened her mouth. Her entire body leaned into him, her skin getting hotter and need flowing off her like the water she could control with her powers.

Axel wanted to drown in it. He plunged his tongue

deeply inside of her, wanting to taste her right down to all seven chakras. The feel of her small hands touching him, caressing his arms and chest inflamed and hardened him until he wasn't sure if he could pull back.

He didn't want to pull back.

When Darcy's hand slid over his shoulder and touched his tat, he growled, slid his hand beneath her bottom, and pulled her into his erection.

"Get away from her!" A demanding digitalized voice blasted through the room.

Axel ripped his mouth from Darcy's, his entire body on alert to find and destroy anything that interrupted them or threatened her.

The starburst screen saver on the laptop was gone. In its place was an older woman with a white bun and two holes with lights shining through for eyes. "Crone." Damn the computer and damn the witch behind the avatar. His head swam with lust, with a longing for Darcy that almost seared him. Every inch of his skin craved her, and even his hawk tat felt tight and hot in a way it hadn't since the first day he'd gone under the needle.

"Let me go," Darcy said.

He released her, stepped back, and looked down.

She wrapped her arms around herself, and inched farther away from him on the stool.

The avatar said, "Yes, I'm Crone. Get control of yourself hunter. If you kill her, your sister will die."

He'd wanted to strip her naked and possess her, not kill her. But for a moment there . . . before the water snapped on and before he'd actually touched her . . . he'd been caught up in bloodlust. He changed the subject. "Why are you hiding? How do we know you're not tricking Darcy?"

"I'm forced to hide because of rogue hunters. I'm helping Darcy. I'm not the one who kidnapped her."

He shifted his gaze back to Darcy. She uncrossed her arms and raised her chin. "Crone is teaching me what I need. The witch loops won't help me."

Crone added, "We haven't been able to remove a death mark in decades. You're demanding that she do the impossible."

If that was true, then he had no other options. He'd have to find the demon witch and kill her. "I won't let Hannah die."

"Then let Darcy work. Let her learn. Maybe we can figure out a way to do the impossible."

Axel backtracked in his mind, going over all that Darcy had told him about chakras, elemental magic, and spell magic. He hadn't realized to what extent the witches were damaged as a result of the curse. "None of you can reach your Ancestors?" Like they couldn't reach their Wing Slayer? Although for hunters, it had only been the hawks that talked directly to the Wing Slayer.

He had the hawk tattoo now. But he didn't know what it meant since he still felt the craving for witch blood.

Crone cut off his thoughts. "No, we can't reach the Ancestors. And we need them for spell work."

Darcy asked, "What exactly are the 'Ancestors'?"

Crone turned to her on the computer screen. "Witches evolved from a very few, special mortals who began to reincarnate when they died, gaining more power and knowledge with each lifetime. In our death cycle, our souls go to Summerland to rest, review, and then move on to the next life cycle. But eventually, some souls became so evolved they chose not to reincarnate. They stayed in Summerland and acted as the witches' spirit guides. They assisted us in spells and helped us learn. When the curse happened, the earth witches broke through the demon witches' shield and entered the cave with the witch hunters. Our souls were torn from us, along with the hunters' souls, and that severed the connection with our familiars and the Ancestors."

Axel watched Darcy as she processed this. Her gaze lost focus and he almost felt her mind turning. "What?" he asked.

She turned to look at Crone. "Before the curse, what was communication like with the Ancestors? Did they talk to any witch, like a conversation?"

"Most witches could have some form of communication with the Ancestors if they could open their sixth charka, the third eye. Sometimes it's voices or sometimes it's signs the witch has to interpret. But some witches, a very few . . ." Crone's gaze narrowed into twin laser beams.

Axel had the feeling Darcy and Crone were communicating in a way he couldn't hear or understand. Either through magic, or Darcy knew Crone well enough to have those instances of understanding, which meant she was lying to him about Crone.

Darcy leaned closer. "A few witches what?"

"Hear the Ancestor voices occasionally without opening their third-eye chakra. They will get a message from them, usually in dreams, but sometimes in waking hours."

"Like email?" She laced her fingers together, then unlaced them, then she fiddled with her hair.

His tension rose with her increasing agitation. "What do you mean?"

She looked over at him. "Remember I told you about the man at the cemetery who scared me and you said it was your father, a rogue hunter?"

He nodded.

"That night, I got an email warning me that the

hunters had found me. That was weird enough, but even stranger was that it was from my own email account. Like I'd sent it to myself. But how could I? I didn't even know anything about rogues or hunters, or that I'm a witch. Then at the mortuary the night you kidnapped me, I got another email, and a phone call with a computer-like voice that said 'Run!' When I went outside, the rogues were there."

His tat warmed enough to feel the outline of the hawk on his back. "You didn't send the emails to yourself, so you're thinking the Ancestors did?"

She jerked her gaze to Crone, then back to him. "I hear voices. I've always heard voices. I used to talk to them when I was really young, but I stopped. Since then, I just hear murmurs, and every once in a while, a single word or two."

She refused to look at him, studying the granite counter instead.

Frowning, she went on. "But why would they talk to me? I didn't even know I was a witch. I was raised in a mortal family."

Crone said, "Maybe the fact that you were raised in a mortal family meant you needed the Ancestors even more than the rest of us. Or maybe you are special somehow, something about you made it possible for them to reach you."

Axel stayed focused on his purpose—Hannah. "So then Darcy could be the witch who can heal Hannah."

Crone looked at him. "This is bigger than just one child's life, hunter. Darcy could be the breakthrough for us to reach the Ancestors."

"Stop it," Darcy said, her voice clear and strong. "Both of you. This is a child's life we're talking about. We will find a way." She slid open a drawer and pulled out two yellow taper candles and one candleholder.

Axel watched her. "What are those for?"

"Fire; my third chakra. I meditate on the candle of the same color as the chakra to help me connect and open it." She took the orange candle out of the holder and replaced it with the yellow candle, then she put the second candle in another holder. Darcy picked up a lighter and lit one candle, leaving the second one unlit. She slid off the stool and took both candles with her. After setting them side by side on the tiled floor, she sat, crossed her legs, and folded her hands in her lap.

The room filled with quiet, broken only by the thrumming of the laptop's hard drive.

Axel leaned back against the granite counter. Darcy's back was straight, her long hair flowing to end a few inches above her rounded ass.

He could see her back expand with each breath.

He realized he was breathing with her, pacing each breath to her rhythm. But he couldn't stop, couldn't look away from her. He didn't know how long he stood there, fixated on Darcy.

Then he felt it; a sizzle deep in his gut, followed by an odd sensation. Like feathers rippling beneath his skin— so quick he wasn't sure that was what he felt.

He recognized the rising hum of the curse, the cramping need, but that was overshadowed by a stronger desire to touch Darcy. To feel her power as he laid her on that tile, stripped her down, and sank into her body, deeply enough to touch each of her chakras.

The second candle lit in a bright flare that must have reached four inches in height. Then the flare settled into a strong one-inch flame.

Sweat broke out on his forehead and back. Blood rushed down, engorging his cock.

She had succeeded in opening her third chakra, but why did Axel feel it? Why was the bloodlust getting lost in a potent sexual lust? What was the witch doing to him?

Axel was restless, edgy, and ready to kill. The pulsing red lights of the club, the throbbing beat of the music, and the snapping flames in the fire pit all fit his deadly mood.

Sex. He needed sex to take the edge off.

But all he could think about was Darcy. Leaving the house tonight, knowing she was down on the bottom floor, had been strangely hard. His gut had wanted to turn back, and each mile that took him farther from her had felt like he'd run it instead of driven it.

The skin on his thumb where he had made contact with Darcy's blood yesterday burned. The tattoo on his back where she had touched his hawk felt oversensitive and empty, like it wanted her touch back. Craved it.

The darker part of him wanted to feel the warm spill of her blood cooling the burning, fire ant–ache eating through his skin.

It had to be the curse fucking with him. He just needed to get laid, help Darcy uncurse Hannah, and send the witch away.

He also needed to get a line on the demon witch as a backup plan in case Darcy didn't succeed in spelling the curse. Or he could beat the information out of his dad. That thought cheered him a bit.

Ram moved up silently next to him and held out an icy beer bottle. "Couple sets of rogues are scouting. They're twitchy as hell."

Axel moved his gaze to the rogues. Two of them were hovering at the other fire pit, their eyes darting around as they whispered to each other like nine-year-old boys. The second pair hovered at the edge of the booths, doing the same thing.

"Hearing about your hawk tat made them nervous

enough. But now you've killed several rogues to protect a witch. They think you are the enemy."

"It's not what *they* think." Axel glanced at the rogues. "They are following orders. Left to their own devices, they'd slaughter witches anywhere they could find them and leave the mess. But that doesn't happen much anymore. The bodies of the dead witches disappear forever. The rogues are organized now."

"And they are growing. Hunters are turning rogue at a quicker pace. Your tattoo of the leader of the Wing Slayer Hunters marks you, to them, as a real threat. I think we need to find out why exactly."

He turned to look at Ram. "Meaning?"

"The direct threats to you started when the rogues learned of the tattoo. It means something. Maybe we need to ask the witches. Maybe it's time we found a way to work with them. We'd have to do it on the Internet or in some way that avoided direct contact. Although you're hanging with a witch now and have not been affected."

Axel drained his beer. "I'm affected. Every damned second." She was in him and he didn't know if he'd ever break free. That one touch of her blood, just a touch, and it felt like they'd formed a connection of some kind. Shifting subjects he said, "My father's behind this. He has guards at his house, like he's some kind of king."

"He needs you to help him keep his throne. You're good at killing and you're good at strategy."

Axel knew that was true. His father had started trying to turn him rogue when Axel had been fourteen years old. After failing that, his dad tried to have another son with Eve, but that child had been a girl. Hannah. Now Myles was back to cooking up ways to get Axel to turn and join him in killing witches and ruling the rogues.

It would never end.

First he had to save Hannah, then . . . he didn't know.

The tattoo on his back warmed. A reminder? Or his imagination? Or had Darcy done something to him?

He handed his empty beer bottle to Ram. "Keep an eye on the rogues." He strode toward the dance floor, his eyes on a tall blonde. He needed to get relief, then he could think. An unwanted memory surfaced, the one of him walking into that building with his dad and seeing that witch tied down, bleeding from multiple cuts and terrified. He had been horrified, felt pity for the witch . . .

And then the lust. Bloodlust. It had shocked him, blasting through his system and making him want dark ugly things.

He would never forget the screams as his father cut the young witch. Or his father taking his wrist and slamming his hand down onto the bleeding wound.

"Axel Locke."

The sharp male voice shoved out his memories. He turned and sized up the man; he was mortal, topping six feet with tightly packed muscle and a steady confidence. Even in the throbbing strobe lights, Axel could see the deep blue of his eyes. "Yeah?"

The man's jaw tightened. "I want to see Darcy. She swears she's fine, but I want to see for myself."

Rage arced up like a massive snake coiling to strike. He knew the man was a mortal, so he wasn't after Darcy's blood. But the need to strike remained. Tightly, he asked, "Who are you?" Did Darcy have a boyfriend? The idea of this man touching the witch had him clenching his fists to keep from grabbing his knife and killing him on the spot.

Unflinching, the man answered, "Joe MacAlister. Darcy's my cousin."

MacAlister only raised his voice loud enough to be heard over the voices and music. He wasn't threatening or blustering, merely stating a fact. But the fact that MacAlister had found him and connected him to Darcy meant one thing: The little witch had contacted him somehow. Clever. Or maybe she got Crone to do it for her.

But now he had a problem.

He had to get rid of the cousin and keep him out of the way. Fixing his eyes on the man, he mentally reached through the optic nerves to short-term memory to shift his memory. "Darcy went on a business trip. She'll be back in a couple weeks. She's never heard of me and neither have you." To do it right, it took a good eight seconds of forcing the subject's brain to concentrate on the new information. It was going to screw with the guy's head because the facts wouldn't add up, and memory holes would cause intense frustration. But MacAlister's mental health wasn't his problem.

Joe stepped closer to him. "Cut the shit. I—"

A scream tore through the nightclub.

Axel stepped away to get clearance, whipped out his knife, and searched the place. He noted that Joe had a gun in his hand, fast for a human but not really a threat to him or any of the hunters. The scream came from the dance floor. Looking that way, he saw that two of the rogues had each grabbed a woman and had their blades at the women's throats.

He shifted his gaze back to the fire pit and saw the same scene; two rogues with blades to two female's throats.

Axel didn't have to look for his men to know they were on the move. The rogues making a stand using his club patrons sent fury pounding through him. Women, always the women that the rogues deemed easy pickings.

The music died and the club went silent, except for the crying from the terrified women. The red and purple strobe lights suddenly looked obscene and more hellish than ever.

As he took it all in, a fifth rogue slid out of the shadows. Recognition hit Axel in his solar plexus. Holden Mackenzie. The boy Axel had grown up with.

Holden stared at Axel and ordered, "Kill the first one."

"Nooo—" The female's piercing plea turned into a gurgle. Several women fainted, thumping down onto the acrylic dance floor under the pulsing colored lights.

Rage, deep and personal, blasted through Axel. What the hell happened to the kid who used to love playing hero? Now he was capable of ordering the slaughter of an innocent mortal woman to make a point.

In his club.

Axel hated that they had come to this, but he would not let anyone, not his father and not an old friend, murder in cold blood. Every nerve in his body went taut as he watched Holden, wearing a long suede coat, stride up to him.

Smug satisfaction rolled through his walk, and made his feminine face ugly. Drawing out his perceived power, he waited a beat before saying, "I want the wit—"

Before the man finished his word, Axel threw his knife, burying the blade dead center in Holden's heart. Because they healed so quickly, the surest way to kill a witch hunter was a direct hit to the heart. He yanked his knife free before the dead hunter hit the ground.

This was what they had become. He just killed a man he'd once called a friend. Cold with rage, he quickly scanned the club to assess the situation.

The other four rogues were just as dead as Holden. Phoenix, Ram, and Sutton were cleaning off their knives.

Key knelt by the woman who had been cut. He looked up at Axel with his gray eyes. "Dead."

Fucking bastards. The woman's blue shiny top was soaked in blood, her mouth frozen open and her eyes staring blankly.

She had died as a message to him.

Patrons started to rumble and talk. They had all seen it. Axel had to control the situation. No time for regrets, he thought, as he glanced once more at Holden's body. His men gathered around, waiting for him to issue orders. "Ram, you're the best at shifting memories, try and shift the memories of what they saw into a jealous boyfriend cutting her throat." He had to force back the boiling anger, the absolute fury that an innocent was murdered in his club. It was done, now he had to deal with the fallout. There were probably a half dozen non-rogue witch hunters in the club. "Sutton, talk to the hunters, get their cooperation or tell them to get lost. Ram, call the police as soon as Phoenix gets rid of the dead rogues."

"Where to?" Phoenix asked.

Axel moved his mouth in a parody of a smile. "Dump them in front of my dad's house." Holden had been his dad's man, so Myles had probably been behind this stunt. The rogues could clean up their mess. And it'd be a message—don't fuck with him or his.

"What have you done with Darcy? Where is she?"

Damn it, the cousin. He stood loose, his gun in his hand by his thigh, his blue eyes hard and determined. Not a flash of shock, fear, or horror. He wasn't the average mortal.

Key stood behind Joe's left shoulder. "A, what do you want done with him?"

Axel considered the options. "What did Darcy tell you?"

Joe met his gaze. "She thinks she's a witch."

"She is, and she's in danger. She's safe where I have her."

"I have no reason to believe you. If she's in danger, I'll protect her."

Axel had two choices left to him: Kill MacAlister or tell him the truth. "She'll be dead within an hour if I let her go." He indicated the bodies being dragged out. "They came here to find Darcy."

Joe holstered his gun, folded his arms, and said, "I'm not leaving until I see and talk to Darcy."

The problems just kept piling up.

8

"How did you do it?"

Jarred out of sleep, the old panic hit Darcy full force. Her heart rate went from resting to run-like-hell. She jerked upright and slammed herself back against the wall and out of reach. "I'm sorry! I won't . . ."

"Too late, you already did."

His voice penetrated her jumbled panic. "Axel?" It all came back to her. It wasn't her dad dragging her out of bed to tell her he wouldn't raise a devil-spawn, it was Axel. Anger overrode her weak fear. "What are you bellowing about?"

"Your cousin came to the club tonight."

"Joe? What club?" She fought to orient herself. She'd worked deep into the night, getting all four chakras to open, but control was another matter. She set off the smoke alarm twice with fires, accidentally spawned a mini-tornado and then she tried to focus her powers and move some of the crystals, but instead she'd melted them into a big mess.

Axel's words finally sank in. Throwing her legs over the bed, she stood up quickly. "Joe's here?"

Axel grabbed her arm. "Not here, at my club. How did you contact him?"

She turned to look at him. In the light from the hall-way, she saw his feathery black hair, his green eyes, and the shadows under his eyes, which made him look tired. His hand was gentle on her arm, very different from the harshness of his face. Something tugged inside of her. "Email. I used my powers to send him an email."

"You're going to get him killed."

Her breath caught, tangling up in her throat. She swallowed and said, "What did you do to him?" Her first chakra whooshed open. Followed by the second; so quickly that she was stunned. It felt like an elevator suddenly dropping.

The hallway lights flickered. The ruined, melted crystals on the worktable thunked together, while all the pieces of metal and rocks in the plastic drawers clattered.

Axel glanced around, then back at her. "Witch karma," he warned her.

"Do you think I'd care? If you killed Joe—"

"He's alive. I didn't touch him. But he was there when some rogues decided to take hostages in my club. To get to you, by the way. They wanted me to trade you for the four women they seized with a knife to each of their throats."

She felt the room tilt, her powers spun in a crazy-eight pattern up and down her spine. She hadn't had enough sleep and the shocks kept coming. "You're trading me? Giving me to the rogues?" She remembered the terror of facing the two at the mortuary, remembered the feel of his knife cutting her while he whispered ugly things to her about wanting her blood. Furious, she jerked her arm, trying to get free of Axel. "You dragged me out of bed to trade me!"

He let go of her arm. "Don't be stupid. We killed the rogues."

She sank down on the edge of the bed, trying to sort out what the hell was going on. "What is it you want from me?"

"Tell your cousin to back off. Do you have any idea what the rogues will do to him if they figure out he's your cousin? They will use him to get to you." He crossed his arms over his chest, emphasizing his hulking muscles, and stared down at her.

Oh, God. She should do it. If Axel was telling the truth, Joe could get killed. "How do I know you're not lying? What club are you talking about?"

"Axel of Evil; it's a nightclub. Mostly hunters hang out there." Walking with confidence in the semi-darkness, he went to her worktable, picked up the laptop, and brought it back to her. "Open it."

She took the machine, opened it, and turned it on. In seconds, she was watching a video feed in full color with sound. A nightclub that looked dark and hellish. The scene split to show Axel talking to Joe on one side of the screen, the second side showed two men each grab a woman off the dance floor and jam knives against their throats.

She watched in horror as the scene played out. A man in a suede coat slid out of the shadows and gave the order to kill.

In sick horror, she saw the woman's throat cut, her blood gushing out on the dance floor.

Darcy slapped her hand over her mouth. "They killed her!" She half rose, holding the computer in one hand. "You let them murder that woman."

Roughly, he said, "Keep watching."

She couldn't watch, couldn't see this. Who were these monsters? How could Axel . . . She sank back onto the bed, her eyes involuntarily drawn back to the screen. She had to see what happened. The man in the suede coat said, "I want the wit—"

He never finished his sentence. Axel threw his knife in a movement so fast she could barely track it. The man went rigid when the knife struck, then boneless as death took him. He collapsed to the ground. She looked up. "You killed him."

"Yes."

Gooseflesh pebbled her bare skin. She wrapped her arms around herself to rub her cold arms. She saw the rest play out, including Joe walking out alive. But her thoughts went back to Axel, to his face when he'd thrown the knife. Cold and hard . . . except she'd seen a flicker of something . . . regret? Grief? "Did you know him? That man you killed?"

"Yes."

She heard it, the tight regret he was trying not to feel. Looking up, she felt caught in his green eyes. "Who was he?"

He clenched his massive hands into fists at his side. "I was friends with him until we were fourteen. Now I killed him. To protect you."

His turmoil and anger licked at her exposed skin like rough sandpaper. She could feel how much he hated what he'd had to do, but he'd done it. At the same time, he was struggling against his own craving. For witch blood, her blood. "Why are the rogues hounding you?"

"They've been quietly organizing for a while, but now they are stepping up their game. Their goal is to wipe out witches completely, and they will do anything to achieve it. They know I'm protecting you, and they want us both dead." He steadied himself. "We're running out time."

"It's only been three days!" She'd been trying!

"Five days since Hannah was cursed on Saturday night. That leaves you five more days to uncurse Hannah before the waxing gibbous moon. Once that moon passes, Hannah's only hope lies in the demon witch being killed before the full moon. She's already tired, unusually crabby, and feverish." He turned and stalked away from her toward the door, then back, as if the room couldn't contain him. "I don't need your cousin getting in my way, Darcy."

The tension in him was winding tighter and tighter. When he'd first woken her up, her fear had been so instinctive that she'd missed how close to the edge he was. She could see it now. Had killing his friend been the last straw? Would he give in to the curse and kill her? "I'm trying! Five days isn't much time! I'm learning as fast as I can." She didn't want Hannah to die! But how could she do this in five days?

He reached behind him. To the place where he kept his knife.

Adrenaline exploded inside her. *Run,* the voices screamed. Darcy jumped off the bed, ignoring the computer that fell to the ground, and raced for the light shining through the open door. Her head replayed the woman's throat being sliced open. She had to reach the door. Get away from Axel, from his knife. Her powers crackled up from her core, but she was afraid she'd hurt herself with witch karma if she used them. Then he'd be on her.

The door was just another step away. Nothing barred her way.

She slammed hard into a rock-solid chest.

Rocking back from the impact, she struggled to keep from falling. Two large hands grabbed her arms, yanking her forward. No one was there—yet someone had a grip on her.

Axel materialized in front of her. "Stop. Damn it to hell, stop!" He was panting, his entire body thrumming. Not shaking, but buzzing as if he couldn't hold all the force bubbling inside of him.

"Let go!" She wasn't going to hold still while he slaughtered her. Her powers escaped in a whoosh, exploding the ceiling lights in the hallway.

Axel reacted in a blur, grabbing hold of her neck and

easing her against the wall, then he slammed his body up behind her. The cold wall pressing against her right cheek barely registered, while the warmth of Axel's body shielding her filled up her senses. Even more shocking, she had the sense of powerful wings folding around her. As if his hawk was protecting her along with the man.

That was insane. Axel wasn't protecting her, he *was* the threat! "I won't let you kill me without hurting you, too." It was a ridiculous threat, he had her immobilized. Anything she did to him with her powers would hurt her three times worse.

"Won't hurt you."

She felt each word rasp out of his chest with tremendous effort. She shivered. "But you were reaching for your knife!"

"No. Cell phone."

"What?" She couldn't move. Damn it, he had her totally pinned. She could see his huge hand flat against the wall, the fingers curling in until his knuckles turned white.

"Cell phone. For you." He groaned, pressing his entire body against her.

She felt his thick erection slide against her lower back. The heat of his body was reaching her, surrounding her. The sandpaper-scratch sensation from his earlier agitation faded to something else, something sensual and intimate.

Probably because she was crazy. Her mind had snapped from the stress. Or it could be Stockholm syndrome. Trying to clarify, she said, "You're giving me a cell phone?"

"Yes."

It didn't make sense. And it was hard to sort out while pressed between him and the wall. "Move back, give me some space."

He eased back a step.

Darcy turned in the small space between Axel and the wall. "What the hell was that?" Once the words were out, she saw the cell phone in his hand. He hadn't been lying.

"You ran from me. I reacted. I told you, running brings out the predator in me." He held out the phone. "Call your cousin. I told him I'd have you call him. You two can talk as much as you like, but just tell him to back off and stay out of the way. Assure him you're safe."

Was she safe? Why had she imagined the wings folding over her, like her dreams when she had been scared and lonely as a child? Maybe it was just seeing his tat that had brought out her old memories. She took the phone, her fingers brushing Axel's. "I thought you were going for your knife." Clutching the phone, she wrapped her arms around herself, hating the uncertainty. The tension. The stirrings of her body that left her restless and frustrated.

His breath came in heavy rasps. "When I catch your smell, the scent of your power, it makes me burn for your blood. Then I touch you and it's something else altogether. A fierce need to protect you. Using your powers to blow those lights . . ." He shook his head. "Don't you get it yet? You'd have been cut three times worse than anything I'd have endured. I can't let you get hurt like that."

She raised her chin. "I'll always fight back."

His gaze pinned her. "I'm thirty-two, Darcy. I've fought this curse since I was fourteen. Self-control is what I live by every day. I won't slip that easily and cut you. But when you run, it whips out my hunter instincts and I'm on you before I can think."

She dropped her eyes, down the flat of his stomach to his jeans. His erection was still thick, twitching as she looked at him. That reaction wasn't about her blood, but sex. She jerked her head to the side, looking away from him. Away from her confusion.

Disgust roughened his voice further. "Christ. I wouldn't have forced you to have sex."

Flushing, she tried to move away.

Axel's hand caught her arm. "Look at me."

She refused to be a coward and lifted her eyes to his. His hand was warm and firm on her arm, but not too tight. "What?"

He touched her face with his other hand. "I can smell your desire."

Her heart kicked in her chest. "You're lying."

His voice slid to creamy. "Honey, your scent tells me everything about you. You use herbal shampoo, citrus lotion, fabric softener. What I can't get the scent of is any sign of sex on you in a very long time." He softened his voice. "Just need."

Of course he'd know what shampoo and lotion she used, he'd brought them to her from her apartment. And yet, she couldn't stand still, couldn't bear the feel of even her clothes rubbing against her. Turning, she tossed the cell phone on the rumpled covers of the bed and said, "Stop it."

He pulled her closer to him. "Stop what?"

She jerked from his hold and rubbed her palms over her arms, trying to beat back the sensations tormenting her. "It was bad enough with mortal men. They didn't know what I was, but during sex they sensed something, or felt something, and it scared them. It made me feel like a freak. That was bad enough." She hated the memories. "But it'd be worse with you. You know what I am, and you . . ." *Shut up!* She told herself.

"I what?" he asked softly.

She whirled around and glared at him. "You hate what I am. And I'd feel it. Emotions that release when a man comes . . ." She had to suck in a breath at the sheer weight of it. She didn't want to feel that from him. "I'd feel it." She would not let herself open up sexually to a man who hated what she was, hated that her blood and power could turn him into a monster. Every single time she'd tried a relationship, and sex, then felt the rejection, something in her had died off. *Hope.* The hope that someone out there would love and accept her as she was. She didn't have enough left to risk.

Axel's face shifted and, for a second, she thought she saw the wings move through his emerald-colored eyes. "I don't hate you, Darcy. I don't hate what you are."

Frowning at the change in him, she answered, "You do." His warmth was drawing her closer to him, closer to something she couldn't name but that she wanted very much, something that made her think if she could just grasp it, she would be whole. She was coming to respect Axel, his fight to stand against the curse, his love for his sister and his mom. But she didn't want to feel this. It scared her.

He shook his head. "No. I hate the curse inside of me. Not you. And I hate that those pissant little cowards calling themselves men hurt you. Do you know why they ran away scared?"

Her stomach clenched. "Because they sensed the witch in me." Her dad had always said she was evil. Or that she brought the bad things like her mom's lupus flare-ups.

"They sensed your power. They know at some instinctive level that you are more powerful than them. Women like you, witches, have always scared mortal men."

He had her attention. "But not you?"

"I'm not scared of you. I'm afraid of losing control of the curse in me, but I am not afraid of you. Right now, I can see your witch-shimmer making your skin glisten a brilliant gold with shots of silver. It doesn't scare me, it makes me hot to touch you all the way to the very core of your power."

Was that true? What if making love with Axel was different? What if he didn't think it was abnormal to want wild and uncensored sex? To need him so deeply inside of her that she was overwhelmed?

He ran his hands lightly up and down her arms. "It's no different for me. When I have sex with mortal women, I have to hold back. I have to hide what I am."

Damn it. She felt the sheer truth of that. His emotional weight was heavy, heavier than her own. The only way she could bear it was his hands on her skin—the contact made her feel stronger, more sure. What was this? Her heart thudded in her chest, making her breathless, while desire made her skin hot, yet her nipples swelled and pebbled. He was making her too vulnerable. "Axel . . ."

He lowered his head, touching his mouth to her ear. "Your scent is tantalizing, mouthwatering. I want to taste you."

His words created feathering sensations, ripples of pleasure she could hardly bear. Need was rising to overshadow her common sense. Her chakras were opening, not to draw power from the earth, but to draw him into her. As if he were some essential part of her. It was too much. "Axel." She reached up to hold on to his shoulders. He had her pressed up to the wall, his body surrounding her. And yet, she could feel that self-control in the taut muscles beneath her fingers. She turned her head to look at him.

He looked down into her eyes. "Taste you," he said, in a low, rough voice, followed by his mouth skimming hers.

Darcy couldn't stop him. Didn't want to. She turned into the kiss.

Axel wrapped an arm around her, lifting her away

from the wall and settling her so that she straddled his thigh. He shifted his hand down to her waist, sliding under her tank to cup her breast.

She arched into his hand, desperate for his touch.

Then he opened his mouth, his tongue invading her with his flavor. Pure Axel, strong and hot, with a trace of beer. Her heart pounded against his fingers caressing her breast. His hand on her lower back urged her closer. His tongue mated with hers, a slow, deep, wet slide that swelled her folds pressing against his thigh. Every part of her body that touched him burned. And every part that didn't touch him ached.

"Darcy? Are you there?" A digitalized female voice called out.

Axel jerked his hand out of her top, and growled low in his chest, "I will kill her. Swear to God, I'll find out who Crone is and kill her. Hang on." He set her on her feet. "I'll close the laptop."

Darcy missed the contact with him, missed the feel of his hand on her breast, his mouth on hers, and his thick thigh between her legs. But common sense finally surfaced. "No, Axel. Let me talk to her. We only have five days."

He took a breath, nodded, and shifted to the side to let her by.

She ran to the bed, scooping the computer off the floor. The Crone avatar looked back at her; was that censure in her eyes? Did she know she and Axel had been making out?

"Darcy, are you okay?"

"Yes, but we're running out of time. Five days until the waxing gibbous moon."

Crone nodded. "I know."

She'd been thinking about this, and she had questions. "What's the difference between an earth witch and a demon witch?"

"All witches are born as earth witches. According to our history, some witches figured out they could summon a demon."

"Why would they want that?"

"Two reasons: more power and the ability to bypass witch karma. There's no witch karma attached to a demon's powers. A few witches experimented with summoning demons and negotiating for harmful powers. Each time an earth witch performs a summoning, her soul is marked by the demon and witch karma is bypassed. The more curses or demon magic a witch uses, or the darker the curse, the bigger the price on her soul. Eventually, the demon will own the witch's entire soul, making her a demon witch."

"What does the demon get?"

The Crone avatar's mouth pulled into a tight line. "Earth witches had the power to banish demons. Since the curse, it's much more difficult and dangerous for witches to do it. Anything a demon can do to get us out of the way is good for them."

"So that's what the curse on hunters and witches was about?" Darcy asked. "Getting us out of the way so demons could have access to earth?"

"Yes. The demon witches were doing what their demon wanted by capturing the hunters. They managed to get one of them to renounce the Wing Slayer, and that set up a loophole for the witches to cast the curse."

Darcy lifted her gaze to Axel. He stood behind the screen of the laptop, close enough that she could feel his body heat on her bare knees. His green eyes glittered with anger as he said, "All hunters knew the risk. We were given immortality and tremendous strength, as well as a high tolerance to pain, and in exchange, we were to never renounce the Wing Slayer. Two of the captured hunters endured torture, refused to renounce the Wing

Slayer and the demon finally killed them. But one renounced him. The coward."

Carla dragged her attention back by saying, "Do you see how dangerous demon witches are? The one who cursed Hannah is going to come after you. When you try to undo her curse, she'll know and she'll come after you to kill you."

She didn't look at Axel, didn't want to show him her fear of the demon witch. "I can't think about that right now." She had finally figured out who she was and what her purpose was. She couldn't walk away.

Crone's image on the screen vibrated with fury. "You think Axel's going to protect you? If, and it's a big if, you can heal his sister, he'll toss you out. His sister's life isn't worth the price of hunting down and killing the demon witch, so why would your life be worth it?"

Hot regret and pain rose inside her. She lifted her gaze to his fiercely determined green eyes. The truth stared back at her—he only had her there to heal his sister. She was a threat to him, to his soul.

"Don't listen to her. I'll figure something out."

"Like locking me in a dungeon for the rest of my life?" She couldn't listen to his empty words, nor would she be shut away for the rest of her life, however long that would be. She focused on Carla on the laptop screen. "First I heal Hannah, then I will concentrate on surviving. Let's keep working." She purposely shut Axel out. She had to, she couldn't be seduced into believing he cared for her when he really just needed her for Hannah.

"Darcy, I'll find a place for you." His voice was harsh and commanding.

She nodded, but didn't look up. "Fine, go do that. I need to work." She heard him walk out.

Carla sighed, and said, "I'm afraid for you if you trust him. You know that, right?"

"Yeah."

"You'll be okay? I have to go take care of some work. I'm also going to talk to the other witches and see what they know about communicating with the Ancestors. I'll check back in a little bit."

She nodded, then Carla vanished.

Darcy was alone. Again.

"I talked to some of the witches."

Darcy lost control of the books she was levitating off the shelves in Axel's office. Five books thumped to the floor. "Car—" She clamped her jaw shut. Even though no one was currently down on the dungeon floor or on the wide screen, someone could be listening. She looked up to see that the Crone avatar had taken over Axel's flat screen. "Don't sneak up on me like that!" She was edgy, sore, and damned tired of being banished to the lower floor. Even talking to Joe with the cell phone Axel had given her hadn't calmed her irritability.

Crone ignored that. "They all agree that it's highly possible that the Ancestors are trying to reach you."

The murmur in her head seemed to agree. Excitement bubbled inside Darcy. All of her life, she hadn't known why she didn't fit in or where she belonged. But now she was finding out. "They'll let me onto the witch loops?"

"It's called Circle Witches, Darcy. Not loops. Earth witches circle their powers to strengthen one another where we can. And they can't let you on. Not yet, not while you're living and working with a witch hunter."

The disappointment filled her throat. Looking away, she focused on a book lying on the floor. She reached out a hand, summoned power through her chakras, and tried to lift the book back to the bookshelf.

The book shot across the room, skidded a path across

Axel's desk, and slammed into the wall. It left a dent the size of a salad plate.

"You lost control. It takes mind, body, and chakra connection to keep control. You can't let your emotions shatter your connection. That's how rogue hunters get control of us—enough cuts will snap our connection to our powers and close our chakras."

Not in the mood for another lecture, she turned and glared at the screen. "Bite me."

"Darcy, I'm sorry. It's not fair that they aren't letting you into the Circle, but they are cautious from experience. You're living with a witch hunter . . ."

"I'm a prisoner in his basement!" And in spite of what Axel said about not being afraid of her, he was. He was afraid of her. Why did she have to feel hawk wings when he touched her? That just made it worse. The hawk wings that always came to her as a child rejected her now.

"Then stop being a prisoner. Stop feeling sorry for yourself and use your powers."

She was being a bitch to the one person trying to help her. "Sorry, I'm just . . . sorry." Taking a breath, she directed her magic to the book she'd just flung across the room. Concentrating, she returned it to the bookshelf.

Then she returned the four other books.

"He's getting to you."

"It's the hawk. I feel a connection to Axel's hawk tattoo. Maybe I am crazy. Not a witch but just plain old crazy."

Silence, then finally Crone said, "I'd be crazy, too, if I was locked up, kept away from the earth elements. You need to get outside, feel the air, the sun, the moon. Just feel it. It feeds our chakras and our souls."

Darcy looked at the avatar of her friend. "Thanks. You're right and I will find a way to get outside." She refocused herself. "What else did the witch loop, uh, the Circle Witches say?"

"Two things. First, you should try to call a familiar and see what happens."

"How do I do that?"

"It's a loose ceremony. You go out at night, under the light of the moon, and ask the Ancestors to send you a familiar."

"I don't just pick some animal?"

Crone shook her head. "No. It's a very close relationship. The animal must agree. They will come to you. Then you take something silver, and magically imprint their likeness on that silver and always wear it close to, or on your body. It's a symbol of a soul bond."

"Silver." She reached up and touched her necklace. She supposed she could imprint the image of her familiar there.

"You'll have to open your fifth chakra to do it. That's where the magic to bond with your familiar comes from. The moon should help you . . . if it can be done."

It all felt overwhelming. "But no witch has succeeded in calling a familiar since the curse?"

"Not that we know of. They've certainly tried, but they've all failed."

"Have you tried?"

"Once. Before . . ." She trailed off. "A long time ago. I can open my fifth chakra though. It can be done."

She nodded and left Carla alone about when she had tried to call her familiar. "What's the second thing?"

"To do the spell, you'll need your witch book."

Darcy dropped her hand from her silver necklace. "I don't have a witch book."

Crone's face softened in sympathy. "It's passed down from mother to daughter. You're adopted, so that's a problem."

"My mom registered me at a biological-parent search agency before she died."

Crone shook her head, her eyes brighter than usual. "I think you probably already have the witch book. Think. Your biological mother would have known you'd need it one day, Darcy. She would have left it with you even if she gave you up for adoption." Crone leaned forward until her face filled the screen. "I *know* she did."

What was Carla trying to tell her? Something her biological mom left with her, something . . .

"Oh!" Of course. Carla had seen it a hundred times.

9

"We have to go to my apartment."

Axel snapped out of his slumber and leapt to his feet. Darcy stood in the archway between his bedroom and his bathroom. "What are you doing up here?"

"I'm done being kept in the dungeon. But that's not the point."

He ran a hand through his hair. "It's exactly the point. I had the door to the bottom floor locked." He'd slept maybe two hours. Three? He hadn't gotten home until nearly five this morning, then he'd had the conversation with Darcy that ended so well. After that he spent the next couple hours looking for safe places for Darcy and trying to locate demon witches. Her voice cut into his racing thoughts.

"I unlocked them."

He saw the witch-glow on her skin brighten with pride. It shoved back the remainder of his sleep-fog. "Damn it, Darcy. You can't startle me awake like that. I could have smelled the power in your blood and lost control before I was fully awake."

"Stop arguing. I need something out of my apartment."

He sucked in a breath. Obviously he wasn't going back to sleep. "Tell me what you need and I'll get it."

"I'm going with you." She dropped her gaze down his length, then added, "Put some clothes on."

He'd slept in his boxers. "Honey, you're the one who

stormed into my bedroom." He walked over to his dresser and yanked out a pair of jeans and a T-shirt. "What do you need from your apartment?" He pulled on the jeans.

"A tapestry. My biological mother left it with me when she gave me up for adoption. I think it's her witch book."

He pulled the T-shirt over his head and turned to her. "What's a witch book?"

She jerked her eyes up from his stomach. "Family spells passed down from generations of witches."

"Okay. It's the tapestry over the fireplace?" He'd seen it when he'd gotten stuff for her out of the apartment the first night. He walked past her into his closet, and shoved his feet into a pair of shoes.

"I'm going with you, Axel."

He walked back out and stared her down. "No, you're not. It's too dangerous. I killed a man who was once a friend to keep you safe from rogues. I'm not jeopardizing your safety now."

"I'm going." She folded her arms across her chest.

Without a word, he walked to his nightstand, picked up his knife holster, and put it on. He wasn't going to argue with her. He could smell her scent, the citrus with the dark underlying spice. He reached for his knife.

It skittered across the nightstand and landed on his rumpled bed.

The scent of rich spices got stronger. The scent of her power, so enticing; it made the blood rushing under his skin burn. "Cut it out," he warned her, then reached again for his knife.

It somersaulted down the length of the bed to the very bottom.

The witch was toying with him. He could grab the knife and be on her before she thought of her next move, but that didn't scare Darcy. Not his witch. Struggling between amusement and staying in control of the curse, he turned and said, "Quit screwing around."

She looked at him, then shifted her gaze to his knife and held out her hand.

The knife flew across the room and landed in her hand. She held it up. "Looking for this?"

His stomach turned over. If she hadn't been accurate, that knife would have sliced right through her hand. "You're getting better with your powers."

She smiled.

Even with the pain of the curse cramping his intestines, he was struck by how beautiful she was when she smiled like that, her skin glowing with power.

"You want your knife, take me with you."

He knew he should get out of the room, get some distance from the scent of her, the call of her rich, power-laced blood. He told himself to walk out of the room.

Instead he walked to her. Strode up to her and reached out to touch her face.

The feel of her warm skin raced through his fingertips and straight to his groin. But it cooled the burn of the curse. "I won't chance taking you, Darcy. The rogues know where you live, and they will watch your apartment. I'm going to slip by them and get the tapestry. But I won't risk you. I won't let them get you."

Her joy dimmed. "It was worth a shot."

He took his hand off her face and moved at high speed. He had the knife in his hand before she could react.

"Hey!"

He smiled. "I could have gotten it anytime. But you were having too much fun tormenting me." Even if it hurt him, ignited the curse, he found the joy she was taking in her new power intoxicating.

*   *   *

Axel wasn't surprised to find Joe MacAlister waiting for him in Darcy's apartment. He'd tried to follow Axel home last night, and he'd finally called Sutton and Ram to cut MacAlister off. The man had some skills, and Axel had recognized in him a bone-deep protectiveness for his cousin. Like a brother, like Axel felt for Hannah.

Darcy had probably called and told Joe that Axel was going for the tapestry at her apartment.

No, MacAlister didn't surprise him, but the woman with him did. She was huddled on Darcy's couch in a jacket too big for her, facing the fireplace where the tapestry hung.

He heard a distinct hiss from the auburn cat sitting on the silver box in the tapestry. Cutting his gaze to the picture, he noticed the cat's color nearly matched Darcy's hair, and that the threads clearly shimmered with magic. How had he missed that the first night he came to the apartment to get clothes and shit for Darcy? Neither Joe nor the woman seemed to notice the feral hiss. For now, he ignored it. He strode into the apartment and shut the door. Directing his attention to Darcy's cousin, he said, "Darcy told you I was coming here?"

Joe stood with his back to the couch and fireplace, his hands loose at his sides while his eyes watched Axel. "Yes. Morgan is sick."

"Morgan?" He looked at the woman. Her scent was sour with fear and illness.

The woman surprised him by standing up. "I'm Morgan Reed."

He figured it was MacAlister's jacket that she wore. "I need to know if my husband is—" She gritted her teeth but went on, "one of you."

What had Darcy told Joe? "What do you think I am?"

"She can't say it," Joe said softly. "Something's wrong with her, whenever she tries to remember, she gets headaches and nausea."

It sounded like a witch hunter had been repeatedly shifting and manipulating her memories. Axel moved around the couch toward Morgan. She stood taller than Darcy, about five eight, and she was too damned thin. Her cheeks were hollow; her eyes sunken.

Morgan stepped back, edging around the couch toward Joe.

Axel stopped, recognizing the deep fear in her light blue eyes. He had seen other women like her. They appeared to be addicts; confused, desperate, and paranoid. But they weren't on drugs, they were victims of rogues messing with their heads. Many of them committed suicide to escape the damage. What he rarely saw was a woman fighting back so strongly. Gently, he said, "Morgan, do you want to know?"

"Yes." She clutched the jacket tighter. Clearly MacAlister's jacket made her feel safer. "What do I need to do?"

"I'm going to come closer and you're going to look me in the eyes." He wasn't going to give her reassurances that he wouldn't hurt her. Why the hell would she believe him?

She sucked in her lips and took a step toward him.

Surprised, Axel stood still, letting her come to him. The woman's courage was evident in her forced steps. It brought home to him a truth he'd been avoiding—that mortals, not just witches, had been suffering from the actions of the rogues. He had done his best in the last years to not get involved. At all. And while he knocked back beers and screwed women in his club, people like Morgan suffered. She reached him, leaving a foot of space between them, then lifted her gaze to his and said, "Do it."

Looking into her eyes, he reached across her optic nerves for her short-term memory. Then pulled back, disgusted to find craters and scarring from repeated invasions by a hunter. He could smell the copper scent left on her from the rogue. Judging by the damage in her brain, he took a guess and said, "He cut you. Repeatedly." It was a brutal way to screw with someone's head, essentially causing a pain-memory reaction. Every time Morgan tried to remember what the rogue didn't want her to, the pain he had inflicted on her with his knife would flash in her brain.

Her face went tight and clammy. "No . . ." She backed up.

Black rage swelled in him. This woman was broken by a rogue witch hunter, the copper scent was definitely rogue. He couldn't even help her by softening her memories, there was too much damage. He looked over at Joe. "I need to see the cuts."

Joe strode to Morgan, taking hold of her shoulders and lowering his face to hers. "I won't let him hurt you, but we want to know, don't we?"

After a long second, she nodded.

Joe let go of her shoulders and eased his jacket off of her. "The cuts are on her stomach and breasts. She believes she cut herself."

"Show me her stomach." Axel knew that if he did this, if he touched those cuts and felt the heat of a rogue hunter's blade, he was going to have to start making choices. He'd been avoiding choices; he'd only been trying to keep his soul while protecting his mom and sister. *How had that worked out?* Yet, this young woman struggled to be strong in the face of serious damage that would destroy most people. Her courage outstripped his and that shamed him.

Joe lifted her shirt. Axel saw his face yank into tight lines of white-hot anger when he looked at the pale scars left from the healed cuts.

Axel blocked out Joe's reaction, and dropped his gaze to Morgan's belly. The cuts were straight lines, two columns of six rows. To distract her as he walked toward her, he said "Morgan, tell me something. Anything. Just talk to me about something pleasant."

She blinked in confusion.

Joe jumped in, "Tell him how we met back in high school. How cute you were in that cheerleader outfit."

A cheerleader, Axel thought. Just a normal mortal. Axel had only gone to elementary school. After that hunters were homeschooled. The curse kicked in around puberty, and they didn't want a witch-hunter kid killing a student who happened to be a witch in school. That would be hard to explain.

In a thin voice, Morgan said, "Joe liked all the girls. He was a big flirt. But he sure was cute with all that black hair, those blue eyes, and that take-on-the-world self-confidence."

While she talked, Axel reached out and laid his hand across the healed cuts.

She flinched.

Joe put his hand on her shoulder. "You used to walk by me ten times a day in your little cheerleader skirt. God, I wanted you. But you wouldn't have me."

Tightly, she said, "I was playing hard to get."

Axel felt the distinct heat in the cuts. The copper scent was stronger, too. She'd definitely been tortured. He lifted his hand, noticing that for a thin woman she had a slight curve to her belly.

Joe smoothed her shirt down. "Darcy told me that you were playing hard to get," he said softly.

Morgan jerked her head to look at Joe. "She told you that? Even when I didn't really stand up for her like I should have?"

Axel snapped up to his full height, something fierce and protective unfurling inside him. "What do you mean?"

Morgan shifted her gaze to him. "We were just kids,

all of us. Darcy was so strange that the kids were mean to her. I tried to stop them when they called her Dark Mac, or did stuff to her, but they just couldn't leave her be. There was something so vulnerable about her and they'd do crap like invite her to a nonexistent party."

It made Axel's chest ache to think of Darcy trying so hard to fit in, and never understanding why she didn't. Wanting so much to be accepted.

Joe said, "You told me when you found out about that. You were upset about it, and even went with me to find her."

Morgan said, "But Darcy was hurt by that creep with the knife! I should have told those kids off and stopped hanging out with them." She stopped, her face drawing in. "Something about that night . . . I keep thinking that's the reason Darcy will believe me . . . but I can't remember what I want to tell her."

Axel saw the connection. "Morgan, you were there when Darcy was cut? Did you see what happened?"

She rubbed her forehead. "Joe and I got there in time to see the knife fly out of the man's hand and stab his arm. Then Darcy's arm burst open, blood was everywhere. The man froze like he'd seen a ghost. He looked right at us and said, 'Help her.' Then he just faded away, like he hadn't even been there."

Joe put the jacket back around Morgan. "Is it important?"

Axel nodded. "Morgan, that night, you had to realize then, on some level, that Darcy wasn't mortal. You saw her use her powers to cut that man with his own knife, then suffer the consequences of witch karma. And you must know what that man was by now. Then when the strange stuff started happening to you, you realized Darcy would at least believe you, and maybe be able to help you. That's why you sought her out." The man who cut Darcy had been a witch hunter, but Axel didn't think he'd been rogue, or at least not then. If he had been rogue, two mortal teenagers wouldn't have been able to stop him and Darcy would be dead. Then Axel wouldn't have her and that was a thought he couldn't tolerate.

Morgan lifted her head, taking in a deep breath. "That does make sense. I'm not crazy."

Joe wrapped his arm around her shoulders and said, "Tell us what you found from touching Morgan's cuts."

Axel looked at Morgan. "You're not crazy, you didn't cut yourself. Your memory has been tampered with using a brutal method. The person that did it cut you repeatedly and simultaneously forced commands into your brain so that every time you try to remember certain things, you feel pain. Extreme pain."

Morgan sank down to the couch. "Is it like hypnosis?"

"It's similar, but far more powerful. Any hunter can do it—we literally travel the optic nerve to the short-term memory and force a new memory over an old one, like a sheet over a mattress. It leaves the person feeling confused and frustrated, but if done only once or twice, it's pretty harmless."

Her thin shoulders stiffened. "But over and over?"

He sighed. "Brain damage."

"Why? Why would someone do this?"

Axel sucked in a breath. "Control, most likely. You said you are married?"

"I am, or was, I ran away. I can't remember why . . ." She squeezed her eyes shut, her mouth thinning with pain.

Axel cut her off. He had his answer. "Don't try. You won't be able to do it. What you need to do is find a witch who can help you. Mortal doctors can't do this."

"Maybe Darcy can help her," Joe said.

"She's just learning to control her powers. Something

like this would take someone with more experience in brain damage."

Joe's frustration spilled out. "Where the hell do we find that?"

Axel walked to the fireplace and reached for the tapestry while saying, "Darcy is in contact with a witch helping her, I'll have her track down . . . shit!"

The cat hissed, spit, and dug a needle-sharp claw into his hand.

Axel yanked his arm back, looking down in disbelief as rivers of blood welled up along three cuts from the base of his index finger to just above his wrist.

"What happened? Did that cat *move*?" Morgan said in a shrill voice.

Axel glared at the cat. It hissed back at him, showing its sharp teeth.

"What the hell?" Joe demanded.

"It's from Darcy's biological mother. All her spells and witchcraft instructions are stored in this tapestry. I am going to bring it to Darcy."

Joe said, "It's never done that before."

"Her mom must have somehow spelled it to protect Darcy from wit—" He'd been planning to say witch hunters, but remembered Morgan, "—people like me." He studied the tapestry. If he grabbed it by the frame, maybe the cat couldn't reach him. He seized hold of the corners.

The cat went ballistic, spitting and scratching like a Tasmanian devil.

Axel stepped back, looking down at the claw-rips in his shirt over his chest. Blood stained his shirt and seeped down to his stomach. "Fucking feline; I'll kill it."

The cat growled low in its throat. The threads along the back of its neck stood up.

Joe said, "Darcy needs this?"

"Yes." And he'd get it to her if he had to stab the cat.

Could he kill a cat made of thread and magic? He'd be damned happy to give it his best shot.

"Let me try." Joe reached up.

The cat bit a chunk out of his thumb.

"Why now?" Joe demanded, while wrapping his shirt around the thumb. "I helped Darcy hang the damned thing, it never so much as meowed."

"It's reacting to me," Axel said. "That cat was probably spelled to go after people like me."

Morgan moved up closer. "Should I try?"

"No!" Axel and Joe said at the same time.

"What if you throw something over it?" Joe said. "A blanket?"

The cat snapped its tail and hissed again. Its whiskers twitched angrily.

Axel figured it was worth a try. He stormed into Darcy's bedroom and ripped the comforter off the bed. Moving at full speed, he hurried back into the living room, spread the comforter open, and grabbed the tapestry off the wall.

The cat fought the comforter, slashing and spitting, moving so damned fast it was like trying to hold on to a Mexican jumping bean. Axel slammed the tapestry to the ground and trapped it with the comforter.

The cat howled its fury. The thing sounded like it was going through a meat grinder.

"How the hell are you going to pick it up and drive with that *thing* thrashing around?" Joe asked.

He glared up at him. "If I can get it off the frame, I can roll it up and lock it in the toolbox in the bed of my truck."

Morgan said, "It's only going to let Darcy touch it. Once you shift your weight at all, that cat's going to rip you to shreds."

He narrowed his eyes. "I could hit it with a hammer. Or run it over a few times with my truck."

"No you won't!" Morgan shouted. "That cat is trying to protect Darcy."

Axel sighed. He was already dripping blood on the comforter. He had to get the tapestry to Darcy in one piece, and if he tried to put it in the truck with him for the drive, one of them wasn't going to make it.

"Go get Darcy," Joe said. "She'll be able to move it."

"Too dangerous." The risk was too great. There had to be rogues watching the apartment. Axel was not going to let them get her. Ever.

"What other choice do you have?"

He turned to look at MacAlister. "You believe all this stuff pretty easily. You believe Darcy is a witch?"

Determined blue eyes stared back. "I grew up with her. I know Darcy better than anyone else. Hell yeah, I believe it. Just as I believe, and it pisses me off to say this, but I may not be the one who can protect her this time."

Axel raised his eyebrows.

Calmly, Joe added, "But if you hurt her, nothing will stop me from finding and killing you."

Axel rose to his feet, ignoring the damned cat's hissing and howling. Joe had been honest with him, so he'd be straight with Joe. "I'm the only thing keeping Darcy alive right now. If the rogues get her, she'll die slowly and painfully. I won't let that happen." No one was taking her from him.

"Darcy has convinced me she's safe with you for now. I'll accept that. But you have no choice here." He gestured to the thrashing mound beneath the emerald comforter. "How important is it that Darcy get the tapestry whole and undamaged?"

Hannah's life might depend on it.

Joe added, "I'll stay here and keep an eye out. I'll call the cell phone you gave Darcy if I spot any trouble."

Axel strode out, thinking that with Darcy, there was always trouble.

"Are you going to make me better today?"

Darcy whirled around. She had found Axel's iPod sitting by his computers and had been looking through his music. She missed her iPod.

Hannah had caught her snooping. She set the iPod down and walked to the door that led to the hallway. The little girl stood there looking smaller and paler than she had before. Gently, Darcy brushed back her bangs. The pink-circle death mark had turned red and was getting darker. "Probably not today, honey. Soon, though. Your brother went to get me something I need."

Hannah looked down at the pretty little ballet shoes she wore with her pink-stitched jeans and white top. Then she shifted her huge brown gaze back to Darcy. "Tomorrow, then?"

"Maybe. I hope so." What did she say to this child?

Hannah stared up at her. "Will you read to me?"

"Uh . . ."

Sutton's voice burst into the room. "Darcy, Axel wouldn't like you being up on the main floor of the house."

She looked back and saw that he had appeared on the computer screen. Had he been spying on her? Watching her while she looked at Axel's iPod? She hadn't done anything, just looked to see his music. "Axel's not here." Annoyed, she waved her hand and unplugged the monitor from the computer hard drive.

Hannah giggled. "Sutton will be mad. He's the boss of all computers."

Darcy looked down at the girl and smiled. "The boss of computers?"

She nodded. "He told me so."

"Well, looks like I'm the boss of him, huh?"

Hannah giggled again and reached for Darcy's hand.

That small hand in hers twisted Darcy's heart. She followed the little girl into the hallway and asked, "Where are we going?"

"To play in my room. Do you like books? I love books. I can't really read, not real good like Mommy and Axel. But I can write my name. I can write Axel's name, too. And I know how to call him, too, all by myself. I know the numbers. Do you have a cell phone?"

Darcy was so amused by the way Hannah's mind worked, she almost missed the question. But she'd learned her lesson the first night when she had been slow to answer. "Axel gave me a cell phone." They passed the opening to the kitchen on her right. It looked like there were more bedrooms on this side of the hallway. They turned into a room furnished with a twin bed with Hannah's Minnie doll in the center, a child-size plastic kitchen, and books and toys spilling out everywhere.

"He gives me his phone to call Key. Key's my friend."

She looked down at the child. "He is?"

Hannah nodded. "He's Axel's friend, too, but Axel doesn't draw like me and Key." She leaned closer to Darcy and whispered, "Axel isn't a very good artist. But don't tell him 'cause his feelings might get hurt."

She nodded solemnly while thinking that no person with a heart could resist this kid. She loved her brother so much she didn't want to hurt his feelings. And Axel? He loved Hannah so much that he'd kidnapped a witch to heal her. And if Darcy failed, Axel would sacrifice his soul to heal her. "I won't say a word."

"How can you with Miss Chatterbox? Hannah, did you ask Darcy if she wants to play, or did you just drag her in here?" Eve leaned against the doorjamb watching them.

"She was standing all alone, Mommy. In Axel's room. I don't want Darcy to be alone."

Darcy's throat ached. Eve was raising an exceptional daughter. Darcy had to amend her thought to include Axel, who obviously spent a great deal of time with his little sister. When she lifted her gaze to Eve, she saw how tired the woman looked. She didn't seem mad to find Darcy with Hannah, but Darcy realized she had enough to contend with and didn't want to add to her burden. "I'll go back downstairs now."

Eve shook her head. "Stay. I don't like you being down there all by yourself. It's not good for you. I'm going to make an early dinner. Can you keep Hannah entertained?"

Her kindness touched Darcy. She knew Eve had been a party to Axel kidnapping her, but she wasn't mean. She was a desperate mother. "Uh, sure. But I should be practicing with my powers."

"Show me witchcraft! Please!" Hannah squeezed her hand. "Can you make my Minnie dance?" She let go of Darcy's hand and rushed to her bed, scooping up the doll.

Eve said softly, "Hannah's feeling a little better, but it won't last. Every episode gets longer and worse."

Darcy nodded, feeling helpless. She wished Axel would hurry. The tapestry would help her, she was sure of it. "I'll figure out a way, Eve."

The woman nodded. "I know you're trying. I'll be in the kitchen." She turned and left.

Hannah walked up holding Minnie out. "Can you?"

"Make her dance?" Darcy asked. "We won't know until we try. But you have to get back. Go sit on the bed, okay?" She didn't want the girl too close in case her powers got out of control.

Hannah climbed up on the bed and sat back against her pillows.

Darcy turned her thoughts inward, thinking of the color of each of the first four chakras: red, orange, yel low, and green. That dizzying elevator-drop feeling whooshed through her and all four chakras opened.

It was getting easier each time.

She concentrated on the air, using it to pull the Minnie doll to a standing position.

"You're doing it! She's going to dance!" Hannah clapped her hands.

Memories of her childhood flowed through her, of playing like this with the voices, and how they would help her make her dolls move around. Darcy hadn't had any real powers then, but the voices had filtered their massive power through her.

The memory surprised her enough that she lost her connection to her chakras and Minnie collapsed onto the bed. *She had talked to the Ancestors!* Who else could it have been?

"No. Minnie get up!" Hannah pleaded.

She'd let the memory interfere with her magic, just as Carla had warned her. She had to control her emotions. Using her power, she brought Minnie back to her feet, then started manipulating the air to make her dance.

While Hannah chatted and clapped, Darcy just let the memories roll over her while keeping her focus on her powers. Memories of the voices playing with her, teaching her, until her dad walked in and caught her.

Minnie stumbled as Darcy remembered her father's fury. The horrible lonely darkness of the closet closing in on her. Her fear, sure that her parents would stop loving her because something was wrong with her.

"You need more practice," Hannah said.

Darcy shoved out the memory and instead, she thought briefly of the hawk who came to her and made her safe. Her powers came back to her control and she got Minnie dancing again, then she added two of Hannah's stuffed bears. It was like juggling, only much cooler!

Ten minutes later, they were both giggling. She'd never have thought her powers could bring her happiness. Finally, she put all the bears down and sent Minnie back to Hannah. The little girl had twin spots of color in her cheeks from laughing, but the color made the rest of her face look even paler. "Tired?"

Hannah nodded. "My head hurts."

"Do you want me to get your mom?"

Hannah scooted over and patted the bed.

Darcy sat down, stretching her legs out alongside Hannah's shorter ones.

The child snuggled up to her side. "Can I tell you something?"

She tensed as a dark, slithering feeling circled around her stomach. Was Hannah projecting it to her? She forced out the cheerful word, "Sure."

"The shadows come at night." Her voice trembled.

Darcy wrapped her arm around the little girl and hugged her. This scared the holy shit out of her, so it had to be beyond terrifying to Hannah. "Oh, baby. It's just nightmares."

Hannah shook her head. "They are going to swallow me!"

"No, they won't. I won't let them." Somehow, she'd stop this hideous death curse. She was a witch, damn it. She had powers.

"My head hurts," Hannah said again.

She put her hand on Hannah's warm forehead. This time, her first four chakras opened with just a thought.

Darcy closed her eyes, concentrating. She wanted to focus narrowly, just draw out the pain and illness. She figured that must be the dark, slithering feeling she'd gotten when Hannah asked if she could tell Darcy something. She just had to look for that. She couldn't break the curse with low magic, but she could try to ease the symptoms a bit.

Waves of feelings came at her: Hannah's love for her mom, Axel, and those other men who must be Axel's friends, she guessed. Hannah's love for Minnie. How much Hannah liked swinging, TV shows, and Axel twirling her in circles. Her favorite books. Drawing. She loved drawing and there . . .

Something dark and painful.

Darcy thought of separating threads and looked for that one dark one. When she had a fix on it, she started imagining pulling.

Her core vibrated.

"Hot," Hannah said.

Okay, she needed to do more. While pulling that out, the headachy dark thread, she sent back gentle cooling energy, like an easy flowing stream. A few seconds later, she said, "Better?"

Axel's voice boomed into the room. "What are you doing?"

Darcy snapped open her eyes. He strode into the room and she jumped to her feet. "You're bleeding!" It looked like he'd tangled with barbed wire or a bear. Long scratches ran up and down his arms, his shirt was torn, spotted with dark wet splotches, and his face had a cut that stretched from his eye to his mouth.

"Damned cat," he muttered.

"Damned cat," Hannah said with a giggle.

Eve walked into the room. "Hannah."

"Sorry."

Eve scooped Hannah up, paused by Axel, and said, "You okay?"

"I'm fine."

She lingered for a second, then left with Hannah.

Darcy gawked at Axel. "What cat? At my apartment? I don't have a cat." He looked more like he'd tangled with a mountain lion than a house cat.

He wiped the weeping cut across his face with the back of his hand. "That cat from the tapestry."

Frowning, she said, "It scratched you? Where is it?" The tapestry had never done anything like that. She reached out to touch the deep scratches. "I can try to heal—"

"No. Forget the cuts." He latched onto her arm, leading her out the door of the room. "The tapestry is still at your apartment."

He led her out of Hannah's room, through the hallway and the kitchen, toward the front door. She struggled to mentally catch up. "You couldn't get it? You're taking me home? To my apartment?" Her blood started to pump with excitement. She would get outside, breathe in fresh air, see her apartment. For just a little while, she'd be free.

He took her out the front door. "I couldn't get it without damaging it."

The air smelled wonderful and a rush of pleasure filled her from being outside. Once they got to his truck, he took her around the passenger side, then stopped.

"Your bio-mom must have put a spell on the tapestry to protect you. It won't let anyone else move it."

Her bio-mom had cared enough to do that? A spark of warmth spilled into her blood. Maybe there was a place that Darcy belonged. She wanted the tapestry to heal Hannah, but maybe it would lead her to her biological mom. Maybe the woman who had given birth to her wanted to see her. She realized Axel was still staring at her, not moving. "What?"

His green eyes hardened. "I'm taking you because I have no choice, you need that tapestry. It's dangerous. Rogues could be anywhere. If they shield their presence, I might smell them, or I might not until it's too late."

She could feel his anxiety. "Okay."

"Don't screw with me, Darcy. No funny-shit witch-craft. No games with your cousin. He's there at the apartment, I'll explain on the way. But know this, if it comes to it, I will bring you back with me by force."

Something thick filled her throat. She'd thought . . . what? That they were friends? That she mattered some-how? That he could trust her to do all she could for Hannah?

10

"Joe!" Darcy spotted her cousin in her apartment and rushed past her comforter, which was spread on the floor in a heap, to him. Tears clogged her throat and made her nose run. Seeing him brought all her emotions to the surface.

Several feet away from Joe, she slowed to a stop. She was a witch. There was no denying now that she didn't belong with the black-haired, blue-eyed Irish MacAlisters. What if Joe rejected her? "Joe, I—" Her voice cracked.

His dark blue eyes crackled with fierce emotion. Joe took a large step, reached out, and hauled her up against his chest. She inhaled his rich leather-and-sage scent.

"Jesus, Darcy." His large hand covered the back of her head. "You're all the family I've got. Don't ever scare me like that again."

She wrapped her arms around him. "You have a witch for a cousin, isn't that going to taint the family name?" She couldn't help it, it was so ridiculous. So unbelievable. For twenty-six years, she'd tried to fit in, to make herself normal enough to fit in. But in the end, it wasn't ever going to happen.

Joe wrapped his hand around her hair to tilt her head back and look down into her face. "You didn't ever shame the family name. Your dad did with his drinking binges and shameful treatment of you. You saved the funeral home the old bastard drowned in debt."

She became aware of Axel's stare on her, and of Morgan, but she couldn't help saying, "And yet he put it in his will that I was to sign over my half of the business when you came home from the service."

"Oh, no," Joe said, letting her go. "You aren't saddling me with that. You're going to come back to work as soon as it's safe for you."

Sadness crept in like a silent fog. She clutched her hands together and got control of herself. *Funeral Director mode,* Joe called it. Quietly, she said, "It's never going to be safe, Joe. All the paperwork is in my office. The mortuary is yours, you're on all the bank accounts . . ."

"Damn it, Darcy, I'm not—"

She met his gaze. "Then sell it. If you don't want it, sell it. Take the money and do something you want to do. It's time you and I stopped living for our dead fathers." Both their dads had owned the funeral home. Joe's dad had died suddenly when Joe was in his early teens. Then Darcy's dad had tried to make Joe his son, his "blood" he'd say, the one who would follow in the family footsteps. The pressure had caused Joe to blow town for the military, hoping to make his mark on the world.

Instead, he'd come back marked in a way Darcy couldn't see but that she could feel.

"Screw them," Joe said. "It's you I'm worried about. We'll find a way to keep you safe and—"

She shook her head. "Don't you see? All the witches are in hiding. The rogue witch hunters are intent on killing every one of us." A moan caused Darcy to step back from Joe and turn to Morgan. She sat on the end of the couch, holding her head. Damn it, Axel had told her about Morgan on the way over. Another incredible thing to digest: Morgan Reed had married a rogue witch hunter. "Morgan." Darcy reached out and put her hand on Morgan's shoulder.

She looked up at Darcy. "I came home because I was scared, and I kept having blackouts. My husband said I was crazy and tried to commit me."

"I might know someone who can help you. I'll check." Carla treated brain-damage victims with her hypnosis practice. But the fact that she was a witch was Darcy's secret for now. She'd talk to Carla first. She turned to Morgan. "Where are you staying?"

Joe said, "With me. I went to her apartment the morning after you went missing to see if she knew anything. She tried to remember what she had to tell you and got sick. Then I saw the marks on her stomach." His jaw bulged with rage.

Joe cared about Morgan. She looked into his eyes and saw something that shocked her. A purpose. Determination. For Morgan. It was happening too fast and for the wrong reasons.

Axel cut into the moment.

"We need to hurry. Grab the tapestry, it's there under the comforter."

In spite of his obvious tension, he'd given her a few minutes with Joe. Axel was more complex than she'd given him credit for. She let go of Morgan and walked toward the tapestry. Axel got there ahead of her and yanked off the comforter. Darcy looked back at the sick woman. "I'll call you, Morgan, as soon as I—"

A loud hiss filled the apartment.

Darcy jumped back and looked down. "Holy cow!" She walked the last couple of steps to the tapestry, which was laying faceup. The auburn cat on the silver box, the one she'd seen a million times in her life, stood arched and ready to attack. It glared at Axel. "I've never seen it move before. It looks real!"

The cat whipped its head around and looked at her.

"Hi?" she tried.

The cat sat down and went back to being inanimate.

But the threads shimmered. Were the spells in that silver box that the cat seemed to be protecting?

She looked at the other three in the room. "What now?"

Axel said, "Pick it up. Carefully."

She knelt down, picked up the edges of the frame, and stood up with no problem. No hissing, no scratching. The tapestry was the same as it had always been. She needed to take it back to Axel's house and figure out how to get the spells out. "Joe, I'll call you about Morgan." She moved toward Axel standing at the door.

Joe cut her off by stepping between her and Axel. "Darcy, tell me where you are going. I need to know you're safe."

She knew Axel would blow a gasket if she told him the location of Axel's house, so all she said was, "I'm safe. He keeps me locked on a level belowground where no one will find me."

"Belowground . . . like a dungeon?" His face turned red. "Jesus Christ, Darcy, you're terrified of being locked up!" Joe whirled around.

Axel was already there, glaring at both of them. "We don't have time for this."

Darcy grabbed Joe's arm. "I'm fine, I swear! It was only the first night that he locked me in!" She could feel his anger rolling off him. She shouldn't have told him about being locked up.

Joe didn't move. "This is how you treat the woman trying to save your sister's life?"

Axel's expression was hard and tired. "I'm trying to keep her alive. Don't get in my way, MacAlister." He moved around Joe and picked her up before she could open her mouth. "Hang on to the tapestry." He strode to the door so quickly, a breeze brushed her face.

"Put me down!" Darcy squirmed in his arms, damned tired of being treated like a piece of furniture.

"Locke!" Joe roared.

Axel opened the door and looked around the small courtyard.

She looked, too. Everything appeared normal, just the courtyard, propane barbeques, and large trees.

Axel inhaled and said, "Shit, rogues."

She caught the faintest scent of copper. Then two men materialized in front of them. Huge men with big knives.

Axel reacted at hyperspeed, turning and dropping her to her feet. He grunted once, then put his hand in the middle of her back and shoved. "Grab her, Joe!"

Darcy flew forward, losing her hold on the tapestry and tripping over her own feet. Joe caught her upper arms and yanked her past him. She fell to her hands and knees.

Voices exploded in her head. *Run! Get out! Hunters!*

Darcy swept her gaze from left to right, taking in Morgan huddled on the floor by the couch and Joe standing over her with his gun drawn.

Darcy looked left.

Oh, God. Oh . . . Darcy's chest ballooned with fear, pain, and rage: Axel stood between her and two rogues. They had to be rogues; huge, with feminine faces and no hair on their beefy arms. But the thing that made her sick was the knife sticking out of Axel's back.

She swore she could hear the screech of fury in her head from his hawk. Blood welled up around the knife to soak his T-shirt and drip down his back. When he turned slightly, Darcy saw that he held his blade. His face was blank, his eyes ferociously focused.

He struck fast, sinking his blade into the chest of the rogue closest to him.

"Nooo!" The man's scream was filled with pain, and with the terror of dying.

Axel yanked the knife out and shoved him aside as if he weighed no more than a small child.

The second rogue threw his knife.

"Axel!" Darcy screamed, knowing there wasn't enough time for him to evade the knife. Oh, God, ohmigod . . .

A gunshot exploded in the apartment. Joe.

The rogue went down.

Darcy shot to her feet. "Axel!" Blood poured from a second wound on his bicep where the other rogue's knife had sliced it as Axel turned away. She fought a wave of hot, sick dizziness, but she made it to him.

Joe handed her something. "Wrap his arm."

It was Joe's shirt. Quickly, Darcy wound the shirt around the slice on Axel's arm and tied it. "His back, Joe!"

"No time," Axel said. "Joe, drive. Darcy, tapestry. *Move!*" His face shone with sweat, his mouth was thin and fierce, and his eyes glittered with pure rage.

"Go!" Joe ordered, "I'll cover." He grabbed Morgan by the arm.

Darcy snatched up the tapestry with one hand, Axel's uninjured arm with her other, and they hurried out to the truck. "Keys!" She said to Axel. She was driving them back, and sending Joe and Morgan somewhere else. Somewhere safe.

"Pocket."

She shoved her hand in the left front pocket and got the keys. Hurrying, she opened the truck, tossed the tapestry behind the seat, and stood back.

Axel heaved himself up to sit sideways, the knife sticking out.

She slammed the door and turned to her cousin. "Joe, you and Morgan get the hell out of here. Away from me!" She raced around the truck, climbed in, jammed the keys in to start it, then fumbled to get her seat close enough to the wheel to drive.

She tried to start the engine but her bloody hands kept slipping off the key. *Axel's blood,* she thought, her mouth going dry and her eyes hot with tears. Finally, she turned the engine over. "Doctor? Hospital? Where?" How could she save him?

"Darcy, it's okay. I'll live. Pull yourself together and drive home."

She knew the way since it had been light out when they left, and Axel hadn't shielded her vision the way he had the night he'd kidnapped her. She put the truck in drive and hit the gas pedal. She turned out onto the main road and accelerated to the speed limit. There was a buzzing in her head, but she couldn't make out any words.

"Turn right here."

She made the turn.

Axel gave her a few more directions, then said, "The only one following us is Joe."

Feeling like her muscles were so tight that one jolt would shatter her, she said, "I'll take you to a hospital or . . ."

"I'm okay. Just drive back to the house."

"You're not okay! You have a knife sticking out of you!"

He reached over his shoulder and—

"Don't! Don't you—"

He pulled the knife out.

Unable to believe what he'd done, she demanded, "Are you insane?" The cab of the truck went hot and sticky. Blood poured from the wound. It was just beneath his left shoulder blade. *Stop the bleeding,* she told herself. She made a right turn, then another into an alley behind a strip mall. Slamming the truck into park, she yanked her T-shirt over her head, balled it up, and shoved it against the wound. For the first time, she noticed he had a big-ass gun resting on his thigh next to his bloody knife.

Lifting her gaze, she saw Axel look around, obviously assessing if they were being followed, then his eyes settled on her. "Nice."

"Now?" She asked incredulously. He was admiring her bra-cupped breasts now? "Are you out of your mind?" One of them was, and she wasn't the one pouring out blood. In spite of her shaking, she pressed her hand hard against the wound to get the bleeding under control. She realized that his pain was flowing into her, seeping from his nerve endings to hers.

Her chakras had opened without her conscious effort.

In reaction to Axel being hurt? Pure fear? Didn't matter, she had to help him. She closed her eyes, struggling to not fight his pain and to let her body absorb it. She forced herself to breathe and let the pain in. She had to calm down and center herself in order to control the powers flowing through the chakras. As the pain traveled through her, she sent energy back to him in exchange. Healing energy that would knit together to heal torn skin and sinew.

"Darcy, stop."

She shook her head as the pain crawled up her arm, and edged across her neck, then slammed into her shoulder blade. It burned to a fiery pitch. She sucked in a breath, losing the connection to her energy. Had she done enough? She opened her eyes. "Let me see." She eased her bloody shirt off the wound.

It barely seeped blood and the edges were coming together, the healing had begun.

"Hold this on there," she said tightly. Turning in her seat, she reached for the gearshift. She had to get Axel home.

He grabbed her hand. "What did you do?" he demanded. "You took the pain, didn't you?"

Her stomach roiled with the pain, but it was starting to recede. She should try to do the same thing to close the wound on his arm, but she wasn't sure she'd be able to drive if she did. The voices were murmuring and fretting in her head, making it hard for her to focus. The rogues had roused them to a fever pitch, and the invasion of the hawk in her mind had them agitated. She couldn't feel the hawk now, but his screech earlier had been real and enraged. "I just tried to close the wound a little."

"Your hands are shaking." He let go of her to turn, reaching in the back and pulling a jacket from the jump seat. "Put this on."

It dawned on her that she was so rattled, she had been planning to drive the rest of the way home in her bra. It wasn't just seeing Axel hurt that shook her up, it was the realization that he had *intentionally* turned his body to protect her from the knife and allowed himself to be stabbed instead. He was protecting her exactly as he'd told her he would. She sucked in a deep breath to calm herself, and looked at her hands on the steering wheel. Her skin was covered in his blood.

Dark spots danced in front of her eyes.

No. She wouldn't get faint or panic. Axel was hurt, she had to drive. The pain was inconsequential.

"Put your arm out," Axel said.

She lifted her right hand and let him slide the jacket on. Then he leaned so close she could smell him. Feel him. His warmth stopped her shivering. His balmy breath eased her fried nerve endings. His jacket was so big, he easily spread it across her back and held it while she slid her left arm into the remaining sleeve.

She faced him. "You have to stop moving. The pain, the cuts . . ."

He snorted. "I heal fast, very fast. But you, little witch, were damned stupid to open yourself up to my pain. Now you're suffering. You have to learn better control."

She turned back, put the truck in gear, and edged out of the alley. Another turn and they were back on Pacific Coast Highway. The ocean spread out on her right in a stretch of rugged, unspoiled beauty. God, she wished she could sit on a rock and just feel the spray of the ocean, the warmth of the sun, or the light of the moon on her skin. Feeling Axel's gaze on her, she said, "I'm fine." The pain was better, somehow her body was breaking down the pain and getting rid of it.

"The hell you are. Your shimmer has dots of red." Axel eased back into his seat. "You're brave, compassionate, and too damned beautiful."

Startled, she jerked her head around to look at him. His voice was throttled to a slow, rich tone that made her stomach jump. Protecting her from that knife, putting the jacket around her, being angry over her pain, those things were confusing her. She understood he needed to keep her alive to reverse the curse on Hannah. But the rest? "Are you bothered being in the truck with me?"

He turned from the side-view mirror he'd been studying, his green gaze latching on to hers. "It's like a humming that keeps growing louder and more grating. Then you touched me, using your powers to call out the pain in my shoulder, and I wanted to push you down on the seat, strip off those pants and . . . possess you. That urge is harder to control than the bloodlust."

She struggled to tear her eyes away and watch the road weave along the Pacific Ocean. She spotted the turnoff, the one she'd never noticed in all the years she'd lived in Glassbreakers, and guided the truck around the corner to begin the journey up into the hills.

"I won't hurt you," he said softly.

She clenched her fingers around the steering wheel. Her skin tingled, her nipples swelled and pebbled, and a clenching need pulsed uncomfortably between her thighs. And the worst of it was that *he would hurt her.* He'd pump himself into her until he lost control with his orgasm, and she'd be helpless against the truth of his feelings. She'd feel exactly how much he hated lusting after a witch—one of those that had cursed his kind. Those feelings would penetrate her skin as mercilessly as a knife, going deeper than a blade to kill off any shred of self-protection she had left. She couldn't risk that.

Even when he'd risked his life to save hers?

What was she thinking? She didn't owe him sex. Both of them were caught in a situation, the trick was to solve the problem and get out. Fast. "Hopefully the tapestry will help me cure Hannah quickly. Free you. Us."

"And go where?"

She didn't know. "I'll think of something." Wouldn't she? It wasn't his problem. Maybe she could find her biological mother, and together they could . . .

Axel cut off her daydream. "Your cousin is still following us. He followed us into the alley and waited, and he's behind us now."

She looked in her rearview mirror and saw Joe's truck. "What should I do?" She turned to look at him. "I don't want him killed. Please."

Axel said evenly, "I'm not going to kill him, Darcy. Nor is he going to back off. You're his family, I get that. We'll sort it out at home. Out in the open, you're too damned vulnerable."

11

Axel got Darcy and the other two safely into the house and took his first real breath.

When he'd seen those rogues holding their knives, seen their eyes alight on Darcy in his arms, something possessive and feral had taken over his brain.

Mine.

He'd have done anything to save her in that moment.

But Darcy was no coward. She'd held it together and drove them home. And she'd even done what she could to heal him.

Damn, he had to get away from her. He knew it. His need for Darcy had gone from bearable to excruciating when she'd touched him with her powers. She was still pale from the amount of pain she'd pulled from him. He couldn't stand it, couldn't tolerate her agony. He'd wanted to shake her and tell her to never, ever, use her powers to ease his pain again.

More than anything, he wanted to yank her up against him and hold her. Take her fear, shock, and pain away. Assure her he'd keep her safe.

But he couldn't do that. Couldn't risk it. He was losing control of himself around Darcy inch by inch.

Eve walked in. "Hannah's asleep. What is going on?" Her gaze zeroed in on the blood on Axel and Joe's shirt that was wrapped around his bicep.

He reassured her. "I'm fine, the cuts are closing. This is Joe, Darcy's cousin, and their friend, Morgan."

Eve nodded. "Come into the kitchen. We'll get some food and coffee."

Axel said, "I'm going to change my shirt and get Joe a shirt. Be there in a second." He needed a minute away from Darcy, away from the feel of her. Sweat broke out on his back and neck, his balls seized up with aching lust and he had the driving need to possess her. Make her his.

He tossed Joe's shirt in the trash and pulled his shirt off to join it. The cut on his shoulder was just an angry red welt below his shoulder blade. Darcy had done a hell of a job on that. The cut on his arm bled only a little; his own recuperative powers were taking care of that. He slapped a gauze pad on it and wrapped a piece of tape around that. Germs weren't a problem for his supersize immune system. The cut would heal by morning.

He ran cold water from the tap and stuck his head under it.

Joe's words about Darcy's terror of being locked up came back to him, along with the memory of what he'd done to her that first night. She'd begged him not to, and even though he'd scented the fear on her, he'd done it anyway.

Then he'd just left her. She'd responded by bashing the lock with the stool and damn near breaking her own hand. Thankfully, his mom and Hannah had gone down there or she would have broken her hand, or worse.

Regret made him sick. But he hadn't thought he had a choice. If she'd gotten away, the rogues would have found and brutally killed her. That wasn't going to happen. He wouldn't allow it.

He sucked in a breath, then washed his hands and dried them off. He turned and walked into his bedroom, dragged on a T-shirt, and grabbed a second one for Joe. He went out into the kitchen.

Eve, Joe, and Morgan sat at the table with steaming cups of coffee. "Where's Darcy?" He tossed Joe the shirt.

Eve looked up. "She went downstairs through the pantry. She said she has work to do."

Down in the basement level alone. He rubbed the ache in his chest. It was starting to feel like he was somehow incomplete. He went to the coffeepot and poured out a cup. "She can eat first before she starts working."

Joe pulled on the shirt and said, "I told her I'd go down with her, but she said she wanted to take a shower and clean up."

Axel slapped the cup down onto the counter. "I didn't know she was claustrophobic. Why is she afraid of locked spaces?"

Joe's gaze turned guarded and he shrugged.

Protecting his cousin's secrets. He could beat it out of him, but then Darcy would probably get mad about that. "Fine, I'll ask her myself." Ignoring the coffee, he headed for his room.

His mom said, "Axel, leave her alone."

He looked at his mom. "Can't."

"Most men are spooked by Darcy," Joe commented.

He stopped and turned. "Mortals. Cowards. They sensed her power and were threatened by it." He went back to the kitchen and picked up the mug of coffee.

"She didn't like being different."

Joe was distracting him, and at the same time, testing his feelings about his cousin. "She likes it now. She used her powers to take my knife from me."

Joe laughed. "Maybe you should give her some space."

He couldn't. So instead, he went to the laptop at the end of the counter, pressed a key, and said, "Darcy." Her image popped into view. She looked tired, and she still had dried blood on her hands. He caught sight of the framed tapestry propped up on the desk against the bathroom wall.

She glanced up at the camera. "What?"

"Come upstairs; get something to eat . . ."

"No. We both know I need to stay down here." She dropped her head back down to stare at the tapestry, shutting him out.

Hadn't he told her he wouldn't hurt her? "Darcy—"

"Busy. Go away."

Damn it, she was busting his balls. "Little witch, if I come down there . . ."

She raised a hand and the laptop screen blanked. He slammed his cup on the dark granite counter.

"She blew the cameras in her room," Sutton said, appearing on the computer screen.

Joe laughed and stood up. "I'll go check on her. Show me the stairs."

Eve stood up. "Sit. Stay. I'll be right back." She hurried through the pantry.

"Let Eve go to Darcy, Axel." Sutton watched him from the laptop screen. "You're barely holding the line."

"She blew my cameras," Axel pointed out. He needed to be able to see her, check on her, make sure she was okay. He needed . . . her. Damn it, Sutton was right. Shifting his focus to a safer area, he reached under the counter and pushed a button.

On the wall behind an oversize rocking chair, a big projection screen rolled down. "Everyone there, Sutton? We need a meeting."

The four other Wing Slayer Hunters appeared on-screen in four separate squares, sort of like the Brady Bunch. Axel said, "That's Sutton West in the top left corner, top right is Ram Virtos, bottom left is Phoenix Torq, and bottom right is Key DeMicca." He gestured to the table. "This is Joe MacAlister and Morgan Reed."

"Hi," Morgan said softly. She stared with huge blue eyes at the screen. "Are you all the same as Axel?"

"They are Wing Slayer Hunters. They have vowed to never become what your husband is." He turned to the screen. "Morgan is ill. Her husband has screwed with her memory. She can't tolerate certain words, and she can't say his name."

"Brain damage?" Phoenix the tackless asked.

Axel said, "Yes. Darcy is going to try to find a witch to help her."

"It may take awhile." Darcy's voice came over the speakers. "Crone hasn't popped up yet."

"Ah, there's my eavesdropping witch." He had figured she'd listen in.

"Darcy," Sutton said, "are you still mad at me?"

Axel zeroed in on Sutton. "What did you do?"

"You told me to keep an eye on her. Hannah came into your room and I told her she should go back downstairs. She used witchcraft to disconnect the monitor so I couldn't see her with the webcam."

"I was just looking at Axel's iPod! I wasn't doing anything to it. I was just looking at his music."

Axel winced. "Darcy, he wasn't accusing you of anything. No one cares if you were looking at my iPod."

She didn't answer. Didn't say another word.

Joe said, "She uses her iPod to block out the noise in her head. I found it outside the mortuary door the night she went missing."

He looked back to the laptop where the mike was. "Why the hell didn't you tell me, Darcy?"

Nothing. She wasn't talking to him, again.

His mom walked back in. "I'm going to make Darcy some tea." She looked at Axel.

He put his hand over the sensitive speaker that picked up their voices.

Filling the kettle with water, she said, "She's desperately trying to get something from the tapestry, but no luck. Crone isn't around and Darcy can't reach her. She's on her last nerve. She's threatened the cat on the tapestry if he doesn't talk to her."

He rubbed his eyes. "Put something in her tea to relax her, Mom. She took a hell of a lot of pain from me to heal the knife wound."

Shutting off the water, Eve looked at him. "It might slow her down."

"We're not trying to kill her," he snapped. Closing his eyes, he said, "If she's in too much pain, she won't be able to center and connect with her powers. I didn't stop her when I should have."

She put the kettle on the stove, and then put her hand on Axel's arm. "It's more than that. She's afraid of what she's going to get from the tapestry."

He shifted his gaze to Joe.

The man's expression was guarded. After a few seconds he got up and walked over. "Can she hear?"

Axel shrugged. "I have the mike covered but your cousin is resourceful."

"Her dad, her adoptive dad, told her over and over that she was evil. That her bio-mom threw her away because she was a little heathen, a pagan, an evil child. He wouldn't let Darcy touch him, ever. When Aunt Eileen, that's Darcy's mom, would get sick, he'd blame Darcy and tell her she made her mom sick because she brought the bad stuff to the family. Darcy would get more scared, and she'd do stuff like talk to people who weren't there, or sneak out back in the middle of the night and talk to herself. When he caught her, he'd lock her in the hall closet away from the moonlight, or any light at all."

Axel heard the roar of his fury, and the scream of his hawk. They both wanted to hunt and kill the man who had hurt Darcy. "Her mother allowed this?"

"Aunt Eileen? Hell no. She didn't know. She'd be in the hospital or laid up in bed. Darcy never told her when she was well because she didn't want to make her sick again. She begged me not to tell her either. It pretty much stopped by the time I got old enough to really understand what he was doing to her. Or I'd have stopped it myself."

Axel believed Joe would have. He knew that Darcy had repressed her powers, and she'd found a way to cope in a mortal family that didn't understand. Now she was facing a new fear. "She's afraid she's going to find out from the tapestry that he was right." It wasn't a question.

Joe nodded, refilled his coffee cup, and returned to the table.

To his mom, he said, "No synthetic drugs, she can't tolerate them. Put in some herbs. When you're down there, find out what more she needs from us." He wanted to go down there and ask her himself, but he was too edgy. The compulsion for her blood burned his skin. And the need to strip her naked and claim her pounded inside of him with each beat of his heart.

He had to go to the club. For Darcy's safety, he had to go find a willing woman. Or two. Though he knew in his gut that there weren't enough women to cool his need for Darcy.

He wanted, he needed the witch.

"I'll take care of her and ask her what she needs," Eve said while crushing some herbs and adding them to the steeping tea leaves.

He met his mom's stare, knew she was reading the tension in him, that she understood as well as any mortal could. It gave him the strength to wrench his thoughts from Darcy. He took his hand off the mike. "Okay, we need to research Morgan's husband. Phoenix, find the bastard."

Phoenix nodded. "Oh, yeah, good times."

Morgan said, "You can find him? I can't even tell you his name."

Ram said from his block on the screen, "We're running a search now. We'll see if you have a valid marriage license."

Phoenix added, "I'll find him, blondie. It's what I do."

Morgan's mouth fell open.

Axel rolled his eyes. "Phoenix's a bounty hunter. He tracks down scum all the time."

Key grinned. "Hanging out with all that scum is why he doesn't know how to talk to women."

Phoenix shot back, "You're all talk, Key. I'm more a man of action, the kind of action that has women coming back for more."

"Enough," Axel said.

Sutton cut in, "I have something." He looked up at Morgan. "Can you read a name and tell me if it's your husband?"

"I don't know. I think . . ." She frowned, huddling deeper in the jacket.

Sutton said, "Don't think about it. I just want you to tell me if this name looks right."

ERIC REED scrolled across the screen, then faded, replaced by the pictures of the four men.

Morgan's square jaw tightened, and lines appeared around her mouth. "Yes."

Joe put his arm around her. "Morgan, how old are you?"

Axel knew Joe was shifting her train of thought to a pattern that wouldn't hurt. "Twenty-eight."

His mom came back upstairs and sat next to Morgan.

Ram looked up from the screen he was working on. "You were an on-air reporter in San Diego?"

Her face eased. "Yes. For almost three years. I was working on a big story about some missing women who never turned up, and my instincts were screaming, 'serial killer' when I started having headaches and forgetting things. It got worse and then I had these cuts . . ." She brought her fingers up and rubbed her temples.

Axel said, "Mom, can you show Morgan a place where she can rest? She's been through enough."

"No, wait. Damn it!" She dropped her hands and took a breath. "I didn't know where the marks on my stomach and breasts came from. My husband told me I was cutting myself. But I'd never been a cutter before." She stopped, putting both palms flat on the table.

"Morgan, easy." Joe put his hand on her back.

"I'm not a cutter."

Axel walked around the counter to Morgan and dropped down to face her. Looking into her eyes, he said, "You're not. He did this to you. The wounds, the memory loss, and the headaches."

"You believe me."

"I believe you," Joe said softly.

"We all believe you," Axel assured her.

She nodded slowly. "I will rest, if that's okay."

"You'll both stay here. It's safer." Axel looked over to Joe. "Darcy will feel better if she knows you're both safe."

Joe nodded and took Morgan's hand as she stood up. "You want me to go with you?"

"No. I'll be okay if I sleep for a little bit."

His mom took Morgan's arm. "There are two bedrooms you can choose from down the stairs. That way Darcy won't be alone down there."

They headed through the pantry and down the stairs.

Once Axel heard the door slide shut, he looked at the screen. "That bastard scarred her brain tissue. He cut her repeatedly to force a pain memory whenever she tries to think of his name and certain other things. I'm thinking it's connected to the last story she was working on about women who went missing."

Phoenix's black eyes narrowed. "I'm going to enjoy finding him."

Joe folded his arms. "I'd like a piece of that action."

Phoenix looked at him. "What are you, another super-mortal like Chuck Norris?"

Leaning his chair back on two legs, Joe said, "Chuck Norris sold his soul to the devil in exchange for his rugged good looks and superior martial arts ability."

Phoenix met Joe's eyes. "Yeah?"

"Then Chuck Norris roundhouse-kicked the devil in the face and took his soul back. The devil, who appreciated irony, said he should have seen it coming. Now they play poker every second Wednesday of the month."

Phoenix grinned. "When Chuck Norris was denied a Bacon McMuffin at McDonald's because it was ten thirty-five, he roundhouse-kicked the store so hard, it became a KFC."

"If you want a list of Chuck Norris's enemies, check the extinct species list."

"Since nineteen forty, the year Chuck Norris was born, roundhouse kick–related deaths have increased thirteen thousand percent."

Darcy cut in, "What's worse than a pissed off Chuck Norris?"

Joe shut his mouth.

Phoenix fell for it. "What?"

"A pissed off witch."

Hurt crawled through his voice. "You don't like Chuck Norris jokes?"

"Do you like Enya, Phoenix?"

His dark eyes widened in horror. "No! That's not music, it's like listening to a cat in heat!"

"Then you probably wouldn't like me zapping your

speakers so that only Enya played. Who I happen to like, by the way."

Phoenix looked at Axel. "Your witch is wicked mean."

Pride swelled through him. "Damn right."

Axel rolled his shoulders beneath the pulsing lights of his club. Already, he wanted to leave, to go back home.

To the witch.

He was at the club to get some relief. Sex. He looked around. "It smells like sex in here."

"Everyone is tense," Key said. He wore jeans that rode low on his hips, a T-shirt, and a vibe of pure anger that drew women to him. Turning his gaze on Axel, he added, "Rumor is that hunters are being forced to choose."

He raised his eyebrows. "To go rogue?"

Key's spiked blond hair reflected the red and purple strobes. "Or die."

Turning his gaze back to the club, he watched the two dance floors. Hot lust pulsed with the lights. He shifted his eyes to the black couches. A young hunter had a woman wearing a short skirt and obviously no panties straddling him. Riding his cock while the hunter held the base of himself to make sure he didn't penetrate her too deeply and hurt her.

At one of the curved, fire-edged bars, he watched a hunter thrusting into a woman on a bar stool. The hunter had pushed the woman far enough back on the stool to limit his access, to keep himself in check and not hurt the woman.

Public sex didn't usually happen in the bar. He didn't give a shit as long as everyone played nice. But it was proof that the hunters were under growing pressure.

He kept his eyes moving, over the redhead with the tight jeans, past the blonde with the tiny dress, beyond the tall beauty chatting up the bartender. He saw them all, but Darcy was in his head. Her pale frantic face in the truck as she tried to heal him. Or earlier when he'd kissed her after waking her this morning. It was her skin his palms itched to touch. Her eyes he wanted to watch lose focus as she came for him . . .

"Hell." He locked his jaw.

"Yeah, it's a real drag to have your pick of hot chicks," Key commented. "Or maybe you're just getting old."

The bastard was yanking his chain. "Not too old to kick your ass." A good fight might ease his tension.

"I'm up for that."

Axel had turned and was headed for the warehouse to do a little sparring when his phone rang. He pulled it out, checked the screen and saw it was his dad. "What?" he answered.

"I have a present for you. Let's see if you're man enough to handle it." The phone disconnected.

He hung up, wondering what the fuck his dad was doing . . .

Before he finished his thought, his phone vibrated with an incoming text message. Snapping it open, he read, "Security breach in . . ."

A loud crash echoed from in the front of the club. He stowed his phone and pulled his knife in one movement. He grabbed his gun with his right hand as a backup.

Screams wailed. Glass shattered. The first bar splintered. Lights exploded.

Then everything came to a halt. He heard only the sound of an idling engine, weeping, groans, and a few snaps of electricity from broken lights.

Axel moved past the chaos to the front of his club where a huge H2 Hummer had crashed through the specially darkened security glass at the front.

"Get everyone out!" Axel yelled, thinking there might

be a bomb in the Hummer. He ran to the idling vehicle to see if it had hit anyone and trapped them. As he got closer, the smell of blood grew. Thick, spicy, intoxicating . . .

Witch blood.

Sweat coated his body in seconds. His grip tightened on his knife. *He had to get to the blood! Feel the blood! His veins burned everywhere, his lungs couldn't get a breath, if he just . . .*

"No!" He backed up, slamming into two young hunters with their knives in their hands; their eyes *glowing* with bloodlust. They were screwed. The witches were alive in the Hummer, he could smell the fresh blood, hear their shuffling and crying. Hunters were circling, and his own need screamed through him.

The two hunters attacked him, desperate to get past him and to the witches. Axel had a split second to decide if he would kill them or try to disable them.

He roundhouse-kicked the first one into the second, sending them flying across the room and into a pool of unconsciousness.

All hell broke loose as the witch blood inflamed the curse. More fists, knives, and bar stools came at him. While Axel fought, he was aware that several women had organized and were dragging the witches from the Hummer. A part of his brain urged them to hurry, get the witches out of there and to someplace safe.

When all the chaos slowed, he turned to see the Hummer was empty, the engine still idling. The scent-trail of witch blood was fading as the blood dried.

Key limped over, bleeding from one eye, his nose, and seven or eight places on his torso. "Fuckfest."

Wiping his hand over the freshly opened gash on his arm, he grimaced. "The women who got those witches out of here, where'd they take them?" He picked his BlackBerry up off the floor.

"I don't know, but I saw Julie in one group, helping the witches."

Julie worked as a server in the club, and was also the daughter of a witch hunter. Her father had secluded himself in a trailer in the middle of a desert to keep from going rogue and had died there. He pulled up her number and hit send.

"Axel." Her voice was out of breath and stressed.

"Julie, do you have the witches, are they alive?"

"Yes. They are helping each other heal. Jesus, Axel, they were cut up pretty bad." Her voice shook.

"Okay, listen, I'm going to give you the directions to a safe house. Take them there. Get them anything they need. And Julie, you and the other women saved their lives tonight."

"Yeah, but for how long?"

"We're going to keep them safe." He gave her the directions and hung up.

He meant it, they would keep those witches safe. But his skin burned with the craving. His gut cramped with the bloodlust. And a little voice whispered in his head, *There's a witch in your house. All yours.*

Hannah. He fought to bring Hannah's face into his mind. He thought of her as he'd seen her before he'd left tonight—sleeping fitfully, dark smudges beneath her eyes, and when he'd brushed back her bangs, that goddamned circle had turned an obscene shade of red. And Darcy had been downstairs, doing everything she could to pull the spells from the tapestry.

He wouldn't kill the witch trying to save Hannah.

He wouldn't kill any earth witch.

Sirens pierced the weird stillness. Axel looked around to see the hunters struggling to their feet. The bar was a mess. As soon as the cops poured in, mortal cops, he talked fast convincing them that a Hummer full of drunks had crashed through the wall, then the drunks busted up the bar and somehow escaped. It was lame as hell but they bought it.

Thanks to the push on their short-term memories.

They got the Hummer towed out, and started boarding up the club, all of them swinging hammers in spite of their injuries from fighting.

Axel's phone rang. He looked at the incoming call then slapped the phone to his ear with a growl of warning.

His dad taunted, "Did you like my gift? Did you run like a girl and puke all over yourself? Or did you take back your balls and harvest the power from the witches' blood?"

He hated his father more than ever, but pulled himself together enough to say, "Why don't you come see for yourself?"

His father laughed. "Bet you smell like puke. Don't you get it? Your little witch is finishing the curse, turning you into her familiar. Then she'll have all the power and you'll be witch-whipped." He hung up.

Witch-whipped was a particularly crude way of saying a witch had bound him as her familiar. Like the demon witches had tried to do with their curse. Darcy wasn't a demon witch, damn it. His dad was screwing with his head. Furious, he shoved his phone into his pocket and hurled the hammer to the ground, ready to go find his dad and confront the bastard.

Sutton shoved Axel back into the freshly nailed boards. "He's goading you, dumb ass! You're so wound up, it wouldn't take but a splash of witch blood to send you over. He's trying to get you to come to his house." Sutton got into his face. "He's trying to turn you. And once he does, your witch is dead, and so is Hannah."

The cold truth of that hit him hard. Axel sucked in a breath.

What if it was true? What if Darcy was doing something to him? When she'd been threatened by the rogues at her apartment, the hawk on his skin had seemed to come to life. The wings had tried to lift off his back. This thing on his back, it wasn't just a tattoo.

"What?" Ram walked over to him, seeing that he was obviously thinking something over.

Hell, if he couldn't tell these four men, who could he tell? "The wings. My hawk tat. I swear the wings tried to lift off my skin today at Darcy's apartment when those rogues attacked. And he screeched in fury."

"Your knife?" Phoenix asked.

Axel shook his head. He'd looked. Repeatedly. "No wings impressed on there. And no ring of immortality around my thumb." Those were the traditional signs that the Wing Slayer used to deem a hunter worthy of being one of his hunters. Yet someone had changed his original raven into a hawk, who was the traditional leader of the hunters. If the Wing Slayer had changed his tattoo, then why wasn't he showing himself to Axel?

He swept his gaze over them and said, "What if Darcy is doing something to me? The hawk tat never did anything until she touched it." God, his hawk wanted her to touch him again. She made both Axel and the hawk feel alive.

Key shook his head. "Your tat isn't charmed by a witch. I'd know. We'd all feel it."

That was true, they'd all feel the residue of her magic. He was letting his father's soulless ramblings get to him.

Ram looked thoughtful. "You were the closest to the witch blood tonight, yet you resisted."

He snorted. "I wanted it. It was too damned close. Only the thought of Hannah kept me from going after it." And memories. Memories he didn't want to deal with tonight.

Ram wasn't finished. "You put the witches in one of our safe houses."

He was changing, there was no doubt. He couldn't let innocent earth witches be killed. He had to act. Was that him rising to the hawk tat he wore or was it something else? There weren't any answers, so he said, "Let's call it a night."

An hour later, he paused the security system to go into the house. Just as he reengaged the alarm, he heard Hannah's cry of terror, "Make them stop!"

Axel threw off his exhaustion and moved at inhuman speed to her room. His baby sister had scooted to the top corner of her bed, clutching her Minnie doll and her blankets. "Don't let them get me!"

Axel scooped Hannah into his arms. "No one's here, baby." He hugged her shaking body to him while scanning the room again. He could see perfectly in the dark, but they'd taken to leaving a night-light on for her.

"The shadows! Please, Axel!"

Her hot tears hit his shoulder and twisted his guts. "No one's going to get you. I swear." She was having nightmares of shadows swallowing her up. The curse was taking hold, tormenting her mentally and physically. Her little body shivered, but her head felt hot against his neck. Axel put his hand on her back to hold her snugly against him and strode out of her room.

He almost ran into his mom.

Axel reached out his free hand and steadied her. She looked exhausted and her arm beneath his hand felt thinner. "I've got her, Mom. Get some sleep."

"Is she feverish?"

Eve's eyes were haunted. Hannah's night-light spilled out just enough illumination to show her in a pair of sweats and a long-sleeved shirt. Her eyes were smudged with fatigue and worry. "Maybe a little, but mostly scared from a nightmare. I'll wake you if she needs anything."

His mom looked over him. "You're hurt."

He shrugged. "Doesn't matter. Go back to sleep."

"It matters," she said softly.

Forcing a smile, he reassured her. "I'll be healed before you get up in the morning. Go back to bed. I'll put Hannah in bed with you once she's asleep." He moved past her and strode out to the kitchen. He didn't bother with a light, but went to the fridge and got out a bottle of water. "Try some water, sweetheart."

"Don't want it." Hannah tucked her face farther into his neck.

Axel bypassed the big table and sat in the oversize rocker. "One drink, Hannah."

It had been nearly a week. Time was ticking by. Tonight, Axel had a list of five demon witches. They were cross-checking to see if they could find out if one of their daughters had been killed the night Hannah had been cursed.

He opened the bottle of water and coaxed Hannah into sipping some.

She looked into his eyes. "Can Darcy make me better now? Please?"

He was asking the impossible of the witch; expecting Darcy to save his sister and his soul for him. Who was really being the coward? Wasn't Hannah worth his soul?

Yes.

He brushed her damp hair back. "She's trying."

"Am I going to die?"

"No. I won't let you." He wouldn't. The problem was that if he went rogue, he'd go for Darcy and kill her. Nothing but his own death would stop him. So he had to time it right. Kill the demon witch and make sure the Wing Slayer Hunters killed him immediately before he went after any more witches.

And Darcy would end up slaughtered anyway. The rogues would find her. He leaned his head back. "Sleep, Hannah."

He was obsessing about the witch. Was it her blood? Her scent? The fact that he wanted her so badly he couldn't sleep?

Or had she done something to him?

Hannah fell into a deep sleep. Axel stood and walked silently into his mom's room. He put Hannah next to Eve. Half asleep, Eve reached out and pulled the covers up over Hannah, then fell back into exhaustion. Silently, he walked out of the room and pulled the door closed.

He stripped off his clothes and got into the shower. Ten minutes later, he got out; he was pulling on a pair of shorts when he heard his BlackBerry beep an alert. He picked it up.

Someone had bypassed the locks and had opened the front door.

12

Wearing just his shorts, Axel walked silently out the door and onto the porch.

Darcy paused at the top of the steps and turned when she heard the door open. The spill of light from the moon touched her skin, changing her witch-shimmer to a sparkling silver. It caught the threads of gold in her hair spilling down her back in thick waves. She wore a green sleep-tank and shorts, leaving her long legs bare.

The sight of her struck him. Drew him. He took a step toward her and stopped himself. "What are you doing out here?" He knew she wasn't trying to escape him in pajamas and bare feet.

"I'm going to try to call my familiar. I need to be in the moonlight." She rubbed her hands over her arms and added, "I can't get anything from the tapestry. Not even a hiss from the cat. I know the spells are in the silver box. I know it!"

Her frustration dimmed her witch-shimmer. He saw goose bumps on her arms. "Hang on." Axel walked back into the house, grabbed the brown-and-tan throw blanket from the back of the couch, and went back outside. "Put this on, you're cold."

She took the blanket and swung it around her shoulders. Then her eyes widened as she looked down his length and back up. "What happened? Your arm is bleeding, your face is bruised, your chest . . ." She went silent as heat colored her face.

He fought a need to grab that blanket wrapped around her shoulders and pull her to him, then strip everything off her so she wore only her witch-shimmer and the faint moonlight. He stepped out, pulled the door closed, and said tightly, "I'm fine. The arm will close back up."

"Here, let me . . ." She stepped toward him, reaching out to touch his arm.

"No." He moved quickly to the edge of the porch by the half wall made of rock. Sitting on it, he sucked in a breath. He'd lose control if she touched him with her powers. He'd been too close to the witch blood tonight, was too on edge. The need to feel her blood was rising. "What do you need to do?"

"Go to the lake's edge." She paused again at the top of the steps. "Did you find out anything tonight?"

Axel watched her. "We have the names of five demon witches. We're trying to determine which one had a daughter killed when Hannah was cursed."

She nodded. "But you'll give me five more days, right? Before you go after her?"

"As long as I can." Was she worried about him losing his soul? Or him killing her if he went rogue?

She turned, made her way down the stairs and walked toward the lake. The blanket draped over her shoulders swung with her body.

He wanted his arms around her, not that damned blanket. If he had so little time left as a man with a soul, why didn't he just take her? Make love to her? For as long as he had his soul, he would sink his knife into his own heart before he cut her.

His gut tightened and his chest felt hollow. He wanted her, needed her, in a way he couldn't grasp. Or maybe he'd just gone too long without feeding the sex part of the curse. He'd been too close to that blood tonight, and the burn still hovered just beneath his skin. Threatening, begging, clawing, promising . . . always promising relief and ecstasy.

It was a lie. A soul-shattering lie.

Keeping Darcy in sight, he watched as she stopped at the edge of the lake. She stood quietly, barely moving. Then she stretched up, allowing the blanket to slide down and pool at her feet on the shore. She tilted her head back to angle her face up to the moon and extended her arms out to the side. Curving her body in a graceful arc, she gave herself to the moon, to the night.

Axel sucked in a breath, her beauty shimmered with heat; her silver necklace reflected the pure white of the moon so that it appeared to be only moonlight weaving a pattern on the skin between her clavicle bones. Her hair flowed in a river of auburn down her back, her breasts rose high and thrust out while the curve of her hips rounded enticingly down to her long bare legs. The moment was so personal he almost felt he was intruding.

He couldn't look away.

She spoke, the pitch of her voice rolling over him like a caress. She arched back even farther, closing her eyes, giving herself over. Then she breathed deeply, and he felt her power surge. Unfurl. Reach out around her, strong enough to send ripples across the dark mirrored surface of the lake.

Axel surged to his feet, unable to stop himself. Not wanting to. Her power, her sexuality, her very center, called to him and demanded that he answer. Now.

The wings on his back fluttered beneath his skin. Animal and hunter instinct took over, and he melted into the night, skimming down the stairs and across the dirt until he stood in front of her. He drew in the scent of her, the full lemony spice now filled with the smell of the moon and sheer joy. And power. He put his hands on her waist.

Her eyes opened slowly, her pupils were enlarged. Her breasts were swollen and her nipples pebbled beneath that little shirt. He could smell the musk of her desire, her need. Her rising power had filled her body, and now it pulsed inside of her. She said, "My fifth chakra opened. I begged the Ancestors to grant me an animal to help me do spell magic and focus my power." Her body shuddered beneath his hands and he felt a wave of energy move through her.

Axel felt it like it were his own. Like he was connecting to her, plugging in, as if unseen parts of their separate beings were fusing. And with it came a sense of hope. Real hope.

Her eyes widened. "Can't control it," she said.

It struck him how he had deprived her of what she had needed, locking her up on the lower floor and away from the elements. She was an earth witch, she needed the earth. Now she was on overload as her power stretched and unfurled and soaked up the earth through her chakras. His own body responded, going hard, tense and reaching with an instinct stronger than any other, stronger than even his bloodlust. A drive to lock up the connection between them. "Don't try," he said. "Let the power have you." He wanted her drenched in the power, swimming in it. Then he wanted to taste that power, feel it, touch it, and finally, sink himself in it while wrapping his arms around her, holding her as she gave herself to the power.

And to him.

"You don't understand." She reached down to pull her shirt from her breasts. Her movements were frantic and unsteady.

Oh, he did. He slipped his hands down her waist and pulled her shirt up and off. "You need to be free. You need to breathe, to feel the moonlight on your skin, and to feel my touch." Her hair slid through the top of the shirt and fell around her.

Dropping the shirt he saw he was right. Her breasts were swollen until her skin was nearly translucent with a silver glow and ethereal blue veins. He cupped their weight in both hands, thumbing her dark and luscious nipples.

She arched, a sound of pleasure slipping from her.

He lowered his mouth to one nipple, dragging his tongue over the hard nub, then drawing it in, suckling. Drawing her into him, feeling their very essence surge and mesh.

Darcy canted her hips, her hands clutching his shoulders, then she shifted to pluck at the fabric of her shorts. "Axel," she breathed his name.

He answered by letting go of her breasts and dropping to his knees. He brushed her fretting hands away and drew down her shorts and panties. Exposing her to the moonlight.

And to him.

Her scent hit him first, spicy and mouthwatering. When he opened his eyes, he saw her dark curls and full thighs. He reached up, gently pressing her legs apart, then separating her curls to see her folds.

The moonlight shimmered on her, showing him the moisture, soaking her and the small bead of flesh stiffened with need. Holding her open with his fingers, he stroked his thumb over that little spot.

She shuddered and made throaty noises that sank into him.

He leaned forward and touched his tongue to her.

Darcy thrust her hips into him. A taste wasn't enough, not nearly enough, and he devoured her. Lapped at her, dipped inside of her, increasing his pace with her movements and cries. Cupping her hips with one hand, he dragged her closer, wanting to be filled with her scent and flesh.

More.

He slid a finger inside of her, feeling the silky hot folds pulse with her witchcraft, then clench and beg. Still suckling her, he added a second finger.

She rode his mouth and fingers, her hands digging into his shoulders until her rich, full orgasm exploded. She cried out, shaking with pleasure and her legs folding beneath her.

Axel caught her in his arms, pulling her to him.

Darcy tasted herself when Axel slammed his mouth onto hers, his tongue probing deep, his arms anchoring her to his body. She could feel his tightly leashed lust pounding at him, his erection thick and hard against her bottom.

Another wave of pure energy undulated from her center outward. Pulsing strong enough to make her shiver. He had licked her into a shattering orgasm, but it wasn't enough. It wouldn't be enough until Axel filled her. She had never before felt these waves of agonizing wanting. Her skin prickled with it, demanded it, it felt like she was splitting apart and needed him to fill her up and seal her soul in her body.

Her cry of frustration broke the kiss.

Axel's green eyes flared. He lifted her from him to lay her on the soft blanket covering the earth. Then he rose, stripping off his shorts.

He was magnificent. His bronzed skin rolled down his stomach then paled at his hips. His hair was inky black and curling around his cock.

Huge.

Like the man himself.

Beautiful in an untamed way. He'd fill her, make her unbearable wanting stop. She looked up to his eyes.

He watched her, his gaze sliding down her body then back to her face. Danger and magic danced in the air between them, drawn to each other like magnets.

Another roll of overfilled power surged through her, forcing her body to arch, her breasts high and her thighs to open. She didn't know what this was . . . but it was sweeping her away, like she was caught in a spell.

She wanted to surrender to its claim, whatever it was. "Please," she commanded, beckoning him to her, to come into her body.

Axel shivered once, dropped to his knees. Settling himself between her legs, he said, "You'll take all of me."

She didn't know what he meant, but then he pressed fingers into her, sliding in slow but deep. And deeper.

"Yes," she agreed. Willing to give him anything. "I'll take it all." She knew the emotional pain would come with his release. It would smother her with the weight of truth about her, but right now, she didn't care. She just wanted him to fill her.

He took his fingers out and circled his cock to guide himself into her.

She spread her legs wider, lifting her hips, accepting him.

"Easy," he growled. His shoulders bunched, his neck corded.

Hot tears of need burned her eyes, thickened her voice. "You said I wouldn't have to hold back with you." She wanted . . . she didn't know, but she had to have it. All of it.

His hard green eyes softened with a flutter of wings that slipped away as soon as she saw them. "Not holding back, sweet witch. You're tight, but Christ, you're opening up for me." He trailed off in a groan as he thrust.

Then thrust again deeper inside of her.

Again. This time so deep her body clenched and a wave of witch energy rippled with the pleasure.

He shuddered, lowered his face to hers and said, "Touch my hawk."

Oh, God, how she wanted to. She slid her hand over his shoulder to the wing tat. The feathers were warm and soft and lifted to her touch.

Axel slammed his mouth to hers, licking her lips, suckling her tongue while pumping his cock into her. Hard. Deep. The sensations pounded her, and she curled her fingers around the feathers, holding on as she soared. Energy snapped, her powers heated and swelled, her soul rose and touched his.

Axel reared up on his hands, his powerful shoulders gleaming with sweat.

She desperately needed him to fill her. She needed to feel the man and the hawk, needed to merge their souls. "Axel," she arched into him.

He stared down at her, his vivid eyes a clear green. Then they filled with the wings of his hawk. "Take what you need, Darcy. Take it all." His words were gentle, but he thrust deep enough to slap his balls against her.

The feel of Axel riding her, totally out of control for her, was too much. She arched, digging her heels into the ground as he drove them both over the edge.

His orgasm burst at the same time.

Darcy wrapped her body around his as the sense of unity and contentment replaced the burning need. The more he released inside of her, the more she calmed. The twitching and pulsing of her powers eased back, settling into a gentle simmer in her chakras. She felt the touch of wings brushing her skin.

Axel's heavy breath stirred her hair and tickled her ear. His chest pounded against her breasts, and his emotions were a steady waterfall of pleasure, triumph, and relief that he hadn't hurt her. That he hadn't lost control and gone after her blood.

Then the waterfall went icy with doubt and distrust. *What had she done to him? He'd gone to her as if she'd pulled the strings that controlled him. A witch. He'd just screwed a witch . . .*

Darcy squeezed her eyes closed, trying to block out the suspicion building in him. The truth of his feelings for her. His distrust. She knew his self-control was how he defined himself, and he'd lost that control with her.

Like she'd been in control?

It hurt to realize she scared Axel. No matter what he claimed, she frightened him. He didn't trust her. Her chakras began to close off, to retreat from her pain.

Then she felt a sensation of wings sweeping around her, comforting her. What was it? Axel's hawk wings? She felt them as real and vividly as she felt Axel's body pressed against her. Was it real or . . .

Axel suddenly pulled out of her and leapt to his feet.

Darcy fought to keep from reacting to his rejection even while it sliced her heart.

He looked down at her and said, "Someone's coming, get dressed." He snatched up his shorts and stepped into them in a blindingly fast movement.

She didn't hear anything, but his urgency washed over her. She grabbed her clothes, dragging her shirt on, sliding on her panties, then standing to step into the shorts. She lost her balance, and started to fall when Axel caught her. "It's Joe."

She could immediately feel his tension ease and his suspicion of her scaled back to an unconscious simmer. There was something odd about how clearly she was feeling Axel. Normally, she just got the fear and distrust; this was more. But right now she had to deal with her cousin. "Joe? Something must be wrong." She shrugged off his arm and pulled up her shorts. Then she lifted her gaze to see Joe striding toward them. It wouldn't be hard to spot them in the moonlight as Joe clearly had. He wore pants and shoes but no shirt. His hair was wild, sticking out at odd angles. The closer he got, the clearer she saw the hunch of irritation in his shoulders.

When Joe reached them, she said, "What's wrong? Is Morgan okay?"

His blue eyes narrowed on her. "It's that damned cat. It started howling about five minutes ago. Woke me up, and I checked in on Morgan, she's awake, too. I went into your room, obviously you weren't there."

"Obviously." She agreed, ignoring whatever he meant as a wave of excitement poured over her. Anticipation. Hope. That cat was the only link she had to her mother and her powers. She took a step. "I'll go—"

Joe caught her arm and pulled her close to him. "Are you all right?"

She lifted her chin and made herself look at him. "I'm fine." She wouldn't explain. Didn't really think she could. She knew it was just sex. Axel had reacted to her simply because of his mega sex drive. But it had meant something to her. He had accepted her, told her not to fight her powers, made her feel safe enough to expose herself physically and emotionally.

Then he'd been suspicious of her. Like she'd somehow tricked him, used him. He was the one who had come to her!

Stupid witch.

It choked her, but she swallowed it down. "Let go, Joe. I want to see the cat." She desperately wanted a connection to who she was, to her mom. Needed it now more than ever.

"If he hurt you or forced you . . ."

She felt Axel's presence loom over both of them with

that weird feather touch when she knew damn well he wasn't touching her at all. But Axel didn't say a word. Keeping Joe's gaze, she said, "He didn't." She had wanted him, craved him, and she wouldn't deny it now. "I'm fine."

Joe nodded and let go.

Darcy rushed into the house. As soon as she opened the access door inside the pantry she heard the cater-wauling noise of a catfight. It raised the hairs on her arms. Quickly, she went down the hallway, turned into her room, and stopped.

Joe and Axel spilled in after her.

The cat stood on the silver box, his hair stiffened along his back, staring at her.

It was cold on the bottom floor, the tile under her feet felt like iced marble. She crossed her arms for warmth and said to the cat, "Tell me what to do."

The cat stared back at her.

Her chakras opened up to the fifth one, but her powers bubbled and popped in agitation, like they couldn't find their mark. Shivering with cold, she considered her options. While she did that, Axel jerked the blanket off the bed and wrapped it around her.

The gesture surprised her, and she looked up into his eyes. "Thank you."

He shrugged.

She turned back to the tapestry. "How do I . . ." She blinked and stopped talking. The threads of the tapestry shimmered brighter than ever. So bright they lost their form, slipping from where they were stitched into the ta-pestry, and moving to the surface of the lake in a swirl of colors. Darcy felt herself tilting clumsily as she tried to make out the threads.

A heavy arm settled around her shoulders and an-chored her. Everything else slid away, the floor, the room, the walls, everything but Axel and the tapestry.

The threads started to take shape on the reflective surface of the lake. Darcy's heart pounded as a woman formed. First the outline, then little by little, she became a solid figure resting on the water.

Recognition sucked the breath out of her. All her life, she'd dreamed about this moment. And now, the woman's auburn hair, brown eyes with the strange cat tilt, the nose, the full mouth . . . "You're my mother." She wasn't sure if she said, or thought, the words.

The image smiled. "Yes. My name is Fallon Lundice. I have only this one time to talk to you before I must go."

"No! Go where? I've only just found you!" Or had she? Was the image real? Was it like Carla projecting herself as the Crone avatar through the Internet? Could it be someone tricking her?

"Darcy," she said softly, the echo of regret, sympathy, love, so many emotions mixed into two little syllables.

She felt herself slip farther, unable to feel the cold tile beneath her feet, or even the blanket around her shoulders. All she could feel was the weight of Axel's arm and a slow tide of grief swamping her. The words scraped her throat as she said, "You're not alive?"

"No. I didn't want to leave you, Darcy. I fought, please believe me, I fought to live. I ran and hid with you, but eventually I had a vision. I knew I wouldn't survive, but you had a chance if I put you with a mortal family; the MacAlisters."

Her chest grew tighter and tighter. It hurt to breathe; it hurt to feel. She looked at the image of her mother; she appeared to be so real and alive, as if Darcy could reach out and touch her. "What are you now?"

"It's magic holding my spirit in the image of the cat in the tapestry. Now I have only this single opportunity to tell you how much I love you, how much I have always loved you, and that I will continue to love you even as I pass over into Summerland."

The loneliness, the wrenching anguish for her mother, took her breath away. Her eyes burned, her throat ached. She was alone. Still alone.

And yet, she felt a set of huge wings fold around her, holding her as they had when she'd been a child and locked in the closet. The comfort of that made her push on. She had only this one chance to talk to her mother. Opening her eyes, she saw that her mother was weeping; the tears rolled down her face and filled the lake.

"You did this for me? Bound yourself to a tapestry for twenty-six years?" She shouldn't cry. She should be damned grateful.

"Time is nothing to me now, and I got to watch you grow up. I thank the Ancestors for that, Darcy. You are all that I could have hoped for and more." The colors of the tapestry darkened. "Had I been able, I would have killed the man acting as your father."

That made her smile. Someone had been there, protecting her as best they could.

Fallon added, "It was an effort to keep from attacking that drunken fool, but I feared it would take too much of the magic left to me."

"You attacked Axel and Joe."

"The witch hunter? I thought he was taking me from you, not bringing me to you. Plus he's a witch hunter. He'd been in your apartment once already. I was terrified he would kill you. I know Joe loves you, but he's a mortal and so I was afraid the witch hunter was controlling him."

That made her smile—no one controlled Joe. But it also made her realize a deep truth. "All those years, you really were with me. I thought I heard a voice singing songs to me. I used to talk to you . . ." She trailed off as she struggled to take it all in. She had a *second* mother who loved her, who'd been there the only way she could.

"I heard you. I wove a few songs into the magic of the tapestry to play for you when you were alone. Something I could give you."

It all made sense now that she knew she was a witch. Now that she knew magic was possible. "And the voices? In my head?"

"Ancestors. They were shocked that you could hear them. Then as you got older, as you struggled to repress your powers in order to survive with that man as your father, their voices receded farther and farther from you. But sometimes you still heard them. You are our hope, Darcy."

"I wasn't crazy."

"Or evil."

She could feel time ticking by, feel the threat of her mom, just now found, slipping away from her forever. "How long do you have? Why did you appear now?"

Fallon rocked gently on the surface of the lake. "I don't know how long, but I have much to tell you. As to why now, you opened your fifth chakra and that is your communication beyond the mortal realm; your powers surged enough to release me."

She nodded, remembering very well just how her powers surged. "I tried to call for a familiar," she said softly.

Her mom's gaze grew wary. "And did your familiar come?"

"No. Not yet. How long does it usually take for one to show up?"

"Before the curse, it could be an hour or a week, it just depended on how far the familiar had to travel to get to you. But now, it's much more complicated. For you to understand just how complicated, and why you are the hope of the witches, you have to know what happened to me."

Darcy's mouth went dry. A fountain of questions gushed in her head. "How did you die?"

"I was murdered."

The white mist closed in on her, trying to draw her into a tunnel and away from the truth. But she stood firm, refusing to let go of this magic that gave her access to her mom. She asked, "Rogues?"

"Yes."

"Oh, God."

"Darcy, I don't remember dying, but I remember fighting to live, to stay in that life to be with you. I would never have left you willingly. But we are witches, we have several lifetimes to live and learn. Our death cycle is really a period of rest until we choose to reincarnate. Or we can choose to stay in Summerland as an Ancestor."

Her heart squeezed at the comfort Fallon was giving her, along with knowledge. It was time for Darcy to listen. She pulled herself together and the mist moved back, allowing her to see Fallon clearly again. "Tell me what happened."

"I thought I knew a way to break this curse, for witches and for witch hunters. I was there when the curse was cast. I was one of the witches who alerted the hunters, through the hawk, their leader. The demon witches were causing chaos and terror in the town of San Francisco. Men killed their wives, mothers killed their children, gossip and lies tore families apart. It took the earth witches awhile to track the spells back to a coven of demon witches. We did this by opening our sixth chakra and using our third eye to see what the demon witches were doing." At Darcy's look of confusion, Fallon added, "Your third-eye chakra is in the center of your forehead. When you open it, your regular sight leaves you, and your third eye opens. Once you learn to control it, you can have 'visions' with that eye. It will show you what you magically summon, or in the time before the curse, we used the third eye to connect with the Ancestors."

"You found the demon witches this way?"

She nodded. "We saw where they were hiding, and called the witch hunters."

"They came?"

"Yes. Three witch hunters were sent, all traveling separately. The demon witches knew they were coming, so they used a glamour to make themselves appear as three young mortal women and approached one of the hunters. The hunter didn't check to see if they were demon and had sex with them, and the demon witches captured him. The other two tried to rescue him, but they were captured as well. The demon witches held them in a deep cave until the full moon that night. Our power is always stronger where two earth forces mesh, for instance: where the ocean touches the shore. Or when the moon faces the earth completely, during a full moon. Those are power points for witches and for demons. Some call them ley lines. For witches, our familiars help us control and focus the power we pull through our chakras from ley lines."

Darcy absorbed this. "The demon witches needed the extra power at a full moon."

"Right. They conjured a magical barrier to the cave to keep us out. To break the shield, we had to open our chakras all the way up to the seventh level—knowledge. Very few witches can do that."

Pride filled her heart. "But you could?"

Her mom smiled. "I could. Together, knowledge and my third eye showed me the demon Asmodeus. He's the demon of lechery, jealousy, anger, and revenge. He appears to have a scrap of human DNA somewhere in his lineage, and that has tied his powers to earth. In the Underworld, that makes Asmodeus vulnerable to other demons who can force him into slavery for them. Asmodeus has to gain as much power as possible to keep that from happening. His powers grow in direct proportion to the misery he causes on earth. The demon witches that had the hunters trapped in the cave were doing Asmodeus's bidding "

"How did you get into the cave?"

"We had to outthink the demon and his witches. That's why we strive so hard to reach our knowledge chakra. Now that I knew the demon, I searched for his weakness. He uses lechery, jealousy, anger, and revenge to create misery, so we set up a circle of love using a ceremony of emotional and physical bonding."

"Sex?" The word tumbled out.

"Sex is a powerful force and is a symbol of love. It can also be a symbol of evil, like rape and domination. Asmodeus thrives on meaningless, degrading, damaging sex. He hates positive, caring sex. We chose a witch and witch hunter who had real love inside of them that the ceremony would bring out. It's a beautiful ceremony; the bodies are symbols, it's the emotion that is real. We pulled that love into our chakras and, with the help of our familiars, funneled it at the dark shield in a steady stream."

"You broke through the barrier to the cave?"

"At moonrise, yes. All the witches and witch hunters poured into the cave and that's when everything went wrong. Too late, I realized Asmodeus had set this whole thing up. He wanted us to get into the cave at exactly the right time—while the demon witches were casting the curse. When we burst in there, the curse ripped out all of our souls and tried to bind them together. We frantically cast a spell to reclaim our souls, but three-headed Asmodeus appeared and, in his fury, sealed the curse with fire. Our souls did our bidding and returned, but they were all damaged. No longer whole."

It was horrible to imagine. She had never realized such evil existed. "You know how to fix this? To break this curse?"

Her mom's brown eyes clouded in grief. "The curse was thrown with these words: 'We bind thee soul to soul; in the blooded power that you crave above all else; in sex to claim your descendants.' We had stopped the demon witches from binding the hunters' souls to themselves, but the wording left the hunters craving witch blood, a craving that drove them to killing madness."

She tried to follow this. "So where did the souls bind?"

Fallon's gaze filled with pride. "My theory was that in that one hideous second when all our souls left our bodies, witch souls bonded with hunter souls. Then the souls halved and went back to our respective bodies. Essentially that made us soul mirrors; two halves of a whole."

"How do we fix this? What part do I play? You said I'm the hope, but I don't see how, I didn't even know I was a witch until a few days ago."

Her mom's eyes grew dark with recollection. "I spent an entire year meditating and thinking about this, and I think there is a loophole in the curse. I believed that if we found our soul mirror and we bonded, our souls would be whole. It was obviously dangerous, since witch hunters were killing witches for the power in their blood. To protect myself, I created a powerful charm to cloak my powers so that a witch hunter wouldn't be able to smell the power in my blood, then be driven to kill me."

"Wait! We can do that? Then we can protect ourselves and—"

Her mom's eyes filled with regret. "It didn't work for

long. I called my soul mirror by the light of the moon just as I would call my familiar. What came was a young man, handsome yet . . ." She shivered. "He had already gone rogue. But he didn't know I was a witch. We had a powerful connection, so powerful that we had sex."

The white fog surrounding Darcy wavered and pulsed with her shock. "But—"

"I know it seems crazy, but once I put things in motion by calling my familiar, I couldn't stop it. Sex was part of it. Before the curse, sex had nothing to do with calling a familiar. But this wasn't a familiar, it was a soul mirror, and sex was part of the curse, remember?"

Darcy nodded. It was all so complex.

"The charm broke as we reached climax. He was furious, leaping up and pulling his knife. But he hesitated."

"Your souls had bonded?"

She shook her head, her hair sliding over the water of the lake. "His soul was gone already, but some part of him recognized me as . . . I don't know . . . part of himself. That hesitation gave me the chance to use a sleep amulet I had made as a precaution. He dropped into a heavy sleep and I ran."

Disappointed, she said, "It didn't work. It changed nothing."

"Except one thing. You were conceived."

The words echoed in her head, *my father is a rogue witch hunter.* Was that the evil her adoptive father had sensed in her?

"From the first moment I realized I was pregnant, I loved you, Darcy. Your father couldn't stay away from me. Something of me got inside him and he tracked me relentlessly. Eventually he learned that I was pregnant. I ran, but he was never far behind. He was furious and believed I had tricked him to get pregnant with you. He was desperate to kill us both. You see, he'd been tricked before."

Her father wanted to kill her. It roiled in her stomach. "Tricked how?"

"By the demon witches. He was the hunter they tricked and captured."

"And he blames all witches." Just as Axel would blame her if he turned out to be her soul mirror. He would believe she'd tricked him. He was already suspicious that she had done something to him. He'd be furious and . . . she didn't know what.

"Yes, and he couldn't stand it. I knew he'd never give up, so when I had the vision I put you with the MacAlisters, then kept running, hoping I could find a way to live and get you back. But he found me."

"He killed you."

She nodded. "My last thought was that you would be safe, at least for a while. I wouldn't tell him where you were, no matter what he did."

"Oh . . . Fallon, Mom . . ." What should she call her? Darcy had loved her adoptive mother very much. But this woman had died for her. Didn't she deserve the title "Mom," too?

Her smiled was luminous. "Thank you for that, Darcy. Hearing you call me Mom . . . thank you." Her voice was thick with years of pent-up emotion.

God. "How can I lose you now when I have only just found you?"

"You never lost me. I've always been with you and I always will be. I am choosing not to reincarnate, but to stay in Summerland as an Ancestor. I'll always hear you, and you will always know I'm there."

"Thank you." She wanted more, she wanted her mother here with her, but Fallon had loved her enough to die to keep her safe.

"I'm leaving you all my spells, all the spells from the

witches in our family. They are my legacy to you, and I hope you can find a way to help that child . . ."

"You know about Hannah?"

She nodded, her long auburn hair floating on the water. "I do." Raising her chin, her dark eyes held a determined light. "How can I help you?"

She had to learn as much as possible to heal Hannah. "Axel says I only have until the waxing gibbous moon to heal her with magic."

"He's correct. The death curse fills the victim with suffocating darkness. Fever, headaches, and nightmares take over. Each day, more and more threads of darkness grow in the victim. The death mark on the forehead darkens to a deeper color as more of these threads form and grow. Before the waxing gibbous, the threads are separate and unorganized. We can draw out these threads with a high-magic spell. Once the phase passes, the threads meld together and form a bond with the demon witch."

The pressure made the swirling fog around her feel like hundreds of pounds of weight were on her. She had to succeed. "What happens if we don't do it by then?"

"Under the full moon, the demon witch will finish the curse and cause the threads to slowly strangle the victim from the inside. Between the waxing gibbous and the full moon, only killing the demon witch will save the death-curse victim."

But if Axel killed the demon witch, he'd lose his soul. She had to figure out how to do this. "What if my familiar doesn't show up? Can I do it without one?"

Fallon said softly, "Maybe your familiar already has. Or it might still show up. You're a witch with a witch-hunter father. You might be the witch who will break the curse and get a familiar. Or you will do it another way. Maybe by a soul mirror."

"You don't know the future?"

"No, but I have faith in you, Darcy." The waters rippled and the image of Fallon began to sink into the pond. "Time is running out. I have to tell you the name of your father."

The white mist pressed in on her again and she began to hear an echo of other voices. The brilliant colors that formed her mom had started to fade. "Who is it?"

"Quinn Young."

13

Axel felt Darcy's magic tumble through him in a continuous stream, vibrating through his intestines.

Then it stopped.

For nearly an hour she had stared at the tapestry. Even stranger, he had heard her talking *inside his head*. He figured out that he was hearing her side of the conversation with her biological mother. That was some weird shit. He could only assume that because he'd touched her blood, and perhaps because they'd had sex tonight, he had been magically pulled into half of the conversation.

Joe moved to stand in front of her. "You were crying. Just staring at the tapestry and crying. You didn't hear me talking to you."

Axel tried to sort out what he'd learned from hearing her side; her mom was dead, murdered. Her mom might have known how to break the curse. Discussion about familiars and Hannah. It fed the dark suspicions rustling in his mind.

Why now? Why could Darcy talk to the tapestry now? Why had he felt her powers vibrating through him?

What had she done to him?

She pulled herself from beneath his arm and moved to

sit on the bed, huddling into the blanket around her shoulders. Lifting her gaze to her cousin, she said, "I saw my biological mother. She's dead, and has been for twenty-six years. She was murdered by my father."

Axel swore his hawk tattoo tried to reach out to her, to ease her grief.

He watched as Joe sank onto the bed next to her. "Ah shit, Darcy."

She smiled wanly at that. "You always know the right thing to say."

He squeezed her in a one-arm hug. "It's my natural charm."

Axel leaned back on the worktable and focused. There was nothing they could do about her parents, or the fact that her mom had been murdered—most likely by a rogue. "Can you access the spells in there now?"

Joe frowned. "Jesus, Locke. She's not a machine."

"It'd be better if I had a familiar." Her face looked troubled as she stared at the tapestry. "Maybe he or she will show up soon."

The familiar comment brought his father's accusations back to him. How had she drawn him into her magic? Her next words snapped him out of his thoughts.

"Who is Quinn Young?"

Axel went stiff and looked at her pale face. "He's the head of the rogues. He's organizing them and determined to wipe out the existence of witches entirely. Why?"

Sharp laughter spilled from her. "Guess that explains why he wants to kill me so badly."

Her eyes were too big in her face, accentuated by dark shadows. "Darcy, what's going on?"

She looked back at the tapestry. "Quinn Young is my father."

"Bloody hell," he muttered. He couldn't help thinking that things were just getting more complicated. Her father was a rogue witch hunter. But maybe that made sense, maybe that formed a bond between them and that was why she was able to draw him into her magic.

Or maybe that gave her an ability to use him to increase her magic. He had to find out more. "Did he know about you?"

"Yes. But my mom put me in a mortal family to hide me. She refused to tell him where I was even when he killed her."

"He wants to kill you. He had you moved up to the top of their witch kill list. But how did he find you?" Things began to fall into place. "Sutton told me you registered to find your birth parents."

"My adoptive mom registered me before she died. You think he found me that way? All she put on the site was my birth date and my picture." She glanced back at the tapestry. "I saw my mother, I look just like her."

Axel worked on the idea. "He could have set something up on the search sites. Probably by your birth date, and when you registered with it, it flagged him."

She shrugged. "He'd recognize me since I resemble my mother."

Axel remembered her telling him that she'd seen his father at the cemetery. "I suspect he sent my father to double-check that you are a witch. That's why he didn't kill you then, he wanted to report back that you're a witch. Far as I know, not many witches are adopted into mortal families. Young would be certain you were his daughter."

She didn't say anything.

He had to know. "Why does he want to kill you this badly?"

She shifted her gaze back to the tapestry. "He believes my mother tricked him. She used a charm to shield her powers and they had sex. The charm failed and she got away. He believes she tricked him like those demon witches did to capture him."

An earth witch that could hide her powers? "The demon witches used a glamour to hide their powers, making themselves appear as young, mortal women," Axel said. "Your mother had that kind of magic?"

"She said it was a charm she made, that she was trying to break the curse. She ended up paying for that with her life."

Had that really been what she'd been doing? Could earth witches even make a charm like that? What had Darcy's mom really been up to? He'd heard Darcy mention familiars. "Was she trying to finish the curse? Bind Young as a familiar? Is that how she thought she'd break the curse?"

Her face went red, her witch-glow darkened to almost black with her rage. "My mother was an earth witch!"

Her fury filled the room with the scent of smoke. Candles on the granite counter began to melt into a waxy mess. Faucets turned on and off. Her outrage rasped against his skin until it felt like the feathers of his hawk were ruffled in sympathetic anger.

"Jesus, Darcy." Joe slid his arm off of her, looking around the room in shock.

Axel drew in a breath and calmed down. "Darcy, you didn't see her in real life, how would you know? She could—"

She jumped up from the bed. "She *died* protecting me. She could have turned to demon magic and saved herself. Then she could have fought back against Quinn Young. But she didn't. So don't you dare suggest anything different!" She stormed into the bathroom. The door slammed, sounding like a gunshot.

"Darcy, I need your help."

Joe's voice sliced through her restless sleep. "What?"

She sat up and shoved her hair out of her face, and tried to blink away the dryness in her eyes.

He loomed a few feet away from her bed, wearing only sweatpants and a deep furrow between his eyes. "It's Morgan. She's locked herself in the bathroom. She's not making sense."

She shoved back the covers and stood. "What do you mean?"

"Just hurry. I'm worried about her." He spun and strode out.

The tile floor was cold, but she ignored it and followed Joe down the hall and into another bedroom. This one had a double bed, a nightstand, and a TV mounted on the wall.

Joe strode up to the closed door that led to the attached bathroom.

"What happened?"

"She had a nightmare and I came in here. I got her to calm down, and she went back to sleep. I must have fallen asleep. When I woke up, I heard her muttering to herself in the bathroom. She wouldn't come out, the door was locked and—" He broke off sharply, and ran his hand through his hair. Then he snapped, "Just open the door! I'm afraid she's going to hurt herself."

"Morgan?" Darcy called out.

"No! I have to protect him, I have to. I, please . . . I can't remember."

Her voice cracked and it broke Darcy's heart. She remembered when Morgan had been an overconfident teenager, so sure she would have a brilliant life in front of her. Darcy had envied that. Envied the way Morgan always knew where she fit. She knew she would be a journalist. She just knew.

In those days, Darcy had sometimes thought about wanting to see Morgan brought down a peg or two.

Right now it made her sad and her stomach pitched in

sympathy. Morgan didn't deserve this. "Morgan, I'm coming in."

"No! I won't let him . . . I won't . . . I had to run, but he'll find me . . . and why can't I remember?"

Joe bounced on his feet. "Move, I'll break down the door!"

Darcy shot Joe a withering look. "Or I could just open it." Putting her hand on the doorknob, she opened her first four chakras with that elevator-drop feeling, focused the power through her fingers, and heard the lock disengage. She turned the knob and pushed the door open.

Morgan stood with her back to the wall between the bathtub and the counter. She had her arms wrapped around herself. An oversize dark blue T-shirt made her look small and lost. "No, don't touch me," she moaned. She slid down the wall, as if standing were just too hard, and curled her arms around her bent legs. "I won't let him . . ." She squeezed her eyes shut, her face contorting with pain. "I won't let . . ." She put her forehead on her knees. "God, I don't know!"

A well of pity filled Darcy. What the hell had broken this woman? She turned toward Joe. He wore a look that bordered between panic and male confusion. He was useless. She walked into the bathroom and knelt down. "Morgan, who are you protecting?"

She looked up, her face bleached of color. "I don't know." Tears sprung up and spilled down her face. Her body shook with emotion.

"Morgan." Darcy reached out and took the woman's hand. Her chakras were open, so she tried to send a calming energy to her.

There was a backwash of emotion and images. *Knives. Screams . . . Oh, God, the screams. Morgan begging him to stop. The pain; razor-like pain slicing through her skin . . . Then Morgan standing in a bath-*

room holding a stick. Her hand shaking, nausea roiling in her stomach, staring at the stick . . .

The realization shocked Darcy out of the connection. She forced herself to breathe through the dizziness and mild nausea. Somehow, she'd pulled in some of Morgan's memories.

And now she knew exactly who she was protecting, even if Morgan didn't know. But, holy crap, the things Morgan had suffered. She shuddered.

"Darcy? What did you do? The fear is better," Morgan said, her voice smoother now.

"It's witchcraft. I sent positive, calming energy to you. Morgan, you need to rest. Drink some tea and see if you can eat." She had to think, figure out what to do. Tell Morgan? Get help? Warn Joe? Joe, who she knew was falling for Morgan. Morgan was making Joe feel alive and giving him a purpose. That was real emotion and connection that was . . .

"I'm broken, Darcy."

Those simple words tore her from her thoughts and filled her throat with sympathy. She had just seen a brief glimpse of what Morgan had endured. She squeezed her hand and told her the truth. "You're not broken, Morgan. You're a fighter." Smiling, she added gently, "Maybe you're a little cracked right now, but not broken. And you're not alone. You have me and Joe. Do you hear me?"

She looked past Darcy to Joe, then back to Darcy. "He's been nice to me."

Darcy snorted. "Nice? You think he feels sorry for you?"

"He was always nice to you, always protected you."

How long had Morgan been alone? Unable to trust her own judgment? "Nice? Hardly. Joe loved me. He still loves me. We're family. He wasn't always nice, Morgan. Sometimes he was downright mean to me. But he loves me and he always stood by me. If he's choosing to help you . . ." She realized that this was true. She knew Joe, knew the man he was, and she was beginning to grasp that what he saw in Morgan wasn't a weak woman needing rescue, but a strong woman struggling to stand against impossible odds. "It's because he cares. Maybe it's as a friend or maybe as something else, but he cares. He's not just being nice. That is something you can count on."

"Thank you."

She nodded, but her mind was whirling with what she had seen. Did she tell Morgan? Tell her now that she'd calmed down? Or wait? She didn't know. What if she was wrong? How did she pull in memories like that? Letting go of Morgan's hand, she stood and said, "I'm going to go talk to Carla. See if she can—"

"Carla? Why her?" Joe reached down to Morgan, took her hands and helped her stand.

Morgan added, "Your friend Carla? The one who helped at your mom's service? She's a hypnotist of some kind. You think that will help me?"

Damn it. She'd been so thrown by what she'd seen and felt, she'd blurted out Carla's name. Her head started to throb. "It's a long story. I'll explain later." She left.

Axel had managed a few hours' sleep and dreamed of making love with Darcy. Of holding her, tasting her, then joining with her and feeling whole.

Then the memory of her hurt expression and furious voice as she'd told him to get out woke him up.

He walked softly down the stairs. She was probably still asleep and he'd leave his iPod on the counter. He had set up an account for her so she could download whatever music she wanted.

Oh, yeah, an iPod would make up for calling her

mom a demon witch. He grimaced, knowing damn well he'd flatten anyone who called his mom something like that.

He paused when Darcy's voice caught his attention.

"I don't understand how it happened. Morgan was terrified, not making sense. I tried to send calming energy to her, but I got a backlash of her memories, her terror and pain from being cut by her husband."

He heard the frustration in her voice. Who was she talking to? Had something happened to Morgan? Axel shielded his presence so she wouldn't see him and walked silently to the doorway of Darcy's room. She sat on her bed with her back against the wall and her auburn hair tumbling down around her. She had the computer on her lap, her long legs stretched out.

He wanted to scoop her up and take her upstairs to his bed. He wanted to slide deeply inside of her and touch all of Darcy, both the woman and the witch.

The digitalized voice of Crone shattered his fantasy as she said, "All witches are sensitive to some degree. All your life, you've felt people's emotions, and if you felt it strongly enough, any of your first four chakras may have opened. Tremendous fear, for instance."

Darcy was watching the computer screen. "Like when the witch hunter attacked me."

"Yes, and you did fear-induced magic and attacked him with his own knife. With me so far?"

Axel kept listening. He wanted to know who Crone was, if she was helping Darcy. Where had she come from and why was she helping Darcy when all the witch loops refused? How could they be sure Crone wasn't a demon witch with some agenda of her own?

"Yeah, I get it. With Morgan, I opened my chakras intentionally to send calming energy to her. But why did I get images back?"

"There's always an exchange. When you send energy

like that, something has to leave to make room. And I suspect you were deeply affected by her misery. You could have been unconsciously looking for answers to help her."

"Was what I saw real? It was awful." Darcy rubbed her forehead as if she could shove back the pictures in her head.

"You saw and felt what Morgan saw or felt."

Darcy dropped her hand to her side. "You work with brain damage, can you help her?"

"I'd have to see her in person. I don't work with this kind of brain damage much anymore, but I'll try. Have Joe bring her to me. Just don't tell the hunters."

"I won't. I haven't told him who you are, or that I know you. I'll figure out a way."

Axel locked his jaw and felt the cool metal of the iPod in his hand. She had lied to him. She knew who Crone was, had known all along.

"How do you know they won't follow Joe?" Crone asked.

He'd had enough. He materialized and walked into the room.

"Axel!" Darcy yelped.

He looked down at her. "Who is the coward hiding behind the avatar, Darcy?"

"You were spying on me!"

"You lied to me. You said you don't know who Crone is."

The avatar shouted, "Leave her alone, hunter. She was protecting me."

He couldn't look away from Darcy. Couldn't stop wanting her. Couldn't stop worrying about her. He'd never felt as connected to another person as he had with Darcy last night. But she was lying to him when his sister's life was on the line. He began to feel like an idiot coming down here with his iPod, trying to give her something that would make her happy. He didn't know what the hell he was doing or why this witch was turning him inside out. He dropped the iPod and the paper with the name and password to download music on the bed, then turned and walked toward the door.

The door slammed. Only his quick reflexes kept the wood from smashing into his face. She'd shut the door before he could leave. He turned and looked at her.

She shoved the computer off her legs, grabbed the iPod, and stood up. "What is this?"

He started to feel even more foolish. He'd ripped her from her life. Yeah, he'd saved her life, but then what? He'd offered her an impossible deal; heal his sister and he'd keep her safe from the rogues for that period of time. And after that? Who would protect Darcy then?

The skin of his tattoo pulled and shifted. What the hell was that about?

He didn't know what to tell her, so he stuck to the obvious. "It's an iPod. I set up an account for you."

She dropped the hand holding the music player as if it were too heavy for her. "Why?"

He felt dumb. Helpless. He looked around the barren room and wondered why the hell he hadn't put in a TV. Or something. Did she have favorite foods she wanted? Drinks? Had he even asked her? "Your cousin said you use an iPod to help with the voices." He shrugged, not knowing what else to say. "If you want anything, I'll get it for you."

"Want?" She lifted her chin, her vibrant brown eyes filling with a raw vulnerability. "What I want is your trust, damn it. Enough trust to do what I need to do to take the death curse off of Hannah." Her voice cracked and she waved her hand, opening the door. "Leave. Go upstairs to the world."

Her pain, her hurt and anger radiated off of her and into him. "Shit, Darcy." He couldn't *not* touch her. Ig-

noring the vibrations of her magic streaming through
him, he reached for her and drew her to him. He
wrapped his arms around her. She clutched the iPod in
her fist against his chest. The skin of his tattoo seemed to
pull and stretch as if the wings wanted to hold her along
with him.

"I can feel your hawk against my skin, as if he was
real, not a tattoo."

He threaded his hand into her tangled hair. "You've
done something to him. Until you, it was just a tattoo.
But now . . ." *What was it?*

She pressed back against his hand and looked up at
him. Strain and worry dimmed her witch-shimmer.
"What do you mean?"

He looked down into her face. "The tattoo was supposed to be a raven. It changed into a hawk. Before the
curse, if the tattoo changed into a hawk, it marked
the hunter as a leader who could communicate with the
Wing Slayer."

Her shimmer brightened with hope, just like her eyes.
"You can do that? Talk to the Wing Slayer?"

He shook his head, feeling the frustration wrap around
his gut. "He hasn't impressed my knife with wings or
given me the thumb ring of immortality."

"Has this happened to any other hunters since the
curse?" She pushed out of his hold and paced to the
granite counter where she set down the iPod, then paced
around the room. "What happened to the hunters after
the curse? I mean I know about going rogue, but what
happened to the actual men?"

He had to focus to listen to her words while staring at
her ass in those little sleep-shorts. He needed to touch
her, to keep touching her, so he caught her arm, sat on
the bed, and pulled her onto his lap. "The tattoos of
wings all faded or disappeared once the souls went back
into their bodies after the curse, and the hunters became

mortal. A lot of them were hundreds of years old, and died within days. The younger ones were saddled with the curse."

She put a hand on his shoulder. "No one talked to the Wing Slayer anymore?"

"The hawks were all older and once their immortality was stripped away, they died. So no. That's why the rogues insist the Wing Slayer is dead."

"Who is the Wing Slayer, Axel?"

He had one arm curled around her waist, the other on her bare thigh. "The Wing Slayer Hunter is half demon and half god. His father was a sentinel god who wanted nothing to do with him. His demon mother raised him in the Underworld, where it soon became apparent that the Wing Slayer had powers of protection and justice that were tied to earth. Basically, the recognition of people on earth—the hunters—brought out his god-powers. But in the Underworld, Wing Slayer's powers were weaker, and he wasn't fitting in. To make matters worse, he grew to look almost exactly like his god-father, who had rejected his demon mother. Eventually, his mother couldn't stand the sight of him and threw him out of the Underworld."

Darcy frowned. "That's terrible. Where did he go?"

"He really had no place to go, so he disguised himself as a human and lived on earth. Then one of the demons found out and exposed Wing Slayer as a half-demon to the witches and they did a banishing spell to force Wing Slayer from earth."

"Which demon?"

That gave Axel pause. "I don't know. I never asked. I just know that he was banished from earth, and the gods were even more annoyed with him. They believed he was meddling where he didn't belong. Wing Slayer wandered for centuries until he stumbled onto Summerland, drawn by the light and beauty. The place was filled with souls."

"Ancestors."

Nodding, he added, "But the souls were sad and troubled. Some of the witches on earth were summoning demons and causing more chaos and destruction."

"And witch karma prevented the earth witches from harming the demon witches."

"Exactly. Wing Slayer had lived on earth and he genuinely cared, and this was his chance to create a real god-position for himself. One that no one could take away from him. So the Wing Slayer made a deal with the souls: He'd create a race of witch hunters for protection and justice to work alongside the earth witches. In return, he wanted to live in Summerland and call it home. They'd all work together for the good of the people of earth. The Wing Slayer called to him the strongest males of earth, branded them on their bodies and knives with his wing mark, and gave them immortality. We became our own race, born of mortal mothers and witch-hunter fathers."

"What happened if a hunter died?"

"As long as he'd been fulfilling his duty, he'd go to Summerland. But if he screwed up, then his soul had nowhere to go—none of the other gods or demons would accept the Wing Slayer's men, and the dead hunter became a shade. All witch hunters knew the score; as long as witch hunters recognized Wing Slayer as their god, his powers were significant. But there was a loophole of sorts and to renounce him could be catastrophic . . . and obviously it was when Quinn Young did it. It broke the communication we had with him, and that's why some believe he's dead."

She looked into his eyes. "He's not dead if he tagged you with the tattoo. He's obviously trying to reach you, you have to figure out what he wants from you."

He couldn't tear his gaze from her. No woman had ever affected him as much as this one. Usually he had sex and moved on, never feeling anything more than passing enjoyment and relief from the curse. But sex with Darcy had turned into a hell of a lot more, a joining that made him feel deeply connected to her. In her brown eyes with the vibrant gold lights, he saw the possibility that the Wing Slayer had seen something worthy in him. His dad's words wormed into his thoughts: *Your little witch is finishing the curse, turning you into her familiar. Then she'll have all the power and you'll be witch-whipped.* Shit, Axel didn't believe that, but what was the deal with Darcy and his hawk tattoo? "If I'm branded by the Wing Slayer, why does the tattoo react to you?"

Her eyes narrowed, her body tensed. "How would I know? I'm just learning to be a witch."

He couldn't let this go. "What exactly is Crone teaching you?"

She slid off his lap, took a few steps, and turned to face him. Her witch-shimmer darkened. "You think I did something to you."

He didn't have an answer. "I don't know."

Darcy turned away from him, staring at the tapestry. "You're just like all the rest. You're afraid of me. Maybe you don't want to be, maybe you're fighting it. But you are. You're like my adoptive father, the men I dated." She stopped talking and wrapped her arms around herself. "I was an idiot to sleep with you, to trust you."

His hawk shuffled and fought to get to her, as if trying to break from his skin. Axel got up and put his hands on Darcy's arms, turning her so he could see her face. What he saw was raw pain. She was tearing him apart. "Trust goes both ways. You're not telling me everything, are you?"

She took a deep breath. "I'm telling you what you need to know. I can't tell you who Crone is; I can't."

He wasn't getting anywhere with her. Thirty years of this fucking curse had created an endless well of mistrust between the witches and witch hunters. "So we don't trust each other." He scraped his hands up her bare arms and cradled her face, unable to stop touching her. "But one thing I'm damned sure of, I'm not sorry about making love to you."

14

"What's up?" Key asked as he strode by Axel, wearing a pair of jeans, work boots, and a layer of sweat. His booted steps rang out on the cement floor of the warehouse next to the club.

Axel held up his bottle of beer. "Calling it a day." They'd all been working on repairing the club along with a group of non-rogue hunters that had been seeking them out in the last week. Suddenly word was getting around about the Wing Slayer Hunters and Axel's hawk tat. The men were asking them if the Wing Slayer was really alive. Asking if they could join them to stand against the rogues.

Asking if they knew how to keep their souls.

Thing was, they'd started off as a group of five men who'd made a pact to refuse to kill witches to keep their souls, and if one of them went rogue, the others swore to kill him. Axel had opened the club as a place to get sex from willing women, and kick back. He'd allowed rogues into the club as long as they didn't cause trouble. It was a good way to keep tabs on them, and hear about what they were up to.

He hadn't counted on the Wing Slayer tagging him with the hawk tattoo. And it hadn't crossed his mind that others would seek them out.

But it wasn't just about their souls anymore. Axel couldn't ignore the damage the rogues were doing to mortals like Morgan. If he continued to do nothing, that would make him just as guilty.

"I sent the men home." Key opened his beer and sat down on the burgundy leather couch across from the chair Axel was in. "Couple more days to finish."

"And?" Axel, Key, and Ram had worked with the men for hours. Hard, thankless work was an excellent way to judge character.

Key drank down half the draft and said, "These half dozen impressed me."

He nodded in agreement then turned to look at Ram, who was methodically cleaning their supply of guns.

Ram looked up with his laser-sharp gaze. "I can start training with them. Give it a little time to see how they shake out."

Phoenix lifted his water bottle. "I'd take some of that action. Don't get enough sparring."

Axel wasn't going to turn away witch hunters looking for a way to stand against the curse. "Set it up. Get a feel for the men." He drank another swig of the beer, and said, "Sutton, what'd you get off Joe's GPS?" He glanced toward the bank of monitors. He had a security detail on the house—hard-ass mortals—along with all his alarms and cameras. The monitors showed all the angles outside the safe house.

"They're secure," Sutton assured him, then added, "Joe and Morgan are at an address that is being rented by a Dr. Carla Fisk. Here's her driver's license photo." He flashed the picture up on one of the screens.

Axel noted the long, silver blond hair, tilted hazel eyes, and, most important, the silver necklace at her throat. "She's not a demon witch, then." Demon witches stayed away from silver. Even silver-plated stuff burned their skin.

Sutton added, "She has a PhD in psychology and has

a small practice specializing in hypnosis in Glassbreakers."

So that was Darcy's friend, Axel thought. Darcy clearly trusted her. But it bugged Axel that Carla hadn't ever said to Darcy, *Hey I'm a witch and so are you.* But then, maybe she figured Darcy was safer living in the mortal world.

Phoenix said, "I hope the witch can help blondie."

Axel shifted from the monitors to Phoenix. "What did you learn while tracking Morgan's husband?"

Phoenix set his water down on the floor by his leather chair. "Eric Reed lived with Morgan in San Diego for two years. Not reporting regular income on his social security number, from all evidence they were living off Morgan's income. But people I talked to all thought he was some sort of computer software consultant. He has bank accounts separate from Morgan and guess where that money comes from?"

Axel knew the answer. "Same place as my dad's."

"Yep, he's on Quinn Young's payroll. I believe he was running a small pack of rogues in San Diego. Morgan was doing a story on a possible serial killer when she be came ill. I talked to her boss at the TV station. I told him Morgan Reed was missing and I'd been hired to find her. He bought it and said that Morgan had been one of his sharpest on-air reporters and then she started losing it. He told me about the cuts on her stomach and that her husband was going to put her in a treatment facility."

Axel thought of the broken, but still fighting, woman he'd met. Eric Reed had underestimated his wife. The prick hadn't destroyed her as much as he'd believed. "Where's the bastard now?"

"No one has seen him in a couple weeks."

Damn it, Axel knew it wouldn't be that easy. "His accounts?"

"Nothing."

Ram said, "Could be that Reed was one of the rogues we've killed, or he might have gone after a demon witch and she killed him."

Phoenix shook his head. "I don't think so. In the last couple weeks, San Diego has had a few gruesome murders. Three different women found cut beyond recognition and their bodies left on the streets."

Axel felt the inked feathers of his hawk stiffen. "Quinn Young runs a tight ship—no bodies left behind."

"Right. So I sniffed out a couple rogues; and damn, if they want to go stealth, they need to do something about that copper stink. Anyway, I prowled the bars until I found two of them and got them alone. Man, those fuckers cried about going shade." He drained his bottle of water.

Axel waited while Phoenix washed down his disgust.

"They spilled that Reed was their rogue leader in the area, and he coordinated the witch kills and cleanup. When someone stumbled onto a witch and killed her, that was fine as long as they called for a cleanup. Reed, they said, was a cold, ruthless, efficient son of a bitch. But he'd disappeared in the last couple weeks and some rogues were getting sloppy and out of control."

Recognition raced through him. "At Darcy's apartment, those two rogues that attacked us were much more skilled than the flunkies my dad sends out. They nearly got the drop on me."

Phoenix nodded. "I don't think Reed's dead. I think he's here in town and looking to prove himself to Young by killing Darcy. Two words: 'Turf war.' "

"Holy fucking shit," Axel snarled, slamming his beer down and standing up to pace off the fury boiling inside him. He stalked alongside the pool table in the center of the warehouse, his footsteps echoing his rage on the cement. His dad was the rogue leader in Glassbreakers. "Young set my dad and Reed against each other."

Ram said, "You and Darcy, you're the goal. The stakes just went up for both Myles Locke and Eric Reed, making things a hell of a lot more dangerous."

Axel nodded and added, "My dad, the moron, thinks if he turns me, he'll have more cachet with Young. Especially if he turns me rogue and I kill Darcy. Stunts like cutting up those witches, stuffing them into a Hummer, then crashing it into my club . . ." He was so furious, it rode over any witch bloodlust he normally felt when his emotions got out of control. He thought of Darcy in the moonlight, her power surging and pulsing until she'd been the most beautiful thing he'd ever seen—until he'd seen her lying naked beneath him.

He would not kill her.

He would protect her.

The need to see her safe was a living, breathing desire inside of him.

Key said mildly, "Your dad probably blows at chess. His strategies are too convoluted, and dependent on too many factors. Instead of just finding a way to kill you, he concocts a comic-book plot of turning you to the dark side so you can rule with him for all of eternity."

Axel let it all race through him. "Rule what? What exactly does my dad have set up there at that house?" Turning, he said, "Sutton, see if you can find the blueprints on the remodel my dad did on his house. Find out what he has set up at that house that drew Eric Reed from San Diego."

"Reed might know that Morgan is here in town," Phoenix pointed out.

"Shit." He couldn't let Morgan get taken by that monster. "I'll call Joe, have him bring Morgan back to the house."

Phoenix leaned back, stretching out his legs. "How's Darcy doing with the spell to heal Hannah?"

"She's trying to get the spells out of the tapestry. Without a familiar, it's a struggle."

Mildly, Phoenix answered, "The rogues believe the witches, the earth witches included, are so desperate to get their power back that they will do whatever it takes. Like complete the curse, bind witch hunters to them, and use them like familiars."

Axel turned, leaning back on the pool table. His hawk tattoo grew tight. "Got a point?"

"There's no witch magic in his tat," Key interjected. "We'd feel it."

Phoenix shrugged. "How do you know a witch can't hide her power?"

Shit, Axel thought. "Darcy said her mother used a charm like that."

"And got knocked up by Quinn Young," Phoenix said, his gaze heavy on Axel. "Quinn Young wants her dead. What does he know about his own daughter?"

"That she's a witch," Key said. "He hates all witches. Blames them for the demon witches tricking him, when the real blame lies with him. He should have checked with his silver knife to make sure those three mortal women weren't actually demon witches."

Phoenix said, "Darcy's mother tricked Young, too, from what Axel told us." He turned to Axel. "I can smell the witch on you. You had sex with her. Did you even feel the bloodlust?"

"Hell yes." Or he had felt it until that moment on the porch when her powers had unfurled in the moonlight and touched him.

"So you had sex with her to control the bloodlust?" Phoenix pushed.

Axel glared at him.

Phoenix shrugged, "It's what we do. Have sex to control the bloodlust."

He hadn't used Darcy like that. And it had been more than sex, full of power, magic, connecting, and filling something inside of them they both needed. They didn't need to know that her power was living and pulsing inside of her, and that he'd touched it, tasted it, and felt it sear his soul.

Or that it had taken every ounce of his will to walk away from her this morning, instead of staying and claiming her the way he felt compelled to do.

Sutton spun around on his chair, breaking the building silence. "Since Darcy's father is a witch hunter, that might be the reason why you can control your bloodlust around her."

Axel had thought of that himself. Could that also be why they had a connection? Why she'd drawn him into her magic so that he could hear her side of the conversation with her mother? Even though she hadn't spoken physically, only magically? He didn't know, but he was left feeling uneasy and suspicious. And other times, usually when he was touching Darcy, he felt . . . whole.

Ram said in his measured voice, "I have one question, and don't turn your laser glare on me. It's a fair question given that we know Darcy's mom used a charm to cloak her powers. Do you think it's possible she cloaked her powers to seduce you?"

"No." He'd felt her power. Plus, he knew how vulnerable she was when it came to sex, and he'd seen her pain this morning when she thought he was afraid of her. "I won't be drawn into the rogue bullshit of blaming all the witches, or believing that killing them will break the curse. We were born to protect earth witches, not slaughter them."

*   *   *

Darcy stared at the box full of sand and wanted to cry. The cat was gone now, leaving the silver box sitting on the hill overlooking the lake.

Using low magic, she'd opened the box on the first try. As the lid began to lift, a real sense of accomplishment had soared through her. She was strong, powerful. She could do this!

The lid raised completely and revealed its contents.

Sand. It was filled with sand.

Disappointment and frustration drowned out her earlier triumph. She'd opened a box of sand. Damn it, the spells had to be in there. Her mom had said so.

How was she supposed to do this? How did she translate those grains of sand into the spells she needed?

She needed a familiar to control her power. Every time she opened her fifth chakra, she lost control.

Since the scene with Axel this morning, she'd trekked up the stairs repeatedly and gazed out the front window, hoping that the familiar she'd begged the Ancestors for would show up.

But she knew deep in her gut that none would.

She was terrified that she knew why: her mom's theory that the witch and witch hunters' souls had merged and split—leaving them with only half a soul. Darcy feared that when she had tried to call her familiar in the moonlight, Axel's hunter soul had responded. But she hadn't sealed the bond by magically impressing his image on something silver like Carla had told her witches were supposed to. Had sex sealed a connection between them?

Her magic had crested when Axel made love to her.

And then the cat in the tapestry had gone wild at that moment, getting Joe's attention so that he went and found Darcy. Once Darcy got inside, she hadn't connected with her mom until Axel had put that blanket around her. Basically, he'd touched her and then she was able to magically connect with her mom.

What if she had accidentally made Axel her familiar?

Nausea swirled in her stomach. She rubbed her forehead and headed upstairs to once more check and see if her familiar happened to be sleeping on the front porch. She clung to a desperate hope that her real familiar would show up and prove she hadn't done the unthinkable to Axel.

How was she going to face him? If she told him what she suspected, he'd either kill her on the spot or he'd throw her out. Then she wouldn't be able to help Hannah. She would have failed. And she was scared, she had no place to go.

She went up the stairs, through the pantry, and into the kitchen. Joe and Morgan had left awhile ago to see Carla. There was only Eve and Hannah in the house. As she started to pass the hallway to head to the living room, she heard Hannah's soft crying.

What now? That poor child was more and more miserable each day. Darcy turned down the hall, following the sounds until she found Hannah's room. The little girl was tangled in her sheets and nightgown, her hair plastered to her sweaty face.

Eve rushed up next to her. "I just ran to the bathroom. I gave her some medicine for the fever, but it's not working."

Darcy could feel Eve's desperation, love, frustration, and rage. It mixed and stewed into something that felt like choking panic. It wound inside of Darcy. Gently, she put her hand on Eve's arm. "Let me try? I might be able to make her more comfortable."

Eve nodded.

Darcy walked to the bed, leaving Eve to watch from the doorway. "Hannah?" She sat on the edge of the bed, put her hand on the child's hot little forehead, opened her first four chakras, and summoned the energy through them.

Hannah moaned and shifted on the bed, scissoring her legs beneath the sheets like she was trying to run.

Darcy sensed a distinct inky gloom coating the child. She couldn't see it, but it felt like the heavy darkness of a small closet, like all that dark energy was rushing and seeking, trying to meld together into some formless entity. Keeping her hand on Hannah, she focused on channeling comfort down her arm and through her hand.

Hannah tossed and muttered. Then suddenly, she grabbed on to Darcy's arm with both hands, as if trying to keep Darcy's hand on her forehead. Her energy rushed toward the sick little girl, much like water from a hose.

Immediately, Darcy felt the *exchange;* dark, thick gloom that felt like it was slithering up her arm. As if a bucket of worms were scuttling over her skin, looking for a place to burrow. She had to set her teeth together and force herself not to fight it. It was just the exchange Carla had told her about. She hadn't even had to search for the dark threads. Forcing in positive, healing energy forced out some of the dark sickness from the curse. She couldn't repress a shiver, but kept her hand on Hannah's warm forehead. Finally the dark worm feeling disintegrated and fell away.

She was left with a throbbing headache and slight queasiness. It was an effort just to stay sitting upright and not slide off the bed into a puddle on the floor.

"You made them leave."

Darcy tried to ignore the lethargy and shifted her gaze to Hannah's face. She took her hands from Darcy's wrist and picked up her Minnie doll, hugging it to her chest. Her eyes were huge in her pale face. "Feel better?"

"Little bit. Tired. Thirsty."

Darcy turned to the nightstand and picked up a bottle

of water. "Have some of this." She got an arm under Hannah to help her sit up. Hannah let Darcy hold the bottle while she drank.

"Done?"

She nodded. "Can I sleep with you? The shadows are afraid of you."

Her throat suddenly ached. "Oh, honey, it's too cold downstairs for you." And Axel would never allow it. He didn't quite trust her. The divide between witches and hunters was deep and steeped in suspicion.

And maybe he was right to be suspicious.

"Can you stay here?" Tears welled up in her eyes. "Please?"

"Until Axel gets home, okay? Then I have to go downstairs." She wasn't going to lie to Hannah then have her wake up and find Darcy gone.

" 'Kay." She closed her eyes and snuggled down in the bed with her doll.

Darcy pulled the covers up over her and said, "Night Hannah."

"Hmm."

"Thank you," Eve said softly from the doorway.

She looked at Eve standing in the light from the hall. "Hopefully she can sleep for a while now."

Eve's face had aged ten years. She looked at her daughter. "We're running out of time."

Darcy took a deep breath, fighting a flu-like feeling of fatigue and general ickiness from touching Hannah's curse. "I can do it, Eve. I will do it. I'll sleep on the floor in here for a couple hours, then once Axel's home, I'll go back downstairs and work on the spells in the box. I'll figure out how to get the curse off of Hannah."

Eve walked to the rocking chair in the corner and scooped up the thick quilt and pillow she had stacked there. She brought them back and spread them out on the floor by Hannah's bed. "I'll wake you when Axel gets home."

Darcy settled onto half the quilt spread out for padding. "Thanks." The thick, pulsing pain in her head was nearly unbearable. Her hand trembled as she reached to pull the second half of the quilt over her.

She had to be strong enough to do this. Whatever happened, Darcy knew one thing: Her mom had fought to her very last breath to let Darcy live. Even when her monster of a father had found Fallon, no matter what he'd done to her, Fallon hadn't told him where Darcy was. She had to be that strong. She had to make her life count. She had to save Hannah, and maybe, somehow, she could live on and continue her mom's work undoing this curse that was destroying both the hunters and the witches.

And harming mortals like Morgan. She drifted off, thinking about Carla, and hoping that her session with Morgan went well.

Darcy woke up when an arm hit her face. Hannah had climbed off the bed and snuggled next to her on the floor. She must have been scared, but she was sound asleep now. Carefully, she moved the arm off her face then climbed to her knees.

God she was tired.

She leaned down to pick Hannah up and put her back in bed.

"I'll do it."

She jerked back, her heart stopping for a second as the voice registered. She looked up.

Axel.

He had walked into the room as silently as a ghost. Her heart pounded with an adrenaline surge. At least it brought her fully awake. He smelled like he'd just gotten out of the shower, and his dark hair was wet and combed back from his hard face.

Getting to her feet, she said, "Hannah wasn't feeling well so I—"

"Mom told me." He hunkered down, scooped up Hannah, and settled her on the bed. He carefully tucked her Minnie doll in her arms then pulled the covers up.

Darcy stood there watching him, watching the play of powerful muscles beneath his T-shirt gentled by his love for his little sister. A lump formed in her throat. She didn't know why. She was ridiculously emotional right now.

Axel turned to look at her. His green gaze seemed to penetrate right to her core.

Time to run. Axel had touched more than her body during sex, and now she felt too vulnerable, too exposed. Her body reacted to his simple look, her nipples ached, her skin grew sensitive, and her muscles softened. It was as if she craved his touch. Needed his touch. She hated that, hated needing something from someone else. Firming up her muscles, she said, "I'll go downstairs."

She turned and walked right into Axel.

"Don't do that!" She hissed in a whisper so she wouldn't wake Hannah. The way he moved with inhuman speed and silence unnerved her. Could he see the truth inside of her? See that she was hiding something from him? He'd suspected something this morning.

He said, "We need to talk."

Oh, God. "I need to work. I've gotten the box of spells open, I just need to figure out how to read them or make them . . ."

Axel reached out and pulled her closer to him. "We'll go outside. That might help you with the spells. It'll make you feel better if nothing else."

He knew that about her. It struck her deeply. Her adoptive dad had known that about her and had used it against her. She inhaled to find her center, but it was Axel's scent that filled her. A cedar aroma and the soap from his shower, mixed with a wild tang that made her want to rip off all of their clothes and feel only the light of the moon and each other's touch. She desperately wanted to go outside. "All right. You can let go of my arm."

Axel released her, turned, and walked into the kitchen.

Darcy followed, pulling herself together.

Eve sat at the kitchen table with a glass of wine and her laptop.

"We're going outside," Axel said.

Eve looked up. "Darcy, are you all right? What you did tonight, it had to have some affect on you."

She shrugged, feeling Axel's gaze turn toward her.

"What did you do?"

Eve answered, "Hannah said she made the shadows go away. I thought I could see something dark moving from Hannah to Darcy. And Darcy got paler and paler."

She didn't want to think about it. "I'm fine."

"Then the moonlight will do her good." He went to the cupboard and got out a couple of wineglasses. He filled them with dark red wine and handed one to Darcy.

She took the glass and followed Axel outside. Her jeans and copper-colored peasant blouse had to be wrinkled. Her hair was a sleep-rumpled mess, her eyes were swollen and most likely smeared with mascara. Her stomach was tight to complement her thick and achy head. She felt like a mess, but once she stepped outside, it all slid away.

The night air was scented with the sea and damp earth, making it rich and sultry. The moon flirted with the cloud cover, brushing her skin with its silver glow, then disappearing. Her blood pulsed stronger and her chest grew warm with the heat of her witch energy. She felt stronger, more alive. More powerful. Without any discussion they headed toward the lake.

"Over there is a hidden garage." Axel pointed to the far side of the house.

"It looks like part of the house."

He nodded. "The hallway downstairs? At the end on the right wall is a mirror. It's actually a hand scanner. I've inputted your palm into the database so you can activate the door to the garage. I have vehicles in there, always ready to go. If I'm not here and the house is attacked, and if my mom isn't here for some reason, I want you to get Hannah and get out."

Surprised, she sipped her wine and mulled that over. The sound of the water gently lapping at the shore drew her. She remembered what Fallon had said about places where the elements mesh, like water meeting land. They were ley lines, a power source for witches. She could feel herself reviving, feel her chakras opening wide, stirring and stretching to reach out into the elements to feed. Filling her. Her skin became more sensitive and her awareness sharpened, making her feel more connected to the world around her.

They stopped at the shore, at the place they'd made love. Turning to Axel, she said, "You're not afraid I'll run away anymore."

"No." He settled his gaze on her, his mouth moving into a confident smile. "You're not stupid or foolish. You know I can protect you better than you can protect yourself."

True.

The smile vanished. "I didn't know you were claustrophobic that first night. I felt your fear, but I wasn't sure you weren't playing me."

She moved a few feet away to a rock and sat down. The sounds of the night were soothing, the water lapping, crickets chirping, trees in the distance swaying in the soft breeze. "You're not very trusting of witches." Idiot. Why had she brought up the trust issue?

"They aren't any more trusting of us." He sat next to her, so close their thighs touched. "That first night, if you hadn't been under attack, I would have tried to ask you first. I had planned to offer you a deal."

He was full of surprises tonight. "And if I'd said no?"

"Then I would have taken you. I knew the rogues were coming after you. I wouldn't have left you there to be slaughtered."

She turned to look at him. He was so close, she could see the faint lines bracketing his eyes, feel his breath stir her hair. His scent, though, the smell of Axel, was what made her want to lean into him and inhale. She craved him inside of her. "Why are you telling me this?" Something was changing in him, as if he was making a decision.

He met her gaze. "You trusted me last night, trusted me with not just your body, but your life. You believed I wouldn't lose control of the bloodlust and kill you." He reached out and touched her face. "You believed in me when you had no reason to. I want you to know I'm never cruel without a reason."

Her heart squeezed. She didn't want to lie to him, to hide her fears from him. But if she told him, he'd throw her out and go after the demon witch. Axel, this Axel she knew, would be gone once he killed the demon witch and went rogue. She couldn't let that happen, not if she had the power to stop it. She would heal Hannah first, and then she'd tell him what she feared she had done to him. "Okay. Is that what you wanted to talk about?" She looked around with the desperate hope that a dog, cat, or whatever form a familiar might take would come running. Nothing appeared.

Axel said, "No, I wanted you to hear it from me—we know that Crone is Carla Fisk."

Her stomach clenched and the wineglass slid from her hand.

Axel shot out his hand and caught the glass before it hit the ground. He handed it back to her.

She stared at the glass in his hand. Carla had risked so much to help her. Clumsily, she surged to her feet. "I have to tell her!"

Axel set her glass down and took her hand. "We're not going to hurt her. I swear it, Darcy. We're committed to not giving into this curse by hurting earth witches. We just wanted to make sure she wasn't a demon witch."

This again! "She's not. I told you she's not. She's my friend!"

"I know," he said gently.

She tried to add it all up. "Did you see her? Scare her? Hurt her?"

"No. Sutton hacked into Joe's GPS system in his truck, got the address where he stopped, and found out Carla rented the house. Then he pulled up her DMV file. We saw the silver necklace she wore—demon witches don't wear silver. Ever."

"She always wears silver. She has a silver armband around her bicep that she's never without." Why the hell was she telling him this? He'd betrayed her. Why didn't she jerk her fingers from his warm, oversize hand? "She'll have to leave. Find a safe place." Carla won't contact her anymore. She'll be alone.

He squeezed her hand softly. "Darcy, I won't let anyone hurt her. The only ones who know are Sutton, Phoenix, Ram, Key, and myself. I didn't have to tell you, but I chose to tell you. Just like I didn't have to let Joe and Morgan come to the house yesterday, then leave today, knowing the location of the house."

"Joe wouldn't tell! He wouldn't risk my life!"

"I'm trusting in that, I'm trusting my mom and sister's life in that. Just like you're trusting that we won't hurt Carla." He tugged on her hand. "Sit down; talk to me."

She could walk away, insist on contacting Carla right

now. Hell, she had enough magic now to lock Axel out of his own house, at least for a while. But he had told her. He had his reasons for finding out who Carla was. Just as she'd had her reasons for keeping Carla's identity secret. Finally, she sank down next to him and said, "I still have to tell her. She helped me when no other witch would."

He handed her the glass of wine. "Your decision."

Not sure what to do now, she took a sip of the wine. As she calmed down, she remembered another secret she was keeping from Axel. Afraid of what he might feel from her, she took her hand from his and scooted a little to put an inch of space between them. "Carla's not going to help me anymore. Not after this."

He turned and looked at her. "I hope to hell that's not true. If it is, she's not a friend."

She stared at the lake. "Carla and I became friends so fast. I met her when a young woman committed suicide after her induction into a cult. Carla had been trying to help the girl and had come to her funeral. She was so sincere in her grief and anger, and so caring toward the family."

"She's a psychologist? Sutton said she has a PhD."

Darcy nodded and watched the play of the moonlight on the surface of the lake. "She works with brainwashing victims through a form of hypnosis. She also helps trauma victims." Darcy lifted her head and turned to look at Axel. "She'll help Morgan. She'll know how to tell her . . ." She trailed off. She hadn't told anyone except Carla.

"Tell her what? What happened this morning?"

She didn't want to feel those flashes of memories again. "Morgan is pregnant. She doesn't know it. Well, Carla says some part of her brain knows it, and she's protecting the child."

Axel's voice roughened. "It's her husband's kid? The rogue?"

"Yes, it's why she ran. I saw her standing in a bathroom, sick and terrified, and looking at the stick that confirmed her pregnancy. This morning, she'd locked herself in the bathroom, rambling about having to protect someone but she couldn't remember who. I went in there and tried to help calm her. But I got a mix of her memories." She closed her eyes, but that was worse, she could see that knife, feel the pain.

"Darcy." Axel took hold of her free hand. "You saw him cut her?"

She nodded, tears prickling her eyes behind her closed lids. She refused to cry. Opening her eyes, she said, "I didn't know what to do, how to help her. I was afraid telling her she was pregnant and that's who she was protecting would be too much for her."

"And that's why you were plotting behind my back to send Joe and Morgan to Carla." He nodded to himself then added, "I'm glad you told me. This complicates things for Morgan, puts her in even more danger. First, it explains why Eric Reed didn't just kill her. He wants that kid if it's a boy. And he's not going to stop until he gets Morgan back—at least long enough to have the kid."

She took her hand from his hold. "Oh, I'll—"

"I've already talked to Joe. They are coming back here later tonight. I told him to be on alert because Phoenix got some information that makes us think Eric Reed is in this area. They are safer here at the house. I don't want them staying at Morgan's or Joe's house. And I don't want you worrying about them."

Did he actually care? Or was it that he just didn't want her distracted from working on spelling the curse off Hannah? She lifted the glass to her mouth, taking a long swallow of wine.

"Do you still regret making love with me?"

Startled, she lifted her gaze to take in his green eyes. She didn't regret it. But she regretted with each cell in her body what she might have done to him. He would hate her. She didn't want to answer him, yet the word slid out of her. "No."

He took her wineglass and set it down. Then he turned back and touched her face. "You said this morning that I'm just like your father. What did he do to you, Darcy?"

His fingers were gentle, but his voice was rough. What did it matter if he knew? She told him. "He was afraid of me and didn't want me to touch him." What little girl didn't want to be held and cuddled by her dad? She'd see TV shows where the dad held the little girl and read a book to her. Darcy would run into her room, get a book, and ask her dad to read it to her. After a few harsh rejections, she stopped asking. But she'd never stopped wanting to be held and to feel safe. It made her mad at herself. She was a woman now, not a child. Time to grow up and stand on her own.

Axel's voice broke into her memories. "Give me an example."

She searched for something a little less pathetic. "If he caught me doing anything he thought was evil, like sneaking out into the moonlight, talking with the voices in my head, or moving my dolls without touching them, he'd lock me in the hall closet." Keeping her gaze fixed on the smooth surface of the lake while squeezing her hands together in her lap, she added, "Or when I was six, and Joe and I snuck into a viewing to see the body of a young man. He had the death mark on the center of his forehead. I guess the mark was covered by makeup but I could see it. The voices in my head told me it was a death mark and to get away." She now realized that it had been the Ancestors warning her. "My dad came in then and I was so scared that I blurted out in front of everyone, including the poor man's family, that the dead man had the death mark on his head. My dad was embarrassed and furious. Later that night he went to a bar, got drunk, came home, and dragged me out of bed. He was yelling that he wouldn't raise a heathen devil-spawn, that my biological mom hadn't wanted me and he didn't want me either. My mom was crying that I was just a little girl." She hadn't meant to tell him that much. It just started tumbling out.

Axel reached into her lap and took her hand. "What happened?"

The feel of his hand, his support, made her want to tell him. "My mom made him leave me alone. Then she put me back in bed and told me that she loved me just the way I was. But I knew something was wrong with me. So I tried to be normal. I didn't want him to send me away." She shut up before she told him how scared she had been, and how hard she'd tried to fit in. To belong.

"He scared you into repressing your powers."

"Evidently," she agreed.

"And your mom let him."

She wouldn't accept that. "No, when she knew about it, she never let him. But she was sick, Axel. A lot of days were a struggle for her. She needed my dad. As much as my dad hated me, he loved my mom more. He'd do almost anything for her, and he took care of her on her bad days when she couldn't get out bed. But my mom loved me and she protected me the best she could." What would Eileen have thought if she'd lived long enough to find out that Darcy was a witch? Closing her eyes, she tilted her head back, letting the moonlight caress her face. She was a witch. Had always been a witch. She let the feel of the earth, the water, the moon soak into her skin and deeper into her very essence.

"You're beautiful when you do that."

The deep tenor of his voice mixed with the other elements and stirred her blood into a longing for him. What? Why did he feel so vital to her? She lifted her head and opened her eyes. He appeared comfortable out here, wearing a black T-shirt stretched across his muscles, his face like carved stone, fierce and yet protective. "Shouldn't you be feeling bloodlust?"

He sank his hand in her hair, tilting her head back. His eyes gleamed in the soft moonlight. "I don't feel bloodlust, little witch."

"No?" Warm sparks lit her veins and heated her stomach, her thighs, and the core in between.

"No." He brushed his mouth over hers with excruciating patience. "I don't know what it is between us, but I want it. And you want it."

Her body melted toward him. "I do?"

"Damn right," he said, his lips, breath, and tongue teasing. "I can smell your desire."

She slid her tongue into his mouth. Tasted him, the rich fullness of the wine and the pure elixir of the man. It shuddered through her. She wanted more.

Axel pulled his head back, then shifted to lift her in his arms and settle her on his lap. He put his arms around her and invaded her mouth, taking absolute control of the kiss.

She had never felt like this, held and kissed in a way that made her feel important. As if for this very second, she was the center of his world and he couldn't get enough of her. His tongue demanded she give back and she did. His arms held her safe so she let him stay in control while her power bloomed hot and wild, making her want to get closer, needing him closer . . .

Axel stopped, lifting his head and staring into her eyes as he struggled to control his breathing. His entire body shuddered. In a thick voice, he said, "Your powers are rushing through me. Sinking into me."

She felt the current of it, the way the hot bloom from her opened chakras had focused. Warm and sensual, it flowed from her to him, then came back in the form of feathers across her skin. It fed every need in her, and made her want more. Need more. Demand more. Without considering it, she said, "Your hawk is touching me."

His green eyes filled with the sweep of brown wings. "You feel him?"

"I do." She closed her eyes, feeling the strength of Axel's arms very distinctly around her. And then the lightest brush of wings everywhere. It swirled her skin to sensual heights that were excruciating and pleasurable. She moved in his arms, arching into the strokes against her skin.

"Damn." The word was low and gruff.

She opened her eyes. The moonlight spilled over his gleaming black hair, but his eyes, they were fully on her. "What?"

"I can make you come just like this. And then I'd come watching you." He shifted her, stood up, and strode toward the house saying, "But when you come, I want you in my arms, skin to skin, while I'm so deeply inside of you that I can feel each tremor of your pleasure, each pulse of your trust in me."

15

Axel didn't understand the bond between him and the witch he was carrying into the house. But earlier tonight, after coming home from working on the club, he'd seen Darcy on the floor with Hannah wrapped in her arms. His sister had been fully asleep, not restless, not fighting dreams, not even suffering night sweats and chills as she had been for several nights. Hannah had been burrowed against Darcy and sleeping peacefully.

What had really shocked him was that Darcy's witchglow encompassed the child, wrapping itself around Hannah while they both slept.

His witch had chased out the darkness tormenting Hannah and protected her with the light of an earth witch.

It had loosened the knot of suspicion in his chest. A woman who protected a child even in her sleep did not try to bind a man to her against his will. Whatever it was that was happening between them, it was real.

Not a lie of magic.

He wanted to believe that, needed to. He wanted to believe there was a purpose to all that was happening to them.

And God he wanted her. He quietly shut the front door, rearming the security and carried her through the living room and kitchen into his bedroom. He turned to shut the bedroom door, but it moved on its own, closing with a gentle snick. Darcy's power brushed over his skin.

He looked down at her. "Showing off?"

Her brown eyes sparkled with gold lights. She lifted her hands and with a sweep of her magic, they were both naked. "Now I'm showing off."

"Someone's been practicing." He shifted her so that she slid down his body to her feet. The feel of her skin against his flamed him to red hot lust. He took her mouth, and debated lifting her up and onto his cock.

Too rough, he decided.

How she took all of him last night he didn't know. She wasn't all that big. Yet with every thrust into her, her body had sucked him in deeper. And deeper. Opened for him until he'd been buried up to his balls.

Christ.

She moved her mouth, trailing kisses to his ear. "I want . . ."

She was going to kill him. He was desperate to know what she wanted, to give her what she wanted. "Want what?"

A beat, then, "Sex."

He felt that lie. And he wouldn't have it. "Tell me."

She looked up into his face. "I want to feel your hawk. Around me. From, umm . . ."

Axel saw exactly what she wanted. While she was stumbling over the words, the image bloomed in his head. She wanted him behind her, wrapping himself around her so she could imagine the wings of his hawk folding around her, holding her, while he pumped himself into her. He touched her face. "Behind. Because you know you're safe if you feel my wings." That he didn't actually have wings didn't matter.

Her eyes went wide. "You heard?"

"Saw. Exactly what you need." He would reach around her, separating her wet fragrant folds, and then

the wings would touch her, feather soft across her cli-
toris. She'd buck against him and just as she started to
come, he'd allow the wings to fold around her, his chest
would be against her back and he'd thrust to her very
core.

She shuddered. Her voice was thick, "Axel . . . you're
in my head."

He put his hand on the back of her head, pulling her
to his chest, pressing her face to that center of him where
he was often hollow. But not now, tonight he was full
and complete. "And you're in mine." He dropped a kiss
on her soft hair. His cock throbbed and wept with the
need to be inside of her. He closed his eyes and inhaled
her.

She responded by sliding her hand down his stomach
to wrap her fingers around him, bringing his body and
mind into bright, rich lust. He desperately wanted to
give her what she desired, what she needed. He picked
her up, quickly covering the distance to his bed. She
worked with him as he arranged her on her hands and
knees, her sweet ass facing him.

Axel's breath left his lungs. *Mine.* The word thundered in time with his pounding heart.

Darcy looked back at him. "I can hear you."

He shifted to look at her eyes, eyes that were drenched
with need. His wings lifted, fluttering beneath his skin.
And he thought, *You touch me where no one else can.*

Hawk?

Yes.

Mine.

Her thought was as fierce as his. She considered his
hawk hers? Hadn't he looked at her backside, the
curves, the folds that hid nothing from him and thought
the same thing? *Mine.* It roared through his head again
and he dragged his gaze from her eyes. He reached out
to touch what was his, what belonged to him.

Darcy arched her back.

He leaned over her, skin to skin, kissing her neck, her shoulder, dragging his tongue along that curve and tasting, actually tasting, her power. His entire body thrummed with it. As he had promised her, he reached around her to part her folds. She was slick and ready, and his mouth watered to taste her. But he'd promised her his hawk. The wings quivered more violently, as if they too scented her. Then, God, he couldn't believe it, he actually *felt* her wet skin against the tips of his wings as they caressed her in this most intimate place. It had to be magic.

Darcy bucked against him, beginning to pant. He saw her mind go moon bright, filled with images of him. Her scent flooded him, and he reached down, grabbing his cock and guiding it into her pulsing center.

She sucked him in. Only with Darcy could he let go and just feel. He pulled out and thrust again, sinking in deeper, the sensation of her power milked him as much as her flesh. She arched against him, the friction driving him to that same moon-bright place. All that mattered was them, their pleasure, their skin, their sex . . . he thrust into her again. Harder. All the while his hawk stretched and folded around her, holding the gentle soul of his witch while he thrust into the wild body of the woman.

"Axel . . ." Her cry was low and fell into whimpers as she came apart.

He held her tight with one arm, and caressed her clit with his free hand, bringing her again. Bringing her harder, brighter until her mind swirled in hot silver. He thrust again and lost himself in her. Gave her everything. He couldn't hold back with her.

The pleasure pounded him, milked him, and pulsed in white hot silver bliss.

*   *   *

She felt him in her head. Darcy had heard voices all her life, but not like this. This blending of their minds, the blending of their feelings was intense and overwhelming. So intensely intimate that it scared the holy shit out of her.

Axel's powerful body finally stilled, his arm around her waist, his mouth against her neck. He whispered against her skin, "I know."

He heard her thoughts. Another tremor of pleasure ripped through her. Sucking in air, she said, "What is this?"

Gently, he pulled out from her body, then lifted her as if she weighed no more than one of his pillows. He laid her on the bed, then spread out next to her. He slid an arm beneath her shoulders and pulled her into him, into the warmth and safety of his chest. "Some kind of mind link."

Fear began to crawl into her mind. She tried to roll out of his arms.

He tightened his grip. "Honey, we're not done here." He brought his free hand up to stroke her breasts and thumb a nipple.

Warm waves of pleasure swelled in her belly but she fought them. "No."

His hand stilled on her breast and he looked down at her. "What's wrong, Darcy? I know damn well you have the stamina to go two more rounds. And I know you want me. So why not?"

Because she was doing something to him! And he was doing something to her. Making her want to be with him. Making her want to trust him. But that was stupid. Foolish. When they had sex, Axel made her feel . . . loved. She burst out with, "Don't do this. Just . . . don't."

His gaze softened while his hand spread over her breast, covering it. "You're afraid."

"Realistic." She struggled to control her swirling energy. To push it back into her chakras, but her powers were responding to Axel's touch. She couldn't get control of them. That scared her more and she snapped, "It's just sex, Axel. I'm nothing to you. You've probably been sleeping with other women all the while I've been living in your basement." That hurt, damn it. She'd given him too much of herself. He could destroy her. Still struggling for control, she said, "We had sex and now I have work to do."

He snorted. "I haven't touched another woman since that night I took you from the mortuary."

Her skin prickled. "Why not?"

His green gaze was hot on her face. "You. From the first, you got under my skin. I thought it was the bloodlust, that I had touched your blood and that touch got me addicted to you. But now I don't feel the bloodlust. It's just gone."

She froze, trying to understand. "How do you think that happened?"

Propping his head up on his left hand, he drew his long fingers around her breasts, down her belly and back up. He turned his eyes to hers. "Maybe we are breaking this curse by turning back to the Wing Slayer. We took the wings, he changed mine to hawk wings, and now we're trying to make the right choices."

She shivered at his touch, her powers followed his fingers like a magnet, creating sensual warm sparks in the pattern his fingers traced. Her body tightened with need. But what touched her heart was the hope in his voice. It was the only time she'd heard that kind of hope in Axel. She might be the one to shatter his hope. Or maybe he was right and this was evidence of the Wing Slayer accepting his hunter. She didn't know. "Do you think that's why the wings feel real to us?"

He moved his hand back to toy with her breasts. "Yes. Wing Slayer Hunters, before the curse, didn't have wings. But the Wing Slayer does. So maybe that makes our wing tattoo feel real."

Or Darcy had completed the curse and turned him into a familiar, essentially an animal. Could that be what was bringing the wings to life? It was so confusing. She was even more confused with his hands on her. She tried to work it out. "Witches evolved. We came from special mortals, evolved into a separate race, and then over centuries evolved into more powerful beings with every generation, every reincarnation. That's what Carla told me. Then the curse happened. Both witches and witch hunters were changed by the curse, we lost a chunk of our powers, you lost your immortality and were saddled with a curse. All our souls were damaged. What if we have to evolve enough to reconnect; us to our Ancestors and you to your Wing Slayer?" Did her mom's soul-mirror theory play a part in that? Or was she just grasping at anything to avoid the fact that she might have turned Axel into a familiar against his will?

His gaze was steady on her face, showing he was listening. Thinking. "What was it about me that got the Wing Slayer's attention enough to change my tattoo?"

Darcy wrapped her fingers around his thick wrist, drawing his hand up to hold it between her breasts. "You told me you've resisted this curse since you were fourteen years old. You were clear on that. Fourteen. Why?"

His green eyes, so fierce and warm, suddenly iced over.

She could feel the cords and tendons of his wrist harden beneath her fingers. "Tell me," she said softly.

"When I was fourteen, my father tried to turn me rogue."

A second passed before she grasped it. "He wanted you to kill a witch?"

His jaw clenched.

She felt the rush of power flowing through her fingers, sending calming energy.

Axel answered, "Yes. She was tied down in a room where no one would hear. He cut her. She screamed . . ."

The backwash images exploded in Darcy's head. *The witch was tied down in a dirty little room, her blond hair matted with sweat and fear. In the memory, Darcy could smell the thick copper scent from her blood and Axel's rogue dad.*

She could see a large man standing next to a tall gangly boy. The man's hand whipped out a silver knife and slashed it across the witch's white belly.

The witch screamed and twisted against the ropes tying her down, begging the Ancestors for help. Begging the boy.

She could see young Axel stood frozen next to his father.

Then his dad grabbed his wrist and shoved his hand into the wound. The boy was horrified, then confused as the pleasure and power tore through him like a rocket. He shivered with it . . . until the witch screamed again.

The boy snatched his hand back, turned and ran. His heart pounding, he ran out of the building into the dirty abandoned lot choked with weeds and trash. Seeing his bloody hand, Axel leaned over and threw up.

Myles came out. "You sniveling little coward!" He backhanded the boy to the ground.

Axel's voice broke through the memory. "Come back, Darcy."

The image broke up into pieces and faded away. Axel's face took its place. The face of the full grown, very powerful man, not the boy.

Her eyes filled with hot tears, but she didn't care. "I saw it. Oh, God. Your dad is a monster!"

He used his thumb to wipe away her tears. "I tried to fight him, I had some insane notion of saving the witch.

But my father was bigger and beat the shit out of me. But even then, when he tried to drag me back in there, I got away. Ever since then I've built my life around self-control, around never letting the curse control me."

Her throat filled again. "Axel . . ." She didn't care if he saw her cry for him, and she clutched his hand tighter between her breasts. "You stood up. For a witch."

"I'm not sure if it was for her, or me. I didn't want to be *him*. I didn't want to be a slave to a curse, or anything like that."

Her throat was full of emotion but she managed to say, "You were born to lead."

"Jesus, Darcy. You make me want to be that man you see." He leaned down, kissing away her tears. "What we have is more than sex, sweet witch." He shifted, rolling on top of her and sliding deep inside of her.

He thrust, shattering her defenses and stroking her body to fiery heat. Darcy put her arms around Axel, holding him to her, desperate to imprint this memory, this moment, of pure acceptance in her mind.

As her orgasm took her, she arched back and forced her eyes open to see Axel. He was watching her, his green eyes burning with hunger. Then he was pounding into her, his powerful shoulders gleaming, muscles popping, and finally he rose up, thrust one last time and let out a roar as he came.

To Darcy's shock, a huge set of brown-and-gold wings opened up in majestic masculine beauty behind him.

Oh, God. What had she done to him? They weren't just feeling the sensation of wings, they were real.

And Axel, in the throes of his orgasm, never noticed.

16

"Axel and his men know who you are, and where you live," Darcy said to Carla, who was on the laptop. She was sitting on Axel's bed with the laptop she'd found in all his computer stuff. After making love again with Axel, she'd fallen asleep and slept straight through the night from exhaustion.

And that damned hawk. Every time she'd almost surfaced from sleep, he'd stroked her while Axel held her in his arms and she'd settled into sleep again. Like he knew she needed the rest.

Darcy watched as the Crone avatar disintegrated and Carla appeared. Her hazel eyes filled with concern. "I should have known they'd find me. They always do."

Her chest hurt. "I'm sorry. Axel swore they wouldn't hurt you, that they've all vowed to fight the curse. They even found a safe place for some earth witches that were cut by rogues and dumped in his club." He'd told her about it last night.

"I know you trust him, but it's harder for me."

Darcy felt the pain in her words. "Why? What happened, Carla?"

"When I lived in San Francisco, we had a group practice. I was the hypnotist in a clinic that emphasized whole body and mind health. We worked with mortals that had been damaged by witch hunters."

"You were all witches?"

Carla nodded. "I was an activist, lobbying that witches had to stop hiding and do what we were born to do. Help mortals and stand against evil, including rogues. I brought in a mortal woman who was having blackouts and other symptoms similar to Morgan's. The rogue who had done that to her managed to track her to my clinic. He killed her and my three partners." Her eyes grew pale and haunted. "He sliced them up, they screamed, it was awful. It was a miracle I got away, but my three partners and the mortal woman were killed." She turned away from the camera and lifted her shirt. A long white scar snaked across her skin.

"Oh, Carla!" The horror of what she had gone through pressed down on her. "That's why you wouldn't talk about why you left San Francisco. I knew something bad had happened and I thought it had to do with your work, but not . . . I'm so sorry."

"Learn from my mistakes, Darcy. I learned that day that we have no choice but to hide."

She understood why Carla was so careful. "But the work you do now is dangerous. Some of these cults do mass brainwashing. They have guns. You're still in danger."

"Yes. But it's a danger I can manage. Witch hunters are much more dangerous."

"Yet you took the risk of talking to me using the Crone avatar."

Carla waved her hand. "You're my friend. And I screwed up. The second you told me about the creepy guy at the cemetery, I should have driven to your house and told you that I am a witch and so are you. You have a right to be pissed at me for not telling you."

Warmth flooded Darcy. She wasn't pissed, not any longer. Carla had done what she believed was best. She'd been attacked by rogues directly. "You thought I was safer living as a mortal. You're a good friend. You took a huge risk agreeing to help Morgan."

"How could I not help her? It's like you and Hannah—some things we just can't walk away from and still live with ourselves." She took a breath and added, "I told Morgan about the baby. Morgan told Joe."

"Are they okay?" She vacillated on Joe. She wished he could find a normal, emotionally healthy woman, but that wasn't the woman he'd found. It was Morgan. Darcy had known it from the first time Joe had seen her after Darcy hired her.

"Morgan is remarkable. I planted some suggestions to help her cope while she was in the astral state."

"What's that?"

"It's where her mind rises to during hypnosis. Where she's safe. And Joe, well, Darcy, he cares about Morgan."

She nodded. "I just don't want him hurt. He came home so . . . disconnected."

"He was connected to you. And taking care of your mother helped him, too. We'll see with Morgan. She's suffered tremendous torture and damage to her brain. But pregnancy is powerful, too, and a mother's drive to protect her child is amazing. That's what has saved Morgan so far. The pregnancy hormones, I believe, had begun rebuilding some of the damaged brain cells even before I started working with her yesterday. That's why she was getting stronger and stronger memory flashes."

Darcy thought of Fallon's drive to protect her. Fallon had died trying to keep Darcy safe. And now, she needed to be as strong and brave as her mother to protect Hannah. Thinking of the tapestry, she asked, "How do I turn that sand in the silver box into something I can understand?"

"You transfer it to something of yours. Something silver. That will bring the knowledge from your mother's spell directly to you. But it is a *spell,* Darcy. Not low magic. It will take time for the knowledge to transfer and for you to absorb it into the silver you choose. During that time, you'll be open to danger from demons. You need a familiar and you don't have one."

"How did you do it then? You have a spell book, right?"

"My mother was alive, and she gave me spells and history a little at a time. It wasn't the same as this—your mother's spells have been stored in a third location for twenty-six years. You're using only your magic to pull them all out at one time and fill the silver you choose. It's higher magic. I don't know if you'll be able to control it without a familiar."

She felt a chill travel down her spine. Looking around Axel's room, she knew that none of the cameras or speakers were on. Just the laptop, which she and Carla were using with magic. She said in a whisper, "Maybe I do have one."

Carla's hazel eyes glowed with excitement. "You have a familiar? We haven't been able to get one in decades. Darcy, this could be a breakthrough for us!"

She slumped against the pillows. "Or it could be something much worse." Quickly, she outlined Fallon's belief that the witches and witch hunters had their souls halved during that fateful night when the demon witches cast the blood and sex curse to bind the witch hunters as familiars.

Carla's eyes widened. "You and Axel fulfilled the curse?"

"He touched my blood that first night. I touched his when he was injured. And we've had sex." Sex didn't begin to describe it.

"And his bloodlust?"

Feeling despair and frustration, she said, "When he's with me, it seems to be gone." She looked up at Carla and said the words she dreaded, "I'm afraid I've bound him to me. As a familiar."

Carla said, "Only animals can be familiars. It's never been successfully done with a mortal or witch hunter that I know of. Look what happened when the demon witches tried it."

Darcy thought of the wings she'd seen on Axel. Had they been real? They had looked real. "What if I've turned him into an animal?"

"Not likely. Any harm an earth witch causes with her powers comes back to her times three, and changing a man into an animal is causing harm. What else did your mother say?"

"She called it soul mirror. The hunters' souls have been searching for witch blood and sex from the curse, and the witches have been searching for a familiar. Neither can fulfill the need. She believed that when we found the right hunter, when the souls mirrored each other's needs, that the soul would be whole again."

"You and Axel weren't there at the curse. You weren't born and Axel was a kid. But we know the curse spread to all witches and hunters from that point on, so all the souls were pulled into this." Carla's hazel eyes lost focus as she thought. Then she reached up and closed her left hand around the ornate silver band that circled her right bicep.

"What are you doing?"

"This is where I keep my witch book. I'm looking for information." She closed her eyes. Her image on the computer brightened then settled. She opened her eyes and said, "All the information I have in my witch book about a familiar says that the familiar always has the right to reject the witch. I'd think that would still hold true even in this soul-mirror scenario."

Greasy sickness rolled in her belly. She thought of Axel telling her about his dad, and how he'd never be a slave to a curse. *Or a witch's spell binding him as a familiar,* she thought. To Carla, she said, "I have to find out. We should all work together, all the witches, I mean. Can't you vouch for me and get the Circle Witches to accept me?"

"I can't, Darcy." Carla looked back at her from the laptop screen. "They won't accept you. Not while you are living with a witch hunter and working with him. And there's another problem."

Her bubble burst with the painful sting of rejection. "Because I have witch-hunter blood from my biological father. They don't trust me."

Carla's face tightened in sympathy. "I trust you. And in time, I'll make them see that you deserve to be in the Circle. But for now, I can be your liaison."

She'd spent her life on the outside of every circle. This wasn't any different. "Okay, thanks. If they'll work on finding out everything about soul mirrors, I'd appreciate it."

"I'll put out a request. There's a lot of knowledge in the Circle."

Her chest hurt but she refused to let Carla see her pain. "That'll be helpful." Carla had been a good friend, was still a good friend. She was doing her best.

"Darcy, you might have more connections than the Circle Witches. They are combining all *our* knowledge, but they can't talk to the Ancestors since the curse. You can hear the Ancestors. Once you get your mom's spells, start working on opening your sixth chakra. If you can do it, and maybe you can if your hunter has bonded to you, then you can ask the Ancestors about soul mirrors. With your third eye in your sixth chakra, you'll be able to understand what the Ancestors are saying."

Even now, Darcy could hear the voices, but not the words. The only time she'd ever heard distinct words had been in moments of absolute terror—like when the rogues had attacked. And then it was simple messages like "Run!" But if she could really hear and understand what the Ancestors were saying . . . her heart jumped in excitement, then thudded in fear. She would have to lie to Axel. Use him for the increased power to access her higher chakras, and then focus that power, but not tell him what she was doing. "I'll try," she said absently, thinking she was headed for disaster with Axel. Heartbreak.

Axel's voice cut in, "Darcy, you awake? Is something wrong?"

She jerked at his voice and yanked the covers up to cover her nakedness. She'd been using magic to project her image to Carla and had projected only her head so she hadn't been worried about her state of dress. "Where are you?" She looked around.

"Desktop computer. I'd be on the laptop but it seems to be blocked by magic."

Carla laughed. "I'll clear the airwaves. I'm going to call Morgan now and set up another appointment." Her image faded out.

Axel's face bloomed on the screen of the laptop. The green light of the camera blinked on. "I wanted to check in . . . wow."

Flushing to her roots, she realized she'd let go of the covers and exposed her breasts to him. She used magic to bring her clothes back from last night. They materialized on her body in seconds.

"Impressive. But I liked you better naked. I like seeing you in my bed."

She sucked in a breath and tried to calm her racing heart. "You let me sleep. I meant to work on the tapestry."

His eyebrows furrowed over his hot green eyes. "You were exhausted. You needed sleep and this morning, you need to eat."

"Thanks," she said dryly. "Not sure how I managed for twenty-six years without you."

He surprised her with a grin that lit up the computer screen. "It's a mystery."

Damn. He was sexy like this. Hell, he was sexy all the freaking time. "Arrogant hunter."

"Prickly witch."

She smiled. "I could probably cast a spell for you to hit yourself with your hammer. Repeatedly. All day long."

His eyes filled with laughter. "I'd have to get even for that. Want to test me?"

She wondered what he'd do. Then she wondered what the hell *she* was doing. She had to focus and get the spells from the tapestry to heal Hannah. Not flirt with Axel. "Was there something you wanted?"

His gaze shifted, sensing her mood change. "I felt, I don't know exactly, I just had a feeling you were upset or something." He shrugged, looking a little uncomfortable.

"I'm not upset. Just annoyed that being a half-breed keeps me out of the witch club."

His green eyes iced and he growled, "Fuck them, Darcy. You're not a half-breed anything. You are fully, one hundred percent earth witch."

"Actually, Carla is working with the Circle Witches for me. I need all the help I can get. I have to get those spells out of the tapestry today. I *will* do it today," she added determinedly.

He ran his hand through his hair, his face lined with worry. "I'll check in later. I'm at the club, call if you need anything. Later." He clicked off.

Even through the machine, she felt the twist of his increasing worry. She knew he was overseeing work on the club, but more important, he and his fellow hunters were tracking the demon witch that had cursed Hannah. And monitoring what the rogues were doing.

She threw back the covers, got up—leaving the laptop on the bed—and headed into Axel's closet to the stairs that would take her to the bottom floor. She needed a hot shower, change of clothes, and then food.

She turned into her room and stopped short. Joe slouched on the stool with his feet on her worktable, watching something on the laptop. He had a huge mug of coffee. It smelled delicious, but coffee left her too wired. She usually stuck with herbal teas. "Why are you in here? I know there's a TV in your room."

He turned to look at her. "I came to talk to you. Obviously, you didn't sleep here."

Joe looked tired and worried. There were taut lines around his deep blue eyes and mouth. "What's up?"

He dropped his legs to the floor, set his coffee on the worktable, stood, and walked to the doorway. From there, he looked back and said, "Morgan's pregnant." Then he turned left out of her room and went down the hallway.

She stared at the tapestry. The cat was gone, the silver chest sat open and was full of sand. But she was thinking about Morgan.

Joe walked back in holding a mug which he held out to her. "You knew she was pregnant, didn't you? That's what you saw in the bathroom yesterday?"

She took the cup and inhaled the fragrant tea. She looked up at Joe and answered, "I saw it."

Joe went back to the barstool. "That's why her husband kept her alive, to breed his kid."

Joe's shoulders were stiff beneath the blue T-shirt he wore. Darcy said carefully, "You care about her."

Picking up his coffee, he faced her. "At first, it was the memory of her in high school. She was hot, and somehow untouchable."

"The one girl who rejected you."

He smirked. "Something like that. But then I went into the military."

Darcy forced her hand to bring the cup to her mouth without pause. Joe hadn't talked about his time in the service, other than funny anecdotes. She sipped her tea and waited.

He shook his head. "It was hell, and after a while I lost myself. I lost my purpose. It was all so fucking pointless." He shook his head.

She went to Joe, putting her arm around him. She could sense his turmoil and deep emotions, the same ones she'd felt over the last few months. "What happened?"

He took a breath. "I fell in love with a woman there."

Darcy stayed quiet, leaving it up to him to tell her what he wanted her to know.

"She was an American Red Cross worker who was killed doing her job trying to help people."

Her chest ached for him. One of those deep emotions she'd been feeling from him had a name—grief. "I'm so sorry, Joe." She hated that he'd gone through this, that he'd suffered, and she hadn't been there for him.

His muscles clenched as he went on. "I wasn't there. I didn't even find out until after they'd shipped her body back home. I was out on a mission and she died alone. Without knowing how I really felt about her." He reached up and closed his fingers over her hand.

Setting her tea down, she hugged him with both arms. The grief and anger poured off him, and Darcy allowed herself to open up and draw it to her. She focused on bright healing light for him.

He put his hand on her arm. "You're doing magic, aren't you?"

She wouldn't lie. "Yes."

He turned to slip out of her hug, and took hold of her

hand. "My world went gray the day I found out about her murder. I lost myself and my ability to see the lines between what matters and what doesn't. Between right and wrong."

She shook her head. "That's not true. The part about your world going gray, okay, that I believe. But you have always been able to stand for right and against wrong. Maybe you're not my blood, but you are my family. I know you." She wouldn't let him cheapen who he was like that.

The pain left his blue eyes.

She smiled. "Tell me about Morgan."

"She brings color to my world. With Morgan I can see the lines. At first, my feelings were based in nostalgia and plain male interest. Carla told me the same thing Axel did—most mortals who have endured what Morgan has completely lose their minds. But here's Morgan, alone and scared, but fighting. Refusing to let that bastard destroy her. She pulls at something inside me that I thought was dead. She makes me want to live again and be the man strong enough to match her courage."

Darcy's hand was still in his and she felt this one emotion more clearly than any other. "You're falling for her."

"I am."

Darcy believed him, but they had to deal with reality. "There's the baby now."

"Yeah." Joe nodded. "Hell of a mess. And yet, I still want her."

She dropped Joe's hand and picked up her tea. "So what now?"

"I'm not walking away, Darcy. Crazy as it sounds, this world, you being a witch, the witch hunters, Morgan being knocked up by a rogue—it makes sense to me. I know my line, and it's to protect and care for Morgan and her kid."

When he said it like that, she understood. Hadn't she spent her life not knowing what she was? Where to fit in? What her purpose was? Learning that she was a witch and taking on the job of healing Hannah whatever the cost—that made sense to her. So if Morgan was what made sense to Joe, then he had her support. "So what's next with Morgan?"

"Carla wants to see her again today. I'm going to take her. We'll deal with each day as it comes, I guess."

Darcy considered it. She had seen a fraction of the torture and fear Morgan suffered, so she told her cousin another truth. "She's going to be physically skittish of you, Joe. Any woman who has been through what she has would be."

His eyes burned a bright blue. "You're sleeping with a man who is cursed with a drive to kill you for your blood. And yet I assume you just came from his bed."

Heat washed through her, not embarrassment, just heat. She trusted Axel with her body. So much. It was the emotions that scared the hell out of her. In the past, she'd always been rejected because of who she was. She hadn't known she was a witch but the men had always sensed her difference and grew scared of her. "Axel won't hurt me. Not like that. He won't give in to the curse."

"And you know this how?"

The way he touched her, protected her, so many things. "I just do."

"Exactly. Morgan had another nightmare last night. This time, before I could get out of bed and go into her room, she came into my room. I pulled back the covers and she got into my bed. Where she feels safe. Where she is safe. When she's ready for more than that, she'll let me know."

Morgan had grown up in a small town and gone to school with Joe. She had to know, somewhere in her brain, that Joe was a man she could trust. "She's a lucky woman to have found you."

Joe's face twitched in embarrassment. "Yeah, well, after growing up with a witch for a cousin, Morgan is downright normal." He picked up his coffee and stood. "You have some serious bed head going on there, cuz. Go take a shower." He strode away, looking ten pounds lighter as he raised his cup to drink.

Darcy lifted her hand.

"Hey!" Joe said, turning empty-handed to glare at her. "You stole my coffee!"

"Sometimes, it rocks to be a witch." She went in the bathroom and closed the door.

17

Axel walked into the house in the late afternoon. Hannah was huddled under a blanket on the couch with Minnie, watching cartoons. She looked up at him; her eyes were sunken into her too pale face. "The TV keeps blinking."

It took a second to get his breath. His lungs burned with fury at how sick she looked. How thin her voice was. How much he loved her. Finally, he asked, "Say what?" Just then the TV flickered, went to black, then flashed back on.

"Blinking." Hannah coughed, curling into a ball with the spasms.

"I see that." He reached down and rubbed her sweaty back until the coughing subsided. Crouching down beside her, he helped her take a sip of water. Then he brushed back her bangs.

The death mark was the color of a port-wine stain. Her head felt hot, her lips were dry and cracked. The anger rushed him in a violent fury.

The TV flickered again.

Taking his hand from her head, he straightened out her blanket. "How long has the TV been . . . blinking?"

"All day. Mommy says Darcy is doing it."

"Ah." He assumed she was having trouble focusing her powers to get the spells out of the box. A familiar had never shown up, and without a familiar, high magic was hard for her to access and control.

But Hannah needed the spell to heal her. And quickly.

"She's talking to herself, too. I heard her say a bad word." She blinked up at him with a serious expression.

"You snuck downstairs?"

"Darcy makes me feel better. She makes me tea and talks to me, too. She makes Minnie dance, too. Minnie likes her."

So did Hannah. Axel could see that his little sister adored Darcy.

The TV flickered and he actually heard Darcy swear through the sound on the TV.

Hannah giggled, then coughed.

It was less violent this time, but she still looked exhausted. His mom walked in holding a half-filled mug. "I made some of Darcy's tea for you." She set the cup on the table, helped Hannah into a sitting position, then handed her the cup. "Okay?"

Hannah took the cup in both hands and nodded.

Eve turned to Axel. "Darcy's been working all day trying to get her spells to transfer. It's not going well."

The two lamps flickered on. Axel wondered what she was doing to all his electronics with her wild energy. "I better go down and check on her."

His mom followed him into his bedroom. "Did you hear about Morgan?"

"Darcy told me last night."

Eve touched his arm. "Her husband is going to come after her. He'll find her. I know he will."

Axel knew she was right. She had stayed with his dad for Axel's sake until his dad tried to force him to turn rogue. Then the two of them had taken off. Evidently, during the thirteen or so years after that, his dad tried to get other women pregnant to replace Axel. It never happened, so his dad tracked down his mom while Axel was gone doing private security for a club. Myles managed to seduce her, which sounded ridiculous for a woman as sophisticated and strong as his mother.

But Axel knew it happened all the time. Witch hunters gave off special pheromones to attract women and fulfill the sex part of the curse.

He also suspected that his mom had been afraid Myles would track down Axel and kill him if she didn't cooperate. She got pregnant with Hannah. His dad was disgusted when he found out the baby was a girl and had left them alone.

But Eve was right about Morgan. Eric Reed would find her.

Axel put his hand over his mom's. "I hope he does, so we can send him to his eternity as a shade. What he did to Morgan . . . I look forward to killing him."

Tears made her blink, but they didn't fall. "That's what the Wing Slayer wants you to do. I'm sure of it. Protect the innocent. It's what you were born to do." The passion strengthened her voice.

She was so sure. "How do you know?"

"Faith. Sometimes you have to have faith to make the right choices. It's always a choice. Before the curse, your dad and many of the hunters were refusing assignments from the hawk. They were making selfish choices, getting lazy in their duty. I don't think it was always like that, Axel. I think the hunters were making fewer and fewer good choices before the curse. Quinn Young wasn't the first hunter to get sidetracked in his duty, he just was the first to actually get caught by demon witches. And now, here you are, making hard choices and you're no longer struggling with the bloodlust even though you had Darcy in your room all night."

Axel wanted to believe. "I can have faith as long as Hannah survives. If we lose her, then I'll know it's a crock of shit."

The passion that colored her face drained into a stricken look. "She won't die!"

"No. She won't. We have leads on demon witches. I won't let Hannah die."

"Axel . . ."

"No. You don't get a vote in this, Mom. If Darcy can't uncurse her, I will. And if the Wing Slayer wants to take my soul for that, then he's as bad as rogues and demon witches." He softened his tone and added, "Have faith. Darcy is powerful, she can do this." He turned and walked through his closet then down the stairs.

As soon as he hit the bottom of the steps, he felt the wave of power. It spread over his skin in a scattershot of mild shocks, moving through him and dissipating.

Totally unfocused. He felt that instantly. Axel strode down the hall and turned into the room. Darcy stood in the middle of what looked like some kind of windstorm. Sand dotted the floor, bed, desk, and worktable. Her auburn hair was pulled back into a sloppy ponytail. She wore a shell-pink tank top, a denim skirt, and no shoes. It tended to be cold on the bottom floor, but she looked warm . . . and hot.

Warm with a slight sheen of sweat on her forehead and upper arms. And hot from the curves of her breasts against that top, and her bare legs. Darcy had muscle in her legs, he loved the feel of them wrapped around him, her thighs tightening and clenching as her orgasm approached.

She whipped her head around as if she'd heard his thoughts, or felt them. "Axel."

Her voice was low and throbbing. He could feel her energy swirling, touching him, dancing away. It was maddening. He moved toward her, his shoes not making a sound on the sand-coated tile. Her scent filled him, and drew him like a charm. All he saw was Darcy.

"I've tried, but I can't do it myself. Carla has been

coaching me as best she can." Darcy shook her head. "I can get my fifth chakra to open, but I can't control it. Maybe I need my sixth chakra, but it won't open. I can't reach it." Her frustration bled through her words.

"I can feel your powers, they're scattered and unfocused. Maybe you need a break?" He wanted, needed, to help her.

"No." She looked dejected. "I need you. I need you to help me."

He felt the wings of his hawk spread in happiness. Responding to Darcy as he always did. It didn't freak him out anymore, it just was. He was only inches from her. "I'll help you. What do you want me to do?"

She glanced away, then back to him, her eyes darkening with resolve. "I need you to touch me. Help me focus. Last night when you touched me, we formed some kind of mind link. I think that will help . . . somehow." She lifted her hand and fingered the silver symbol that rested flat against the skin between her clavicle bones.

He reached out to touch the necklace. "It's warm with magic." His body went tight with need, with silvery lust, but he ignored it. He felt the tat on his back stir again, the wings fluttering with the desire to touch her. Protect her. Help her.

Darcy tilted her face, looking up into his eyes.

He leaned down, and keeping his fingers around the necklace, he kissed her. He sank his tongue into her mouth, tasting her.

She wrapped both her hands around his arm that held on to the necklace. She kissed him back with enough heat to make him groan. His body flooded with her magic, it felt like warm light that vibrated. He couldn't touch it but he sure as hell could feel it. His raging hard-on felt it. But Axel forced his mind away from sex and lifted his head. "We'll do this. Together. Ready to try it again?"

Her eyes shimmered bright gold lights, and her skin glowed silver. "Yes. I need you close to me. Touching me."

He was a second away from lifting that skirt and being as close as a man could get to a woman—deep inside of her. He let go of the necklace.

She clutched his wrist. "Don't let go of me."

Ah, hell, her voice, her tone, reached deep inside of him, so deep that it had to be real and not a trick of magic. "I've got you, sweet witch. I'll hold on to you while you set your magic free." He shifted around the back of Darcy, then put his arms around her, folding them beneath her breasts.

"Hawk?"

The wings fluttered beneath his skin. "He's here. Feel him?" He tried to open his mind and let her feel what Axel did. Tried to let her feel him with her as she had last night when they had made love.

"Yes." She leaned back into him. "I don't know the spell, so I'm just opening myself and calling the spells."

She was where she belonged—in his arms, where he could guard her. It crossed his mind that those were odd thoughts, but he shoved it away. Darcy needed the spells to heal Hannah. He said into her ear. "Go ahead, call the spells to your necklace."

She raised her arms above her shoulders and stretched them out toward the tapestry, her fingers spread and extended. Her witch-shimmer began to brighten. "I beg the Ancestors, help move the gift of my mother's spells from the silver box into my silver necklace."

The hum of her powers rose inside of him. The connection opened between them. Good God, her thoughts and memories swirled, and for a second, he could see her as a young girl locked in a dark, small space. Then it vanished, but Axel grasped that the memory held her back and tripped up her power. She'd been told she was evil when she did anything weird or magical.

It pissed him off, and he heard the echo of his hawk's furious screech.

Words flowed from him, "There is no evil in you, love. You're a witch, embrace it. Show me, Darcy. Open for me," he said softly, his body shuddering at the mental image of her when she opened for him. "Let the power have you."

She arched her body into a graceful, beautiful line. Her head angled back against his chest, her breasts and hips thrust out. He couldn't tear his gaze from her.

Until the clap of thunder.

Axel looked up at the tapestry while keeping Darcy supported in his arms. The box in the tapestry glowed, and the sands began to melt into a thick, sparkling liquid. He sucked in a breath at the power in those threads.

Darcy's body arched further, her eyes were closed now and her witch-shimmer lit to a glow as bright as any star.

The entire room shivered.

Axel felt like he was on the ultimate amusement ride. His insides came alive, the throb and beat of her witch-energy streaming through him. The sexual energy between him and Darcy grew sharp and bright with the magic in the room. It brought him to the painful edge of release, but he didn't care. All that mattered was the witch in his arms. Her scent was burgeoning with desire. She began to sway slightly. He knew if he touched her, if he skimmed his hand under that skirt and into her panties, she'd come.

He had to force himself to breathe, to keep his hands where they were and just hold her. But damn, he wanted to feel her come, feel her wet pleasure.

A sudden atmospheric shift chased out his sexual thoughts. The shimmer in the room dimmed. Danger screamed through his body, honing every one of his senses to intense awareness. A stutter and gasp of the witch energy streaming through him warned him that another force was trying to get in. Axel whipped his head around, looking for the source. In the opened doorway, he saw a shadow of something with three heads.

Demon, his hawk shrieked.

The thought exploded in his mind, *Mine! I'll kill anything that threatens her.*

With his gaze pinned on the opening to the room, the door trembled, then slammed shut. The oppressive force vanished.

Hawk settled on his back.

The shimmer in the room brightened allowing Darcy's witch energy to flow freely once more. What the hell was that? A demon? With three heads . . . Asmodeus. How had Darcy summoned a demon, the demon that had taken part in the curse?

A loud crack caught his attention. He shifted his gaze to the tapestry just as a stream of lightning arced from the silver box in the tapestry to Darcy's necklace.

He'd never seen, or felt, anything like it. The pure energy of that continuous beam of lightning sizzled, crackled, and flashed brilliant colors. It fed the necklace for endless minutes.

It ramped up both their sexual urges. Darcy moaned with need.

Axel leaned down. "Soon, Darcy. I swear. Just let the magic fill you."

She shuddered. Her skin was so hot, he felt the heat through her thin top.

Finally the beam of lightning thinned, then disappeared.

The box slammed shut.

*   *   *

Darcy hurt. It felt like her organs were going to burst open like an overripe watermelon. Her skin was hot and tight, and there wasn't enough room for her to get a full breath. The necklace was heavy and hotter than her skin. "It's done."

"Not yet." Axel skimmed his hand beneath her shirt and under the bra to cup her breast, using his thumb to stroke her swollen, sensitive nipple.

She couldn't help but moan.

He slid his other hand down her abdomen, over her hip, and down her thigh. He snaked under her skirt, sliding up the inside of her right thigh.

Her powers shot to where his hands touched her, making her writhe. "Too much!"

"You need release. And I have to touch you. God, I have to feel your wet need, your pleasure." He pulled her damp panties from her and replaced them with his long, warm fingers. He parted her folds.

Her breath shot up into her throat and she arched into him. "I can't control it."

"All you have to do is feel." He shifted his hand on her breast to grasp the nipple with his thumb and finger, rolling gently. Sparks of pleasure lit from her nipple to her core.

He slipped a finger inside her body. Then two. Thrusting into her. She bucked against him.

"Darcy, honey, give it to me. Everything." He slid his thumb over to caress that swollen nub. And kept thrusting his fingers in and out. While tweaking her nipple. She let him have her, letting her body go, moving against his hands, desperately seeking relief. The pressure built and throbbed to a crescendo. When she exploded, he locked one arm around her while he stroked her to orgasm. "More. Pour it out, let it go." He kept rubbing her more and more, until the excess energy poured out of her with every pulse of pleasure.

She was limp when he finally pulled out his fingers and scooped her up in his arms. He walked into her tiny bathroom, set her on the closed toilet, then leaned in and started the shower. "Want me to strip you or . . ."

She let her powers get rid of her clothes. Then his. Axel stood in front of her naked. His dark hair hung nearly to his shoulders, his face suffused with color, his chest rippling, and his cock . . . the thick head beaded with need. She reached out and used her thumb to spread his semen, coating the broad head. Immediately, her powers surged, reaching.

His cock twitched hard.

She leaned forward and drew her tongue across the sensitive tip. Then she had to have him all and closed her mouth around him, drawing him in as far as she could take him.

Axel hissed in slowly, then let out a breath with a groan. Hearing his pleasure excited her, but the feelings washing off of him and sinking into her ripped open her guts. He loved the feel of her mouth, he loved the feel of her hand, but even in the intense sexual need, his first thought was her. Her protection, her comfort . . .

Just her.

Tears burned her eyes and she closed them, letting her mouth draw him in while she brought up her hand to cup his balls and poured her magic into her fingers and tongue.

Axel slapped his hands on the mirror behind her. "Christ, Darcy."

Except she didn't think he said the words out loud. She thought in her head, "Come, Axel. Come for me."

He shivered, his entire body rocking with the intense pleasure. He dropped his hand to the back of her head, tugged the band from her hair and sank his fingers into the strands. He thrust into her mouth, once and again.

"Darcy . . ." He gave it to her then, spurting into her mouth. Letting her take as much of him as she could.

With his orgasm came his overwhelmingly fierce need to help and protect her. Along with how much he wanted to drive his cock into her even though he'd just come.

And the suspicion. Just a thread that hadn't yet risen all the way up to his consciousness.

But it would. The sorrow of it was just too much for her to bear. She didn't want to hurt him and she didn't want to lose this intimacy, trust, and connection with Axel.

He leaned down, putting his mouth on hers, and her thoughts shifted once more into silvery pleasure and joy to feel him merge body and soul with her.

He pulled back, looked in her eyes and said, "I can't get enough of you." He lifted her in his arms, stepped easily over the side of the tub and put them both in the warm stream of water. With the water pouring over her hair and down her back, he said, "Again. Now. Put your legs around me." Then he lifted her to take him deep into her body.

Darcy stayed downstairs while Axel went up to check on Hannah. She wanted some time to think. It was all so overwhelming. During the transfer, all the knowledge in her mom's spell book had poured through her. Some knowledge stuck, and some she wasn't able to catch as it flowed through her chakras.

Now she had to see if she could access the spells in her necklace. Usually witches learned magic as they grew. Even if their mother died, another witch took them in. They filled their own spell books, or got the spells from their mother's, one at a time.

She sat on the floor wearing jeans, a white shirt, and no shoes. One by one, she pointed at each candle, using her fire chakra to light the flames; a red candle for earth, orange for water, yellow for fire, and green for air. Then she moved to high magic, lighting the blue candle for communication beyond the mortal realm.

Her fifth chakra opened at her throat, creating a spinning sensation around the length of her spine as low magic and high magic met. As soon as that settled, Darcy pointed at the indigo candle for her sixth chakra.

Nothing. That chakra located at her forehead remained closed.

She took a deep breath, feeling her power rise through her first four chakras, and flow down through her fifth. She held the connection. She would get her sixth chakra open eventually. For now, she focused and pointed at the violet candle for knowledge. It lit.

The chakra at the top of her head remained closed.

Darcy faced forward, letting the candles surround her, and closed her eyes. She placed her hands in her lap and focused on the necklace at her throat.

The silver warmed and expanded against her skin. She directed more and more of her energy into the necklace. Carla told her it was the same backwash principle as when she saw and felt Morgan's memories and emotions. By pouring her energy into the necklace, she was forcing an exchange.

She saw her mother's memory of summoning a familiar: Fallon stood beneath the moonlight on a secluded beach somewhere. Darcy could see the pale moonlight dancing on the water. See her mother raise her arms high and arch her back, her long hair picked up by a breeze and blown around her.

Words flowed through her head.

Time hung still and endless as Darcy watched. Her stomach clenched in worry, she already knew this story. Her mother had told her.

A man walked toward her mother, he wore black, was

tall, and had windblown hair. When he got closer to Fallon, she saw his face. The delicate lines and soft skin of a rogue. His eyes were dark, his mouth full.

She opened her eyes, forcing the connection to break. Her hands shook in her lap. She'd seen her father.

Her mother's killer.

The man who wanted to kill her.

Her hands were cold and clammy. Her head throbbed from tremendous sadness. Acid burned her stomach.

But she had to try again. Had to find a spell to break the death curse. She centered herself by looking at each candle, touching each chakra, except the two that remained closed. Then she closed her eyes and concentrated, directing her energy into the necklace.

This time she tried to let the different images just move through her. It was hard not to focus on her mother, but she let the impressions keep passing by her.

Until she came to one where her mom was younger, about nineteen. She was on the beach facing a man who had the mark.

The death curse.

Darcy focused hard on the image, stopping it, then playing out that specific one. She saw witches gathered behind her mother. Staying focused, she watched her mother do the spell to break the curse.

She had what she needed, it was time to pull out.

Opening her eyes, she was shocked to see Axel. He was crouched down on the other side of the candles, watching her. "What are you doing?"

"Checking on you, but you were in some kind of trance so I waited. I don't want you staying down here, Darcy. Come upstairs, I'm making spaghetti."

Her stomach growled viciously.

"What were you doing?"

"Finding the spell to heal Hannah." She lifted her

hand, closed her fingers, and all the candle flames went out.

"Your hand is shaking." Axel wrapped his fingers around her hand, rose, and pulled her to her feet. Threading his fingers through hers, he tugged her out of the room and turned left down the hall toward the stairway.

"I saw my father, then I pulled out. I was in my mother's memory."

"That's in your witch book?"

Darcy realized she was on dangerous ground here. She couldn't tell him about soul mirrors yet, not until she healed Hannah. "It's not like an actual book. My mother couldn't teach me the spells one by one, so she transferred her memories of doing witchcraft. I saw the first time she met my father, which was the time she used a sleeping charm on him to get away." Or she would have seen it if she'd stayed in the memory long enough. They walked into the kitchen. The smell of spaghetti sauce filled the room and made her stomach rumble again.

Axel let go of her hand and walked over to the stove, then he said, "Can you make this damned water boil?"

A large pot filled with water sat on a flame, next to a pan of simmering sauce. On the counter next to that was a package of spaghetti noodles, along with an open bottle of red wine and a couple of glasses. Axel moved to stir the pan of spaghetti sauce, then he picked up a cookie sheet.

She asked, "Is that garlic bread?"

"Yes. It's going to burn because that water is taking too long to boil."

She smiled at his aggravation. "Put it in the oven," she said, then lifted her hand over the pan of barely warm water and directed her energy into it.

Axel stuck the bread in the oven, then moved around her and poured the wine. He handed her a glass.

She took it while keeping a steady flow of energy directed toward the water. A minute later, the water simmered into a full boil.

"Put in the spaghetti."

She added the spaghetti then turned to see him at the other end of the counter slicing a rich-looking cheese.

Damn, she was starved.

A slice of cheese lifted off the cutting board and sailed toward her. She snatched it from the air and took a bite of the sharp cheddar. Delicious. She washed it down with a sip of wine.

His lips twitched into a quick grin. Axel stirred the spaghetti, then the sauce.

The fragrances made her mouth water.

He picked up his wine and said, "Did you find the spell for Hannah?"

She nodded and handed him a cheese-topped cracker. "I saw the spell to break the curse, but I'd like to study it more tonight. And I'm going to have to try to get my sixth chakra open to see if I can communicate with the Ancestors. We need their help to break the curse."

Axel swallowed a bite of cheese and cracker, then asked, "How do you open the chakra?"

She traced the rim of her wineglass. "I don't know. Keep trying. Maybe it's in my necklace somewhere. Carla is asking the Circle Witches—some of them are old enough to remember before the curse."

"Okay, tell me about the spell."

"It's a ceremony. I need to do it someplace in the moonlight and with ley lines, a place like the beach."

Axel pulled out the colander of noodles from the pan, drained them, and poured them into a large bowl. "Ley lines?"

"They are power points where earth's power gathers.

Where the sea meets the earth, old graveyards where life meets death . . . they just are. The magic comes in bringing the power of the earth from the ley lines up through me to meet the pull of the moon, then I add to that the power of the Ancestors. I focus all that power on Hannah and chant for healing."

Axel filled two plates with spaghetti, sauce, and bread, then placed them on the bar. "Sit and eat."

Darcy sat on a bar stool, rested her bare feet on the rungs, and picked up the fork. She was oddly calm about the magic. It was Axel that had her worried. How had she come to care about and need the man who'd kidnapped her? If she was right, the curse had ended up giving him the power to destroy her.

"How dangerous is this spell?"

"To Hannah?" She sipped some wine and went on. "Moderately dangerous. I don't think any more harm will come to her."

Axel set his fork down and caught her chin to force her to look at him. His green gaze fastened on her eyes. "To you. While you were doing that transfer earlier, I'm pretty sure a demon tried to appear, but it seemed to be unable to fully materialize."

She dropped her bread, causing spaghetti sauce to splatter onto her white shirt. Cold fear coiled deep in her gut. "You're sure?"

"Something was there. I could only see a shadow in the doorway, but it had three heads. I think it was Asmodeus. Then the door slammed and seemed to break its connection to us. I'm not sure how."

She shivered. "I felt you tell me to shut the door." She frowned, thinking about it. "Maybe I heard you say 'shut it out,' so I think I did it. But would that keep a demon out?"

He let go of her face and picked up a napkin to wipe away the spaghetti sauce on her shirt. "My hawk screeched at it. Maybe that warned off the shadowy bastard."

"I heard that." She took the napkin from his hand. Her powers rushed to the places he touched, making her feel odd. She wiped at the sauce stains, then realized she had magic. Passing her hand over the stains, they disappeared.

"You'll be in more danger when you do this spell, won't you?"

She looked up into his eyes. "I'll use a consecrated salt circle. I think the salt will protect me. Maybe. Either way, Hannah is worth the risk."

Axel turned away, picked up his fork, and ate. After a couple minutes, he said, "I will be there when you do the spell to protect Hannah and you both."

She needed him there, so that worked for her. "Okay."

He lifted his right hand to slide it beneath her still-drying hair and caress the back of her neck. "I won't stop protecting you once Hannah's well. You're not alone any longer."

She dropped her head, staring at the remains of dinner. He cared about her, truly cared. Made her feel like she belonged. The elusive love and acceptance she had always craved was within her reach.

But she didn't know if it was real. Or a bond forced on him by a decades-old curse that she'd accidentally completed.

"Darcy."

God. She lifted her head, unable to resist his call. She looked into his face.

The face of the man she'd fallen in love with. Her heart beat simply to hear his voice. Feel his touch. She'd sacrifice everything for him. Even his love. "What?"

Before he could say anything, Eve's voice shattered the moment. "Axel! Hannah's seizing!"

18

He ripped his hand from Darcy, leapt off the bar stool, and raced to his sister's room. The small light by the bed showed Eve holding Hannah's shoulders while her body convulsed. Her eyes were rolled back in her head, her jaw was locked, and sharp guttural noises came from her throat. He hurried to the other side of the bed, fighting a dark rage that made him want to hunt down and rip apart the demon witch who'd done this to Hannah.

Darcy burst into the room. "Move!" She edged Eve up toward Hannah's head, threw back the covers, and shoved up his sister's nightshirt. She put her hand on her small chest, right in the center, and closed her eyes.

The air was sucked out of the room, as if all the molecules rushed to Hannah in such a hurry that they left a vacuum. Energy danced around Darcy's hand like dust mites in a beam of sunlight. Darcy jerked and nearly stumbled.

Axel reached across his sister and grabbed her shoulders to steady her.

Hannah's seizure slowed and stopped.

"Darcy, your hand!" His mom cried.

Axel looked down at her hand still on Hannah's chest. The skin had turned dark and grayish. Her fingers looked swollen and misshapen. As he watched, they pulsed as if some living thing was snaking under the skin.

Darcy met his gaze, her mouth tight. "It's the death curse. I'm pulling out what I can reach without a spell."

Her voice was tight and breathy. How much pain was she in doing this? How much pain was Hannah enduring?

"The convulsions are over, but she's getting sicker and . . ."

Her words cut off when the house went dark.

"Shit," Axel snarled. He snapped upright and grabbed his knife. "Mom, are you armed?"

"Yes."

Her voice was calm, hard.

"It's just a power outage." Darcy sounded scared.

He moved to the door, keeping his mom, Hannah, and Darcy behind him. "Generator would have kicked on. It's rogues, they've found us. Darcy, pick up Hannah."

"Got her."

"Get behind me, Mom, bring . . ." An explosion rocked the front of the house followed by glass shattering. "Follow me!" He turned right into the hall.

A rogue armed with a gun swerved into the hallway and cut off their escape. Axel reacted instantly, throwing his knife into the man's chest. The rogue hit the ground.

Hannah started to cry.

Axel ignored her, took a step, and yanked his knife out of the body. Then he grabbed the rogue's gun, a Glock, and turned in time to shoot a second rogue skidding around the corner.

Hannah screamed, then cried out, "I want Minnie!"

"Hush, baby," Darcy said.

Axel felt the push of her powers as she charmed Hannah into silence. "Get downstairs!" He quickly turned into the kitchen to provide cover while they ran into his room and downstairs to escape. His senses were on high alert. He could see in the dark and his hearing was better than ever. He estimated there were four rogues coming into the house.

The kitchen was clear.

He looked at the living room and spotted two more stealthily making their way through the big hole that had been blown where his front door used to be. Moving silently, he turned to kill the bastards that threatened his family.

Terror pounded viciously against Darcy's rib cage. Hannah clung to her neck and had her legs wrapped around her waist. She clutched the railing as she hurried down the stairs.

Gunfire erupted upstairs.

Hannah sobbed, but didn't scream.

"Darcy, hurry to the end of the hall!" Eve said behind her.

She rushed to the end. The walls were beige and the mirror Axel had told her about was hanging at the end. It looked lonely and out of place there. She put her hand up against it.

The wall at the end started to glide open.

Eve slipped past her, going up into the garage. "There's five steps up, Darcy. No lights. Follow me."

The garage was dark, cold, and smelled of oil and leather. Thin lines of light came in from the far wall, leading Darcy to believe it was actually a garage door. Combined with the light spilling out from the hallway, she could make out a three-car garage. She followed Eve's dark shape.

Her knee smashed into something cold and hard. Pain shot through her kneecap and froze her. Biting her lip, she managed to keep from crying out.

Hannah squeezed her harder, whimpering.

Darcy shifted the sweaty girl and freed one hand to touch whatever she'd smacked into. A car. Big enough to be an SUV. She'd hit the driver's-side fender. Carefully, she went around to where Eve waited.

Quietly, Eve opened the door to the backseat.

Darcy set Hannah inside.

Hannah started to squirm and protest.

"Shh, Hannah." Darcy climbed in and put her arm around the trembling child. The smell of leather was stronger in the SUV.

Eve quietly closed the door. Then she got in the driver's seat and the door locks engaged. "Keep Hannah down."

She laid Hannah on the seat with the girl's head in her lap and worked to keep feeding her calming energy. No child should be this terrified.

Eve started the car, put it in gear, and hit a button that raised the garage door.

Darcy held her breath as the door rolled up. The SUV lurched forward and slid out of the garage. Just as they turned left to edge around the front of the house, two rogues with guns ran toward them. They both fired at the car.

A bullet tore through the front windshield and another one went through Darcy's window. She pitched her body over Hannah to protect her from broken glass.

A tire blew out. Eve lost control of the SUV. Two more tires were shot out.

It was happening so fast!

The rogues closed in, their pale faces looming in the headlights, huge hairless arms holding guns pointed at them while they stalked the car.

Panic clawed at her. She didn't want to die! But worse, a million times worse, was the chance that Hannah and Eve might be killed. "I can hold them off, Eve. You and Hannah get to Axel's truck! Hurry."

"But . . ."

"Go! Go out the passenger side and grab Hannah!"

Darcy took a deep breath. She could do this. Axel would save her.

Or she would die.

But she couldn't let Hannah die. It was Darcy the rogues wanted. She took a deep breath and tried to calm her panic and focus her energy. Then she said, "Ancestors protect us." She grabbed the handle, shoved open the door, and jumped out. She raced a few feet toward the house and looked back.

The three rogues looked at her, then looked at Eve dragging Hannah out of the SUV and running toward Axel's truck. She needed them all to want her.

Crave her.

Blood! She frantically searched the ground. Spotting a fragment blown out from the front of the house, she scooped up a long chunk of wood with a jagged tip. Glancing up, she saw one rogue had grabbed Eve, who was struggling to get to her gun while holding Hannah.

No time to think. Darcy jammed the piece of wood into the inside of her left arm and dragged it up her elbow. The pain bloomed hot and fierce. Blood welled up and spilled over her arm. She held it up and yelled, "Hey! Witch blood! Come and get it!"

The rogue holding Eve turned his head.

Eve shot him point-blank in the stomach. Hannah screamed, a high-pitched sound of sheer mindless terror.

The other two rogues turned toward Darcy and inhaled. Their entire attention focused on her.

Then they disappeared.

Holy shit! She knew they were running at her, but she couldn't see them. Her heart beat frantically, her lungs burned. She turned to run toward the house. Toward Axel.

Behind her, she heard the truck roar to life and peel out.

She raced to the steps, reaching out a hand to grab the

rail, when the smell of copper made the hair on the back of her neck stand up.

A hand grabbed her outstretched arm, jerking her to a halt. Both rogues appeared at the same time. The one that had grabbed her yanked her other arm behind her back, immobilizing her. "Cut her!"

The second rogue had a silver knife the size of a cop's nightstick. It flashed so fast, it took a second for her brain to register the cuts—first a razor-sharp slash on her left bicep, followed by one on her right thigh.

Then came the shock of pain. Her eyes burned with tears. She tried to fight them, kicking out blindly.

That knife flashed again, a third cut, this time through her shirt to her side. Warm blood flowed everywhere. The burning pain rushed along her nerves and cut off her concentration.

The stench of copper made her stomach heave.

Her chakras closed up as she lost the connection with her powers.

The first rogue picked her up and threw her over his shoulder. Then he broke into a run.

In her mind, she screamed, *Axel!*

The screech of a hawk answered.

The gunshot to his left thigh slowed Axel down and really pissed him off. He'd killed the bastard who'd shot him then fought through two more, killing them, too.

He heard Darcy's scream rip through his chest and guts.

Racing through the big gaping hole where the front door used to be, he rushed to the balcony in time to see two rogues running down the road with her. His truck was gone, his leg was bleeding and weak, but he didn't even pause. Putting one hand on the rail, he leapt over.

His hawk screeched again.

In a blinding instant of confusion, wings burst free of

his back and spread to catch the wind currents. He was jerked from a jump that should have landed him on his feet into a horizontal position.

Axel was so shocked, he damn near slammed face-first into the ground. But the muscles in his back, chest, and abdomen reacted, flapping his wings until he rose from the ground.

He was fucking flying! He soared with powerful sweeps of his wings, but stayed low enough to use the copper scent to guide him. He saw his two security guys, mortals, dead on the ground, and farther up the road he spotted his truck hauling ass. He was relieved to see a head that looked like his mom's through the back wind-shield. She must have gotten away with Hannah.

Now for the bastards that had his witch. He spotted them loping down the road, easily going twenty miles an hour. The biggest one had Darcy clamped over his shoulder.

Mine! Instinct had him bank his wings into a dive. He saw the blood on the side of Darcy's shirt and his mind went red with rage.

She twisted her head, angling to look up at him. Her brown eyes widened in shock, and he could see the ripple in her dulled witch-shimmer.

Thirty feet away.

Twenty.

Ten feet away when the hunter who was holding Darcy looked up.

Axel shifted in the wind currents so that he slammed his boots directly into the bastard's face, instantly snap-ping his neck. Then he landed on the ground and caught Darcy as she fell.

The other rogue turned with a roar.

Axel set Darcy on her feet, folding his wings into his back, and stalked toward him.

The rogue attacked, going for Axel's heart with his knife.

Axel kicked the knife from his hand with a bone-crunching roundhouse.

The rogue grabbed his injured hand, but his gaze landed on Darcy. He bellowed and started running toward her, pulled by the fierce craving.

Axel slammed into his back, knocking him to the ground before he could reach Darcy. He jammed his knee into the man's back, grabbed his head and twisted viciously, snapping his neck.

The rogues were dead. Darcy was safe for the moment. Rising, he strode to where she stood frozen. Her witch-shimmer was the color of soured milk. Blood flowed from several wounds. And yet she cried out, "Your thigh! Are you shot?"

He stopped in front of her long enough to say, "Yes." Then he scooped her up in his arms. "Put your arms around my neck."

"Your leg hurts!"

She could feel it, damn it. "Close it off, Darcy. Are my mom and Hannah in my truck?" He wasn't exactly sure how the flying thing worked, so instead he strode down the road to where the rogues had parked their cars to attack on foot.

"Yes. They got away, but I don't know where they'll go. Put me down."

Once he reached the cars, he tried the doors until one on the black Chevy S10 opened. Popping the remaining lock, he walked around and settled Darcy into the passenger seat.

She looked up at him. "You had wings. Where did they go?"

Yanking off his shirt, he saw that it had a rip in the back where his wings had burst through. "Hell if I know. How many cuts?" He tore the shirt into strips and quickly tied one around her arm. Left bicep. He knew the next cut would be right thigh. Then the trunk of her body, most likely her side, judging from the blood on her white shirt. They did it that way, cuts on different points of the body, to confuse the body and disconnect the witch's powers.

"Three cuts from the rogues and one I did myself."

He grabbed the edges of her jeans to rip it apart so he could see the cut. Her words sunk in and he looked up. "You cut yourself?"

Her eyes were dry and haunted. "I had to. They were going after your mom and Hannah. But it's me they wanted."

She'd turned herself into witch-blood bait! "You . . ." He couldn't even say it. Un-fucking-real. He wrapped her thigh then lifted her shirt. That wound went a little deeper. The bloodlust frenzy had been taking hold. It's a wonder they hadn't fallen on her right then. The thought made him sick.

"Axel, your thigh is worse than these cuts."

Her powers kept trying to reach out to him, then falling away. Despite her own hurt, she wanted to take away his pain. "Stop, Darcy. I don't feel pain like you do. You feel it vividly. To me, it's just irritating. Don't waste your powers on me. I want you to concentrate on healing yourself."

"Is that true?"

He didn't smell any more rogues, but it was still dangerous to stay out in the open. And yet, he took the time to lean in and touch his mouth to hers. "Yes, I swear. We're meant to handle physical pain." But he wasn't built to handle seeing her in pain. He knew the cuts hurt her badly enough that she couldn't get her chakras to stay open so she could establish a connection. He could feel her power rise, then slip away. He took the last strip and wrapped it around the jagged wound that obviously hadn't been caused by a sharp knife. "What did you do this with?"

"A broken piece of the house."

Christ, she was brave. Her pain was dotting her witch-shimmer with red. He tied it off, then took hold of her face. "Look at me."

She lifted her gaze to his.

"Breathe Darcy. In and out. Follow me." He took in a breath.

So did she.

He exhaled softly.

Darcy did the same.

Their breathing fell into sync and her heart rate calmed. "Perfect. Now open your chakras and connect to your powers. Go with it Darcy, let the powers have you."

Her witch-shimmer slowly warmed from sour milk to a more natural tone. "That's it. I want you to lay your head back and rest now. I'm going to get us out of here." He closed the door, went around to the driver's side, and climbed in.

Darcy said softly, "Your tat looks the same. Your back looks the same." She ran her fingers lightly over the hawk.

He felt the feathers ruffle and preen. Looking over at her, he was surprised to see her witch-sheen getting brighter. "You feel better touching my hawk?"

She dropped her hand. "I . . . yes." She looked at the steering wheel, then frowned. "How are you going to start the truck?"

Shit. He'd have to go back and search the dead rogues to find the keys. He reached over to open the door and said, "I'll be right back."

"No! Tell me how to do it."

Her fear stirred his tat. Axel shut the door, reached

out, and took her hand. "It's okay, I won't leave you."
He told her how to direct her powers to start the truck.

She focused her energy, and he felt the hum travel
through him as the truck rumbled to life.

He kept hold of her hand, still awed by what she had
done. "You saved my mom and sister's lives."

Her eyes filled with tears. "I didn't know what else to
do. I knew you'd try and rescue me. You need me to
undo the curse."

"I need you. Period."

19

Darcy took in the huge warehouse located next to Axel's club. Three excessively large men stood behind the man she recognized as Sutton. They all turned to watch as she and Axel walked in. Axel had his arm around her and his knife in his hand. "Where's Mom and Hannah?"

Sutton rose from the keyboard slowly, with his hands in clear view. "Easy, Axel. They're upstairs in your condo. Eve told us you were attacked and the rogues got Darcy. Obviously you got her back." He shifted his gaze to her. "Relax, I'm not going to hurt you, Darcy."

"Me either," said the one with the military-short haircut and blue eyes. "I'm Ram."

"Not really feeling it. I can smell the witch blood but it's just a buzzing feeling, not pain," said the man dressed all in leather. "I'm Phoenix," he added.

"So this is the witch chick." The last man was the smallest. His spiky blond hair caught the overhead lights as he took three steps toward her.

Fear washed through her. She didn't know what to expect from these witch hunters.

"Key," Axel warned, then his body jerked and a whoosh filled the room.

Darcy felt the feathers explode past her, then curl protectively around her shoulder; the tips rested against her cheek.

Axel had sprouted wings. Again.

Key stopped short, his gray eyes taking in the entire wingspan.

The other three men moved closer behind Key.

"Holy shit, Axel," Phoenix said. "Forget to tell us something?"

Darcy looked up at his face. A fleeting surprise softened his features. "Hell of a night." Axel pulled her tighter into his side, his left wing curling in a little more. "None of you are feeling the bloodlust?"

Sutton shrugged. "No more than usual. Not the spike and pain we get when there's a witch around, particularly a witch with drying blood on her clothes."

Key dragged his gaze from the wings. "I wasn't threatening your witch. Just getting closer to see her."

"When did you get wings?" Ram asked.

"When the rogues grabbed Darcy—I leaped off a balcony and found out I could fly." Axel's voice was flat.

Phoenix moved around Axel's side, then returned to the front. "That's fucked up."

Key slammed his elbow into his ribs. "Language, dumb ass."

Phoenix looked at her and grinned. "Oops. But wings? Real fucking wings? What's that about?"

The boyish grin on the man with death-dark eyes wearing black leather and never-met-a-rule-he-didn't-want-to-break attitude surprised a smile out of her.

Axel seemed to ease a notch. He shifted beside her, sliding his knife into the holster at his back. "The wings didn't come with an owner's manual."

"Never heard of a witch hunter getting real wings," Sutton said.

"Things change. Ever since the curse, everything has changed."

"They are hawk wings," Key pointed out. "They match

your tattoo exactly. You're not immortal, no thumb ring that I can see. Any appearances from the Wing Slayer?"

"No."

Darcy could feel Axel's confusion mixed with deep anger over the attack, and hope. She also felt the gruff affection in the room; these men were clearly family to Axel, like Eve and Hannah. Softly, she broke in. "Can you control the wings? Put them away?"

He looked down at her, his green eyes full of curiosity. "I didn't try to make them come out. They just did."

"Because you thought I was threatening her," Key said.

Her stomach clenched. She wasn't controlling his wings, she couldn't be. She hadn't called them out, had she? "Please, Axel, try."

"Okay, you'll need to move. I don't want to hit you."

She didn't want to step out of the embrace of his hawk. The feel of the soft feathers touching her made the night bearable. But she had to prove to herself that she hadn't done this to him. That she hadn't turned him into a familiar. She forced herself to move toward the men, but stood off to the side. Alone.

Axel turned and took a couple steps to his right, closer to the pool table.

"Damn," Key said. "Look at that."

Darcy couldn't look away. The wings jutted out where his shoulder blades were, huge and majestic, while all the muscles of his neck, shoulders, and the torso below his wings corded and rippled with incredible strength. There was no sign of the tattoo.

"Move the wings," Ram suggested.

Axel fisted his hands on his hips; the wings did a slow flap, fanning the room with their powerful sweep. Then the wings lifted high, folded, and melted into his skin as his hawk tatoo.

She swallowed down her relief. She wasn't controlling

his wings, she was sure of it. The room echoed in silence. Everything had happened so fast, Darcy could hardly catch her breath. With Axel's help, she'd managed to heal her cuts most of the way, and get the bullet out of his leg while he was driving. But she was sore and drained. Finally she broke the silence with an inane question. "Do you all live here?"

"Nah." Phoenix snapped out of his shock the quickest. "We have homes, but we hang here if we're not busy. I was out with a pretty woman when I got the call to get my ass to the warehouse."

His leather vest left miles of massive arm bare. She was relieved to see the coarse hair on his forearms, and the large wing tattooed over each bicep. "I see."

"We thought we were going to have to go after you, Darcy," Ram explained. "But Axel got the job done."

Stunned, Darcy looked around at all the men watching her. "You would have rescued me? But—"

"Bet your ass we would've," Phoenix said. "First off, Hannah needs you. Second, I hate rogues. No rogue snatches a witch under our protection. Not happening. Got me?"

She blinked. She'd been so scared when the rogue had had her. She'd prayed Axel could save her, but it hadn't occurred to her that these men, these witch hunters struggling with the blood curse, would try and save her. "Thank you," she said, feeling overwhelmed. The only other person she'd ever been able to count on was Joe. Oh, God, Joe! "Axel! What if Joe and Morgan go back to the house?"

Axel strode to the men. "Give me a phone."

Key handed him a cell phone.

He walked it to her. "Call him."

"Thanks." She dialed Joe's number.

"MacAlister."

"Joe, it's Darcy. Don't go back to the house. We were attacked—"

"Slow down. Are you all right?"

"Yes. I had some cuts, but I'm alive. So is Axel. Can you stay with Carla? What if they go after her?" Tears started to well up in her throat.

Axel put his arm around her, and took the phone. "Joe, she's okay. Scared, a little hurt, but okay. Darcy has a point, though. I can't send a witch hunter to watch over Carla. And then there's Morgan."

Axel listened, his face hardening into grim lines.

"It's a strong possibility. This was a well-staged attack. Reed could have been behind it."

Axel listened then handed the phone back to her. Darcy took it. "Joe, please be careful."

"I will. Darce are you okay there? I'll come get you."

"I'm good here. I love you, Joe." She knew she was probably embarrassing him, but she didn't care.

"Back at you. But seriously, Darce, can you stay out of trouble for a while?"

She almost smiled. "Doubtful."

"Yeah, I figured. Later." She hung up. Axel and the men were talking, looking serious.

Sutton said, "I got the blueprints for your dad's place. I put them on the big screen when we were planning to rescue Darcy and possibly you. It was the most likely place we could think of to start searching. We were just starting to study them when you two came in."

They all looked up to the biggest screen in the bank of monitors. The computer-drafted blueprints showed a big house with an even bigger building behind it.

"These are the original blueprints." Sutton put another set of blueprints on a smaller screen.

"He expanded the building behind the house," Axel said.

"We know it used to be a veterinarian's office. I pulled

the notes from the architect. He had two barracks added on at the end," he said, using a laser pointer to show where the buildings were added on. "A control room wired for high-tech computers, then there's notes about a conference room, some smaller rooms, but the thing that really stood out . . ."

Axel tensed beside her. "What?"

"He kept and updated the surgery room and the kennels."

Darcy had no idea what it meant, but shivers ran down her spine.

Axel seemed to stop breathing. Then he said in a viciously cold voice, "He's building a compound to turn witch hunters rogue. The surgery room is to slaughter witches, the kennels are to hold the witches until they have the witch hunter they want to turn." His body vibrated with rage. "He's creating an army of rogues for Young."

Phoenix's boots rang out on the concrete as he stalked closer and stared up at the blueprint. "Eric Reed would want in on that action."

Darcy's chakras flung open. Power surged up through her first four and slammed into the power rushing down through her fifth chakra. The power spun around her spine and voices pounded and screamed at a spot in the middle of her forehead.

"Feel that?" Key said. "Axel, your witch is doing something."

"Her power is surging through the room," Phoenix added.

She heard them talking but she shut her eyes against pain and dizziness.

"Darcy!" Axel grabbed her chin. "Look at me."

She couldn't. She kept her eyes closed as the vortex spun harder in a crazy-eight pattern around her spine. The pressure intensified inside her, compressing painfully against the center of her forehead. Then it suddenly burst, blowing open her sixth chakra.

Fallon appeared. She was lying on the ground with blood running from shallow cuts on her arms and legs. Pain-etched lines around her full mouth; her hair was caked with blood and grime. She was in a graveyard, illuminated by a full moon shining down on huge crumbling headstones rising out of unkept grass.

Quinn Young stood over her with a gleaming silver knife in his hand. "Your tricks are worse than the demon witches'. They made me want sex. But you, you used something else, you made me want something that isn't real."

Fallon met his gaze. "It would be real if you hadn't gone rogue and lost your soul. I would have cared for you, loved you and our child."

Quinn Young's smooth feminine features twisted into a haunted expression. "Witches, you're all liars."

"Yet you can't kill me."

"Tell me where the baby is!" he snarled.

"Our daughter is dead. Stillborn."

Young crouched down. "Liar." He slashed the knife across Fallon's still-swollen abdomen.

Her mother screamed in a cracked voice. "She's dead!"

Young put his hand in the warm blood, closing his eyes, absorbing power. "This is real. Power is real. I have enough witch blood to summon Asmodeus."

"No," Fallon whispered.

Young kept his hand in Fallon's blood, leaned back and said, "Asmodeus, demon of lechery, jealousy, anger, and revenge, appear! I summon thee from the Underworld by the blood of a witch! Appear!"

The earth trembled, then a hole burst open in the ground, and a dark form slithered up and took shape, three heads on a large body. The smell of burned skin mixed with sulfur.

"Asmodeus," Quinn said reverently. "You honor me by appearing."

The demon spoke. "The daughter lives. Somewhere. Kill this witch and find the child."

Young, still crouched, shifted his gaze to Fallon.

She looked back at him. "Feel inside you, Quinn. You can still make the right choice. Let me go, let your daughter and me live, and the better part of you will live on in your child."

"Choose." The demon's voice crackled through the graveyard, making the trees sway and cast bony-fingered shadows. "The power of the Immortal Death Dagger is yours if you kill the witch. You'll be able to kill even an immortal with the dagger." The three heads talked as one, then raised one hand holding a black knife the size of a man's forearm.

"Ancestors protect us," Fallon began to chant in a whisper.

One of the three heads turned to look at Fallon, while the other two watched Quinn. "They don't hear her, do they, Quinn?"

He stared at the black knife moving as though it were alive. Writhing in the thick fingers of the demon. "No, you destroyed the Ancestors and the Wing Slayer. That's real power."

"Take my knife. Kill her."

Quinn's eyes filled with greed, the pupils dark with lust as he looked at the knife. "What's the cost?"

"Three things. You raise an army, lead them, and kill the witches. You find the girl witch you sired and kill her. Kill any witch hunter who takes wings or they could resurrect that half-breed god, Wing Slayer, and challenge our power."

Young looked down at Fallon then up at the gleaming

black death dagger. Then he chose. With inhuman speed, he grabbed the black dagger and stabbed Fallon.

Darcy heard screams.

"I've got you, come back now."

She felt Axel's arms around her, her face buried against the hot skin of his chest. Her raw throat told her she'd been screaming. Her head throbbed as if she'd been stabbed with the dagger. Axel ran his hand over her back. She couldn't hold still and realized she was shaking violently.

"Quinn Young summoned Asmodeus with my mother's blood. He killed her and now he has the Immortal Death Dagger."

"The attack tonight on my safe house wasn't my dad's gig," Axel said. He had gotten Darcy settled in his condo, set her up with his computers to talk to Carla, then went back down to the warehouse. "It was carefully set up. They knocked out our power and our backup generators. They had a plan."

"Eric Reed," Phoenix said.

"Where's Quinn Young?" Ram asked. "What triggered Darcy's vision with your dad's house? Is she connecting Young to the house?"

Key said, "Darcy's vision must be a warning that Quinn Young has the Immortal Death Dagger."

"We aren't immortal, a regular knife can kill us," Phoenix pointed out.

"Axel has wings, immortality might be next," Key answered.

They all looked at him. Axel rubbed his neck. "I don't know. I don't fucking know. But Darcy's vision tells us that Young is more dangerous with that Death Dagger, able to kill an immortal now. We know Young's the one calling the shots. Maybe my dad took Reed as a partner at Young's direction."

"Could be," Sutton said. "But I'm wondering why you haven't heard from your dad since the cut-up witches in the Hummer?"

Axel frowned, trying to make sense of it all. "You think he's dead?"

"I think it's possible there's been a hostile takeover by Eric Reed. In the last day or two, the path I used to hack into the Rogue Cadre computers has been cut off. New security is in place."

Axel reached for his cell, flipped through the numbers, and called his dad.

It went straight to voice mail. His phone was off.

"I think you need more from your witch. She's having visions and shit. Show her the blueprints again."

Axel turned to look at Key. "She needs to save her strength to heal Hannah."

Key nodded. "Got that. Hannah was terrified when she and your mom arrived, and she looked bad. Pale, shaking, sweaty. The waxing gibbous is three days away. So when is Darcy going to do the spell?"

"She'll try tomorrow at moonrise. On a beach; she says she needs to be at the edge of the ocean for better access to the ley lines." Darcy was exhausted and sore, and he knew her head still hurt. But she was trying to reach the Ancestors. His hawk wings were fretting in his tattoo, not liking being this far away from her. The feeling created an itching sensation that only Darcy's touch could ease.

"If the spell works, then what?" Phoenix asked. "You'll keep the witch around?"

Axel dropped his cell and turned to fix his gaze on Phoenix. He sat in a chair, his long legs stretched out, peeling an orange with his knife. "I'm not throwing her to the rogues. And there's going to be a pissed-off demon witch looking for her."

While still stripping the rind, Phoenix said, "Your

wings sprang out when Darcy was in danger, and now you're talking like you can't walk away from her. It's as if you are bonded to her in the way of a familiar."

Axel measured the man with his eyes. "I'm protecting her in the way of a Wing Slayer Hunter."

Slowly, Phoenix lifted his gaze. "All I'm saying is that we are in uncharted territory and we'd better have our priorities clear. No matter how hot, I won't let this witch use Hannah's life for her own agenda; for instance, to regain power lost by the curse."

That sliced through him. Darcy wasn't using him like that, but he recognized that the men who were protecting Eve, Hannah, and now Darcy, had a right to make sure he had his head on straight. "Hannah is my priority."

"Thought so." The bounty hunter tossed the rind into a trash can.

Darcy sat on the floor in the middle of Axel's sleek modern office at the front of his condo. On her left was a mahogany desk with a black lacquered top. On her right were two sleek black leather recliner-and-ottoman sets. Above those was a large flat-screen where Carla was projecting her image and watching as Darcy tried meditation to open her sixth chakra.

"You're resisting; afraid of what you'll see. Or maybe you're worrying about doing the spell tomorrow. You have to block it all out."

She opened her eyes and looked at her friend on the screen. "I'm trying. I can hear the voices but just can't reach them." Hell yeah, she was afraid. She had seen her father murder her mother for possession of a demonic knife. "I can't control it. What if the third eye shows me something else horrible?"

Carla's face softened. "You're doing great, Darcy. But the Circle Witches said you have to get past the fear."

"Easy for them to say. They're afraid of me. Tell them to get past their own fears."

"Darcy," Carla said, "I know it seems cruel, but they have to be careful. However, they do want to help you heal Hannah. They will gather at moonrise tomorrow and send as much of their energy to you as possible to help with the spell."

"Thank you," she said tightly, then asked, "Did the Circle Witches say anything about soul mirrors?"

"They don't know the answer. And not understanding what your bond is with your hunter, they are being cautious. But they did say that if you open your sixth chakra and talk directly to the Ancestors, they'll be happy to bring you into the Circle."

That burned in her stomach. They'd accept her if the Ancestors did, but they didn't hold any other witches to that standard. Darcy pulled her knees up beneath her chin. "And what if I've bound Axel to me? Is that okay with them?"

"They swear you can't bind him as a familiar."

"Yeah? He has wings, Carla. Do the Circle Witches remember any other witch hunter having wings?" Tears filled her throat. After her vision, Axel had lifted her up and carried her to his big marble bathroom and put her in a giant spa tub with him. He'd touched each of her still-healing wounds, drawing her powers to his touch so that she'd finish healing. He made her feel cared for and safe.

And it was all probably a lie.

Soul mirrors. He hadn't agreed to anything, he'd just had sex with her. How was that an agreement?

Her throat hurt.

"Darcy."

Not Carla this time, but Axel. He'd walked in with his eerie quietness and now he filled up the room. She lifted her chin off her knees. "What's up?"

He crouched down. "You're tired."

"I need to talk to the Ancestors." She had to know.

"For the spell?"

"Yes. I can't do the spell without them." That was true. If she could reach the Ancestors, they would help her heal Hannah.

He took hold of her elbows and pulled her to her feet while saying, "I was with you the first time your third eye opened, maybe you can do it with me close to you." Then he turned to Carla on the screen. "I've got a witch hunter outside your house tonight. He won't come in, he won't be that close. But he's there if something happens."

Darcy turned her head and felt her heart twist. "Who?"

"Sutton. Joe already knows. We're not taking any chances."

He was guarding the people she loved. "Thanks."

He put his arm around Darcy. "Say good night. We're going to bed."

"I have to work on opening my chakra."

"You will open for me, little witch. Trust me." He pulled her out of the room.

She heard Carla's choked laughter.

Darcy let him pull her into his bedroom, then he walked across the room to a nightstand and pressed a button. A whirling sound engaged and the blackout drapes along an entire wall parted to reveal floor-to-ceiling windows.

Moonlight spilled through and illuminated a bed draped in a dark burgundy comforter.

Awed, she said, "It's beautiful. You live here?"

"Usually." He walked back to her and used both hands to brush her hair back off her face. "Use your powers, take off your clothes."

His abruptness surprised her.

And excited her, damn it.

Still touching her face, he added, "Honey, you've tried it your way. I can see the strain in your eyes and feel it in your unfocused powers. Trust me, Darcy. Let me help you open your sixth chakra." He stepped back and pulled off his shirt.

His huge shoulders and chest filled up her vision.

Then he kicked off his shoes and yanked down his jeans and boxers.

Clothed, Axel looked strong and amazing. But naked he took her breath away.

"Do it, Darcy."

She closed her eyes, calling her roaming powers back to her and magically sliding her clothes from her body to a neatly folded pile on the floor.

When she opened her eyes, Axel stared at her with fire in his green eyes. He reached out and took her hand, drawing her to the window side of the bed. He sat down and pulled her down on his lap, her back to him, her front to the moonlight. She looked out the window, seeing the outline of the buildings against the night sky, but—

"No one can see in. The windows are specially made." He said it against her ear, making her shiver. "Lean back against me, close your eyes, and feel the moonlight."

She felt him, felt his rock hard thighs beneath her, his already hard dick pressing against her, his large hands anchored on her waist, and his breath touching her skin. But Axel was right about one thing—her powers responded to him. He could help her; but she had to tell him. "I'm afraid of what I'll see. What if I can't control it?" She didn't want to see her mother murdered again.

She felt a ripple of something go through him. He lifted a hand to her forehead, tilting her back to look down into her eyes. "I'll try to direct you. But I need to get into your mind and we both know how that happens. Once I'm there and your chakra opens, you can tell me what you're seeing and I'll pull you out if it's wrong."

He was protecting her. Helping her. She faced the window and leaned back into his chest.

Axel slid his hands down her sides to her thighs, pulling them wide. "I want you to feel the moonlight, let it feed you. Here." He moved his hands again, cupping her breasts from beneath, and lifting them like an offering.

Her powers rushed and bubbled while the moonlight caressed her nipples and she began to fill with incredible energy as her chakras fed from the moonlight and other elements. Her breasts swelled, her stomach clutched.

"Oh, yeah, Christ, I can feel you responding. The scent of your desire . . ." He leaned down, caressing her shoulder with his mouth and tongue, biting gently.

Each and every nerve ending came to life. She shifted and moved, and reached for his wrist, tugging his hand down to where she burned for his touch.

His laugh was dark and sensual, tumbling through her insides. "Greedy little witch." He teased her by trailing a hand down her stomach then back up.

Two could play this game. She shifted, ready to turn and straddle him.

He anchored an arm around her waist, pinning her to him. "Open up, Darcy. Pull me in." He skimmed his hand down her belly, reaching down until he separated her folds. "You're so wet, so swollen," he whispered.

She thrust against his hand, needing more from him. The ache between her legs began to build and cause more pressure all the way up through her chakras. A heaviness formed between her eyes. *I feel something.*

Don't think about it. Think about the moonlight, and this . . . he slid one finger inside of her.

She arched back, her body responding, her mind absorbing him.

Christ, you're pulling me in. His breath went hot and heavy, his arm around her tightened as he slid in a second finger.

He knew her rhythm, pumping into her, his thumb teasing her clit.

The pressure grew where he touched her, and raced through her chakras. She was losing herself . . .

I'm here, I've got you, let it happen.

His mouth was hot and wet on her neck, his words in her head, his fingers stroking her, the moonlight filling her, until she exploded. Ripped apart by hot silvery pleasure, the pressure between her eyes blew open.

She couldn't get her breath.

Go with it honey, keep going.

She kept riding the silver light of pleasure so intense that she grew scared.

Hawk wings wrapped around her, soothing her and making her feel safe.

Open, Darcy. Open your third eye.

Darcy opened her eyes but her regular vision was gone. It was her third eye that took over. This time it didn't hurt. Her mind filled with formless shapes of light. Bright and warm entities that she wanted to get closer to. *Ancestors.*

Go to them.

A chorus of voices said, "You hear us."

"Yes."

"You did it, Darcy. We're so proud of you."

"Axel and his hawk helped." The thought brought her back to what she needed. "We need your help. I beg you. To save Hannah."

"Do the spell and call on us. We'll reach you through your blood. Don't forget the blood, whole soul blood, Darcy."

Relief poured over her. "Thank you. I don't know the rules, can I ask more questions?"

"Yes, but we can't answer all of them. You only have a short time. You're using powerful high magic."

She got to the point. "Did I bind Axel? Are we soul mirrors?"

"Yes. All hunter and witch souls were merged and halved at the curse. Soul mirrors are the two halved souls finding each other. If blood and sex are exchanged, the two souls bond as one and break the curse."

Darcy had already known it. She'd known it on some level since the night she'd attempted to call her familiar.

Axel had answered the call.

Fighting her emotions to keep her third eye open, she asked what it meant. "Is Axel a familiar?"

"No." The souls moved and shimmered on a plane of existence she couldn't quite understand. "A soul mirror is not a familiar. He mirrors and channels your powers, and you do the same for him. It was your desperate call to him tonight that brought out his wings. You mirror each other's strengths. He's protection, and you are healing."

Did it matter what they called it? "I want to know if I have taken away Axel's self-control. His choice. His free will to do as he chooses." She couldn't live with that.

The voices answered, "No. The witch hunter is free. He can walk away from you. He'll be cured of his bloodlust. He won't fall in love with anyone else. He'll always be missing half his soul. He won't be fulfilled, but he can live his life any way he chooses."

She wanted to feel relief. She could tell Axel that, she could make him believe he wasn't a familiar. But her stomach hurt with the fear of him rejecting her. "What about his hawk?"

"If he rejects you, the hawk will die off. He'll be a man, a very strong man with unusual abilities. Enhanced eyesight, hearing, the ability to turn invisible . . . all of it. But he won't have wings."

He won't be an animal. He'll be a man. But . . . "What about his soul? If he kills a demon witch, will he lose his soul?"

"That we can't answer. It's time for you to go."

"But—" Everything faded to a white mist and she had the sensation of sliding through a long tunnel. Time lost meaning as she moved through warm fog that made her think of the Ancestors' love, until it gave way to the hard security of Axel's arms. Her third eye closed, and she could see with her regular vision once more.

Axel had moved her so that she was sitting sideways, and he held her against him. She realized that his hawk's wings were surrounding her. Had she brought out his wings?

He looked down at her face and answered, "You got scared; I knew my wings would make you feel safe." He lifted them off her and folded them until they melted and formed back into his tattoo.

Talk about powerful magic. But would he accept it as his own? She couldn't risk finding out yet. The stakes were too high. "I talked to the Ancestors."

"I know. I couldn't hear it, but I felt the light of them filling your body."

"They'll help me. Tomorrow at moonrise, I can heal Hannah."

His face shifted into relief, then tensed with worry. "Will you be safe doing it? Asmodeus wants you."

"I didn't ask them that. But I'll use a salt circle, it'll be safe enough. And blood, they reminded me that I will need my blood to bring them into the spell." They'd said whole soul blood, and now that she understood that she and Axel were two halves of a whole soul, that meant her blood was whole soul blood.

He kept his gaze on her face. "What are you not telling me?"

Suspicion coated his words, made the air between them heavy. "I wasn't there that long, was I?" She'd lost all sense of time.

"Few minutes." He ran his hand up her arm, studying her skin. "Your witch-shimmer went brilliant, nearly blinding white while you talked to them. Now it's dull and your powers are backing away. You're upset and withdrawing from me."

She was, she realized. Like a coward. Because he could hurt her, she was backing away. It disgusted her when Axel was doing everything he was capable of to help her do the spell. He hadn't even freaked about the hawk wings. Instead, he'd used them to comfort her.

She was tired of being afraid. Instead, she reached out with her powers and her hands to touch him. And then she put her heart and body into loving him. What she couldn't tell him with words, she told him with her soul.

20

Axel sat behind his desk in his condo office. Setting his coffee cup down, he said, "No trouble at Carla's?"

Sutton leaned against a wall. "No, it was quiet."

"I don't like it," Phoenix said, popping open a can of Coke. "Reed should be looking for his wife. She's knocked up with his kid. He didn't kill her when he could have, so what's he doing?"

"Waiting. Patience. Strategy." Ram lifted his cup of coffee and drank.

Sutton turned to him and asked, "You try your dad's phone again?"

Axel nodded. It was an odd feeling to consider that his dad might be dead. For the first fourteen years of his life, he'd been okay. He wasn't always there, but when he was, he'd treated Axel all right. When he'd decided it was time for Axel to go rogue, that's when he had fully understood what his father was. Since then, Myles had been a menace that he'd fought constantly.

Now, was he really gone? Or was he playing another game?

Axel said, "And where is Quinn Young? He can't let the rogues find out he has a witch daughter. He's built his rep as a witch-hater, convincing his growing cadre that the witches must be killed to break the curse. Add to that the fact that Asmodeus ordered Young to kill Darcy, and it has me wondering—where the hell is Young?"

Pheonix said, "You think Young will make a move tonight when Darcy does the spell?"

Axel frowned. "It's possible."

Ram said, "We've got it covered. She'll be safe enough. It's a deserted stretch of beach, there's four excellent lookout places for Sutton, Key, Phoenix, and me. We'll be far enough away that the witchcraft shouldn't bother us. Joe will be right there and so will you. I've got a half dozen other witch hunters as backup."

He nodded. They'd been over the plan several times. Axel settled back into his chair. "Darcy said she'll set a salt circle and that the Circle Witches will add their powers, that should keep her safe from Asmodeus." He went on to the next problem. "What do we have on the demon witches?"

Sutton said in a tight voice, "Only one fits, the one named Linette Olsen. She has a twenty-two-year-old daughter who disappeared the same night Hannah was cursed."

"Good. Ram"—he turned to him—"find her. I need to know exactly where she is. Don't get too close, just find out where she is."

Ram studied Axel. "Do you think Darcy's spell will work?"

He hoped so. "She said it will. She reached her Ancestors and they said they would help. She'll bring them into the spell with her blood."

"Then what's worrying you?" Ram asked.

"She's not telling me something. Either way, I need to have a backup. If the spell doesn't work tonight, I'm going after the demon witch, Linette." He set his mug on the desk and looked up. "If that happens and I go rogue, all of you made a vow. I expect you to follow through on it. Clear?"

"Clear," Sutton spoke up.

Axel shifted in his chair. His hawk wing tat warmed but nothing else happened. Darcy had reached her Ancestors, but Axel had still fallen short. No Wing Slayer appearance.

Sutton pulled out a handheld device and keyed in some information. "I'm sending what I have on Linette to Ram's phone."

Ram nodded, rose, and set his empty mug on the desk. "Leaving now. I'll be back in a few hours." He strode out.

"Phoenix, you and Key see if you can get close to my dad's place, see what you can find."

"Can we kill rogues?"

The tattoo warmed again. "Yes. You find a rogue, kill him."

They walked out.

Axel turned to regard Sutton. "You're tied up in knots."

He lifted his blue eyes. "It's under control."

He was getting closer and closer to the edge. And something was tipping the balance. "You need a couple hours, go find some women friends, get some release."

Sutton started for the door then turned back and locked his gaze on Axel. "Last night, I couldn't get the picture of her, of Carla, out of my mind. I walked around the outside of that house and I could smell her. I went back to my car and I could still smell her. I can almost feel her on my skin."

Axel sat up. "Christ, why didn't you leave?"

He ran a hand over his face. "Because I might not be able to have her, but I sure as fuck won't let a rogue get her." Then he was gone.

Axel stared after his best friend; silently praying that

the Wing Slayer would not force him to follow through
on his vow.

But if Sutton went rogue, Axel would kill him.

Everything was ready. She had the items she'd need to
focus her elemental magic placed in four strategic points
on the sand. Darcy smelled the sea air and felt a measure
of calm.

She had to be calm. She had to be in control. She had
to heal Hannah.

Carla walked up to her. Her close-fitting dress was as
white as her hair. With the moon just beginning to rise,
she looked both sexy and ethereal.

She looked like a witch should.

Darcy didn't have many changes of clothing with her,
so Carla had brought her a dress, also white. Spaghetti
straps, soft lace at her breasts and at the hem. No shoes.

No underwear at all. Spell work required drawing
power through her chakras, and clothes could tangle up
the flow. So a simple dress worked best.

Some witches did spell work sky-clad. Darcy knew
once she was into the spell-casting, she wouldn't care.
But before and after, standing on a beach naked in front
of all the gathered people, such as her cousin Joe? She
didn't think so.

"Five minutes to moonrise," Carla said gently.

Darcy nodded. Carla was there to channel the energy
the Circle Witches were sending to support the spell. But
she was also there as her friend. They both turned to
look at Hannah.

Axel had his sister wrapped in a blanket and held her
in his arms. She was too weak to lift her head. She
coughed, her chest visibly contracting in pain. Axel
rubbed her back, his hand ridiculously huge against the
little girl.

Darcy looked at the two of them in the rising moonlight. Axel with his midnight-black hair, his bearing huge and fierce, cradling his blond little sister against his chest. It choked Darcy up and made her focus.

Whatever happened, healing Hannah was what mattered. When she told him later about the soul-mirror phenomenon, he might hate Darcy, might turn away from her, but she would have given him his sister's life. And made sure he kept his soul so he could stay around and protect Hannah and Eve, and lead the Wing Slayer Hunters.

He suddenly met her gaze then walked over to her. "What's wrong?"

She was projecting to him. Unconsciously. Their link kept strengthening. "Nothing. I'm focusing." She reached up to Hannah's face buried against Axel's neck. "I guess I was thinking how much I want this to work."

"It will work."

She nodded. "Yes. Are you okay?"

"Why wouldn't I be?"

"Carla's a witch. I wondered if you were feeling any bloodlust from her?"

He shook his head. "Nope. I can feel her, smell her, but it's just a buzzing. Now you." He dropped his gaze down her length and lowered his voice. "Your scent is tormenting me. No underwear?"

She couldn't help her body's instant reaction. "No."

He closed his eyes, color rising to crest his cheekbones.

She remembered what happened when she did the transfer of her mom's spells, and then when he'd helped her open her sixth chakra and talk to the Ancestors. "Axel, I need your help. But we have to stay in control. Your men are out there, far enough back so that Carla doesn't incite their bloodlust, but they swear they can see everything."

"They can." He touched her face and calmed the whirling energy in her chest.

She leaned into his hand, needing the center he gave her. She added, "Joe and Morgan are here, along with your mom, Carla, and Hannah."

"I'm here to protect you and Hannah, not ravish you. You do your work, and let me worry about everything else."

She nodded.

"Darcy."

She took a breath and met his stare.

"Don't fight it. You're a witch, which makes you a very sensual woman. Don't fight the sexual feelings when you open your chakras. Let them have you and know I'm standing right here with you. There's nothing embarrassing or wrong about it. It's part of your power. It's part of who you are."

He knew her so well. All the years she'd yearned for acceptance and she'd found it with a witch hunter. Unable to stop, she raised up on her bare toes in the damp sand to press her mouth to his. She just brushed his lips.

In return, she felt his wings brush her skin. His actual wings were resting in his tattoo, but she could always feel them through their mental link.

"It's time," Carla said.

Darcy turned to Carla and took her hands. "Thank you. You're more than my friend, you're my sister." They were bound as witches.

"Sisters," she agreed, kissed Darcy on the cheek, and moved to her place next to Hannah.

Axel walked to where Eve knelt on a blanket in the sand. He settled Hannah so that she sat leaning her back against Eve. "Is Darcy going to make me better now?"

"Yes, baby." He rose to his feet. The rising moon caught the blue-black of his hair.

As Darcy had requested, Axel stripped off his shirt

and laid it by Eve. His tat gleamed in the moonlight, the rich brown-and-gold feathers of the hawk looked vivid and real. She needed his hawk as close to her as possible.

Then he came to her. "Ready, witch?"

She nodded. The moonlight was caressing her skin, making her warm and full. Her first four chakras were opened already, her powers stirring and surging. Now it was time to gain control. Darcy turned to the ocean, lifting her arms to form a circle and said: "Pure in its whiteness, born of the earth, consecrated by the sea, feared by the dark, embraced by the light, salt rise and circle your protection."

She formed the circle in her mind.

A huge wave rose and slammed into the shore. A white line of chalky salt separated from the water, rising into the air and traveling in a straight line to the shore. Once there, the line of salt settled into a perfect circle around her, Axel, Eve, Hannah, and Carla.

Releasing a breath, she thanked the Ancestors for helping her set a protection circle to keep demons out. Her senses sharpened. The air was heavy with salt. Waves crashed and broke in a comforting rhythm. Hannah coughed. Eve breathed loudly. Carla chanted softly to establish her connection to the Circle Witches. And Axel stood behind Darcy, not yet touching her, but she could feel every beat of his heart.

Hannah coughed again and said, "Did you see, Mommy?"

She blocked out Hannah for now. She blocked everything but Axel behind her. The feel of his body, the smell of his skin, the pulse of his breath twining with hers. Even without his touch, their bodies fell into sync. It reassured her that he would know when she needed him.

Now to focus the first four chakras and connect them to the ley lines. She turned to face north and commanded, "Earth."

Sand swirled up into a funnel then poured itself in the red crockery dish sitting just inside the salt circle.

Darcy pivoted to face east, her arms wide and her spirit open. "Air."

The wind swirled her dress high on her thighs, caressing her skin, then rushed to fill the green balloon tied to a silver weight.

She turned to the west. "Water."

A wave rose from the sea, reaching higher and higher until the wall of water blocked off the moonlight.

Hannah began to cry.

Darcy ignored the child. Keeping her chakras open, she let the power of water reach into her. Her skin grew damp, her hair wet, her body fluid as though she were one with the wave.

Then the wave receded, allowing the moonlight to illuminate the water that filled the orange goblet.

Finally, she faced south. "Fire."

There was a hiss and crackle as the yellow candle in the gold holder flamed to life.

All four earth elements started to flow to her. Her pulse began to beat in her ears, thick with rising energy. Her breasts swelled until her nipples throbbed. Her hair lifted, filled with static.

Darcy closed her eyes, raised her arms, and opened her fifth chakra. This was where she would draw down the power of the moon to meet the ley lines running up through her. She arched, leaning back to allow the moonlight to touch as much of her as possible, and chanted softly, "Ancient as time, powerful as the sea, the moon is our source, let her light guide and fill me." The rays poured into her through her skin, filling her senses and creating a magnetic *pull* in her body. She would use that to draw up the elements of the earth.

Soon it was hard to breathe, and she began to ache. Her skin stretched.

Her feet began to tingle and warm. The earth was sharing more of her power! She'd tapped into the ley lines and could feel the thrumming energy rushing up.

Her thighs grew damp from a pulsing need. Even her womb throbbed, but she didn't let herself think about it. Just accepted as much as the moon and earth were willing to give her. She recalled Axel's words that her sensual nature was part of being a witch.

As she grew dizzy with the swirling, pulsing power, she felt Axel's warm hands settle on her waist. She steadied, drew in a breath, and then turned her mind inward; reaching for all that swirling power from the ley lines and the moon, and funneling it straight up through her chakras.

A low pressure pinged in her forehead. She closed her eyes and pushed the powers, just as Axel had done last night using sex. She built the pressure, adding more and more until the spot between her eyes felt like it was bulging.

She gave herself to it, to the earth and the moon and the Ancestors.

Her sixth chakra flew open and her powers started the crazy-eight pattern up, down, and around her spine.

Only Axel's hands held her upright. Concentrating, she slowly opened her eyes. But her regular eyes were blind now, and she saw only with her third eye.

Everything looked bright but blurry, like she was seeing through an aura of light. She couldn't see anything beyond the circle, it was all fog.

Her entire existence was in the circle.

She walked to Hannah and knelt.

Axel went with her, kneeling down so that his thighs cradled Darcy's body, his hands still on her waist. She felt his erection press against her back.

It fed her more strength. She didn't understand it, she simply accepted it.

Eve raised her hand and pushed back Hannah's bangs.

The spot stood out against all the beautiful white light like an angry black hole. It looked . . . lightless. Not the beautiful black of Axel's hair, but a dark, evil smudge.

Darcy blindly reached into the pocket of her dress and pulled out the small silver knife that Carla had given her. She pulled off the protective cover with an audible snap.

She raised her hand and pricked her right thumb. "With the blood of generations of witches, I beg the ancient souls for their healing and knowledge. Enrich my blood to chase out the darkness and heal the innocent Hannah Locke."

Darcy could see her blood welling up rich and red.

She touched her thumb to the death mark.

Axel brought his arms up to cradle her body and reached out to take one of Hannah's tiny hands in his fingers.

Darcy felt the jolt as her powers focused and channeled, reaching through her pricked thumb into Hannah. She chanted in a strong voice, "Ancestors, I beg you to heal this child. Moon Source, I beg you to heal this child. Earth, I beg you to heal this child. Sister witches, I beg you to heal this child."

Flashes of light came into existence, moving around the circle. Darcy silently thanked the Ancestors for lending their ancient strength.

The wind whipped up the sand. The ocean roared. Flames crackled on both sides of them.

Darcy chanted louder. Sending all the healing energy she had through her thumb into Hannah.

A dark ugliness began at the tip of her thumb, burrowing up past the first joint, then it slithered farther up her wrist.

The pain slammed into her, trying to cut off her energy and close her chakras. It hurt! It felt like her blood was starting to burn. Tears filled her eyes, blurring her vision. The agony wormed up her hand, fired through her arm, and clutched her chest.

Darcy forced herself to breathe while holding her chakras open to keep her connection with the moon, earth, and Ancestors. "I accept the pain. I accept the sickness," she said over and over. Her witch energy would break it down and expel it back into the atmosphere. She just had to endure.

"Darcy," Eve cried. "The spot is getting smaller. It's working."

She heard Eve's voice thicken with hope, but all she could concentrate on was the dark sticky threads filling her lungs, making it harder to breathe.

"Blood, Darcy. Blood of a whole soul!"

She heard the Ancestors but it didn't make sense. She was using her blood. But everything was slowing, weakening . . .

Then it all just . . . stopped.

The candle facing the south went out.

The water in the west dried up.

The balloon deflated.

The sand in the crockery disappeared.

The lights of the old souls faded away.

Extreme fatigue weighed down her muscles and her entire body hurt as the connections slammed closed. She struggled to reopen the connection, crying out, "Not yet!"

Hannah wrinkled her forehead beneath Darcy's thumb. "Am I all better?"

Darcy didn't know, but the forces channeling the healing energy inside of her were gone. The dark lines burrowing up her hand and arm had faded and vanished. It took all her energy to lift her thumb from Hannah's forehead. The blood smear shielded the spot where the death mark was.

Eve's hand shook as she used a wet wipe to clear the blood.

The spot was a little smaller, back to dime-size. The color was candy-apple red. Shades lighter than when she'd started the spell, but still there.

Axel went rigid behind Darcy. She could feel his anger and frustration building.

She felt his suspicion break through.

He jerked his hands off of her and surged to his feet.

Carla shifted closer to look at Hannah. "You've pushed back the curse."

It wasn't enough. Dully, Darcy said, "I failed. Something went wrong. I couldn't sustain the forces. I was missing something. The Ancestors said blood, but I was using blood."

With an edge of despair, Carla said, "We'll figure it out."

"No," Axel said.

As Darcy tried to get to her feet, Joe rushed to her and crouched down, got an arm around her, and hauled her up. "Jesus, Darcy, you can barely stand."

"I'm fine. It'll pass." She shouldn't be this weak but she didn't have time to worry about that. She took a breath and said, "Axel, let me try again. I can do it. I'll figure out what went wrong."

He met Darcy's gaze. "There's no more time. You did your best."

The doubt behind his words told her he didn't believe that. But his disconnection scared her more than anything. She knew what it meant. He was going after the demon witch. He could lose his soul, and she could lose him. No! This wasn't about her. Hannah and Eve would lose him. His men would lose him. They all needed Axel. "I'll do better! I have to talk to you. Listen to me, there's something I have to tell you." Would it help or hurt? Maybe if he knew about their soul-mirror connection it would help the spell? What had she missed? Why did she feel so weak?

He didn't even look at her. "Go back to the condo with my mom and Hannah. One of the men will be there to protect you." He strode away.

She couldn't believe it. "No, damn it!" She ran after him, her feet churning up the sand, but there was no way she could catch him. He was moving at a blurring speed. Panic clawed up her chest until she yelled, "Axel, come back!"

He materialized in front of her so quickly she ran right into him.

Stumbling back, she fell on her ass in the sand.

He towered over her, his green eyes blazing fury, and his wings spread out behind him. The moonlight revealed him in stark clarity; his powerful chest and shoulders rippled with muscles and tendons to support the incredible brown-and-gold wings spreading out behind him in a wingspan that was almost as wide as he was tall. He was overpowering just to look at.

Axel clenched and unclenched his massive fists. His wings beat the air in time with his palpable anger. Finally he spit out, "What did you just do?"

"I don't know! I mean I screamed at you to come back . . ." She scrambled up to her feet.

Wrenching fear dripped down her spine. She was afraid for him, afraid for Hannah, and afraid she'd screwed up too much to be forgiven.

"Start talking, witch. You called, my wings sprang out, and I felt the need, the compulsion, to return to you. What have you done to me?"

The suspicion sliced through her skin and into her heart. "I didn't know, Axel. Please believe me, I didn't know!" Her nose clogged, her eyes burned, and desperate, futile hope beat in her heart. She wanted him to believe her. To believe *in* her. Like he had tonight before she failed.

Axel crossed his arms over his chest. His wings lifted an inch in obvious impatience. "What have you done?"

She hadn't wanted it to be this way. She'd hoped he would be so relieved and happy when she healed Hannah . . . but she had failed. Now she owed him the truth. There was no hiding, no delaying. She told him bluntly, "We're soul mirrors. When the curse happened, all the hunters' and witches' souls were halved. It's complicated, but the simple fact is that for decades we've been trying to fulfill the curse. Hunters by craving witch blood and sex, and witches by searching for a familiar to do powerful magic."

His green eyes blazed. "You turned me into a familiar."

"No! You're not a familiar! We're soul mirrors! It's not the same!"

The seconds stretched out, broken only by the sound of the waves crashing. Everyone stayed back.

Finally, Axel said, "No? I'm not bound to you?"

She had to convince him. "No! The choice is yours! You can reject me. You won't ever have the bloodlust again. But Axel, we don't know about your soul. You can't kill the demon witch!"

He tilted his head, his jaw bulging with rage. "This was your plan? Keep Hannah just sick enough for me to need you? For me to keep you around until I accepted my role as your familiar? Your pet? Your goddamned flying monkey?"

She grabbed his arm, unable to bear the awful gulf between them. His muscles flexed dangerously beneath her fingers. But she pressed on. "It's not a plan! I didn't know for sure about the soul-mirror connection until last night!" Her heart poured out of her. "I love you,

Axel! Please, please, you have to believe I wouldn't do anything to hurt you."

His face was cold. Heartless. "Go with my mom, Darcy. Keep my sister alive until I can kill the demon witch. And when this is done, when Hannah is well and if I'm not rogue, I'll find you a safe place. Somewhere far away from me and my family." He ripped his arm from her touch, took a few steps, then leapt into the air, his powerful wings taking him away from her.

21

Darcy wanted to drop to her knees and let the pain of Axel's rejection have her. But she couldn't.

She had more to do this night.

She'd accomplished one thing—she'd told Axel she loved him. He would know that. Maybe he didn't believe it now, but later, maybe he would believe it. Maybe he'd remember her without the hatred, maybe even with a little affection.

Joe's hand settled on her shoulder. "I'll kill him for that."

Fighting back her lingering fatigue, she turned to her cousin. "No, you won't. You won't touch him. Axel didn't deserve this. He's right, I bound him to me. I didn't mean to, but it doesn't change anything. He would never have chosen me of his own free will. I turned him into my puppet. He's right, leave him alone."

"Don't lie to me, Darcy MacAlister. That man is no one's puppet. Not now and not ever. He chose you, then when the going got tough and his pride took a hit, he hit back. He doesn't deserve you," he snarled.

She smiled. "Thanks, Joe." He had always loved her, always stood up for her. How could she tell him what he meant to her in her life? How could she express that kind of love? She settled for, "You've always been there for me. I'm very lucky."

Narrowing his eyes, his hand tightened on her shoulder. "You're coming with us to Carla's."

She shook her head. "I can't. I have to stay with Hannah. I'm not going to let the death curse have her. I'll be safe enough; the Wing Slayer Hunters will keep me safe for Hannah's sake, if nothing else."

His face darkened, his jaw stubbornly set.

"Joe," she said softly. "I have to do this. I'm fine. But you have to get Carla out of here. There are too many witch hunters around and everyone is upset."

"I don't want to leave you."

She forced a smile. "I know you don't. But you need to keep Carla and Morgan safe." Putting her hand on his arm, she added, "Morgan is making you happy. I love her for that alone."

His eyes caught the moonlight, brightening to something she hadn't seen in Joe in a very long time—hope. "She makes me care, she makes me want to fight to create a better place for her, and for her child. I haven't felt like this since I left Glassbreakers all those years ago."

"You deserve happiness. Now get Carla out of here." She glanced into the night, desperate to get everyone she cared for away from the coming danger. "Hurry, Joe."

He studied her, "You'll go with the Wing Slayer Hunters?"

"Yes." There was too much at stake to worry about lying.

Joe kissed her cheek and left.

She watched him walk away with Morgan and Carla. She stared at Joe until she couldn't see him any longer.

"We need to get Hannah back to the condo," Eve said, her voice flat and troubled. Hannah was asleep on her shoulder.

She turned to Axel's mother. "I'm not going. But you need to hurry, get Hannah out of here."

"Darcy, I know you didn't turn Axel into a familiar and I'm not leaving you out here."

She loved Eve for that. "Yes, you are. I'm going to

make sure Axel doesn't lose his soul. The demon witch will come to me. I'll kill her."

"You can't. You're an earth witch."

"That's not exactly true. The cost of doing harm is witch karma, but I can do it. And I will. Just get Hannah out of here and take Sutton, Ram, Key, and Phoenix with you. I don't want any of them losing their souls in this fight. It's my fight. I made the choice to do the spell for Hannah, I'll deal with the demon witch."

Eve paled further, her brown eyes unsure, her arms wrapped around her daughter. "Axel said . . ."

Eve was a mother who loved her kids, but she was also a decent woman. It was clear she didn't like leaving Darcy in this situation no matter what. She pushed a charm into her voice. "You need to get Hannah home, Eve. Take the men and go. Hurry."

Eve blinked, then nodded, turned, and walked away.

Finally she was alone.

Axel soared over the night skies while shielding himself so no one saw him.

The demon witch's name was Linette Olsen. She had walked in on Axel's dad while he was slaughtering her twenty-two-year-old daughter, Kristen. Furious, she'd cast the death curse, but since hunters were immune, the curse bypassed Myles and Axel and struck Hannah.

They'd found Linette's house but she hadn't been there. Ram had followed his instincts to the run-down house on a barren street where Kristen had been killed. The house was empty, but the bloodstains were surrounded by black candles that had clearly been lit. The place stunk of death and demons. Linette and possibly her coven, were holding some kind of ceremony around the blood of her murdered daughter.

Axel was sure he'd find the demon witch there.

It's what he should have done in the first place, gone

after the demon witch that had cursed Hannah. Trusting Darcy . . .

Even now, he didn't want to believe it. Darcy had used a child, used Hannah's illness, to manipulate him. She'd turned him into her flying monkey and he'd let her. But since he had the wings, he'd use them to help him kill the demon witch.

He didn't care if he survived. What did it matter? It was all a lie. He'd wanted to believe his wings were a gift from the Wing Slayer. He had begun to believe that the Wing Slayer cared about his hunters, that he was trying to reach them once more. That the men he cared about meant something to their god. And that their efforts, their daily struggle to resist the curse and turn back to the Wing Slayer Hunter meant something to the god.

It all meant nothing. Not a goddamned thing.

Maybe the witches had killed off the Wing Slayer.

Maybe all the witches ever needed was a dumb-fuck witch hunter to tattoo the wings that would allow them to finish the curse.

Axel banked and headed down toward the lonely looking house set back from the street on the corner lot. As he landed he sniffed the air.

Death. It smelled like old blood, decay, and faintly of sulfur. But he didn't smell any sign of life, which meant the house was empty.

He decided to check to be absolutely sure. He strode up the pathway lined with overgrown shrubbery to the front entrance.

The door hung open. His mind exploded with the image of the night he'd rescued Darcy from the two rogues at the mortuary. They'd been trying to get her through a door like that.

His hawk screeched, the sound full of suffering. It was a sound of such grief and pain that it nearly split open his head with the agony.

"Shut up," he snarled. "She doesn't love us." *Us? What am I thinking? There's no us. The hawk is her creature. She'd turned him into an animal.* "And yet," he said out loud, "she's lying to keep us bound to her." The memory of her face when she'd said she loved him . . . so desperate and pleading . . . was imprinted on his brain. He had wanted to believe her. In that second, he'd wanted to, but he couldn't.

Logic told him that Darcy had known what she was doing to him. She had known when she couldn't transfer the spells herself. *I've tried, but I can't do it myself,* she'd said. She had known she couldn't do it without him. He'd gotten so damned horny, he hadn't thought it out.

But Darcy had known, just as she must have known what she was doing the night she called her familiar. There was no way she couldn't have known—he'd been so compelled to go to her. How could she wield that kind of power and not know?

No, she didn't love him, she loved using him to control her tremendous power.

Axel was no one's familiar. The hawk fretted and made disgusting noises of pain inside his head.

Ignoring the stupid bird, he furiously kicked open the door, slamming it into the wall, just to hear the satisfying crunch of wood. The house was dark inside, but his eyes adjusted in seconds. He strode into the front room, his gaze drawn to the main puddle of dried blood on the old scarred wood floor.

The candles surrounding the blood had dried wax drips running down onto the wood planks. He heard no sound, sensed no movement.

He looked down at those candles and his anger, his fury, and his hurt at Darcy's betrayal collided into a knot of vivid worry. Where the hell was the demon witch?

Darcy. Even now, he couldn't stop the fierce protective worry for her. But she was safe, she'd gone with his men. He would track Linette right to the gates of hell if he had to in order to make sure that demon witch died tonight. Axel started to turn—

Something shifted in the atmosphere.

His senses went on alert. Even his hawk quit its miserable keening.

Whipping out his knife, Axel whirled to his left—and his mouth fell open. A huge man with bronzed skin and deep gold wings floated on the air. He had to be well over seven feet tall. His hair matched his wings. Bronzed bands circled his massive wrists and upper arms, and they were stamped with wings. Only a strip of bronze cloth that wrapped around his hips and over one shoulder covered him. The Wing Slayer had finally made an appearance.

"Linette isn't here." The being's voice had a vibrating bass timbre.

Axel stared at him, feeling each word spoken deep in his chest. He fell to his knees. The witch hunters were not alone; their god lived. "Wing Slayer." He bowed his head.

"I chose you as my hawk, Axel Locke. And until tonight, you were a valiant hawk, refusing to let this curse destroy you or the other men."

"Until tonight?" He raised his head. "Because I'm going to kill the demon witch?"

"No. That is exactly what you should do. After bonding with the witch and binding your damaged souls into a whole, your decision to kill the demon witch tonight was the final step that allowed me to appear to you now."

He tried to understand. "That's what you wanted?"

Wing Slayer said, "Needed. It's always been the single rule hunters must abide by—never deny me and always do the right thing in my name. That's what invokes my god-powers. You had to have enough faith in me to kill the demon witch despite the costs to you personally."

Axel knew he was missing something. "You've appeared now—what do I need to do?"

"Asmodeus and his demon witches cast the curse to separate the hunters from me and the witches from their Ancestors. That got witches and hunters out of his way. Asmodeus is dependent on creating enough misery on earth to feed him greater power in the Underworld. If he fails to do that, he will be enslaved by other demons."

His chest got tight as he grasped the stakes. "What do I do?"

"There's a loophole to the curse. Soul mirrors."

His head spun with the vivid memory of Darcy trying to tell him that they were soul mirrors. He sprang to his feet as a foreboding sensation made his heart pound. "Soul mirrors really exist? But the wings . . . I thought she . . ."

Anger trembled in his voice. "Enough. You earned those wings to protect a very special witch. The wings weren't the gift, the real gift was Darcy. You rejected her. And yet, she still loves you enough to do your work for you."

What? His work? Christ, not the demon witch! Axel tried to open his mouth, but his entire body was frozen leaving him helpless in the face of the Wing Slayer's fury. His heart was writhing in his chest with the weight of what he'd done. She'd loved him, told him the truth, and he'd walked away. Rejected her.

The Wing Slayer said, "You wanted to be free of the curse, here's the price Darcy will pay to free you." He stepped aside and the wall behind the door opened up to show the beach. Darcy was on her knees, blood pouring from her side. Witch karma, Axel realized, she'd tried to cut the demon witch and now suffered a cut three times worse. The demon witch taunted her by changing her glamour into people Darcy loved.

He could feel Darcy's pain, her physical pain and her emotional pain. He felt the wealth of her love for him flowing through her even though her heart was broken into a thousand pieces.

Broken by him.

He tried to look away, to find the Wing Slayer and beg him to help Darcy. The demon witch would kill her! But the freeze held him. Forced him to watch as he saw the look he knew so well take hold of her.

Determination.

Oh, God. No.

He heard her voice. *Ancestors willing, all I ask is that Axel live. Give him my soul and make him whole. Let me take his place as a shade.* No! His mind screamed it, with every fiber of his being, he tried to stop her, to stop it.

But Darcy unfurled her powers and reached her arms up against the hideous pain of her injuries, then her witchcraft exploded. Flames erupted . . .

"No!" The word fought past the paralysis. Grief and regret choked him, drove him back to his knees and broke something inside of him. His hawk screeched and clawed, trying to get free, to get to Darcy. He bellowed, "Stop this! Stop it. Take my soul, not hers!"

His wings burst from his back and he suddenly found himself in the air. Flying with a speed that was impossible.

Did he have time? Could he get to Darcy and save her?

He had to. He had no illusions, he had fucked up and it was going to cost him his soul. But if he saved Darcy, it would be worth the price. She was worth any price.

22

The moon slid behind the clouds, leaving the ocean a dark angry mass. The sand was cold beneath her feet. Goose bumps rose on her skin.

Darcy had the weirdest sense of déjà vu. Perhaps she was being fatalistic. Perhaps this was how her mother, Fallon, had felt knowing her death was coming.

"Darcy, I have missed you."

That voice. My god. Darcy whirled to look behind her.

The clouds parted to reveal her mother standing there, not Fallon, but Eileen, whom she had buried only a week ago. Only her hair was black, not streaked with gray and brittle as it had been at the end. Her blue eyes were vivid and full of life. "Mom?" It was torn from her and tears burned up her nose and into her eyes. She had missed her so much. She wasn't alone!

The voices surged in her head.

Her powers raced, spun, and bounced but now that Axel had rejected her, she couldn't get control of her high magic.

Eileen reached her hands out to Darcy. "I came back for you."

Those words turned the voices in her head painful. But she didn't need to hear the actual words, her own heart told her the truth. She was still alone. "Stop it. You're not my mother." It was the picture of her mother that Darcy had chosen for her obituary. "You're a demon witch."

The creature that looked like Eileen snapped her hand up, palm facing Darcy, and grunted out an unfamiliar word.

She jumped back as the danger slammed into her. With brutal suddenness, she couldn't breathe. The witch was strangling her! She clutched her throat, fighting to breathe.

The necklace at her throat warmed against her skin, reminding her that she controlled the elements. She ripped her hands off her own throat and flung open her chakras. She was abruptly able to breathe as if she had resurfaced from being underwater.

The thing laughed. "Slow reflexes. That's what got me killed."

What did that mean? Darcy thought as the clouds moved past the moon and darkened the beach for a few seconds. Then they parted.

Fallon stood there, looking just like Darcy. Long auburn hair, brown eyes, and she wore the bloody clothes she'd had on when Quinn Young had murdered her. Wounds started to burst open and bleed. Then her belly split apart.

Pain lanced Darcy's forehead. Her third eye burned with the memory of seeing her mother murdered. Nausea churned. "Stop it!" The pain, the hurt, the utter loneliness made her want to reach for Axel. Her powers wept, her heart begged, but Darcy pulled back. Axel had told her many times she had to learn to protect herself and not let her powers escape her control.

And he'd made his choice. He'd rejected her.

She didn't dare look away from the dying image of Fallon for fear of what the demon witch inside the glamour would do.

And if she didn't act, if she didn't end this, then she

would fail. She'd die while the demon witch lived. And
Axel would have to kill her and lose his soul.

She couldn't fail.

She had only one weapon—the knife Carla had given
her to cut her thumb for the spell. She had to use it to
shock the witch into her own form. Pulling the knife out
of her pocket, she focused her powers . . .

The knife was magically ripped from her hand and
jammed into her thigh. Pain bloomed hot and furious.
Blood welled up around the blade, staining her white
dress with a growing red splotch. Dizziness assaulted
her. *No, damn it, she wouldn't make this easy.* She
grabbed the knife and yanked it out.

"Darcy! It hurts!"

She looked up, and saw Fallon on the ground, sliced
and bleeding.

No. Don't believe it. It's not real. Darcy concentrated
enough to close off the wound in her thigh, relieved that
she could heal wounds caused by dark magic.

The creature leapt to her feet, the image of Fallon
melting into an image of Carla, dressed as Carla had
been tonight. "I wanted to tell you to—"

Darcy only needed to see the missing silver armband
that Carla was never without to know for sure. It wasn't
Carla. Deep rage, and a need to end this, to stand for
what was right, drove her. Darcy pulled her powers
through her chakras and blasted the silver knife toward
the creature's heart.

She screamed in fury and the stench of burning skin
tainted the night air.

Silver burned a demon witch so she must have hit her,
Darcy thought just as the skin burst open over her left
rib cage. The bone shattered. Muscle ripped apart. The
agony speared her, dropping her to her knees. The blinding hurt of it wrapped around her ribs, causing her to

sway and stars to burst behind her tightly squeezed eyelids. Unbearable pain relentlessly pounded at her.

Witch karma.

Damn it, the witch must not be dead. If Darcy was alive enough to hurt this much from the triple punishment of witch karma, then the demon witch still lived, too. Her powers slid from her control, the pain cutting off her connection to her chakras. If Axel was here, he could help her focus and . . .

But he wasn't.

"Stupid witch," the creature snarled, coming closer.

Darcy had to kill her. She had to make sure the demon witch died with her, or Axel would . . . *Don't think about him!* She fought to block the image of him, to hold out against the need for him that lived inside of her. Instead she concentrated on her options. Water? Fire? Earth? She could drown them both. Or burn them both. Or bring down an avalanche of earth to bury them both. Which would kill the demon witch? She had only one more chance.

Fire. Fire destroyed everything.

Darcy rose on her knees. She had to reach her powers, and the only way to do that was to accept the pain and make it a part of her. Her broken ribs, torn skin, and ripped muscles filled her mind with red-hot agony. She accepted it, as she would accept her death. She prayed her last prayer: *Ancestors willing, all I ask is that Axel live. Give him my soul and make him whole. Let me take his place as a shade.* Without her soul, she'd be stuck between worlds. She accepted that, too.

She reached up with a bloody hand and touched her necklace.

Instantly she felt the warm light touch her deep in her chest. Her mother, Fallon, was with her. It was enough to reconnect her to her chakras and reach her powers. This time she knew her control and focus wouldn't be accurate without Axel. She had to bring an inferno of fire to make sure she hit the demon witch. As she raised her arms to summon the element of fire, she heard the screech of the hawk.

Darcy opened her eyes and snapped her head up. Her sense of déjà vu and fatalism shattered, as if her destiny had shifted. The clouds parted as a massive winged shadow bore down on them from the skies.

Axel! Her entire being reached for him, her heart swelling beyond her pain. In return, she felt the brush of his hawk wings, a brush filled with fierce protection.

The demon creature yelled a word and flames burst from the bowels of the earth.

"No!" Darcy summoned the water of the sea, pouring it on the flames before it could touch Axel. Her aim, her focus, was dead-on and the fire sputtered out instantly.

Axel shifted in his flying dive to land on his feet in front of where she knelt. His huge wings were fully expanded, blocking her view. From the back, he was awesome. There was no tattoo, just his wings bursting from his back and all those powerful muscles controlling them.

She saw a blur as Axel took the knife from the holster at the back of his pants. Ducking down to see under his wings, she saw the demon witch facing him.

The creature took on the image of Eve.

"Trick," Darcy warned.

Axel never faltered. He stabbed his knife into the heart of the image of his own mother.

The image shattered as the witch screamed. The glamour fell away, revealing an average-looking woman, her face contorted with pain.

Axel's voice thundered around her. "No one hurts my witch. No one."

The smell of burning flesh grew sickening. But Darcy

couldn't move. The pain of her injuries kept her pinned down in the sand.

In seconds, a hot, sulfur-smelling wind whipped around them, forcing her to close her eyes. Then it was gone.

Darcy opened her eyes in time to see Axel's wings fold up and fade into his skin as the tattoo reappeared. It was truly magical. Still on her knees, the pain trying to steal her consciousness, she watched as he turned.

Where was the demon witch?

"Gone," Axel answered her unspoken question. "At her death, the demon pulled her into the underworld." He dropped to his knees in front of her. "Darcy, we don't have much time." He reached for her, lifting her in his arms and onto his lap. "We have to get you healed quickly."

"Can't, Axel. It's witch karma. I can't heal it." She tried to keep her eyes open to fill her mind and body with him and take the images with her into death.

"You have to." He took her hand and placed it onto the wound bleeding through the dress.

The small touch tore a wretched groan from her. Her shattered ribs screamed. Darkness closed in on the edges of her vision.

"Darcy, look at me. Come on, sweetheart, you have to do this. Breathe with me."

Just like that, her panting calmed and her breathing fell into sync with his. Her wounds wouldn't heal, but calming her breathing helped her stay conscious and allowed her more precious minutes with him. She couldn't believe he'd come. Saved her. But would he keep his soul? "Please," she begged softly. "They have to let you keep your soul. Our souls are bound. With my death, you'll be whole." The words hurt but she had to stay focused.

"No! Darcy, damn it, you're going to live." He gently laid his hand over hers.

Her powers reacted in spite of her pain, rushing to his touch. The energy went around her wounds, reaching up through their joined hands to slip into him. Was her soul leaving her and joining with his?

"No!" Axel snapped, his eyes blazing. "Pull them back. Heal!"

"Doesn't work that way." She felt the pain in him and tried to reassure him. "It's okay. You'll be free. I promise." Cold shivers wracked her. The tremors hurt her crushed ribs and torn muscles. She closed her eyes, squeezed them closed, not wanting to cry in front of him. She didn't want him to remember her as weak.

Axel pulled her in closer to his body.

The heat of him felt good. He smelled good, so solid and real, so Axel. She heard a sound, then felt his wings fold around her, cradling her with their warmth. He'd brought out his wings to warm and comfort her.

Like when she'd been a child.

He stood up with her in his arms, his wings cradling her. "I'll get you to Carla. She can heal you. I don't know how much time we have . . ." He stopped walking as a huge shadow fell over them.

Darcy opened her eyes and saw another winged man hovering in front of them. Was she hallucinating?

The hallucination spoke. "The death curse is broken; your sister will live."

Axel bowed his head, then asked in a hushed tone, "You'll see Darcy well and safe?"

Fresh fear for Axel rushed through her. "Axel? What is this?"

He looked down at her, his face gentling, his eyes going bright. "This is good-bye." He leaned down and kissed her. His mouth was tender but his feelings were wild and fierce, tumbling over her in wave after wave of love, passion, possessiveness, and sacrifice. Tears filled her eyes and ran down her face in hot streaks. His hawk stroked its soft feathers up and down her back and arms. He lifted his head and said, "You are my gift, Darcy. I love you and I will continue to love you for eternity. Always remember that."

He loved her? Was it possible that he really cared for her? Accepted her? Even if she had accidentally bound him to her as a soul mirror? In spite of the pain of her injuries, hope sprang to life. But it didn't make sense. "Then why are you saying good-bye?"

"Because I chose you. Your life and your soul. You'll live your life and when you die, you'll go to Summerland to see your mother. You can reincarnate if that's your wish. But you will have the choice."

Her heart beat frantically, making her wounds burn with pulsing agony. He was dying for her, going shade. "No!" She turned her gaze to the winged creature. "The Wing Slayer."

He nodded.

She stared at him, taking in the wing-stamped bands wrapped around his huge arms. Clearly he cared for his hunters—maybe he could be swayed. "It's not fair to take Axel's soul. He didn't choose me of his own free will. He didn't offer his soul for me from free will. I bound him with magic. It's me that should be punished. I give him my soul freely, I give him my life. I give him everything."

Axel was struggling to speak, but Darcy figured out that his maker had silenced him. She turned and looked up into his face. She saw sheer pain and fury that turned his eyes into glittering emeralds, his jaw and throat working against the freeze. He was huge, powerful, and she loved him with all of her soul. "I give you my love and my soul freely. No spell, no magic, no compulsion. You and your men have to work against this curse destroying all of us. You won't need me. You're free of the bloodlust." All the emotion, all the words drained her.

She was dying. She had intended to kill with her powers and she would pay the price for that. She had no idea what eternity in the between-worlds would be like. Already she was fading, feeling the darkness closing in on her, taking her away from the light she loved so much. She supposed she'd never feel the moon or sun again, but that was a small enough sacrifice for Axel. She would know that he lived on free of the curse.

She hoped her mom had forgiven her for failing and that Axel would remember her with . . .

Axel's voice tore free. "Save her! I gave you my soul, my life . . . I'll give you anything you want!"

Darcy wanted to soothe Axel, but she couldn't think of the words.

The Wing Slayer said, "Enough. Axel, cut your hand and lay it on her wound."

Darcy felt him drop to his knees, laying her in the crook of his left arm. Forcing her eyes open, she saw him take out his knife and slice the palm of his right hand. Bright red blood welled up in a straight line. Then he lay it on her side. "Take my blood, sweetheart. Let it give you the strength you need to heal."

She lifted her gaze to his eyes. Her powers stirred from the ashes in her chest, gaining life as his blood mixed with hers. It filled her up, making her arch in his arms and groan with the pain.

Hawk wings slid around her, caressing her skin as the energy welled inside of her. The pain lessened enough for her powers to reconnect and surge up to her control. The shattered bones and torn muscles grew hot with what felt like pure light shining down on them. This was what she'd been missing when trying to heal Hannah; she needed Axel's blood mixed with hers to make the spell work. Whole soul blood, the Ancestors had said.

That's what had drained her, she'd needed the strength of Axel's blood mixed with hers.

"That's it, Darcy, you're healing." Relief coated Axel's voice.

She lifted her gaze to his face. "I'm going to heal, Axel, then I'm going to kick your ass. And your Wing Slayer's ass if I have to. I am not letting you sacrifice your soul for me."

"Silence." The word thundered, drowning out even the sounds of the ocean. "Kick my ass, indeed," he said. "Did you hear that?" He looked up, his face absorbing the light of the moon until it glowed. "Your witch has a fighting spirit. She brings hope."

Who was he talking to? The Ancestors? She glanced at Axel, then she heard his voice clearly in her head. *He likes you.*

Wing Slayer sighed. "Even now they talk to each other. No respect."

Darcy couldn't help smiling. *Because we are of one soul, whole and powerful together.*

He turned to look at them. "Yes, you are. Your souls have joined and bonded as soul mirrors. You have both proven your honor and selflessness this night." He shifted, moving so close that Darcy caught the other-worldly scent of metal and flowers. He reached out and touched the necklace at Darcy's throat. "So that your power may have wings. You belong to the Ancestors, but you are my child, too. I will always hear you."

The silver warmed and shifted at her neck, while her throat filled with emotion. She didn't need a mirror to know that the intricate loops and swirls had shifted into a pair of hawk wings spread wide in flight. She had no voice so she bowed her head in thanks.

"Your Ancestors are here with me. I am the only one who has form, but they lend their power, their light."

She nodded, overwhelmingly grateful.

"Axel, give me your knife."

Axel handed him the knife he'd used to cut his palm. The knife with the silver grip.

Fear skittered up her back. What if he killed Axel now?

Hush, sweetheart. Whatever he chooses, he will not harm you. But I have taken his wings, and I pledged myself to the Wing Slayer.

The Wing Slayer said, "Hold your right hand out, palm down, thumb extended."

Axel held his hand out.

The Wing Slayer moved with a speed Darcy couldn't see. All she saw was the half-moon slice at the base of Axel's thumb. Blood welled up. Axel stayed still.

The Wing Slayer said, "Darcy, your left hand."

Axel wrapped his left arm around her reassuringly.

The fear left her and the clean sense of sheer faith filled her. Out here in the moonlit night, with the ocean roaring behind them, the sand beneath them and the Wing Slayer god before them, Darcy held her left hand out. Again she didn't see the knife move, but a half-moon slice appeared painlessly in the flesh at the base of her thumb. The blood ran down her hand.

"Put your palms together."

A quiet reverence filled her, and she felt the same from Axel. She turned on her knees and pressed her palm to Axel's, their thumbs lining up. The cuts matched up seamlessly, forming a perfect ring around their two thumbs pressed together.

"Call your Ancestors to you, witch."

Axel helped her push her powers through her chakras until her sixth one opened. Her third eye showed her the collective light of the Ancestors surrounding them.

The Wing Slayer wrapped his hand around their thumbs. "As true soul mirrors, may the two of you reflect the faith, courage, honor, strength, and cunning to fight the curse and protect the innocent. We give you the gift of time to aid you."

Thunder exploded overheard, lightning arced from the sky to the ocean and sand-covered ground beneath them rumbled.

Darcy's third eye floated shut and they were alone on the beach. The Wing Slayer and the Ancestors were gone. Axel's knife gleamed on the sand between their bodies. "Your knife," Darcy said.

Axel reached down with his left hand and lifted the knife. The silver handle was stamped with hawk wings. Raising his gaze, he said, "It matches your necklace."

They would both live, and Axel had achieved the position of Hawk, the leader of the Wing Slayer Hunters. She was glad for him, filled with joy, except . . . "You forgive me? For binding you to me? I honestly didn't know at the time, then when I began to realize, I was too scared to tell you. Too scared you'd throw me out and go after the demon witch."

With their palms still touching, Axel twined his fingers with hers. "Never fear that I will reject you. Ever. You are a part of me, the best part of me."

The truth of his words seized her heart. But she still wanted him to understand that she hadn't known what would happen. "When I called a familiar . . ."

"I answered. I came to you. Not because I was compelled, but because I saw you clearly that night. And deep down, I knew I belonged to you. Familiar, soul mirror, no matter what it's called, I belong to you."

She wanted him to know everything. "I saw your wings that night in your bed. They spread out just as you climaxed. God, Axel, I'd never in my life seen anything more majestic or powerful. I wasn't sure I didn't just imagine them."

He smiled, easing her fears, then he lifted their joined

hands to his mouth and kissed her hand. "I didn't feel them, but every time I'm inside you, I lose control. There's no feeling like it."

They both looked down at their joined hands. The blood from the cuts was gone, and in its place each thumb had a perfect unbroken line circling its base.

Darcy brought her other hand up and saw the same perfect ring.

Axel said in a thick voice, "Immortal lifelines. They have given us immortality."

She couldn't grasp it. "So you're stuck with me for eternity?"

He dropped her hand to cradle her face. "I choose you for eternity. You are my love and my gift. I will always protect you, Darcy. Always." He took her mouth in a kiss.

The rush of need arrowed through her tightening her skin; her nipples were swollen and aching. She sank her hands into his hair and kissed him fiercely.

Axel responded with a barely contained violence, growling low in his throat and pushing her back onto the cool sand.

Some sense returned. "Wait! Someone might see us."

Axel rested his hands on either side of her shoulders, his dark hair falling over his uncompromising face. "No one is around." His gaze dropped to the necklace resting at her throat. "You wear my wings, witch."

"And you have my heart." Her witch energy surged, warming her already tight skin until her torn and bloody dress seemed to be strangling her. She wanted his skin on hers, his hands, his mouth. It pulsed in her, fed by the sound of the ocean, the feel of the moon, and the man looming over her. "Join with me, Axel." She used her powers to get rid of her dress.

He reared back on his knees, his eyes raking down her body clothed only in the silver hawk wings and moonlight. "Mine, Darcy." He slid a hand between her thighs. "Spread yourself open."

This was what she loved. She could feel Axel using his hearing and vision to assure they were alone. But he meant to claim her. Not make love, not have sex; he meant to claim and mark her as his own. She spread her legs. And while he looked, she magically took his clothes, all but his knife, which she left within his reach.

The moonlight spilled over his tight bulging shoulders, his stomach rippled with tension, his dick huge and thrusting out between his powerful thighs. He moved between her legs, scooping her thighs in his arms and lifting her to his mouth.

Darcy felt the touch of his tongue and cried out. Her powers rushed to meet his mouth, feeding him . . . love, energy, she didn't know. She felt his wings caress her breasts, feathering back and forth over her swollen nipples. She sank into a world of tongue and feathers and Axel. The sensations raced through her, circling into a whirlwind of pleasure until she was writhing and panting.

And then his voice in her head. *Mine, sweet witch. Your taste is mine, just like your heart.* She burst into an orgasm, crying out as Axel growled his approval against her wet folds, milking more pleasure from her.

She barely started to catch her breath when he rose up and covered her body, burying himself in her with a single deep thrust. Her powers swirled, racing down and wrapping around him.

Axel jerked, his body going rigid, his dick growing harder inside of her, his back bowing with intensity. Sweat popped out on his skin. But he didn't move, just accepted what she did to him.

She looked into the hard and ferocious face of the man she loved and squeezed him again with her powers and with her body.

"You own me, Darcy." He said the words with a thick groan and then began pumping into her, harder and deeper with each stroke until he was pounding into her with raw passion. Until he completely lost control and his hawk shrieked with joy. Darcy heard it and shattered, surrendering everything she had to Axel. The pleasure burst over her in hot silver rivers streaked with shimmering colors. Her heart pounded, her core pulsed around Axel as he came in rich hot spurts over and over deep inside of her.

And in her mind, he whispered again, *You own me.*

23

"Axel!" Hannah raced out of her room as soon as she heard his voice.

He scooped her up in his arms. She was wearing a pink and white nightgown and smelled like baby shampoo.

She threw her skinny arms around his neck. "I'm all better! No shadows! But I don't want to go to sleep. What if the shadows come back?" She leaned back in his arms to look into his face. "Key got Minnie for me! But I still don't want to go to sleep."

His head spun with all her chattering. "Let me see your forehead."

She happily shoved back her bangs. Her forehead was perfectly smooth with no mark. Thank the Wing Slayer for that.

"See? No mark! Can I have hot chocolate? Or cookies?" She kicked her legs against his chest.

Axel looked at his mom. She stood by the couch in the living room, tears running down her face. He shifted Hannah and held out his arm to her. Eve rushed up and Axel hugged her to him.

"Mommy's been crying all night. I think she needs a cookie, too."

Axel laughed, holding his mom tightly.

"Hannah," Darcy said, "how about I get you a cookie and a glass of milk? If it's okay with your mom."

Hannah held her arms out to Darcy.

"Eve?" Darcy hesitated, her voice uncertain.

Eve raised her head, reached out, and took Darcy's hand. "Thank you. I can't believe I left you on that beach."

Axel saw Darcy's flush. He sighed. "She charmed you into leaving her, Mom. You can't trust witches, they are sneaky."

"Hush, Axel. Part of me knew what she was doing. I chose you and Hannah over her." She turned back to Darcy. "You belong to us, and we won't ever leave you alone again."

Axel saw Darcy's eyes fill.

Hannah threw herself into Darcy's arms and hugged her. "You can be my sister. Like Axel. Only he's a brother not a sister. Do you want a cookie? We can both have cookies . . ."

His sister's voice trailed off as Darcy carried her into the kitchen, but he could clearly feel Darcy's delight and love for Hannah.

"What happened?" Eve asked.

"I'm curious, too," Sutton said behind him. "I can see the wings on your knife where it's sticking out of your holster."

He turned as his men walked into the condo. "First thing, the next time any of you leave my witch unprotected, I will kill you."

All four men nodded. No excuses, no explanations.

"I went to kill the demon witch, Linette, but she wasn't at the house of her murdered daughter as we'd thought. But the Wing Slayer was."

"You saw him," Sutton said, his blue eyes fastened on Axel. "He's alive." His voice was thready with amazement.

Next to Sutton, Phoenix said, "Your wings, they are from the Wing Slayer, not Darcy."

Axel nodded, feeling the emotion radiating from the

men. They had waited and hoped for this day. And here it was, but there were still so many unanswered questions.

Ram cleared his throat. "Your curse is gone?"

"Yes. The curse has a loophole; soul mirrors. Darcy is my soul mirror, the other half of my soul, and together we are whole. Then all the Wing Slayer needed was a sign of faith from me—and going to kill the demon witch was it."

Key took a deep breath. "There's hope for us. If we find our soul mirrors?"

"Let's go into my office," Axel said, more to give the men time to collect their thoughts than for any real need. He took his seat behind his desk. His mom stood beside him while the men all settled into the room. He recapped the events of the night.

Eve put her hand on his shoulder. "You're immortal now?"

"It doesn't mean I can't die, Mom. Quinn Young's Immortal Death Dagger is one way to kill me. But I'm even harder to kill than I was." He would outlive his mom. That was hard, but natural enough. Children were supposed to outlive their parents. But he would also most likely outlive Hannah. She would grow old while he would not. If he had Darcy with him, he could handle that. Knowing that afterlife existed made it easier to bear, too.

His mom smiled. "You've become the man you were born to be. You did it, Axel. You fought the curse and won. Your soul is safe. You killed the demon witch who cursed Hannah, and you're not rogue."

Key said, "That's some deal, you get a mate and you're free of the curse. But the Wing Slayer turned your raven into a hawk before you knew Darcy. Our tats stayed the same."

The others looked at him. They all needed some reassurance, some sign that they were as important to the Wing Slayer as Axel was. He was the leader, and he would lead. "The Wing Slayer had the wings of each of his hunters branded on metal bands that he wore. Not just hawk wings, but all the wings. You are Wing Slayer Hunters." He paused, then added, "He hasn't abandoned you. The more we believe in him, the stronger he is."

Pheonix said, "You believe our soul mirrors are out there?"

Sutton added, "How are we supposed to find our soul mirrors? It's not like we can hang out with the witches. Just being near them . . ."

Axel knew Sutton was struggling since being near Carla. "We don't have all the answers, but I do believe each of you has a soul mirror." He met each of their gazes. "Which is all the more reason for us to try to protect earth witches. They are our salvation."

Sutton said, "We've already started. We set up the safe house for the witches that were in the Hummer. I've been thinking about that, too, since it's hard for Ram, Key, Phoenix, and myself to get too close to witchblood, we could send Joe when earth witches are attacked by rogues. He could get the witches to safety while we go after the rogues."

"I'm down with that," Phoenix said.

Axel nodded, pride in his men filling him. "For now, I'll take care of the demon witches we run across. I don't know what would happen if one of you killed a demon witch before you found your soul mirror, so we'll play it safe. We'll keep the club. You all need a place to control the bloodlust." He saw in the face of each man the private hell they fought every day. While he was grateful as hell to be out from under the curse, he wouldn't rest until all of them were free.

Key said, "We need to find a way to work directly with witches. We could set up a system to warn them if we get intel that a rogue is going after a specific witch. Maybe Darcy can help us with that."

"We can ask . . ." Axel stopped talking when the flat-screen on the wall over where Ram and Sutton sat flashed on.

He looked up and went still, then absolute fury pumped through him. The camera was mounted in a corner so that he could see three steel examination tables equipped with restraints gleaming coldly under the lights. On a far wall were three cages that held five women.

They had to be witches. The camera showed the bright red blood oozing from wounds and some darker stains that were drying. All their eyes had the witch tilt. While he watched, they were chanting softly, either praying, or trying to summon their powers. But rogues knew how to shut down a witch's power with their knives, and there were other methods, too. Drugs, stun guns, anything that would create confusion.

Axel shot to his feet. "It's my dad's place." He turned to Sutton. "Confirm that."

The bald-headed man shot out of his seat and took Axel's place at the desk, his fingers flying over the keyboard. He opened a laptop and worked on that, too.

Phoenix shoved off the wall he'd been leaning against. "They are going to kill the witches."

Key's face darkened. "They are taunting us. Why send this?"

Axel knew the answer. "To bring us to them. This looks like a plan of my dad's. But I don't think he's alive or he'd be on the phone to me—or on-screen."

"It's coming from your dad's place," Sutton announced.

Ram stood. "We can't let this happen. We can't . . ." His words trailed off as something on the screen got their attention. The double doors to the surgery opened. Two rogues dragged in Joe MacAlister.

"Fuck," Axel snarled, his wings shoved hard beneath his skin as he realized they had Darcy's cousin. She loved Joe. And damn it, Joe was family to her, all the real family she had left.

He'd screwed up, letting Joe, Carla, and Morgan go back to the house. He hadn't even thought about them once the spell failed on Hannah and . . . He shut down his thoughts and watched the screen.

Phoenix said, "He fucking tracked her. Reed tracked Morgan, he's had a bead on her this whole time. That's how he found your safe house. Morgan had been there." He sucked in a breath and spit out, "We slowed him down but we didn't stop him."

More rogues carried in Carla Fisk. Her long, snowy blond hair was matted with blood, her hazel eyes wide with terror.

Sutton shoved himself up and out of his chair. "Oh, hell no. Not Carla."

Axel whirled to see Sutton had his knife in his hand, his eyes locked on the screen. *Shit.* He looked at Key and Phoenix, jerking his head slightly toward Sutton. They both moved to flank the man.

Axel turned back to the screen. Eric Reed walked in, dragging Morgan by the arm. "Let them go!" she cried.

He ignored her and directed the rogues. "Put MacAlister on the table. And the witch on the other table. Strip them both."

Joe fought them. He caught one rogue with a kick to the balls, dropping the bastard. Caught another with a fist to the chin, snapping his head back into the cages holding the witches.

Six rogues jumped him, beating, hitting, cutting until they got Joe on the table and in metal clamps.

It was a fucking nightmare. "I'm going," Axel said.

"I'm with you," Sutton said.

Axel turned, ready to object.

Sutton thrust out his chest, his shoulders tensed and his blue eyes fixed in determination. "You can kill me if it happens. I want you to kill me if I go rogue. But I'm taking a whole shitload of those bastards with me."

Axel wanted to protect his men. But what had the Wing Slayer told them? *Protect the innocent.* He lifted his gaze to find Phoenix, Key, and Ram lined up behind Sutton.

A witch on the screen screamed. Axel turned to see her being dragged from the cage by several rogues. Reed was giving the rogues the caged witches as payment for bringing him Joe, Morgan, and Carla. Rage whipped through him. "Let's go."

"Oh, God, it's Joe! And Carla!"

He turned to see Darcy staring at the screen, her face dead white, her brown eyes wide with horror. Grabbing her, he said, "I'll get them free, Darcy. I'll bring them home to you."

Ram said, "The other men are coming to stay with Eve, Hannah, and Darcy. They'll be safe."

Axel dropped his mouth to hers, a reassurance, and then they left.

Darcy stood in the modern office of Axel's condo, her gaze riveted on the TV screen on the wall. Desperate fear churned in her stomach for Joe, Morgan, and Carla.

What were they missing? Axel was immortal now, did Reed know that? No. Darcy didn't think he did, but she bet someone else did.

Her father. Quinn Young. He was in league with a

demon, a demon who gave Young the means to kill Axel. He was using Reed to lure her and Axel to him.

The voices pounded in her head, bile rose in her throat, but what she thought of was Fallon. What her mother had told her. *We have to outthink the demon and his witches. That's why we strive so hard to reach our knowledge chakra.*

Darcy stood quietly, letting her powers work. Her first four chakras opened with the elevator-drop sensation.

Her fifth chakra at her throat opened.

Her sixth chakra at her forehead opened with a starburst as her vision faded and her third eye took over.

Her father, Quinn Young, raised his arm, and the hideous blackened thing on his forearm bulged, raising the burned, dead skin, stretching and stretching . . .

Nausea rolled in her stomach and shot up her throat as she watched.

The thing burst from Quinn Young's arm in a sickening whoosh. Darcy couldn't see where it went.

Until it slammed into Axel's chest, directly into his heart. She saw her mate's shock of pain, then felt him mentally reach for her.

Checking to make sure she was safe before he died, leaving her alone.

Driven to her knees with grief and pain, her third eye went blind and her ordinary vision came back. But before she could think, or focus, a violet mist swirled around her and the very top of her head felt like it had slammed into a brick wall.

Chakra seven. The knowledge was there, she'd opened chakra seven. The violet color stayed in front of her eyes, but the knowledge was incredible. There were gods, demons, spirits; so much more to the world than just the earth. It was incredibly seductive, and she had to see it all, had to keep watching . . .

Darcy felt a prick from her necklace that jerked her out of the compulsive studying and absorbing. Now she understood the danger of the seventh chakra; it was mesmerizing enough that she could lose control and re main in the seventh chakra trance, just studying and studying endlessly.

Axel was in danger, he would die!

Her love for Axel kept her focused and she let her seventh chakra help her work it out, help her understand what she knew: Her father had planned for Eric Reed to send the video to lure in her and Axel so that Quinn and Eric could kill them.

She had to be smart, had to understand what she was fighting. Why did Quinn Young need to kill her and Axel?

The answer hit her hard. Asmodeus had decreed it. The ancient demon and Wing Slayer had grown up in the Underworld, where they learned that both their powers were tied to earth. Wing Slayer had created the witch hunters to bring out his god-powers and give him a place to belong. He cared about earth and her people. Asmodeus needed earth to increase his powers to survive in the Underworld. The demon had cast the curse three decades ago to break Wing Slayer's god-powers and destroy the witches and witch hunters. But soul mirrors were the loophole that would bring Wing Slayer back to power and threaten Asmodeus's quest for power. That was why the demon had appeared to Young and bribed him to kill her mother. He'd decreed that Young kill Darcy because without Darcy, Axel would never have been whole. There would be no soul mirror and no threat to his power.

Darcy understood that the gods and demons were only as powerful as their subjects made them. All their choices either strengthened or weakened the demon or god.

She had a choice. She could panic and lose, or she could do as her mother had done once before and out-think the enemies. She had the tools. She understood exactly what Asmodeus was now, and what she had to do. If she used her magic correctly, she would save Axel and together they would help the witches and hunters defeat Asmodeus.

The violet fog dissipated.

She jumped to her feet and whirled to Eve standing behind her. She grabbed the woman's shoulders. "I have to go! He'll die if I don't! I saw it!"

Eve's face paled, but her brown eyes stayed calm. "There's two witch hunters here. I'll send them with you."

"No." She shook her head. "They can't help. My blood will save Axel, Eve. If I've learned what I should, then my magic will protect me. Oh, I need salt."

"I've got that." Eve grabbed her hand and pulled Darcy behind her. "You'll take my car. Do you know how to find them?"

With her free hand, she touched the necklace at her throat. "Always."

Between Sutton's blueprints and the reconnaissance work Phoenix and Key had done earlier that day, they had a very good layout of the place. Axel flew ahead in order to get a bird's-eye view, while his men drove, but everything he saw matched up with what Key and Phoenix had discovered.

Axel put away his rage at what his dad had set in motion. Whether his dad was dead or alive, it ended tonight.

He landed at the meeting place about a hundred yards from the house. The black SUV skidded to a stop next to him and the men poured out.

Ram said, "I've got a group of witch hunters on

standby for cleanup. First we have to see how many witches are in there and if we can get them out." He paused for a second and added, "Alive."

"Once we kill off Reed and any other rogues inside, I can take care of the witches." Axel was not going to let his men go rogue if he could possibly prevent it. "Tell the other hunters to stand down until we give the order."

Ram relayed the order. "Done."

He nodded. "Let's do this."

Moving with predatory silence, Axel and his men shielded their presence and reappeared only when they killed the guards patrolling the grounds. They dumped the bodies of the dead rogues out of sight. Next they grabbed a rogue crossing from the house to the out-building and used his face and retina to bypass the so-phisticated facial recognition and retina scans to get into the building.

Then they killed him.

Entering through the barracks, they stayed invisible. The barracks held two rows of twin beds neatly made, but no rogues.

"Don't like this," Ram said.

Axel silently agreed but kept moving, using the blue-prints on Sutton's handheld as a guide.

"Shit, smell that?" Key snarled.

Axel did. Witch blood, but it was dying blood. He turned to the door on his right.

"Private room," Sutton said. "They used to be exam rooms."

"They're using them to kill the witches they dragged from the cages." If he opened that door and the witches weren't dead yet, the blood smell would be overpower-ing. He had to make a decision. "Sutton, you and Key check ahead, make sure it's clear to the surgery room."

They moved on.

Axel knew Phoenix and Ram were standing next to him, although he couldn't see them. "I'll go in first." He reached for the door, but it was pulled open before he touched it.

"Let's hit the clubs and . . ."

Phoenix materialized and jammed his knife into the throat of the speaker.

The rogue gurgled, his brown eyes filled with fear.

"What the . . ." The second one whipped out his knife.

Ram sliced straight into the rogue's heart and twisted.

Axel moved past the dying rogues into the room. Two exam tables held dead witches. One had short red hair and a scattering of freckles, splattered with blood. The other had been a chunky brunette. Now they were naked, drained of blood, with gaping cuts all over their bodies. The desecration of these two women infuriated him.

"Nothing we can do for them now."

Ram was right. Axel nodded and turned away. They pulled the door shut behind them.

The next private room had three butchered witches. The rogues who had murdered them were already gone. Axel closed that door, his pulse pounding in his ears. Phoenix and Ram were doing okay since the blood was dead or dying. Or their anger kept the bloodlust at bay.

They moved down the hall when a voice said, "Found the control room."

Axel stopped at Sutton's voice. They were all invisible but Sutton must have heard or smelled them. "Go on."

"I checked the cameras. Joe and Carla are on the tables. Morgan's on a chair. Four guards in the room, more guards in the kennel room that opens into the surgery."

"Trap. Knew that."

"One more thing," Key said.

Axel waited.

"Your dad's body is in the conference room. I believe that Reed made his stand there in front of an audience and left the body as a message to anyone who thought to take power from him."

His father murdered in his own masterpiece of a compound. Fitting. Axel wasted no pity or grief on him. Three people who deserved his protection were in trouble. Two of those were people Darcy loved and he couldn't bear her pain if they died.

And it was time to make their stand. Show the world the Wing Slayer was back and the Wing Slayer Hunters would kick rogue ass in his name. "Let's go."

Going to the door, Axel opened it enough for them to watch for a second and get the lay of the room. The guards were so fixed on Reed they weren't paying attention to the fact that the door had opened slightly.

Reed had dragged Morgan up by the arm with his left hand, while holding his knife in his right. She had blood running from her mouth, her eyes were wide with horror.

"Don't hurt Joe! He didn't touch me!" Morgan said.

"Can you blame him? Who would want to touch you? You're a crazy-ass cutter." He laughed at his own joke.

"I'm not!" Her face turned red. "I'm not! I didn't . . ." Her body bowed with pain.

Reed smiled. "Forget what you were saying, sweetie?"

Morgan curled forward, as if trying to get into the fetal position. Then she slammed her fist up under Reed's jaw, knocking his head back.

"Morgan, no!" Joe roared at the same time. He thrashed on the table, snapping one of the restraints.

Axel took advantage of the distraction and burst into the room, his men at his back. They couldn't hold the shield that made them appear invisible and fight at the same time, so they dropped it as they entered.

Reed threw Morgan into the wall and whirled. "Get them!"

The rogues rushed them with several more pouring out from the kennel room where they'd been hiding.

Axel turned right, avoiding the oncoming rogues, and swiftly killed the two who had been standing guard at Joe's and Carla's feet. Then he turned back.

Phoenix and Key worked back to back, killing with brutal swiftness. Key took a slice to his left arm, whipped around, and killed his attacker.

Sutton worked his way around, killed the two guards at Carla's head, then turned his back to her, crouching to take anyone who came near her.

Ram fought off a swarm of rogues that were protecting Reed. He got close to the man when a shot rang out, dropping Ram to the ground.

Axel saw it happen, and watched as Eric Reed turned the gun on him. "Where's Darcy?"

Darcy. Furious, Axel leapt up into the air, unfurling his wings. His left wing slammed two rogues into the ground. His wingspan took up half the space in the room. Axel caught a handful of Reed's shirt, lifting him into the air with powerful pumps of his wings. The rogues started climbing tables trying to rescue their leader.

Reed roared his rage, swinging his gun around and firing.

The bullet went through Axel's arm and pissed him off more. In a lightning-quick strike, he buried his knife in the bastard's heart and threw him at the rogues.

He landed, ignoring the blood pouring from his arm.

Key, Phoenix, and Sutton were taking care of the rest of the rogues. Axel dropped to his knee by Ram. The bullet had torn through his rib cage, maybe nicked his heart. Goddamnit. He'd die if they didn't get the bleeding stopped. He ripped off what was left of his shirt and pressed it on the wound. *Too much blood.*

Hold on, Axel, I'm coming. I won't let Ram die.

Darcy! She was in his head.

At the same time, he felt a new threat. Rising from Ram's side, Axel turned to the opened doors of the surgery.

Quinn Young stood there. Tall as Axel, with brown hair and black eyes, he took in the scene, then looked at Axel with calm curiosity. "Where is Darcy? It's sad, pathetic really, that one witch can bring down so many men."

Darcy, do not come. Don't get near this place. It's too dangerous. She was with him, he knew she heard him.

She didn't answer.

Young crossed his arms over his chest, his short-sleeved golf shirt revealing the black Immortal Death Dagger that lived in the burn mark on his right forearm. "Nice wings, by the way. Do you enjoying serving a witch? Being turned into an animal?"

Axel just needed to figure out how to get past that dagger on Young's arm and strike him in the heart. Crossing his arms had looked casual enough, but Axel knew he was protecting his heart with the Immortal Death Dagger.

His men were behind him with Ram, who would die if they didn't get him out of there and to help. Shit. "Darcy sends her regrets but she's not interested in meeting with you."

"She'll show." Young walked into the room and looked up at the camera. "You know why, Locke? Power.

And if she doesn't get her witch ass over here, I'm going to kill her power source. You." He dropped his arms and turned.

Axel brought up his arm for a death strike with his hawk-embossed knife.

Instantly, the smell of burned skin grew, and the black knife burst from the flesh of Young's forearm and rocketed toward Axel's chest.

Axel hit the floor, rolled over two dead rogues, and leaped to his feet.

Shit. The Death Dagger had already returned to Young's hand. He controlled it enough to call it back to him without touching it, meaning he had some high-stakes demon magic. Keeping his own knife in his hand, he considered how to win against that Death Dagger. Young was stalling, toying with them, using them to draw Darcy to him.

"We have the witch!" A voice called out in triumph.

Two young rogues dragged Darcy into the room. She had three wounds; a knife cut to her bare right arm, one to her left thigh through her jeans, and a slice through her black T-shirt that pierced her side. Her eyes shone with pain and determination. Her right fist was tightly closed—was it cut, or was she holding something? She glanced at Joe, and the remaining restraints snapped open.

She had her powers! Axel felt them vibrate in his intestines as she released Joe's restraints.

"Darcy!" Joe used his elbow and one unbroken hand to get to his feet.

She ignored her cousin. Standing up to her full height, both the rogues holding her slid to the ground as if drugged. "Guess I'm late for the family reunion."

"How did you kill them? You're an earth witch." Young's voice pinged with irritation.

"I didn't. I used a sleep charm I learned from my mother. Remember that sleep charm?"

"Darcy," Axel warned in a low voice. Why was she baiting Young? She knew he had the Immortal Death Dagger, she'd seen him kill her mother to get it. He glanced at Phoenix and inclined his head to the two sleeping rogues.

Phoenix moved in a blur, killing both of the hunters.

Darcy didn't even flinch, and that's when Axel grasped what she was doing. She couldn't kill with her powers, but he and his men were very capable of killing. Fierce pride in her warred with fear and anger. She'd *let* herself get captured to find him. With his body between Darcy and Young, he said through their mind link, *Run Darcy, it's too dangerous.*

I have a plan. Trust me.

Darcy . . .

Young said, "So you're clever, but you're still an earth witch. I learned not to be played by witches. Cleverness won't win against real power."

She tilted her head and answered, "Here I am. Come and get me."

Young smiled and in the time it took him to smile, he blew by Axel and got behind Darcy. By the time Axel tracked him, Young was already throwing his arm around Darcy's neck. Then he shoved the Death Dagger against the bleeding wound on her side.

Darcy screamed, her face going white, her witch-shimmer turning gray. She pounded at Young's arm with her still closed fist.

An obscene slurping sound filled the room.

The Dagger was sucking her blood! Feeding the demon that owned it. They could see it *growing* fat and glistening with her blood.

Axel's heart stuttered then kicked into born-to-kill

predator mode. He growled deep in his throat, while the screech of his hawk bounced in the room. He pumped his wings, propelling himself into the air. He landed and struck in a blinding flash, slashing bone-deep into the arm that held the Dagger against Darcy.

"Axel, no!" Darcy cried.

Too late. The Dagger ripped off of her wound with a sickening wet sound and disappeared.

Where the fuck did it go?

Pain exploded in Axel's chest, knocking him back and slamming him to the cement floor. Stunned, he lifted his head and looked down.

The Immortal Death Dagger was embedded in his heart. Buried to its glistening black hilt.

A shock of white-hot agony boiled through him. The effort of breathing became a struggle. He felt blood running down his chest and onto the floor. His vision started to darken . . . and he saw the wings of death coming for him.

He struggled to push death back, desperate to protect Darcy with his last breath.

Darcy felt Axel's pain and shock like it was her own. Red hot, then icy cold as his life bled away. His love though, his love wrapped around her and kept her anchored to her powers. His love made her strong, strong enough to fight the evil of her father.

"Immortality isn't all it's cracked up to be," Quinn laughed. His arm was still around her neck.

Phoenix, Key, and Sutton let out roars of fury and rushed toward Axel.

The Dagger rose from Axel's heart with a wet pop and swung at the hunters, forcing them back. Three against one, they fought the Death Dagger. Joe had Carla on the floor by Morgan, protecting them despite a crushed hand and various other injuries.

While Young gloated and tormented, talking about *the real power of demons,* Darcy whispered, "Pure in its whiteness, born of the earth, consecrated by the sea, feared by the dark, embraced by the light, salt rise and circle your protection." She tossed the salt she had clenched in her fist, while mentally forming the circle of protection around the room, running the line between Young and herself.

Young's arm was shoved off her neck, his entire body pushed back several inches. He bellowed in rage, lunged for her, then bounced back off an invisible barrier.

The Death Dagger was pushed outside the circle.

"What the fuck did you do! I have the dark powers, you can't do this! You can't trick me with your witchcraft! Not this time!" Young bashed into the barrier over and over.

She ignored him, dropping to the ground by Axel. Terror clawed at her heart and mind. She could feel him separating from her, feel his soul being torn from hers. She grabbed his knife from his limp hand and sliced her palm.

Key moved up next to her. "Darcy . . ."

"Shut up, I won't let him die!" Axel had no shirt on, so she slapped her bleeding palm to the stab wound. Her chakras were wide open and weeping with her. "Please," she begged the Ancestors. "Save him."

Carla, wearing a too-large shirt, dropped to her knees and added her power and light.

Darcy touched her necklace with her free hand. "Wing Slayer, hear me, I give your hunter blood, I beg you to give him breath."

Light bloomed where her hand lay on Axel, bright against the bronze of his skin mixed with the scarlet of his blood.

His eyes opened, the clear and fierce green she loved.

"Thank you," she told the Ancestors and Wing Slayer.

He sucked in a breath then snarled at her, "You won't be thanking them when I throttle you, witch. You risked your life coming here!"

She smiled, feeling his life force grow strong and the connection between them sizzle. "And I saved yours." She kept her hand on Axel giving him as much blood as he needed. "Phoenix, bring Ram over here. Gently."

Carla put her arm around Darcy's shoulders. "I'll help."

Phoenix and Key gently carried Ram.

"Where's Sutton?" Axel asked, moving her hand from his healed wound and holding it while sitting up.

Phoenix said, "He went to oversee the cleanup." He glanced at Carla, then added, "He ripped his shirt off and threw it at Carla to cover herself, then left. He was in a bad way. Sweating bullets. The curse had him by the balls." They both set Ram down.

Key ripped the bloody shirt away from Ram's chest. The hunter was unconscious and his breathing was shallow.

Darcy took her hand from Axel's hold, "Go over there by Joe, get some space." From Carla's blood. Key and Phoenix appeared in control, but she and Carla were going to use magic. While the hunters didn't seem to feel Darcy's too much now that her soul had bound with Axel's, they would feel Carla's magic.

They nodded and moved back.

Swiftly, she cut her other hand. This time, she winced at the hot streak of pain.

"Stop that!" Axel snapped, clearly coming back to his full strength.

Laying her hand on Ram, she called for the light of the Ancestors. The power rushed down to collide with her low magic then poured out of her hand with her blood.

Axel put his hands on her waist, settling behind her and next to Carla. "Need my blood?"

"Just your strength. Your blood is already mixed with mine from healing you."

Ram's pain slammed into her, knocking her back. Axel's arms caught her while Carla let go of her shoulder and quickly grabbed her wrist and kept it anchored on Ram's wound.

"Give me the pain, Darcy. Now," Axel demanded.

She felt her energy obey him, the pain moving through her to him.

"Darcy." Ram opened his eyes and looked up at her. "What are you doing here?"

She smiled down at him. "Pissing off Axel."

"Thank you. For healing me and pissing off Axel."

"He's fine," Axel growled behind her.

But Darcy heard the sheer relief and gratitude under his gruffness.

An icy foul wind with the stench of burned skin blew through the circle. "This isn't over, Darcy MacAlister. Your mother tried to run, too. I found her and by Asmodeus's Death Dagger, I'll find you."

Darcy whipped her head around in time to see Quinn Young's eyes blaze red fire. The Immortal Death Dagger was back on his arm and it was cauterizing the wound from Axel's knife.

Bile rose in her throat.

"I'll find you!" He turned away and vanished.

Clean air returned.

Axel pulled Darcy closer to him. "Exactly what did you do?"

"I set a circle to keep demons out. He wears the mark of the demon, Asmodeus. It was a risk, but I had a vision and I knew . . ." She shuddered. "I can't lose you. I won't. I'll find you every damned time you need me."

Axel wrapped his arms tightly around her, making her feel safe and secure once more. "I'll always need you."

She leaned into his strength, feeling the hard ridges of his muscles covered the heat of his skin. And the touch of his hawk brushing her mind and her body. It was incredible to be valued for her power and ability, then allowed the luxury of needing comfort.

"Darcy!"

She lifted her head and turned toward Joe's wretched cry.

"Morgan's bleeding. She's losing the baby!"

24

"I've missed you, Mom." Darcy touched the headstone that she had magically conjured for the woman who had raised her, loved her, and taught her an important lesson. The headstone had her name, date of birth and death, and her true legacy:

Love is the Real Magic.

"I wish I could have met her." Axel put his arms around Darcy, pulling her back to his chest. The cemetery was empty, but the moon spilled her light over the rolling grasses and stately headstones. "I want to thank her for loving you and keeping you until I found you."

"She knows." It wasn't her third eye or knowledge chakra telling her that, but faith. Her mother's soul had moved on, but her love stayed with Darcy. She turned in Axel's arms and looked up at him.

He touched her face with love and possessiveness. "It's time to go home, Darcy. You spent all last night and today taking care of Morgan and Joe with Carla. It's time to go home."

It had been a long night and day. Joe had been badly hurt and had fought them on trying to heal him, insisting they put all their energy into saving Morgan's child. Finally, when they'd gotten Morgan's bleeding to stop, he allowed them to heal the most serious of his injuries.

No one knew if the child would survive to full-term.

When Darcy left, Joe had been asleep on the bed with Morgan, cradling her, his freshly healed hand resting on her stomach.

So much pain. But they were fighting to overcome the curse and make things right. It wouldn't happen with one person, or in one day. But each choice mattered.

Each choice counted.

Darcy leaned her cheek into Axel's chest, felt the beat of his heart. "I've never felt at home or like I belonged, until now. With you, I am home."

He buried his hand in her hair, tilting her head back. "You're a hell of a woman, Darcy. I love you, witch." He kissed her.

She closed her eyes, sinking into the feel of his mouth.

Axel lifted her in his arms and broke the kiss. "Put your legs around me and hold on."

"Why?"

He smiled down at her. "We're going to fly." His wings burst from his back as he took a couple of steps and leapt into the air.

Darcy twined her arms around his neck and felt the air dance around them as his wings propelled them through the night. "Wow, you really know how to sweep a witch off her feet."

He kept his gaze on the horizon, but he smiled and tightened his arms around her. "You are my mate, Darcy. We'll always fly together."

Read on for a sneak peek at

SOUL MAGIC

by
JENNIFER LYON

Coming soon from Ballantine Books

DAY ONE

Sex wasn't working for him anymore.

Sutton West stood next to a black acrylic bar etched in fiery red lights. The nightclub, Axel of Evil, had a whole hellish theme going on. The music pounded, the colored strobe lights bounced and the smell of sweat and alcohol coated the room.

It was last call.

A few mortal women lingered on the dance floor, and some witch hunters lounged by the two fire pits watching them with pointed interest.

Sutton returned his attention to the dancers, looking for one to take to bed to ease the pain of his cravings. He spotted a woman with long, shimmering black hair, chocolate eyes, and long legs. His interest barely twitched.

He shifted his gaze to the two blondes, one in a yellow dress, the other in tight jeans and a black top. Both were hot, but when another male walked up and started dancing with them, he moved on without a stitch of regret.

One redhead stood out. She was taller, curvier, and she danced with her whole body. She practically burned up the dance floor. He watched her the longest since she was normally his type—a woman who threw herself into life with untamed enthusiasm.

But he knew he couldn't match her zeal. Sutton had an absolute rule about women: they were helping him beat back the curse, and he would treat them with the respect they deserved. The redhead deserved more than he had to give tonight, and his gaze wandered around the club. This lack of interest in sex worried him. Sex was how the hunters controlled their compulsion for witch blood. If they gave into the compulsion and killed a witch, they lost their souls and went rogue—living only for the next "fix" of witch blood. For Sutton, losing interest in sex meant the curse was getting a foothold in him. He'd touched the blood of a witch and now he was on the edge of losing control. He tightened his jaw in determination. *Never.* He'd never give in to the curse. His father had set the standard and Sutton would live up to it.

Which meant he'd die before he let the curse win and take his soul.

Pushing his dark thoughts aside, he focused on the three men returning from hunting rogues. Key and Phoenix went to report to Axel, while Linc headed toward him.

Linc was one of their two candidates set to be inducted into the Wing Slayer Hunters. They both had the outline of their wings tattooed on their bodies: Linc Dillinger had chosen a falcon and Brigg Cusack had chosen a crow.

Now they all waited. Each of the two men had to face a test that would prove him loyal to the Wing Slayer. The test was an unknown, but Axel Locke, their leader, would recognize it when it happened.

Linc came to a stop next to Sutton with barely a whisper from the perfectly cut slacks and coat over an open-collared shirt. His professionally cut, mixed brown hair was expertly tousled. His gold eyes were dark and troubled under the pulsing strobe lights. "You heard anything from Brigg?"

Sutton shook his head. Brigg had left the club two nights ago and evidently no one had seen him since.

"I looked for him tonight. I couldn't find anything, not a goddamned trace of him. It's not like him to just vanish like this."

The tension of waiting for their mysterious test was taking a toll on both men. "Maybe he found a party and hasn't come up for air." They all had their times when the curse drove them to extremes. Sutton took himself off to the most isolated spots he could access. He climbed, hiked, ran, and swam trying like hell to sweat out the curse. Then he'd return to civilization and find a willing woman. As many as it took.

"He should have checked in," Linc said.

Sutton silently agreed. It was giving him a bad feeling, too. "Could be getting cold feet about becoming a Wing Slayer Hunter. It'll make him a target for the rogues."

Linc shook his head. "No. Brigg is hardcore about passing the test and getting fully winged at the Ceremony of Induction. We both are."

"Might be that Brigg is facing his test now," he pointed out. "There are some things a man has to do alone." Sutton knew that Linc was really worried about Brigg, but under that was the resentment that Brigg might be facing his test and would be ready to take his wings first.

Linc let the silence stretch out, then he shrugged, looked around, and said, "Any claims on that redhead?" He tilted his head toward the woman Sutton had noticed earlier.

"Nope. She's yours if she'll have you."

He looked at Sutton with a gleam in his gold eyes. "Thousand bucks says she does."

"Sucker bet and I'm not a sucker." The man was throwing off pheromones so heavy that women across the club were glancing his way.

Linc chuckled and strode off to the dance floor.

Sutton turned back to the job at hand, closing down the club for the night. He glanced at Key, Ram, Axel, and Phoenix. They were spread out around the club, checking things out, closing down the bar, saying good night to patrons, and making damned sure a rogue hadn't gotten in. The rogues had been quiet for the last couple of months. Witches still disappeared but they weren't challenging the Wing Slayer Hunters openly. They were scurrying in the shadows.

He knew from his constant efforts to hack into their new databases that they were rebuilding the Rogue Cadre. They had created new and better firewalls, clearly showing a sophistication that did not bode well. They were also trying to recruit witch hunters to go rogue and fill their ranks. Quinn Young, the rogue leader, had to find a way to kill all the witches. He had a very demanding master—a demon—who wanted all the witches dead. Young and his rogues were out there, strategizing and planning.

Sutton got the all clear signal from the others. He dropped his crossed arms and raised one hand.

The music cut off, the colored strobes died, and the house lights went on.

Witch hunters and the women started making their way out.

One woman hung back, a mortal with wavy brown hair and bright brown eyes, wearing an emerald green dress that swirled around her thighs. She was rooting around in her purse with a frown. He walked over to her. "Lose something?"

She lifted her face, and he saw the sheen of sweat from dancing. Flashing him a smile, she said, "I don't think I should drive home."

He nodded. "We have several cabs out front."

She moved up closer to him. "Or you could drive me home."

She smelled of peppermint blended with her natural scent. Maybe he should take her up on it. Take her home, give them both a little pleasure and leave.

Too much effort.

He'd rather go to the warehouse to work on cracking the firewalls into the Rogue Cadre databases. "Maybe another night. But I'll help you to a cab."

She shook her head, looking embarrassed. "No, thanks. I'm fine. I just got a little overheated from dancing." She started walking away, putting her hand back into her purse, probably looking for her car keys.

He regretted embarrassing her and turned away to make a last circuit of the club.

He heard a click.

By the time he turned, the woman had already fired.

Everything happened at once. Ram pulled his knife out. Sutton bellowed "No!" at the hunter, while turning to protect his heart just as the bullet tore into his right shoulder.

Key wrenched the gun from the woman's hand and Axel appeared at his side. His green eyes furious, his face tight. "Sit down, let me look."

Sutton snorted. "You've seen a bullet wound before." He walked by Axel to where the woman stood, her eyes wide, sweat coating her face, and her hands trembling. "I shot you. My God, I shot you!"

"Why?" Sutton asked. The pain in his shoulder was burrowing into the nerves and firing his compulsion for witch blood. But this woman wasn't a witch, she was a mortal. A harmless little thing, she barely reached his shoulder. Why the hell had she shot him?

"I don't know! I don't remember! I . . . I don't even have a gun!"

Sutton watched as Axel faced the woman and looked into her eyes. Witch hunters had the ability to travel the optic nerve mentally and shift memories. Axel was seeing what he could get by touching her memories.

He turned to meet Sutton's gaze, his face grim. "Rogues."

The scream jerked her from a light doze.

Dr. Carla Fisk jumped up off the couch, her head spinning at the sudden movement. Her small office was dim, lit only by her desk lamp.

Another scream.

She kicked aside the shoes she'd taken off before lying down and raced out the door, lifting her long skirt out of the way as she took the stairs two at a time. On the second floor, she could hear broken sobbing.

Then Max Bayer's soothing tones. "Josie, honey, wake up. You're safe."

Carla slowed her steps, composing herself. She loved to listen to Max gentle their residents. The transitional clinic was Max's baby. His specialty, though, was tracking and extracting people who had been indoctrinated into cults.

Whether they were lured, seduced, or forced, if he could find them, he got them out.

Carla had worked closely with Max to design the program to reverse the brainwashing. She admired him, respected him, liked him. . . .

But she didn't feel anything romantic toward him, only admiration for his work and friendship.

As her heart calmed down, she turned and walked into the room.

In the light from the nightstand lamp, she saw that Josie was sitting up in the bed closest to the door. She had her knees drawn up tightly to her chest, her arms wrapped around them. Her face was tight and splotchy from crying.

Max was on his knees, his back to Carla. He wore a pair of gray sweat pants and nothing else. His back was lean, his arms wiry and strong. "Josie, you're hyperventilating. Try breathing with me, like Carla taught you."

Josie kept her eyes fixed on the wall across the room. "They'll find me."

She saw the muscles ripple across Max's back. She could feel his need to pull Josie into his arms and swear to her that he would never let that happen.

But Max resisted the impulse. Josie had only been out of the cult two days. Men frightened her. In the place she'd been, men had total, brutal, and humiliating control over the women. She couldn't even look at Max.

It always killed Max that these young women were afraid of him. Eventually, they came to trust him. And then he let them go.

Carla put her hand on Max's shoulder.

He looked up at her, his dark eyes full of impotent fury. Max had once had a scientific curiosity about cults, and had worked closely with a young research assistant trying to infiltrate a cult. Then the research assistant had gotten in too deep and the cult killed her. The curious sociologist in Max died, and this man, full of passion, grief, anger, and guilt was born.

She squeezed his shoulder. "How about getting Josie some water?"

He rose. "I'll be back in a few minutes."

His bare feet made little sound on the wood floors.

"Is he mad at me?"

Carla sat down on the side of Josie's bed. It was a child's question. "No. Max isn't going to get mad at you for being scared or having nightmares." She reached out, putting her hand over Josie's cold fingers. Opening her first four chakras with a swift popping sensation that started at her pelvis and rose to her solar plexus, Carla sent calming energy to the frightened girl.

Her eyes widened. "How do you do that?"

"In our hypnosis sessions, I've been giving you calming suggestions. When I touch you, your brain remembers the suggestions." And, of course, she was a witch. But Josie didn't need to know that. Few mortals did. What Josie needed was healing, and Carla could do that with her powers of hypnosis.

The girl's breathing settled down to an even, healthy rhythm. "Do you think they can find me here?"

"No. You were in Arizona, out in the desert. This is Los Angeles, they wouldn't even know where to look. But more important, do you think Max or any of his men wandering around here would let them take you?" Max's team doubled as protection for the clinic when they weren't out on a mission to extract someone from a cult.

"Yesterday, that big guy, umm, Rich?"

Carla nodded.

"He watched me walk in and out the front door. Never said a word, but he smiled."

Testing to see if they'd stop her from walking out. To see if she was a prisoner. "Did you think he'd stop you?"

She shrugged, then picked at the blanket. "I'm free now and safe, but I can't seem to understand that."

Carla had to control her anger at the bastards who had done this to a nineteen-year-old girl. "Honey, they brainwashed you. They tried to destroy your individual self. But you are an amazing, strong, and smart young woman and they failed. Your brain is fighting back and nightmares are a part of that."

She took a deep breath. "Really?"

"Really. Ready to go back to sleep?"

"I don't know if I can."

Carla glanced at the bedside clock. It was just after two a.m. Then she said softly, "I can help you sleep."

Josie nodded.

Carla concentrated to funnel the elemental power of the earth up through her four opened chakras. That was the easy part.

The hard part was trying to open the top three chakras. Actually it was nearly impossible since the curse had destroyed the witches' bonds with their familiars. Carla could open her fifth chakra, which was her communication with other realms, but she couldn't open her sixth chakra, which was her third eye, or her seventh, which was knowledge.

She needed her fifth chakra to guide Josie's spirit to the astral plane. She concentrated and pictured the blue chakra at her throat, then she began funneling her powers up faster and faster, concentrating on that one spot.

The vibrations grew stronger, and she felt a choking sensation. She pushed harder, her body trembling as she struggled to control her magic. Then the sudden relief as the chakra flew open. Her body dropped away and she floated on a plane of blue.

The astral plane.

"Doctor?"

"I'm right here," Carla said, and her doppelganger body took shape. The astral plane was spiritual and their actual bodies were down on the physical plane, but for reasons known only to the universe, a mirror image body usually appeared with the subconscious. Perhaps because it was the only way the human mind could grasp the reality of this level of existence. But, in Carla's experience, what happened to the bodies were separate. For instance, if Josie's body on the physical plane were to be hurt, her body on the spiritual plane wouldn't know it. At least not until her subconscious returned to the body to experience it.

Josie appeared standing next to her. "I love this place." As soon as Josie said it, a large green pasture opened up before them, dotted with grazing horses. They'd practiced creating these places that Josie loved. "Can I ride the horses?"

"Of course. Your body on the physical plane is asleep already. This is your dream. You're safe here, you control what happens."

"I'm asleep?"

"Yes."

"How do you do that?"

"Magic," she laughed. "Now go ride your horses."

While the girl moved off toward the horses, Carla kept a tight hold on her spirit, and began guiding all but the dreaming fraction of her spirit back to Josie's sleeping body.

Dreams were actually a part of the spirit leaving the body and exploring other realms. The small portion of Josie's spirit on the astral plane would return without a hitch once the girl woke up.

Returning to the physical plane, Carla settled back into her own body, feeling heavy and tired. It took a tremendous amount of energy to control the magic of her fifth chakra.

Josie was asleep where she sat, her face relaxed. Carla laid Josie down and covered her. She glanced at the light, and it went out.

Then she turned and walked into the hallway.

Max leaned against the wall, holding a cold bottle of water. He handed the water to Carla. "You might as well drink it. She's not going to wake for hours now."

Carla took the bottle.

"Have I told you lately how amazing you are?"

Many times. "Josie wouldn't have the chance to recover and live a full life if you hadn't found her and got her out."

He studied her, raising an eyebrow. "Same shirt and skirt you wore today. You haven't gone home. Let me get dressed and I'll take you home."

"I'm fine. I have a change of clothes in my office."

"You slept on the couch again."

She drank down a gulp of the cool water, avoiding his gaze. "I worked late, and—" she had nothing to go home to. The loneliness was a constant ache. Insomnia was bad enough, but when she slept, the nightmares caught up with her. The memory of the knives, the pain, the helpless terror . . .

And then the witch hunter who saved her.

Her dream always shifted then, the horror giving way to being touched and stroked and filled until she felt whole. When she woke, she was left aching for something that wasn't real. Carla had spent her life trying to find a way to meld together the two parts of her psyche; the logical scientist and the emotional witch. Always pulled in two directions.

Max reached out, laying his palm on her bare arm.

The warm touch hurt her all the more because she didn't feel the connection he wanted. She cared about him, but he didn't stir her passion.

And if he ever found out she was a witch, he'd want to use her like her father had. That thought surprised her, caught her off guard, making her stiffen beneath Max's hand. She tried to smile and said, "Go back to bed, Max."

He dropped his arm. "Try to get some sleep," he said and walked away.

Carla took her bottle of water downstairs, ignored her office and turned left, passed through a dining room and went to the small, walled courtyard with the fountain. She keyed off the alarm system for the slider door, then opened it and slipped out in the cool night.

She sat in the chair, propping her feet on the edge of the stone waterfall. There were large pots of geraniums dotting the patio. Soft colored lights in the center illuminated the bubbling stone waterfall cascading down into comforting splashes. The tiny sliver of moonlight barely touched her skin, but it was enough.

It fed her chakras, eased her exhaustion.

Two years since her sister's murder, and the grief, guilt, and regret still took up too much space inside her. She had to let Keri go, had to accept that her sister's soul had gone on to her next life. The scar across her lower back, the one she'd gotten trying to save Keri, ached slightly. It was time to let it all go. She breathed deeply, drawing the cool damp night air into her lungs.

She was just releasing the air out when her cell phone vibrated. Reaching into her skirt pocket, she pulled the phone out and opened it.

The image of her best friend, Darcy, stared back at her. "Carla, where are you?"

Darcy was using magic to project her image through the phone. She spoke to the picture. "Transitional Clinic. What's wrong?" It was after two in the morning, she wasn't calling for a chat. "Is a witch missing?"

Darcy shook her head. "Not that I know of."

Darcy and Axel had broken the thirty year old curse on the witches and witch hunters, making Darcy the most powerful witch they knew of. She was struggling to find her place among the witches, while her mate, Axel, led the Wing Slayer Witch Hunters in their fight against rogues. Like the rogues who had killed Keri. So if Darcy wasn't calling about a missing witch . . . "Then what is it?" Her worrying pulled tighter in her stomach.

Her face was troubled. "A woman shot Sutton tonight."

Carla dropped her feet from the edge of the fountain, sitting up. Her skin tingled from her neck to her thighs—all the places that Sutton West's T-shirt had touched her when he had rescued her from the rogues. The dreams of him were making her restless and needing something she could have. "Is he alive?"

Darcy's brown eyes glinted with silver lights. "Yes. He's fine, she missed his heart."

Her own heart skipped a beat and caused her to struggle for her breath. Finally, she said, "Why did the woman shoot him? Was it, uh, personal?" And why did that make her chest burn?

Darcy shook her head. "A rogue has been in her head, Axel is sure of that much. But he's never seen this kind of thing before. He can't tell if it's brain damage from some witch hunter repeatedly shifting her memories or . . ."

"You think the rogues are trying to kill the Wing Slayer Hunters using a mortal woman?" Carla processed that. "Like some kind of mind control? Do witch-hunters have that kind of power?"

"We've never seen it, but I'm worried. We have the

woman but she's in shock. I can't get much out of her. The rogues have been fairly quiet since Axel and the men took a stand against them. But this . . ."

She remembered that night too well.

"What if the rouges are reorganizing and using some kind of brainwashing on mortals?" Darcy continued. "How many others are out there? What's going on?"

"Bring her to me."

"Too dangerous. The rogue would be able to track her and we don't want them to find the clinic or the house you're staying in."

Carla couldn't endanger their residents, Max, or any of them. She made a quick decision. "Where are you? I'll come there."

"I was hoping you'd say that."

Prickles of unease skittered up her spine. "What do you mean?"

A large shadow passed overhead. Carla jerked her head up in time to see a huge creature with wings fill up the night sky. He swooped in, his gold and brown wings catching the moonlight as he shifted on the air current so that he landed on his feet a yard away from Carla. His wings spread across most of the courtyard. Then he lifted his wings up and folded them until they disappeared into the tattoo on his back.

Carla turned to Darcy. "No way, I am not flying!" She still couldn't get used to the idea of a man with wings who could fly.

"You'll be safer with Axel. Please, Carla. Let him bring you here."

Carla turned to look at the man in question. He stood well over six feet, and without a shirt, his muscles gleamed in the moonlight. His wings ripped holes in his shirts, so he usually flew bare-chested. Lifting her gaze, she looked into his green eyes. "We could drive my car."

He smiled. "We could try, but Darcy will magically disable it."

Her curiosity outweighed her fear. She looked at Darcy. "You so owe me for this."